LONG SHADOWS

JODI TAYLOR

HEADLINE

First published in Great Britain in 2021 by
HEADLINE PUBLISHING GROUP

2

Cataloguing in Publication Data is available from the British Library

ISBN 978 1 4722 6752 8

Typeset in Times New Roman by CC Book Production

Printed and bound in Great Britain by Clays Ltd, Elcograf S.p.A.

Headline's policy is to use papers that are natural, renewable and recyclable
products and made from wood grown in well-managed forests and other
controlled sources. The logging and manufacturing processes are expected
to conform to the environmental regulations of the country of origin.

HEADLINE PUBLISHING GROUP
An Hachette UK Company
Carmelite House
50 Victoria Embankment
London EC4Y 0DZ

www.headline.co.uk
www.hachette.co.uk

To my comrades Sansie, Anu and the Tiny Iron Bear –
a sincere thanks for all your help.

PROLOGUE

My name is Elizabeth Cage. I don't know who I am. Or even what I am. My adopted parents are both dead but they didn't know either. No one does – although there are those who would like to find out.

I used to be able to say that I'd never caused anyone any harm in my life but that's no longer true. My life took a strange turn after my husband, Ted, died, and now there are several people – alive and dead – for whom, because of me, things did not turn out well. Because I have a 'gift'. Michael Jones calls it a talent. I call it a curse. I can see things. And yes, I can see dead people, but mostly I see people's colours.

Years ago, when I was a child, I'd never heard the word aura, so in my head I called it a colour. Everyone has one. Usually they're beautiful – a shimmering outline that constantly changes shade and shape as people react to what's going on around them. Sometimes there's a dark or dirty patch – usually around their head or their heart – and that's never good. And they're all different. Each colour is unique. Like fingerprints. Some are thick and vigorous and clearly defined; strong, throbbing, rich and deep. Some are pale and insubstantial.

It's not unknown for some people to have very similar colours to their family and close friends. I recently encountered an

1

entire village where everyone's colours were all variations of the same blue, turquoise and purple. The colours of a mother and her baby are almost identical for the first weeks and then, as the child develops her personality, her colour develops too.

You might have come across people for whom you feel an instinctive liking – that's because your colours are similar. Other people might repulse you – you feel an urge to keep them at a distance. You might not know why, but your colour does.

Your colour tells me things about you. Things you might not even know yourself. Perhaps things you'd rather keep secret, but give me a few minutes and I'll know whether you're happy or sad. I'll know if you're lying. I'll know if you're afraid. I'll know whom you love and whom you hate. You don't have to say a word but you're telling me just the same.

And no – I'm not that happy about it, either. It's a talent that hasn't done me any favours at all. Think about it for a moment – do you actually want to know what people think of you? What they *really* think of you?

I've done my best to live a normal life. I married Ted and settled down to what I hoped would be peace and happiness. And then, suddenly and very unexpectedly, Ted died and my life changed overnight. I began to crash from one situation to another. I was imprisoned in a government-sponsored mental institution. I'd be there still if Michael Jones hadn't got me out.

I've no idea what will become of me. Not only do I not know who I am or what I am, I don't know where I'm going, either.

Well, no – that's not strictly true. I was going to Scotland.

CHAPTER ONE

'Well, this makes a nice change,' I said as Jones shifted up a gear and we joined the motorway heading north.

'What does?'

'Us. In a car. Unthreatened. Unpursued. Undead.'

'I think you might be slightly confused as to the precise meaning of undead, Cage, but, worryingly, I understand your drift.'

'Well,' I said, 'I don't think I've ever been in a car with you when we haven't been fleeing something horrible. Most recently, three homicidal standing stones and an impossibly peripatetic red armchair.'

'And let's not start on the dastardly Dr Sorensen.'

I shivered. 'No, let's not.'

'Cage – why so gloomy? We're on holiday. Scotland beckons. It's going to be great. Men in skirts, good fishing, beautiful scenery, fresh air, good fishing, great food, more alcohol than even I can handle – by the way, Jerry says to bring him back a bottle or two of something powerful – and did I mention the good fishing?'

Jerry is a friend of Michael Jones. He's also a very successful thief. I probably shouldn't say any more.

'It's a fishing holiday,' I said. 'It would be hard not to mention the good fishing.'

'Come on, Cage, cheer up. A well-deserved bit of peace and quiet for both of us. Although I'll tell you now, if anything odd happens – people rising from the grave, long-haired weirdos with a sword and a puppy, curses, ghosts, funny-looking people – then we're out of there at top speed. This is a holiday. Got it?'

'I don't know why you're blaming me,' I said, indignantly.

He turned to grin at me. 'Because you're weird, Cage. There's no getting around it.'

'Just watch the road,' I said.

He laughed, put his foot down and we headed north.

'Are we there yet?' I said, opening my eyes.

'No.'

The engine purred, the tyres hummed. I fell asleep again.

'Are we there yet?' I said, opening my eyes.

'No. Wipe your chin.'

I closed my eyes again.

'Are we there yet?'

'*Yes.* For God's sake – yes. And wipe your chin again.'

We left the high hills and followed the road down into a thickly wooded valley, still lush despite the hot summer. The air was cooler and fresher under the trees. We'd had an amazing summer and it wasn't over yet, even in Scotland. The leaves were turning red and orange and gold but they were still on the trees.

The road was narrow and steep and Jones drove slowly. I could see dilapidated buildings dotted around among the trees. I opened the window, enjoying the cooler, fresher air as we approached the river. I could hear the sound of rushing water somewhere close by. I could smell leaves and wet earth and water. This place was beautiful.

We emerged from the woods and there, on the riverbank, stood an old, abandoned mill. The leat – the millstream – had long since dried up and dark green ivy clambered over everything.

'Brace yourself,' said Jones and I looked ahead. We were approaching an old stone bridge. A very picturesque but very old stone bridge. Very, very old. I hoped it would bear our weight because there were a worrying number of metal ties holding it together. I wondered if it was actually safe for vehicular traffic and mentioned that to Jones.

'It'll be fine,' he said. 'The hotel's somewhere on the other side. Keep your eyes open.'

He changed gear and we crept cautiously across. The bridge was barely one car wide. I disobeyed him and closed my eyes – all the better not to see the inevitable catastrophe if something approached from the other direction.

'It's probably been here for the best part of five or six hundred years,' said Jones, amused. 'I doubt it's going to collapse just because we've turned up. Have you gone to sleep again?'

'No, of course not.'

'Only your eyes are closed.'

'No, they're not. Well, maybe a little bit.'

And then we were across. The hotel almost sprang out of the landscape at us, nestled among the trees on the banks of the white foaming river.

'There it is,' I said, excited. 'We're here. We've arrived.'

'Well, of course we have. What did you expect?'

'Death, catastrophe, blood, fire . . .'

'That's what I love about you, Cage. The way you always look on the bright side.'

I wasn't listening. This was beautiful. A large sign among the trees welcomed us to the Old Bridge Hotel.

'Fully licensed,' said Jones, who has different priorities.

I suspected this had once been an old Edwardian hunting lodge. Its roof was thick with chimneys and gables. The front bedrooms would have spectacular views out over the river. I felt happier just by looking at it. There would be walks and scenery and good food. There might even be fish. This was going to be a wonderful holiday.

We pulled into the hotel car park which was carefully camouflaged with trees so as not to spoil anyone's view. There were only two or three other cars parked there. I wondered if perhaps the other guests were all out taking advantage of the lovely weather and touring the area, but it wasn't a large hotel anyway. Probably not more than ten or twelve bedrooms. They might not have full occupancy at this, the end of the season.

Jones switched off the engine and for a moment, we just sat. The way you do after a long journey.

He turned to me and grinned, his red-gold colour flaring up around him with excitement. 'All right?'

'Yes. I'm so looking forward to this.'

'Me too.'

I opened the door and climbed out to see an elderly man marching determinedly across the gravel towards us. He wasn't very big and most of him was covered in an Edwardian hall-porter coat in dark red that fell past his knees. A row of medal ribbons – to which I guessed he was certainly entitled – ornamented his chest. Golden epaulettes worthy of the generalissimo of the People's Utopia of Somewhereorother adorned his shoulders. It was a miracle he could stand up under all the weight. His peaked cap rested on top of his very large pale ears and bore the legend Old Bridge Hotel.

Disregarding Jones completely, he stood in front of me and inclined his head in what might have been interpreted as an actual bow.

'Good afternoon, madam. Welcome to the Old Bridge Hotel.'

'Thank you,' I said, closing the car door. 'It's very nice to be here. The hotel looks lovely.'

'It is, madam. A beautiful spot. If I could introduce myself – my name is Clarence. May I assist you with your luggage?'

Jones, having thrown an assessing glance at Clarence's less than imposing physique, was already pulling the cases from the car himself.

'Is the hotel very old?' I asked, more for the sake of conversation than information – and also because I didn't want to hurt Clarence's feelings.

'Built in 1905, I believe, madam. As a private hunting lodge.'

I frowned. 'The reign of Edward the . . . Seventh?'

'That's right.'

'Did he ever stay here?'

'Several times. For the fishing and the shooting. We don't do the shooting any longer but the fishing is as good as ever.'

'Well, that's good news,' said Jones, closing the boot. 'What can I expect to catch?'

'At this time of year, sir, trout. Plenty of them around. Practically throw themselves out of the water, they will.'

'They'll have to,' I muttered.

'I heard that,' said Jones.

'You forget I've seen you fish.'

'Most importantly,' said Jones, turning back to Clarence, 'and not as stupid a question as you might think – are there any spooky goings-on? Moving furniture? Carelessly concealed bodies?'

I blushed but fortunately Clarence laughed in genuine amusement. 'None of that, sir.'

'No headless Highlanders or wailing ladies looking for their lords? No clocks striking thirteen?'

'Not at all, sir,' he said, entering into the spirit of the game. 'No ghostly battles fought in the dead of night. No mysteriously levitating objects hurling themselves across the room. Not even a Black Dog howling at the moon foretelling a death in the family.'

'Did you hear that, Cage?' said Jones, wheeling the suitcases across the gravel as Clarence trotted alongside. 'Nothing for you to get your teeth into here. You might as well wait in the car.'

He and Clarence began to talk fish. I dropped back to give them room, grinning at their backs.

Clarence abandoned us at the front door, which stood open to welcome guests. The porch was full of boots, waterproofs, walking sticks, dog leads, umbrellas, wicker baskets and odd bits of what I assumed were fishing equipment. A polite notice requested muddy boots and wet outerwear not be worn inside the hotel; a drying room was provided.

Jones rummaged in his pockets.

'Oh no, no, sir,' said Clarence, backing away. 'No gratuities expected. Enjoy your stay.'

Spotting another car pulling into the car park, he trotted off, presumably to watch them struggle with their suitcases as well.

I don't know what made me do it, but I paused for a moment to watch the car manoeuvre itself into a parking space and the passengers alight. They were a young couple, by the looks of them. She looked very frail, emerging from the car and looking uncertainly about her. Definitely not capable of handling her own luggage. He, on the other hand, looked more than able, so I turned back to the hotel.

We pushed our way through the inner doors. 'It's like stepping back in time,' I said, looking around in delight.

'No, it's not,' said Jones, firmly, possibly remembering our encounter with Evelyn Cross when she'd whipped us both back to a moment in WW2. 'Nothing like.'

We were standing in what had surely been the original hall. Fashionably shabby rugs covered a stone-flagged floor. To our right, a magnificently ornate wooden staircase curled off out of sight. You had to hand it to the Edwardians, they could certainly do a staircase.

To the left of the staircase stood a matching wooden counter – obviously more modern but nicely done. Two rows of pigeon-holes faced us from the back wall. An ornate but electric chandelier hung from the high ceiling and the two full-length windows were curtained in a tartan material that contrived to be both traditional and modern at the same time.

A gleaming circular table with a striking arrangement of bronze, orange, cream and yellow chrysanthemums stood in the middle of the room. I couldn't help thinking that apart from the desk, the telephone and the computer screen, the hall must look very similar to the way it had a hundred years ago.

A slim, grey-haired woman sat behind the desk. Her soft

heather colour was almost motionless. Very serene and still. She looked up as we approached.

'Good afternoon. I am Emily Kirk. My husband and I welcome you to the Old Bridge Hotel.' She had a lovely, soft, lilting accent that matched her colour.

'Good afternoon,' said Jones. 'We have reservations in the name of Jones and Cage.'

'That's right,' she said, clicking away at the keyboard. 'If you could just complete and sign these, please . . .'

She passed over two sheets of paper.

'I'm afraid you're too late for afternoon tea,' she said, to Jones's everlasting regret, 'but dinner is served from seven onwards so you'll have plenty of time to unpack and settle in. Have you come very far?'

'Rushford,' said Jones, handing her his completed paperwork.

'Quite a long journey then. Now, I've given you Rooms Six and Nine. They're opposite each other. One looks out over the river and one across to the mountains. I'll leave it to you to decide who has which.' She looked up and smiled. 'Please, no bloodshed.'

'Does it often come to that?' enquired Jones.

Her colour swirled towards him, soft and gentle. 'More often than you might think, Mr Jones. Let's just say we've found it advisable to take down our collection of antique weapons. The lift is behind the stairs.'

'I can manage the stairs, I think,' said Jones, hefting the suitcases.

'I'll bring the keys,' I offered.

10

'Don't strain yourself, Cage.'

'I don't intend to,' I said, heading across the hall.

The stairs were what I call luxury stairs. Very wide and shallow and thickly carpeted with lovely old-fashioned brass stair rods. Getting up them was easy, although as Jones pointed out, I was burdened only with a handbag and two keys.

The corridor at the top stretched left and right. We turned right. Portraits hung on the walls. Pale faces peered out of dark canvases, watching us look for our rooms. Their expressions were uniformly gloomy.

'They probably didn't catch any fish either,' I said.

I unlocked Room Six first. This was the room at the front with the view over the river. Jones followed me in. The furniture was dark and old-fashioned and very solid. Everything was polished to a high shine. A green and gold bedspread matched the curtains hanging at the windows.

'Nice,' he said, looking around.

'Hm,' I said, crossing the corridor and unlocking Room Nine. This one was almost identical except the bathroom was on the other side and the colour scheme here was red and gold. The view from the window was full of rolling heather hills and jagged mountains.

'Nice again,' said Jones, dropping the suitcases. 'Which one do you want?'

'Your holiday – your choice,' I said.

I'd bought him this fishing holiday as a Christmas gift and he'd asked me to join him on it. Since then, we'd had what Jones frequently referred to as an incident-heavy year and this was the first opportunity we'd had to get away. Plus, we were

11

avoiding the law after a red armchair had shown us where a woman's body had been concealed. No, don't bother reading that again – you got it right the first time.

And as if that wasn't enough, both of us were also avoiding the attentions of Dr Sorensen after Jerry, Iblis – don't ask about Iblis – and I had broken Jones out of Sorensen's clinic. And then the Three Sisters had had a go at us – so all in all, quite a crowded year. And that's not even mentioning the troll. And it wasn't over yet. For someone who only ever wanted a quiet life, I did seem to attract trouble wherever I went. To be clear, I don't actually do anything. Things are done to me. There doesn't seem to be anything I can do about it.

As I said, I'm Elizabeth Cage and I was married to Ted Cage. My lovely Ted. We lived happily and quietly, and I had no idea how much he sheltered and protected me until he died, when all sorts of things began to happen to me. I only escaped with the help of Michael Jones – yes, the same Jones currently complaining about the weight of my suitcase. Before anyone feels sorry for him, he's the biggest man I have ever met. He could probably lift both cases, me, and half the hotel without even breaking a sweat. He has fair hair just beginning to grey at the temples and works for the government, in which capacity he knows a large number of very dodgy people. And seems quite proud of it. As he'd once said to me, 'I work for the government, Cage, of course I know some dodgy people. Have you ever actually met an MP?'

He's irritating but cooks like a dream so one makes up for the other. He's friendly, outgoing, and for some reason, people like him.

Unlike me. I'm not friendly and I'm definitely not outgoing. I like to keep my distance from people. At school I was the weird one. At work I was the one shoved down into the basement by myself to digitise the council's records. The job no one else wanted to do. It didn't bother me. I liked being on my own. Sometimes, for me, people can be a little difficult to handle.

Once, when I was a child, I saw a woman. She looked perfectly normal. Nice, even. Well dressed and smart. But her colour was black and oily and full of violence and instead of swirling gently around her, it stabbed in and out in vicious spikes. I hid from her. She stopped. I knew she was aware of me. I held my breath and after what was, to me, a terrifying few minutes, she went on her way. I ran all the way home to my dad.

It's important to say there are no good colours or bad colours. Nice people do not necessarily have pretty colours and bad people are not necessarily a sinister and murky black like the woman I saw when I was younger. Philip Sorensen's colour, for instance, is a kind of bluey-white, like thin, greasy milk on the turn. Jones's is a golden red, so thick and vigorous that it can light up a room.

Or sometimes a colour is faint and fragile – like Mrs Barton's, my next-door neighbour, whose mind is usually somewhere else these days. Her robin's-egg blue colour grows thinner and more brittle by the day. I don't think it will be very long now.

My own colour? I can't tell you. I can see everyone's but my own. I don't know why. Perhaps I don't have one, which is worrying because every living thing has a colour. Except, possibly, me.

I was roused by Jones demanding to know if the furniture

13

was communicating with me again and were we going to stand here all day. I said, 'No, obviously not,' and to show him I was in complete control of everything, took the key to Room Six and its view of the river.

CHAPTER TWO

It was dark outside when we went down to dinner. They'd drawn
the curtains to the dining room, which was done out in the same
misty purple and grey as the mountains and was welcoming and
cosy. Circular tables were scattered around, each with a crisp,
white cloth. Light winked off the cutlery and glassware.

We weren't the first people in. Two of the other tables were
already occupied.

'Please sit wherever you like,' said the very young waiter, his
chest swelling with importance in what I guessed was probably
his first job.

Jones selected a corner table. I knew he would. He never
sits with his back to a room. Especially one with an open door.
He seated himself to face the room. I took the seat opposite,
which gave me a very nice view of the wall and curtains, and
looked at the menu while he busied himself with the wine list.

'What do you fancy, Cage?'

'Tonic water, please,' I said vaguely, my mind already on
whether to have the pâté or the prawns, followed by the pulled
pork or the salmon. Or even the venison. Or the steak. Not all
problems are a problem.

He sighed. 'Am I drinking alone?'

'You usually do.'

15

'We're on holiday, Cage.'

'A glass of white wine then, please. And the pâté and the salmon.'

'Are you sure you want fish tonight?' he said. 'It'll be trout tomorrow, don't forget.'

I put down the menu. '*You'll* be catching tomorrow's dinner?'

'Of course,' he said, offended. 'Didn't you read the brochure?'

'Only the relevant bits. You know – descriptions of the hotel, the facilities and surrounding area.'

'We bring home our catch . . .'

'Not sure who you mean by *we*. Or even what you mean by *catch*.'

'. . . And they cook it for us. There's a tray with your room number on it in the tackle room by the kitchen and we just leave them there.'

'Them?'

'It says in the brochure I can expect to catch anything up to six fish a day. Although I have to throw the little ones back. Which reminds me – think of a number under ten.'

I regarded him with some misgivings. 'Are you going to start doing conjuring tricks?'

'No – we have to choose a beat number. The place we'll fish from. Normally they hold a draw to allocate beat numbers but there aren't too many of us staying at present so we can choose. Which number did you think of?'

'Three,' I said, on the grounds that the lower numbers were probably nearer the hotel.

'Three it is,' said Jones, cheerfully, filling in a card.

'Have you ever actually caught a fish?'

16

'Catching fish is not the point.'

'What is the point?'

His colour subsided a little. He didn't look at me. 'To sit in peace. To drink in the silent hills. Listen to the murmur of the river. Breathe in the clean air. A chance for the things I've seen or done to be picked up and rolled away and buried deep.'

In a way I knew what he was saying. Once, when my world had become too dark to endure, my mind had taken refuge in a box where everything was white and still and safe and no one could find me and I didn't have to come out until I was ready.

I smiled at him. 'You go ahead and not catch all the fish you want.'

He grinned and his colour brightened around him. 'How's your room?'

'Very comfortable. Nice bathroom. Great views.'

The waiter arrived to pour our wine.

Jones lifted his glass. 'To us, Cage.'

I nodded and sipped. 'Actually, I'm really looking forward to this. Life's been quite difficult recently and it will make such a pleasant change not to be menaced by trees and trolls . . . and other things.'

'Don't think about any of it, Cage. We've got five days here. A spot of R & R for both of us. And much needed, I think. No one's going to drug us or kidnap us . . .'

The young waiter waiting nearby to take our order was trying so hard to maintain a professional indifference but I was certain I could feel the draught from his flapping ears. His face was quite still but his browny-green colour, shot through with gold, was swirling with excitement.

'Mr Jones is a writer,' I said. I didn't see why Jones should get to tell all the lies. 'He's trying out a plot.'

'Ah.' The waiter nodded wisely and his colour retreated a little and became tinged with disappointment. We might have been his first serial killers.

We placed our orders and settled back.

Jones was toying with his cutlery – straightening it, lining it all up in a row, moving it and then lining it all up again. His colour, now more red than gold, was twisting around him. He had something to say, and for someone who always gave the impression of knowing exactly which words he wanted and the effect he wanted those words to create, he was having some difficulty getting going. I waited.

'Cage, do you remember, back in that café in Rushby . . . I said I wanted to ask you something?'

'Yes, I remember.' And I did. We'd sat in the sun, under the striped awning, watching the fishing boats come in, and he'd said he wanted to ask me something. He never got around to it because, once again, we'd been overtaken by events. 'Wasn't it about spending Christmas at my place? That was what you said later.'

'Yes, but that was because I bottled out.'

I was conscious of my heart beginning a slow thump. It wasn't like him to bottle out of anything. His colour was deepening by the moment.

'The thing is, Cage, I want to talk to you about something quite important and I'm not sure what you'll say.'

I put down my glass. His colour was massing around him. To protect him. He wasn't sure of my reaction to whatever it was he wanted to talk to me about. His unease made me uneasy. Suddenly, I didn't think I wanted to know.

'Look, Jones, you don't have to . . .'

The waiter arrived with our starter. We sat in silence as he served us. I think he was disappointed we weren't discussing disembowelling someone or plotting to overthrow the government.

We ate in silence for a while and then Jones said, 'How's the pâté?'

'Good,' I said, shovelling a slab of it on to my toast.

He frowned. 'It's pâté, Cage, not tarmac. Have some finesse.'

I watched his colour settle down around him. He'd bottled it again.

We ate our starters in silence. It wasn't an awkward silence. He was concentrating on his food. I was concentrating on mine. Which was delicious. Everything was perfect. The setting, the food and that lovely first-day-of-the-holidays feeling. I finished my starter first and looked around while I waited for Jones to finish.

We'd come down to dinner early and the room had filled up while we'd been eating. I could hear people chatting behind me, hear the chink of cutlery on plates. Occasionally, someone would laugh. I was feeling so relaxed it took me a while to notice, but there was something . . . At first, I ignored it, but it was growing . . . A red thread of cruelty curdled the room.

I felt a sharp stab of resentment. This was my holiday. Why couldn't I just be left in peace? But this wasn't something I could ignore. Under cover of sipping my wine, I let my mind drift . . . just a little . . . frustration . . . red . . . anger . . .

Jones started to say something. I can't remember what it was, but before he could get more than three or four words out, I said, 'What's happening behind me?'

I sometimes forget he does this sort of thing for a living. Without even looking up from his plate, he said quietly, 'A couple. Rings – so married. Probably to each other. They look miserable enough. Late twenties. He's some sort of young executive, I think. Wearing too carefully casual clothes. Not sure about her. Long hair hiding her face. They're having a row. Very quietly. He's furious. She's in tears.'

I sipped my wine again. Only a sip because I don't like getting drunk. There are things out there that lurk on the edges of our consciousness. Sometimes they stay quietly in the background, but sometimes, in the no man's land of not quite drunk but not quite sober, they can make their presence felt, so I don't drink a great deal.

I'd like to have ignored the young couple and their problems. I was on holiday. I'd had a tiring year. I deserved a little peace and quiet. But something was happening in this room. Something that couldn't – shouldn't – be ignored. I could feel it building. Something very nasty was in here with us. I risked a look around. The couple were two tables away to my right. They'd been served but neither had even started their meal. He was gulping down his wine, his face flushed. His colour was a deep crimson with scarlet and orange flitting around the edges. She was sitting, head bowed, twisting her napkin in her lap. I could see tears on her cheeks. Her colour was grey, tight, still and watchful.

I turned back again.

Jones continued to eat, saying quietly, 'Problem?'

I sighed. 'Actually, I think so, yes.'

'What do you want to do?'

'I don't *want* to do anything but I might not have a choice.'

'We,' he said.

'Sorry?'

'*We* might not have a choice.'

'It might not come to that,' I said.

'You sound doubtful.'

'I am. What's happening now?'

'He's a very angry man,' said Jones calmly, still eating. 'I should imagine that if he ever loses control, we'll be watching the furniture fly in all directions.'

To look at Jones, you'd think we were discussing the weather.

I nodded. Violence was curdling the room. Tragedy waited in the wings. I could see the young waiter, just a little bit out of his depth, standing over by the door and wondering what to do. Sobbing guests probably didn't happen every day. The gold in his colour had disappeared, to be replaced by streaks of orange anxiety.

'Has anyone else noticed?'

'Yeah, heads are beginning to turn. I suspect our waiter will be off to get the owners in a minute. We're building up to a nice scene.'

'No,' I said, suddenly alarmed. 'That mustn't happen.'

'What do you want to do, Cage? Intervene? I suspect everyone else is about to become very British and pretend they haven't noticed a thing.'

I had a choice. I could do nothing. I could ignore everything and let events take their course. Except it doesn't work like that. I don't know why I see these things. I don't know why this happens to me. I only know that if I don't at least try to do something, then it's like an unscratched itch, which gets worse and worse until it stops being an itch and becomes a pain and

21

I have to do something to relieve the pressure ... I shifted in my chair. Something dark was building. There was blood in the air tonight.

I heard a crash behind me. Now I could legitimately turn to see what was happening. Somehow, she'd managed to drop her glass on to her plate. Dark red wine flowed across the white tablecloth. It was actually quite an unpleasant image. She cringed back in her chair. His face turned an even darker red of embarrassment. His colour began to deepen to purple, rolling and boiling, reflecting his rising anger. He was losing control of himself. Flinging down his napkin, he pushed his chair back and strode from the room, leaving her all alone at the table.

'Now what?' said Jones, placidly, buttering his roll.

I pushed my chair back. 'Keep her here. Don't let her leave, whatever you do. She mustn't be left alone. Not even for a moment.'

'Wouldn't it be easier to do this the other way around? You stay with her?'

'I don't think so,' I said, standing up slowly. 'I need an urgent word with her husband.'

He nodded. 'One day we'll have a quiet meal, Cage.'

'Don't hold your breath,' I said darkly and followed the young man out into the hall.

He'd paused for a moment, as if wondering where to go next, then turned abruptly left, colliding with an armchair and start-ling Emily Kirk, who was talking to two guests at the reception desk. I made *it's all right, I've got it* gestures and she nodded.

I thought he'd go into the bar, or perhaps up to his room, but he didn't. He made for the gents. I stopped at the door. This was unknown territory for me. My mum used to suffer agonies of embarrassment even walking past a gents' toilet. She would make me avert my eyes in case I ever saw anything unsuitable for young eyes. Once or twice I'd asked her what she meant by that, but she wouldn't say, simply chivvying me quickly past the offending facility. She definitely wouldn't be happy with what I was going to do next, but I had to do it. Because something awful was going to happen tonight and possibly only I could prevent it.

I took a deep breath for courage, slipped in through the door and leaned against it. He was standing at the urinal. I averted my eyes, staring around at the smart blue and white colour scheme while I waited for him to finish.

He looked over his shoulder, saying curtly, 'You're in the wrong toilet.' He had a strong Yorkshire accent.

I took another very deep breath. His purple and red colour was boiling with anger and something else. Yes . . . frustration. There was so much frustration pent up inside him, all ready to blow and I didn't want him taking it out on me. He was wound up tighter than an elastic band. He could lose control at any moment. I had to make him calm down and listen to me before events spiralled further downwards to disaster.

Still keeping my distance from him, I said very quietly, 'You need to leave. Now. Don't go back into the dining room. Don't even stop to pack. Take the car and go now. She means to kill you tonight.'

He missed the urinal. Most of it went on his shoes. They were suede and I still feel bad about that. They would never have been the same afterwards.

He zipped himself up. 'You what?'

'She means to kill you. She's setting the scene. Another

23

furious row in public. She's in tears in the dining room. Everyone hates you. With no evidence whatsoever, they're already convinced you've been knocking her about. And then, sometime tonight or possibly tomorrow, she'll kill you. She'll stab you, probably. In your sleep. She'll say it was self-defence. You were about to attack her. Everyone in the dining room will testify to the argument tonight. How afraid of you she was. Everyone will be terribly shocked but no one will be surprised. This isn't an isolated incident, is it? How many times has something like this happened? I suspect she's been setting this up for some time. Do you have somewhere you could go tonight?'

He was gawping at me. I couldn't blame him. I was just a mousy little woman, with unfashionable clothes and hair, standing in front of him and telling him unbelievable things. 'Who are you? What are you talking about?'

'Listen to me,' I said sharply. 'I'm saving your life.'

'How do you know . . . ?'

'Never mind how. You *must* stay away from her. She's deadly. Answer me. Do you have somewhere you could go tonight?'

He nodded vaguely. His eyes were far away. I wondered if he was suddenly seeing past events in a different light.

'Do you have a solicitor?'

He nodded again.

'Get yourself to safety *now*. That's the most important thing. First thing tomorrow, make an appointment. Tell them everything. And make very, very sure you're never alone with your wife. Remember – she's made you the villain.'

He was struggling to take all this in. His mind was literally struggling. I could see his colour seethe and surge as he tried

24

to process my words. To make sense of this suddenly different perspective. I guessed there were events in their past that were suddenly making much more sense to him but, even so, I suspected he was very conventional – definitely not a deep thinker – and here was a strange woman in the gents' toilets telling him his wife was planning his death. That sort of thing didn't happen in his world. I swallowed down my impatience because this was taking too long. I had every confidence in Jones's ability to keep his wife in the dining room, but for his own safety, this young man should get out at once.

I took a pace towards him. 'Look. Suppose the two of you are alone in your room tonight. There's a shout. A crash. A scream. She emerges holding her face and crying. What do you think people will say happened? Who do you think will get the blame? Or she falls down the stairs. Everyone will look at you. Did you just push her?'

He threw a panic-stricken glance at the door. His colour had stopped writhing and was coiling around him like a blanket. Protecting him. He was almost convinced.

I turned to go. 'I can't do any more for you. Leave now and save your own life. Otherwise . . .'

I let the rest of the sentence hang in the air. I had no idea how this would play out. For all he knew I was some madwoman. For all I knew he was right.

'I'm in a nightmare,' he said suddenly, his colour flying around him as some of his inner tension released with the relief of being able to tell someone. 'It's like being tangled in a sticky web. No matter what I do or say – everything twists. All my friends have gone. My parents aren't speaking to me. I've somehow found myself in a job I hate and that I can't do very well. Every part of my life is going down the tubes and I don't know why. The more I struggle, the worse it gets.'

'What's her name?'

'Leanne.'

'There's your answer.'

'But why? Why would she?'

'Do you have life insurance?'

'Well, yes.'

'And a nice house?'

'Yes.'

'And a big bank account?'

'We're comfortably off, yes. Is that why?'

I said quietly, 'A little, yes – but mostly I think she does it because she likes to play.'

I could see that hit home. His colour recoiled, twisted for a moment and then subsided. He was beginning to see clearly.

He leaned over the basin and washed his face. Crossing to the machine, he pulled out a paper towel and held it to his eyes for one long moment, shutting out this suddenly unfamiliar world. I didn't blame him in the slightest but he was wasting time he couldn't afford.

The seconds were ticking away. I had no doubt that Jones could keep Leanne in the dining room but I wanted this young man out of here. I wasn't sure he would be strong enough to withstand his wife. I tried to put some authority into my voice. 'Stop hiding. You have to go. Right now. Don't look back until you're safe. And never be alone.'

He screwed up the towel and threw it in a bin. 'You think she'll come after me? I'm ready for anything she could do to me.'

26

'Nothing so straightforward. I think she'll injure herself and God help you if you don't have an unbreakable alibi. Do you understand now?'

He nodded, took a breath as if to say something, thought better of it and then pushed past me to the door. Yanking it open, he stopped and muttered, 'Thanks.'

'What's your name?'

'Tony.'

'Good luck, Tony.'

'Do you think she'll let me go this easily?'

'I'm hoping she'll write you off as a bad job and move on. I think she will if you protect yourself. There are plenty of other victims out there.'

He nodded without looking at me and let the door swing to behind him.

I gave him a minute or two and then slipped out as discreetly as I could. Once outside, I took a moment to let my breath out. It wasn't over yet. Suppose he hadn't believed me. Suppose, even now, he changed his mind and decided to ignore the very strange woman who had followed him into the toilet.

Emily Kirk was still at reception. The other guests had gone and there was no cover for me at all. I smiled weakly at her raised eyebrows and made my way back to the dining room.

I walked past Leanne without a single glance.

'All right?' said Jones as I sat down at our table and picked up my wine. My hands were shaking.

'I shouldn't be doing this,' I said in a low voice. 'I'm a housewife. I shouldn't be confronting strange men in wrong-gender toilets. I should be at home, making jam.'

He swallowed his mouthful. 'Have you ever made jam?'

27

I hesitated. My mum and dad brought me up to be truthful. 'I've made jam tarts.'

'Not for me, you haven't.'

'I'll make you some when we get back.'

'I look forward to a tart-laden future. But again, are you all right?'

I shook my head. 'I don't know.'

I stared down at my food and blinked back a stupid tear. I'd really looked forward to this little holiday. I'd never been to Scotland before. I just wanted to be an ordinary person – even if only for a few days. I pushed my plate away. I'd lost my appetite and that was a shame because the salmon was first rate. I wondered if it had been caught locally. Although not by Michael Jones.

He reached across the table and placed a warm paw over my cold one. His red colour reached out and touched me once, just briefly. My jangled nerves subsided. I took a deep breath, the world slowed down, righted itself, and my appetite came back. I smiled at him and picked up my knife and fork and asked him what she was doing now.

He wiped his mouth with his napkin. 'Just sitting there. Waiting for him to come back.'

Yes, she would, wouldn't she? She'd wait for him to come back so she could embark upon the second act. With lots of nice, respectable, reliable witnesses around. And Michael Jones, of course.

I shivered. I'd never before encountered such concentrated malice in one person. I risked a quick glance. Even now, her colour was still a flat grey. There was very little variation of shade and almost no movement. Her public face was one of dis-

28

tress and fear but inside she was perfectly composed. Perfectly in control. Manipulating the people and events around her and enjoying every moment.

I continued with my meal, straining my ears until, in the distance, I heard a car start up. Headlights showed briefly through the curtains. I heard the sound of wheels on the gravel. The car passed the window and then pulled away into the night. The sound of the engine died away. He was safe. That had been the easy part.

I patted my mouth with my napkin, said, 'Back in a minute,' stood up and walked over to where she sat, hunched and alone among the ruins of their meal. 'You poor thing,' I said, trying to sound sympathetic and motherly. 'Why don't we see if we can't get you tidied up a little?'

She lifted a pathetically woebegone face to me. 'Oh yes. That's a good idea. Tony doesn't like me to be untidy.'

'Well, in that case, let's get you fixed up before he comes back. He looks as if he likes to get his own way.'

'Oh no,' she said. 'He's so kind and caring and he does everything for me. I'm not allowed to lift a finger.'

Damning him with every word she uttered. I looked at her colour again. No movement. No change. If she was even a fraction as agitated as she would have us believe, then it should be jumping about all over the room, riddled with anxiety and fear and distress, and instead it simply moulded itself around her. Rather like armour.

I helped her out of the dining room. Every eye watched us go. Jones continued to eat.

I took her to the ladies. The toilet I could legitimately be in. This one was done out in pink, white and grey. Quite nice, actually.

She sniffed artistically and peered at herself in the mirror. Her colour encased her, rigid and still. Distraught she might appear to be, but she was in perfect control of herself. And the situation.

I was careful not to get between her and the door. If she wanted to make a bolt for it, I wasn't going to stand in her way. Although she'd have a job now Tony had taken the car. I took a moment to gather myself and then said, 'He's gone, you know.'

She turned her head to look at me and just for a moment there was a flash – like a door opening on to something nasty – and I saw the real person beneath. It was rather horrible, actually. Like the opaque surface of water with something very unpleasant lurking just beneath. It dawned on me that perhaps she might not experience emotions in the normal way. Or even at all. It also dawned on me that I was alone with a very dangerous person.

And then she smiled bravely through her tears. 'I'm sorry?'

I was assailed with sudden doubt. Suppose I was wrong? Suppose I'd just made things a hundred times worse. And then I looked at that flat, unchanging, uncaring colour again and was more convinced than ever that I had saved a life tonight.

I clasped my hands together so she wouldn't see their trembling. 'He's gone. Tony. He's left the hotel. He didn't feel like hanging around waiting for you to murder him so he pushed off.'

For a long second, she did nothing but stand and stare at me and that was the moment when, just for a very tiny moment, her guard came down and I saw. I saw how she had planned it all. The build-up. The so-called threat to her life. And then the murder. The shock. The horror. The sympathy. And throughout it all – the attention. All the little puppets dancing around her. Dancing her dance to her tune. And then, when she became bored she would move to a new area to begin the dance all over again. With different puppets this time. Because that's what it was to her. A dance. Entertainment. Fun.

I came back to the present. She was clutching at the wash-basin as if she hardly had enough strength to stand. 'I don't understand. You say he's gone? Where? Why would he do that? Oh God, was he very angry?' Her voice trembled. 'Sometimes he gets so angry and it frightens me.'

The door opened. Jones walked in and looked around. 'So this is a ladies' toilet. Nice.' He closed the door behind him.

She stared at him as if horrified. 'You can't come in here.'

I think she'd just about written me off as no use but here was someone she could weave into her schemes. I wondered if I should tell her she was wasting her time.

Jones held up his wallet. There was some kind of official-looking card in the pocket, but knowing Jones it could just as easily have been his library card. I didn't care. I was just so pleased to see him because it was only when he turned up that I realised how scared I'd been. There was something seriously wrong with this woman.

She turned to Jones, pitiful and afraid. I suspected she found men much easier to manipulate. 'Oh, help me, please. I don't understand what's going on and I want my Tony.'

Jones had once said to me that we often reached the same conclusion but by different routes. I prayed that tonight espe-cially he really was on the same path as me and not free-walking

31

through the foothills of misunderstanding. Sometimes I think I should have more faith in him. I didn't have to say a word.

'Leanne Elphick?'

She stared at him, her eyes huge in her pointed, fragile little face. 'How do you know my name? Who are you? Oh God, what is happening?'

I suspected he'd done nothing more sinister than ask her name from Emily Kirk, but she clung to the washbasin, every inch of her terrified and bewildered and overwhelmed. Even now there was still no change in her colour. I would say she wasn't experiencing any emotion of any kind.

He put his wallet away. 'We've been watching you for some time.'

He bluffs very well. Part of his job, I suppose.

She stepped back. 'Why? Why would you watch me? I want to go home.' She began to cry. The frightened little woman completely unable to cope with the world about her.

I stared at Jones, worried he might not realise just how dangerous this woman could be and trying to convey my concerns to him.

'Pack it in, love,' he said to her with barely concealed contempt. 'You're not impressing anyone.'

That got her attention and reminded me again just how good he was at his job. And he was right. I read colours but Jones reads people. Like a book, it would seem.

He didn't give her any time to recover. 'Anthony Elphick has left the hotel, I'm pleased to say. And in such a hurry I'm afraid he's stuck you with the bill. And don't bother sobbing all over Mrs Kirk – it turns out she never liked you, from the moment you stepped through her front door.'

32

He was bluffing, but his bluff was cutting the ground from under her feet with every word he spoke. And rather taking the wind out of my sails. 'Well,' I said to him. 'Obviously I'm not as special as I thought I was.'

'I think you're very special,' he said softly and then moved fast as she came at him with the soap dispenser. As he said afterwards, 'The shame of it, Cage. Clubbed to death with a Palfrey and Herman's Lily of the Valley Luxury Hand Soap dispenser. I'd never have heard the last of it.'

He reached out, grabbed her and twisted her arm. The soap dispenser fell to the floor. I picked it up and put it back because I've been brought up to be tidy.

'Now then,' he said, holding her firmly because she was trying to go for his eyes – and still that solid grey colour of hers never moved. 'That's enough of that.'

She was panting but only because her struggle had left her out of breath. 'You don't have anything on me.'

'Wrong again,' he said, but without elaborating so I guessed he didn't. 'Did you not hear me say we've been watching you for some time? This isn't your first go, is it?'

That hit home. Her colour jolted.

'Now,' he said. 'I'll tell you what's going to happen. You'll pay the bill like a good girl – why should the Kirks suffer just because you're some kind of psychopath? – and then you'll leave. First thing tomorrow. Quite quietly. And I'm going to pass on your details to some interested parties. I'd keep my head down for a bit if I were you. Over here, Cage. Stand behind me and don't get in my way.'

I stood beside him as he let her go and pushed her away from him.

She stared for a moment, assessing her chances, I suspected, and then wrenched the door open and stalked out of the toilet.

I watched the door close behind her. 'Are you just going to let her go?'

'What can I do? She hasn't done anything.'

'Yet. Will you really pass on her details?'

'Oh yeah. Someone will be interested in her.'

'They'll arrest her?'

'Perhaps. Or, given her nature and skill set, possibly employ her. Could go either way.' He put his hand on my shoulder. 'Sorry if this spoiled your evening but I think you might just have saved a life tonight.'

'I think you did that. You didn't need me at all, did you?'

'Well, I suspected something – that scene in the dining room didn't sit right with me – but it took you to show me the way. Shall we finish our meal? They were just bringing round the sweet trolley when I left.'

CHAPTER THREE

We returned to the dining room where our young waiter, clearly a little bit out of his depth, was dithering at our table, obviously wondering whether we'd abandoned our meal and were ever coming back. I felt quite sorry for him.

'I think we'd like the dessert menu, please,' said Jones, picking up his napkin again. His colour seemed brighter and more solid. 'Cage, I want to talk to you for a moment.'

I don't know why this filled me with such foreboding. To delay the moment, I said, 'You're not going to do a Tony – abandon me and stick me with the bill – are you?'

'Any man who knew what was good for him would have abandoned you months ago, Cage, but I am made of stern stuff.'

He said no more until after he'd given the dessert menu a thorough perusal and placed his order. We sat in silence until our waiter arrived with the desserts. I was sticking to a sorbet but Jones had gone full sticky toffee pudding. In a spirit of gratitude, our waiter – Rory, his name badge said – had been generous with Jones's portion. I could barely see the plate. Actually, I could barely see Jones.

I relaxed a little. That would take him some time to work through. Whatever he wanted to say, I was safe for a while.

I had forgotten how easily he could eat and talk. 'So, Cage . . .'

He paused for another mouthful. Whatever it was he wanted to speak to me about was obviously nowhere near as important as eating his pudding.

I sighed. 'Was there something specific you wanted to say?'

'A couple of things, actually.'

I put down my spoon. 'Go on, then.'

He deliberately fixed his attention on his pudding. 'It was the anniversary of Clare's death last month.'

Clare had been his partner. Professional partner, although I think there had been a deeper relationship than that. She died, but not before she'd betrayed him and the people he worked for. They'd held Jones responsible and, although he never said much about it, I knew he'd had a pretty tough time for a while. Dr Sorensen of the Sorensen Clinic had been part of that tough time.

I thought he was mostly over that now. In fact, he *was* mostly over it. The two of us had been inching our way towards . . . I don't know. I don't know what Jones and I had. I don't think he knew either, but whatever it was, I liked it and I didn't want anything to happen to it. And now he wanted to talk to me . . .

I looked at him. 'Are you all right? About Clare, I mean.'

'Yes, I am. I've accepted what she did. In a way I can even understand why she did it.'

He busied himself with his custard. I could see he wasn't finished talking so I signalled to Rory for some coffee, please. Because while Jones might not have a problem with Clare, I did.

I am aware that a lot of what I say makes me sound unbalanced. Not normal. It's normal for me but not for anyone else, so I've learned to conceal my supposed talent. My dad taught me to get through life as peacefully as possible and that's what I've

36

always tried to do. Only then my husband died and everything started to slide out of control and then, last Christmas . . . oh God . . . last Christmas there'd been an accident. I banged my head. And reality . . . something went wrong with reality. There was Jones's version – which, to be honest, was everyone else's version as well – where I'd banged my head, had a wonky moment and been carted off to the hospital.

Then there was my version – where I'd been attacked by something that looked like Clare and yet wasn't. I'd been hunted through my own house. Even now, if I closed my eyes, I could see that thing reaching for me, its dislocated jaw swinging in that evil wind; I could hear the telephone ringing on and on and on and Ted's voice telling me I was going to die. And all the time the angry snow swirled, covering the world in white silence.

Except it never happened. It couldn't have, because in my reality I'd exploded in a frenzy of rage and grief and fear and I'd brought down the whole clinic in a vortex of blood and destruction. I saw Sorensen's broken body caught up in the whirlwind as I lay in the white silence of the snow, looking up at the stars as the world ended around me.

Except it hadn't. I'd woken up and the snow had gone and the world was still here and so, obviously, it had all been a dream. 'You banged your head, Mrs Cage,' they said. And yet, deep down, I was sure it had happened. Except that it hadn't. Yes, I know – unbalanced.

Jones had finished his dessert while I'd been busy with my thoughts. 'Anyway,' he said, 'the reason I'm bringing this up now is because it kind of ties in with something I wanted to say to you. I've been waiting for the right moment – only I suspect that with you, Cage, there will always be something happening – so I'm just going to go ahead and say it now.'

The coffee arrived.

'All right,' I said, my heart pounding. 'Go ahead and say it.'

He stirred his coffee. 'My boss was none too happy over Sorensen grabbing me last summer. When he thought he'd use me as leverage to get to you. Sorensen's been told, in no uncertain terms, that his obsession over you has led him to act inappropriately and to pack it in.'

'Obsession is putting it rather mildly.' I looked at him. 'When I met you, I thought you worked for Sorensen.'

'I've worked *with* him. I've been seconded to him on several occasions. But no, I work for another department. And I rather think my boss is going to have something to say about Sorensen attempting an unauthorised interrogation on a member of her department. If she hasn't already.'

He brooded for a while and then roused himself. 'The thing is, Cage, I've been told to make myself scarce. Take myself out of the picture, so to speak.'

I was horrified. 'They've sacked you?'

'Oh no. Full pay and so on. I'm not sure how official unhappiness with Sorensen is going to manifest itself and I must admit I'm very happy to keep my distance on this one and find something else to do for a while.'

'For how long?'

He shrugged. 'Not sure. I think it depends on what Sorensen has to say for himself, but it could be anything up to a year.'

'A year?' I said, hoping I didn't sound as dismayed as I felt. 'Mm.'

'What will you do?' I braced myself. 'Where will you go?' I

had visions of him island-hopping through Greece or mountain climbing or exploring the rainforests or ... something. Not living quietly in Rushford, anyway. For anything up to a year.

'Well, that's one of the things I wanted to talk to you about.'

He stopped again and sipped his coffee.

'Go on.'

'Well, I was thinking – when we go back to Rushford ...'

'Can you go back? I mean, we were ... on the run. We were living quietly and ...'

'Actually, Cage, no, we weren't. There was nothing quiet about it. We were holed up in a very pleasant seaside cottage where no one would ever have found us and then you set the furniture off. And barely had we got over that than those bloody weird women at Greyston had a go at us again. I have to tell you that your idea of living quietly is very different to mine.'

'I mean,' I said, patiently, 'that we were going to avoid Sorensen. Possibly go abroad and live.'

'Well, now we don't have to. He's in serious trouble at the moment and he's got more to worry about than us. And you heard what he said – he doesn't want you any longer. And if he doesn't want you any longer, then why would he want me? I suspect he'll concentrate all his efforts on burying the last few months and pretending they never happened. And he's never going to want to admit he lost a valuable patient – that would be me – to a housewife – that would be you – an old crook – which would be Jerry – and whoever or whatever that weird blond bloke is.'

'Iblis?'

'Yes, him. And his bloody dog.'

'Nigel?'

He sighed. 'He's called that mongrel Nigel?'

'Nigel the Ninja and actually, I rather think that was your suggestion.'

He sighed. 'Anyway, to return to the topic, I think it's safe for us to go back.'

'And if not?'

'Then I'm sure we'll get to know about it soon enough. And at least we'll have had a lovely holiday in Scotland. Have I thanked you?'

'Many times. And I should be thanking you for bringing me. It's been lovely so far.' I remembered Leanne Elphick. 'Well, mostly lovely.'

He looked at me. 'That's the other thing I wanted to talk to you about. It could always be like this, you know.'

'What – being in Scotland?'

'No – I mean the two of us. Together.'

'What are you saying?' My hands were shaking again and I dropped them into my lap, out of sight.

He looked around the dining room, nearly empty now. Rory was beginning to clear the tables and lay for breakfast. No one was within earshot.

'Cage, I've been thinking. We could do this full-time. Together.'

He was nervous. His colour was shooting all over the place. I, on the other hand, was simply bewildered.

'Do what all the time?'

'Help people, Cage. I think we should help people. Together.'

Still slightly at sea, I said cautiously, 'Define together.'

'Not sure how I can make it much clearer. I mean working together. What did you think I meant?'

I rushed to cover up my blunder. 'That's what Sorensen said. That you and I could end up working together. Is that what you meant?'

'No. Forget Sorensen.'

'I wish I could.'

'Look, you saved that kid in the tree. And then there was Evelyn Cross. Not that she was a person but you know what I mean. And Hélène Rookwood. I know you panic because things happen around you, but have you ever thought that that's what's supposed to happen? That you turn up and things happen so you can put them right. We sometimes say we arrive at the same conclusion but by different routes. We complement each other. You could sort out the weird stuff and I can do the muscle. We'll have to charge because I didn't have a husband to leave me well-off and I need the money, but we could tailor the fees to people's resources.'

I was completely at sea. He was proposing I overturn the habits of a lifetime and I couldn't take it in all at once. 'But how would that happen? I mean . . .' I tailed away.

'Well, let's say someone comes to see you saying they think Great Aunt Mary is haunting the spare bedroom. We pop along, I stand in the doorway – well out of harm's way – you firkle about a bit, doing that funny thing you do, and report that Great Aunt Mary's told you her will is hidden in the chimney breast. I pocket the fee and we both shoot off down the pub.'

He'd lost me. 'Who is Great Aunt Mary and why would she have hidden her will in the chimney breast?'

'I don't know but I expect you could make everything clear on the last page – you know, like one of those thrillers where everything's tied up in a neat bow.'

41

I shook my head. 'But it's not like that for me. I only see flashes of someone else's story. I don't usually know how things start, let alone how they end. I've no idea how Leanne and Tony Elphick will turn out. And besides, I couldn't have done anything without you along to enforce things.'

He beamed triumphantly. 'Exactly the point I'm trying to make, Cage. Teamwork. Why don't you take a while to think about it? Are you going to finish your sorbet?'

I pushed over my dish and, to save time, my after-dinner mint as well.

'Exceeds expectations,' he said thickly, spooning up the sorbet. 'I like that in a partner. Have you thought about it yet? What did you decide?'

'Only that you shouldn't talk with your mouth full. It's not attractive.'

CHAPTER FOUR

'Well,' he said the next morning over breakfast, 'apparently Leanne Elphick has already left the building. Mrs Kirk says she was quite unwilling to be reasonable about the bill until the police were mentioned and then, very grudgingly, she settled.'

I remembered that nasty, implacable grey colour. 'Good.'

'Yes, an excellent result all round. But best of all, I think we can assume yesterday's events have fulfilled our quota of one unpleasant experience wherever we go, so we should be able to relax and enjoy ourselves from now on.'

'I've ordered our packed lunches,' I said. 'And I told Mrs Kirk that one of them was for you so we'll probably need a pack mule to carry it all. Did you bring your own fishing gear?'

'No, I'm hiring theirs. Do you want a rod too?'

I shook my head. 'I've brought some books.'

He blinked. 'You're not going to catch many fish with a book.'

I buttered my toast. 'Bet I catch more than you.'

We collected our lunches from reception and Jones loaded himself up with fishing paraphernalia. I had a neat backpack with lunch, water, sunglasses, sun cream, and two books. He shouldered his fishing stick and away we went.

It was another beautiful day. Still hot, but with a breeze strong enough to move the topmost branches on the trees. Golden leaves fluttered around us, landing on the ground with a whisper. The river was on our left and we followed it upstream along the wide path. The air was soft and fresh. I took a deep breath and felt my spirits rise. This was going to be absolutely lovely.

'Ours is Beat Number Three,' said Jones, consulting the small map provided by Emily Kirk. 'As selected by you last night. It's on this side of the river and about two miles upstream.'

We didn't rush, happily ambling along the riverside, pointing out the occasional squirrel or scuttling rabbit. Just for once, we had all the time in the world. No one was after us and we had nowhere else to be. Just for once, *now* was more important than the past or the future.

The river flowed past, wide and fast and noisy. Trees hung over the water's edge making patches of deep shade. I recognised ash, elder and willow. It was all a bit of a tangle, broken by the occasional stony beach marked with numbers in red. We passed Beat One and after a while, Beat Two.

The water was browned by the stony bottom but beautifully clear. Larger rocks and gravel banks had formed pools, and dark shapes moved placidly in the depths.

'Trout,' said Jones happily. 'Look at them panic. They know I'm on my way.'

Four or five buzzards glided in great circles overhead – 'Not terribly reassuring,' commented Jones – uttering their strange kitten cries. Other than that, there was nothing but the sound of the wind and the river.

'Here we are,' he said, shrugging off his gear at a little wooden jetty with the number three painted on a small plaque.

The bank was quite wide here. A verge of close-cropped grass swept up to the remains of a low stone wall just right for leaning against. I unpacked my own stuff, laying out my books and a small cushion. Adjusting my sunglasses, I leaned back against the warm wall and sighed contentedly. This was the most beautiful spot.

I spent a few minutes watching Jones set himself up. He screwed his rod together, optimistically assembled his keepnet and prepared to lure a perfectly happy fish from its natural habitat. This could take hours. I opened my book.

Nearly two hours later and it began to look as if his, 'I'll only catch two for our dinner tonight and throw the rest back,' might have been a little over-optimistic. I remembered his previous attempts at fishing when we'd been held in the Sorensen Clinic. They'd been spectacularly unsuccessful as well. Not least because there were no fish in that part of the Rush anyway. I strongly suspected that should a fish unexpectedly find itself on the end of Jones's line, both it and Jones would be equally surprised and very probably neither of them would know what to do next.

'What are you doing?' he said, throwing himself down beside me.

'Making plans for a steak meal this evening. I ask again – have you ever actually caught a fish?'

'Oh, I've pulled all sorts of things out of rivers, Cage. Is it time for lunch yet?'

I looked at my watch and to my surprise, it nearly was.

We lunched lengthily. Sandwiches, crisps, fruit and cheese, chocolate, hard-boiled eggs, juice and water. I laid it all out.

There was a lot of food here. The hotel seemed to have packed enough for six people. On the other hand, five of those people were Michael Jones so it all worked out in the end.

I leaned back against the wall and munched my sandwiches. The peace was complete. I listened to the unending music of the river and the wind in the trees. Every shade of orange and russet was represented in this early autumn pageant of colour, contrasting vividly with the brilliant blue sky overhead. There wasn't a cloud in sight. If I'd wanted to design the perfect day and the perfect spot, I don't think I could have done a better job. And I had a good meal and comfortable bed to look forward to at the end of the day, as well. This holiday was just what I needed.

The second day was a repeat of the first except we chose another beat so Jones could not catch any fish in a completely different part of the river.

I'd picked Beat Seven, which was on the other bank. We trailed across the bridge with Jones leaning over to watch the water and, he said, plot his strategies.

We walked through the woods this time. They were alive with birdsong. On Beat Three we'd had more grass and open countryside and a view of the woods. Today we were in the woods and looking across the river at open fields. The ground was hard and dry. Mrs Kirk had told us they'd had no rain for nearly a month now.

I found a nice spot under a tree, unpacked my book and prepared for another day of massive hardship, eating, reading and watching Jones as he armed himself for the fray.

As before, the morning flew by. I finished my book just in time for lunch.

Obviously, considering I wasn't moving fast enough, Jones unpacked lunch himself.

'Bridies,' he uttered, incomprehensibly.

'What?'

'Scottish pasties,' he said. 'Like the Cornish pasty but without the potato. And with flaky pastry. There are two types of bridies – ones with one hole and ones with two holes.'

I refused to ask.

'Holes signify the filling,' he said, telling me anyway. 'One hole for no onion and two *for* onion. What did you think I meant?'

I refused to tell him.

They were massive. The bridie with one hole was mine and the two with two holes were for Jones. I never thought he'd manage two but I was wrong. Sitting under the trees, watching the river flow past, it was one of the nicest lunches I'd ever had. Followed by fruit for me and crisps for him.

Actually, the bridie might have been a bit of a mistake. Half an hour later I was in danger of falling asleep over my new book so I clambered stiffly to my feet and told Jones I was taking a short walk to go exploring.

He nodded vaguely, staring hard at the river, obviously contemplating his next strategy while a shoal of giant trout swam contemptuously past.

I left him to it, walking back the way we'd come. I thought it might be fun to have a closer look at the bridge and explore the old mill and dilapidated buildings I'd seen as we'd driven up to the hotel. I moved quietly, trying not to disturb the birds who'd come down to drink. At one point, I thought I saw the flash of a kingfisher's wing.

I passed the hotel on the opposite bank. As I did so, Mrs Kirk appeared from the garden with a basket full of vegetables. She saw me and waved and disappeared in through the kitchen door. There was no sign of Clarence. In fact, there was even less happening here than downstream with Jones. The whole world dreamed in the hot sunshine.

I stood on the road, near the bridge, watching the water flow underneath, breathing deeply and fortunately not having to dodge any vehicles. Like many people, I'd never realised how silent the world is when the persistent, ever-present background noises of traffic are removed. Just water, wind and birds. As it had been for hundreds, if not thousands, of years.

The ivy-covered remains of the old mill stood to the right of the bridge with the remains of what looked like a village on the left, further up the hill. I thought I'd explore the village first and set off through the trees, listening to the birdsong as I went, my footsteps silent on the soft, pine-needle-strewn path. Rays of sunlight shafted diagonally through the trees, highlighting the dust hanging in the air.

The path climbed gently, but not enough to make me pant or sweat. I passed several of the outlying buildings I'd seen from the car, and then, quite suddenly, I was out from under the trees with open land in front of me. It looked as if I'd found the village.

The deserted buildings were in surprisingly good condition – like the hotel, they'd been well built of local stone – but not one of them had a roof. I don't really know very much about Scottish history, but was this evidence of the Highland clearances, when they forced people to leave and then removed the roofs of houses to prevent rehabitation? Surely, we were too far south for that. Mrs Kirk would know. I must remember to ask her this evening.

What I thought could have been the main street curled away to the left. As far as I could tell, the village had been built around a rising rectangle of open land, where, presumably, the villagers would have grazed their livestock. There was an old well in one corner, its wooden covering well and truly rotten. Cautiously, I peered down the shaft. It wasn't that deep and seemed perfectly dry now, but there would be others around the place. I must remember to watch where I put my feet.

I wandered between the crumbling buildings, stumbling over hidden stones and extricating myself occasionally from clinging brambles, until I thought I'd explored most of it. Not that there was very much to see. After a while, one crumbled cottage looks very much like another. I perched on a bit of wall in the shade and tried to count the buildings. There were more of them than I had thought. Unless some of them had been outhouses – sheds or pigsties or whatever.

In front of me was the centre of the village – where the few shops would have been – butcher, baker, blacksmith, grocer, and so on. And the inn. What looked like the village church – no, the kirk – a small, stocky building, was at the top of the slope. With the mill and the bridge, this must have been a thriving little community. In my mind's eye, I peopled it with men going about their business, women gossiping at their gates with vegetable-filled baskets over their arms. There would be lines of washing, hung out to dry in the sun. Children and dogs running everywhere. Or perhaps there would be a school for them? Yes, a school with the bell ringing in the distance. Near the church, probably. And there would be farmers driving their

49

flocks down to cross the bridge or bringing in their produce on a cart. Perhaps there had even been a market here on the green. My village was clean and neat with happy, healthy people.

I smiled to myself. It probably hadn't been like that at all. There would have been rain. And mud. Lots and lots of mud. And leaky roofs. And sickness. And the perpetual fear of a bad harvest. There would have been the usual feuds and disagreements raging. People would have fallen out with each other in the way that people always do. Every Sunday the minister would have chastised them for unseemly behaviour – if not downright sin – and the local laird would almost certainly have been a tyrannical despot, grinding his tenants' faces into the mud for extra profit. Just to add insult to injury, he would probably have been an English tyrannical despot. Again, I must remember to ask Emily Kirk. Perhaps there were some local history pamphlets back in the hotel.

As far as I could see, though, this hadn't been a bad place to live. What catastrophe could possibly have caused the inhabitants to abandon it?

I stood up, brushed the dust and cobwebs off my bottom and took the still faintly visible path around the left-hand side of the village green. I carried on up past the church, which did have its roof intact – although obviously no one had been inside for a very long time. I could see the door but brambles made it inaccessible. If there had been a churchyard, it had long since disappeared under spindly saplings and undergrowth. I walked on past the building I thought might have been the school and out the other side of the village.

What was either a narrow road or a broad path ran ahead of me. The left side was bounded by an ivy-covered stone wall which had completely collapsed in places. This was exciting. Walls enclose property and all that was missing from this set-up was the local manor house, which must surely be around here somewhere.

I walked on into the silent woods. When had the birds stopped singing? The trees began to cluster more closely together. The air was stifling and I was getting hot. I decided I'd just go a little further and if there was nothing interesting around the next bend then I'd turn back. The glittering river seemed suddenly very attractive indeed. I could sit on the bank, dangle my feet in the cool water and tell Michael Jones exactly where he was going wrong. He would appreciate that.

I came upon it quite suddenly. A pair of stone gateposts reared up out of the dry, dusty grass. I suspected the gates themselves had been stolen long ago. Beyond them a short, unkempt drive led to a large house, its roof and chimneys barely visible behind its own overgrown garden.

The house must have been a lovely place once upon a time, set among the mature trees and with spectacular views down over the river valley. I could just see the lady of the manor wafting around her gardens, wearing a pretty bonnet to shade her complexion from the sunshine, and cutting flowers to put in a basket over her arm.

A tall cedar tree reared up out of the undergrowth and giant clumps of – I think – rhododendrons jostled almost everything else out of existence. Such a shame. It must have been a beautiful place, once.

I peered around the gateposts but didn't go in. The garden looked quite impenetrable and somehow unwelcoming, so I left everything to doze in peace and walked a little further up the

51

road. Concealed among the trees I found a second entrance – the original entrance, probably – with what I assumed were the remains of the lodge house. Here though, there had definitely been some sort of damage. A fire, perhaps. The stones I could see looked scorched and blackened and were scattered over a wide area. Had they pulled the lodge house down to prevent the fire spreading further? Or had it collapsed by itself? The two surviving walls were no more than head height. Perhaps the cottage had exploded for some reason. An illegal still, perhaps. Brambles scrambled over everything. I picked a rich, ripe, glistening blackberry and spat it back out again. It was so bitter that it made my teeth turn furry.

I contemplated the scene before me. The wrecked cottage. The tumbled stones, half hidden in the stalky, dry grass. The blackberry-laden brambles. No birds squabbled over this fruit. Everything looked untouched. Only plants and trees lived here. There was complete silence all around me. No breeze blew to cool my face. Just hot stillness everywhere. For a moment my head swam with the heat. I put my hand on the wall to steady myself and closed my eyes. Dear God, it was hot.

The sudden blast of heat made me step back. I opened my eyes and as I did so, everything around me exploded into life and colour and catastrophe. I stared in disbelief. The world was on fire. Red and orange flames leaped everywhere. The little cottage, somehow miraculously restored, was being enveloped in a great wall of flames. I could hear them roaring. This was no dream or vision. This was real. I had to step back because the heat was searing my face.

My first instinct was to turn and run. To raise the alarm. There hadn't been any rain for weeks. This whole area could go up. All the trees, dry grass and undergrowth – everything was tinder-dry. And the people. I should alert the local people. Like an idiot, I'd left my phone behind. The nearest telephone would be at the hotel. I could call from there. I went to turn. To crash back through the trees and run down the hill. To get help.

And then I stopped. No – this wasn't right. What was happening? The flames were so bright that I hadn't noticed daylight had disappeared and it was dark. A slim, silver moon shone in the sky. The crackling flames sent golden sparks streaming upwards, bright against the black, night sky – like tiny temporary stars.

And then the sound kicked in. Someone was screaming. I could hear voices. Men were shouting. A group of people were running towards me, bringing buckets and containers – anything that would hold water. I looked around. From where would they get water? Wasn't the well too far away? Or would the cottage have a pump in the garden? And would they be able to get close enough to use it? And from where had they come?

I looked back over my shoulder. The big house, now clearly visible without its surrounding jungle, blazed with light. Lights shone in nearly every window. The front door stood wide open and a warm yellow lamplight streamed across the dark ground.

Five or six half-dressed men were running towards the fire, shouting instructions to each other, with what looked like their nightshirts stuffed into their breeches and their boots unlaced. They must have just rammed their feet into the nearest footwear and run to help. One man was wearing one boot and one shoe.

There were women here as well – maids, perhaps, with shawls or coats thrown over their long white nightdresses. They too were laden with pots and saucepans.

Someone ran right past me. Automatically, I stepped back out of his way. He couldn't have missed me but there was no collision. I don't think he even saw me. I looked down at myself. Was I invisible?

They might not be able to see me but I could certainly see them. And – my heart lurched – I could see a figure silhouetted in the tiny upstairs cottage window. I squinted. Only her head and shoulders were visible but I was almost certain it was a woman and she was trapped.

I shouted and pointed but my voice was lost in the commotion around me.

I looked around for whoever was in control here. Someone would be giving the orders. I could tell him. I scanned the crowd of scurrying people, looking for the person in charge.

I found her. A woman with a cloak thrown over her nightdress was shouting commands. I could hear her voice over the clamour.

'Form a chain. Form a chain. Humphries, there are people in the house. Break down the door. Break it down. For the love of God, we must save them.'

I could feel her fear, her helplessness, her panic. I could feel it from all of them but especially from her. Standing on a half-buried rock, she urged them onwards. I felt she would have seized a bucket herself if she thought it would help.

Her people did their best. Two men – one of them would be Humphries, I assumed – ran to the cottage. They had cloths tied around their faces to protect them from the flames and

54

smoke but they were beaten back by the heat. They couldn't even get close.

I could feel her impotent frustration. There just weren't enough people here to be effective. They'd found water somewhere and formed a chain; slopping buckets were being passed from hand to hand. Even the maids had joined in. The flames held the cottage in their grip and they weren't letting go. I could see people flinging water at it but they were wasting their time. It was painful to admit, but I couldn't see how anyone could possibly escape that raging inferno.

Now they were concentrating all their efforts on the front door, hurling bucket after bucket at the flames there. I think they had some plan to force their way through. I wondered if there was a back door. Yes, there must be. Perhaps there were people trying there as well.

All the time, the flames were roaring around the little cottage and the figure in the upstairs window – yes, it was a woman – was beating her hands against the tiny panes. They'd seen her. They knew she was there. We could all see the panes of glass were too tiny to break. It was very possible the window didn't even open, and even if it did, I suspected it would be too small for her to climb through. They were shouting at her to come downstairs. I don't know if she could hear them. I couldn't hear her screams over the roaring flames and if we couldn't hear her, then she probably couldn't hear us.

A great feeling of helplessness washed over me. There were so few of us to help. We couldn't do anything. We needed more people. More men. More buckets. More water.

The woman's face was still at the upstairs window, dark against the flames now climbing the walls behind her. I could see her hair tumbling around her face as she tried to force the window open. Not that it would do her any good. We needed a ladder. Perhaps they could climb up, rip out the entire window frame, somehow, and drag her through.

There was no time. The flames were consuming everything in their path. How much longer could she possibly survive the smoke and heat?

More people arrived at a run. From the village by the looks of it. Again, all of them were dressed in whatever clothes had first come to hand. They stood in the road, chests heaving after running up the hill. I thought they'd come to help. Relief flooded through me. There were enough of them to make a proper chain. And there were some big men there – they could force the front door open somehow and get her out.

They did nothing. Not one of them. Having arrived, they stood motionless, drawing tightly together in an uneasy group. Sullen and silent, they watched events unfold in front of them. I could see the reflected flames flickering across their faces. The women clutched their shawls around them, hands to their mouths. The men just stood and stared. One turned his head and spat. I was standing some distance away and I could still feel their sullen hostility.

The woman in the dark cloak jumped down off her rock and ran towards them, her hair tumbling from under her nightcap. She shouted at them, gesturing wildly towards the burning cottage which, by now, was almost incandescent. A massive heat haze rippled around it. Tiny flames were running along the ground. The grass was alight. Even the surrounding trees were beginning to catch. This was not a safe place to be.

Two running men appeared – grooms, I suspected – carrying an unwieldy wooden ladder between them. They tried to get close enough to prop it against the cottage but the heat kept driving them back. Even with wet cloths tied around their faces the heat was so intense that they simply couldn't get close enough to prop the ladder against the wall.

Still the people from the village stood and stared. Their faces were closed to all emotion but I could feel their surly resentment. There would be no assistance from any of them.

The woman in the cloak was frantic. So was I. Her emotions were mine. I felt the same panic, the same fear and deep frustration. The same helplessness. And, deep down, a rising fury that they wouldn't do anything to help.

I turned to face them. 'You must do something,' I shouted. 'There's a woman in there. Help her. You can't do nothing. You have to try.'

A man carrying two slopping buckets ran past me and I reached out to grab his arm. 'You must help her.' He brushed me aside. I don't think he even saw me. No one could see me. No one could hear me. I looked wildly around. What else could I do? What could anyone do?

The heat was scorching my skin. I could feel the hair on my arms begin to singe. The smell of smoke was making my eyes and nose run. I began to cough. I was dangerously close to the cottage. I should move. Burning myself would not help the woman inside, but surely there was something I could do. I stared around, as impotent as everyone else.

I think that was the moment when I realised it was all hopeless. Even if we'd had a modern engine and twenty firefighters, I don't think anyone would have been able to do anything. I felt my shoulders sag and my legs tremble. I leaned forwards and put my hands on my knees, sucking in smoky air. My chest hurt with the smoke. The fire had won. With the villagers helping, we might have had a fighting chance. Without them we had nothing. The woman in the cottage was lost.

She was standing quite still now, her hands pressed helplessly against the windowpanes. She'd stopped shouting. She'd stopped beating at the window. Had she also realised it was futile? That she could not be saved? As I stared, the flames roared up behind her. She half turned. I saw her mouth open in a dreadful soundless scream as the flames enveloped her. I caught just a fleeting glimpse of a fiery halo around her head and then, with a mighty crash, the whole roof came down and any inhabitants were beyond saving. Beyond everything. The window blew out and flames belched into the night. Slowly, with a crash, the whole cottage fell in on itself, one wall after the other, sending great showers of sparks and burning embers in all directions. Flames erupted heavenwards. The heat was even more intense. People screamed and shouted and then everyone, including me, was running to get away. Burning slates and timbers crashed to the ground around us. I covered my head with my arms and ran blindly.

The woman in the cloak was shouting at her people to get back to safety. The villagers, presumably, saved themselves. Everyone regrouped at a safe distance, out on the road. Even from here the heat was intense. I could feel it drying the sweat on my face. Would I ever be cool again?

Cloak whirling, the woman spun around to face the villagers, still standing apart in their sullen clump. They flinched. I didn't blame them. Her voice cracked with emotion. 'You could have tried to save the children.'

Oh God, there had been children in there. Had they been in the same room as the woman? I hadn't seen them. Perhaps they were just babies. And now I could feel my own anger rising – a reflection of hers, perhaps. These people had let them die. They'd stood and watched. They'd done nothing. They'd let a woman and her children die.

She turned back to the burning cottage. I could still feel her anguish but it was fading. In fact, it was fading fast, replaced by a deep, deep purple fury that frightened me with its intensity.

The flames roared and twisted, feeding off whatever they could find. People were slapping at the grass. To try to prevent the flames spreading, I suppose. She stopped them, holding up her hands and shaking her head. She no longer cared.

'Let it burn.' She deliberately turned to look at the villagers, saying, 'Let it all burn.'

The men stood together, their hands thrust deep into their pockets, shoulders hunched. Their women stood behind them. Now that it was all over – now that it was too late – there was fear and something like regret. Although whether regret at their own failure or regret at the deaths of innocent people, it was hard for me to say.

Silently, she regarded them – almost speculatively – rather like a scientist observing his subjects. She said nothing at all but one or two shuffled uneasily. Were they feeling remorse?

She stared at them in silence. I watched her. That she was in charge was very apparent. She was accustomed to being obeyed and tonight, for some reason, she hadn't been. I had a very strong feeling the people from the village would be made to regret that.

That was the moment I should have left. My heart was

pounding in my chest and my legs were shaking with the shock. I should have run away. Back through the trees into the real world with its daylight, cool river, and Michael Jones. Every instinct I had was telling me to leave. Because something was gathering and that something was finding a very unwelcome echo within me. Something overwhelming was here. I couldn't stand against it. It would consume me. Grief. Rage. And . . . something else. Yes . . . impotence. A strangely familiar feeling of powerlessness as dreadful events unfolded around me and there was nothing I could do about it.

But I could. I could do a lot about it.

I could make them sorry.

Best of all – I could make them pay.

Something drifted down from the sky. Ash, probably. Or, impossibly, a tiny snowflake.

Like an ominous wind, something dark and dangerous twisted its way between the smouldering trees, swishing through the long grass, winding through the motionless people. Something was here. Blind in its desire – no, its *demand* – for revenge.

I'd known that sensation. That familiar urge. To visit revenge on those who deserved it. To lash out. To hurt. To destroy. To obliterate everything in my path. Once again, the thing that lived inside my head began to uncoil itself. I was helpless to prevent it. The world blurred before my eyes. The force of emotion threatened to burst my heart straight out of my chest. For one moment I thought I would die. That the power of it would kill me.

But no – stop. Stop. No. It wasn't me. I wasn't the one. This was something else.

The woman with the cloak stood about twenty feet away, still staring at the villagers. On the surface she was standing quietly but inside . . . inside she was a vortex of raw, uncontrolled emotion. She was the source of all this . . . this . . . this rage of revenge. And the thing about revenge is that although it might be sweet, it's always too late. The worst has already happened. Revenge is . . . yes . . . now I had it. Revenge is *punishment*.

Until this moment, I'd only caught glimpses of her, darkly silhouetted against the flames as she alternately organised her people and raged at the villagers to join in the fight against the fire. That she was a person of consequence in the area was obvious. She must be the lady of the manor then. There was no sign of a man, so she'd be a widow, a mother, or a sister – in charge anyway. This was no feeble woman, screaming helplessly as people died. She'd commanded and people had scurried to do her bidding.

Except for the people from the village, still standing silently apart, surly but afraid. Yes, at this moment they were very afraid of her and rightly so. They were her tenants. They owed her their livelihoods. They'd seen her. They'd certainly heard her as she shouted her orders at them and yet they'd hadn't moved. They'd disobeyed her and people had died.

Her emotions were boiling inside her, burning hotter than the fire still consuming the remains of the fallen cottage. The force of it hurt my chest and I could feel the response within myself.

Because this had once happened to me. Not long ago there had been an occasion when I'd felt that all-consuming rage. That urge to destroy. To rend. To hurt. To kill. To punish. And I had. I'd brought down the Sorensen Clinic. I'd killed in anger. I'd killed *with* anger. And it was happening again. I couldn't drag my eyes away. Couldn't move my feet. I was rooted to the spot as my own red rage burned as brightly as hers.

I wondered afterwards if my rage had been a reflection of hers – or whether it had been the other way around. Whichever it was, emotion called to emotion. A molten thread connected her to me and me to her. I knew it. And so did she.

Slowly, as inevitably as time itself, she turned to face me. She could see me. Unlike everyone else here, she could see me. The world receded. It was just the two of us. Despite the massive heat coming off the burning stones, I turned cold all over. My blood congealed. My breath caught in my throat.

Because I was looking at myself.

CHAPTER FIVE

The legend of the doppelgänger is worldwide. Everyone has one, apparently, and if you're lucky, you never see yours. To meet your doppelgänger is to die. To see your own face is a sign that certain death is coming for you. In which case it was coming for me, because I was definitely looking at my own face.

Don't misunderstand me. This wasn't someone who looked like me. Or someone with a strong resemblance to me. This was me. Myself. I. I was looking at me. My own eyes, red-rimmed and sore with smoke, stared back at me. The same eyebrows – with the small scar over one of them where I fell as a child and cut my forehead. My dad had picked me up and carried me home. There was the same small freckle on my cheekbone. The same ears. The same chin. I looked at my own self and my own self looked back at me. And the thing that lived inside my head opened its eyes.

For a moment the world whirled around me again. I was looking at a cloaked woman. And then the viewpoint altered and I was looking at a woman in T-shirt and jeans. And then I was looking at the cloaked woman again. As if in a mirror, slowly, we both reached out, fingers extended. Right hand to left hand. Closer . . . closer . . . Our fingers were millimetres apart – the moment froze – and then I was standing in an empty clearing with the remains of a small stone cottage around me. The sun was blazing down and I could smell dry grass and dust, and everything was as it had been before.

Except for me. I was drenched in sweat and still unable to move. I sucked in one or two deep breaths and slowly let my arm fall to my side. I dragged myself to a nearby stone, sat, and waited for my heart to stop trying to hammer its way out through my chest. I pulled out my water. There wasn't much left – I should have brought a fresh bottle – and it was unpleasantly warm after spending so much time in my backpack, but it would do. I closed my eyes, tried to slow my breathing, and waited for the cold sweat on my skin to evaporate.

When I thought my legs could hold me, I stood up and walked back out on to the overgrown road to stand on the exact spot where *she* had stood. I looked back. The ruined stones lay quietly. The sun shone. There was no breath of wind. Nothing moved.

Turning away, I made my way back through the abandoned village, past the village green, and out on to the proper metal road. I quickened my pace and by the time I reached the bridge, I was nearly running.

There I paused, leaning on the parapet and waiting for my heartbeat to return to normal. I watched the river go past, feeling the fresh, wet air on my face, concentrating on the way the water eddied around the rocks. I watched the bubbles swirl away downstream. I looked at the trees overhanging the banks, gently touching their own reflections in the occasional still pool. The temperature was much cooler down here. I leaned on the warm stonework and breathed it all in.

A family of ducks stood on a gravel bank in the middle of

the river. An adult and four younger ones – their fluff almost disappeared among their adult feathers. I watched them waddle into the water, swim a little way, upend themselves so they were just a row of duck bottoms, and then paddle back to their starting point. There they would shake themselves, preen a little, and then do it all over again. I have no idea how long I stood watching them.

My heart was still pounding in my chest. My hair was glued to my forehead. And the back of my neck, as well. I thought about going down to the riverbank and splashing my face with cold water and then realised I was an idiot because the hotel was only just over there. I could wash properly, inspect myself for any burns, and change my T-shirt.

I trotted across the bridge and down to the hotel. I saw no one on the way. Everyone else was out enjoying the lovely day. I'd handed in my key rather than risk losing it by the river, but no one was around so I nipped behind the desk and grabbed it and then ran up the shallow stairs.

Once in my room, I ripped off my T-shirt and found another. I washed my face and the back of my neck. My skin was completely unburned. I sniffed my discarded T-shirt and there was no smell of smoke. In fact, there was nothing at all to show I'd just witnessed a major conflagration. Slowly, I dressed again. This T-shirt was very similar to the one I'd been wearing before. With luck, Jones would never notice.

'You've changed your T-shirt,' he said, as I approached.

'Blackberry stains,' I said. 'I had to put it in to soak.'

'Very good,' he said admiringly. 'I very nearly believed you. Now tell me the truth.'

I said nothing.

He laid down his rod, took my arm, led me to sit under a tree and handed me a bottle of water. This one was cool because he'd been standing it in the river. Along with a couple of beer cans. Because, apparently, you can't fish without beer. There's some kind of rule.

'Well, something's happened,' he said. 'I can see by your face. And you've changed your clothes and your hair's damp. Did you fall in?'

I was tempted to say yes. He'd make unkind remarks for half an hour but that would be the end of it and I could pretend it never happened. That I'd never seen that slow turn of her head. Never seen myself looking back at me. Never had that awful moment when I'd not been sure who was who. Not been sure which one was the real me.

I'd been silent too long. Jones interrogates for a living. And I am the world's worst liar. And looking at him, his concern was genuine. His colour swirled gently around me. Not too close. Just enough. Just right.

I took another swig of water and, screwing the cap back on again as an excuse for not looking at him, I told him what I'd seen on the other side of the bridge. Except for the bit about seeing my own face. I don't know why I didn't mention that. I told myself I needed to get things straight in my own head before talking about it with anyone else.

He took the bottle off me and screwed the cap on properly because, he said, I was annoying him with my clumsiness. 'Do you want to go back with me? We could go and have a proper look?'

I shook my head. I've seen some nasty stuff over the last

66

few years but that was too unsettling. I'd seen myself. More than that – for a moment in time I'd actually been that other person. Suppose it happened again and I couldn't get back into the proper me. Or was she the proper me? In which case – who was I? Or even worse – *what* was I?

'I don't think that would be very helpful,' I said.

'OK,' he said cheerfully. 'Well, you sit there in the shade and I'll do all the packing away as usual.'

'Have you finished?' I asked.

'The light is too bright,' he said, which I gathered was angler-speak for 'the fish are running rings round me again'. 'We missed tea yesterday so why don't we go back and sit in the garden and scoff scones. I can entertain you with tales of the ones that got away. Seriously, Cage, you should have been here. It was massive. The struggle was epic. I made Beowulf look like a girl. You could make a movie of our heroic battle. I wrestled them all to the shore and then had to subdue them with my bare hands.'

'You sound just like Iblis,' I said, amused despite myself.

'What, Blond Boy with the awful dog?'

'Yes,' I said dreamily, just to annoy him. 'Do you remember, he saved us all and then he went back and saved the little dog. He's such a hero.'

Jones began to pack away his gear, muttering to himself, and slowly, because it was still so hot, we left the riverbank and made our way back through the woods to the hotel.

'We'll need to go through the garden so I can put my gear back,' he said.

'And deposit your fish in the specially marked trays,' I said. 'For cooking and serving at dinner tonight. Mm-mm.'

67

'You're a horrible woman, Cage,' he said.

The gardens were to the side and back of the hotel and surrounded by a deer fence. We let ourselves in through the gate and followed the path past a dilapidated little wooden shed that could more accurately be described as a hut. A very elderly hut. Although only until the next strong wind, after which it would be described as a heap.

'Hello there,' said a voice, and Clarence emerged from the gloom, still in his uniform. I never saw him out of it. 'I thought I heard voices. Have you had a pleasant day?'

One of us hadn't caught any fish and the other had had a nasty experience in the woods so we both remained silent.

'Oh dear,' he said, looking at me. 'Why don't you come in and I'll make us some tea?'

I think Jones had visions of finger sandwiches and scones and little cakes and silver teapots, none of which we were likely to find in a garden shed, but Clarence had already disappeared back into his dark domain. I couldn't wait to see what he came up with so I went with him. Sighing, Jones dumped his gear by the door and followed me in.

Actually, it was rather nice. The smell of wood and creosote took me straight back to my dad's shed where I used to help him with his woodwork and we would talk. I would hold his pencil, his screwdriver or his spirit level – whatever was required – and tell him about my day at school. The sun would stream through the window highlighting the wood shavings and sawdust. All around the walls were shelves stacked high with tins of paint and creosote and wood stain and the jars of old nails and string that he always kept – because you never knew when they might come in useful, he would always say,

68

to the great exasperation of my mum – and the two battered kitchen chairs where we would drink our tea and eat chocolate digestives. Smell is evocative and, just for a second, my dad was right there with me, and then it all faded away as Clarence offered me an old wooden stool to sit on.

I was glad to sit down. Jones made himself comfortable on a stack of fertiliser bags. We waited a moment, and then, since Clarence made no move, Jones winked at me, and made the tea himself. A dusty light bulb hung from the roof so I assumed the shed had power. He switched on the kettle and found some astonishingly clean mugs. I thought they'd be horrible and chipped and brown with tannin but they were spotless. There was even a tiny fridge with a tray of bolted seed potatoes resting on top, their too long yellow stems reaching out towards the window.

'Good work with that nasty woman by the way,' said Clarence to me. 'I really didn't like her. Ignored me, she did. As if I wasn't there.'

'Perhaps she didn't see you,' I said, wondering why I was making excuses for her.

'Oh, she saw me,' he said grimly and just for a second, I saw him in his younger days, in the army, perhaps, given the medal ribbons he wore. 'I made sure of that.'

Jones put mugs of tea in front of us and sat down again.

'Well now,' said Clarence, looking closely at me. 'It's just a wild guess, but I'm thinking you've been up in the woods and saw something you wish you hadn't.'

I stared down at my tea and nodded.

'If it helps,' he said, 'you're not the first. Not that many people go there now – there's no need to, after all – but occasionally

69

someone will trek up there on their own and come back down again with that look on their face. A nice mug of tea usually sorts them out.' He nodded at my tea.

Obediently, I sipped. It was good tea and I said so.

'Thank you,' said Clarence, obviously much gratified.

'I think you'll find I made the tea,' murmured Jones.

Clarence waved this aside. 'It's usually local people, of course. Those with roots in this area. Those whose families have always been here. Sometimes they see something. A glimpse of the past. Or a voice echoing down the years. It's usually a very fleeting glimpse.'

I shook my head. This hadn't been an echo or a fleeting glimpse. This had been real. I'd been there.

He was watching me closely. 'I can tell you the story if you're interested,' he said.

I sighed. In books, the young and beautiful heroine – so not me then, as Jones would be the first to point out – has to force people to tell her what's going on. In my world, people fight to tell me things I don't want to hear. I was on holiday. I was here to relax and enjoy myself. The memories were fading. Well, apart from the moment she turned around and I saw myself, but I'd told myself that as long as I stayed down by the river and never went up the hill again – and why would I? – then no major harm would have been done. I would lie around watching Jones fail to catch our supper, read a book, eat a massive packed lunch, and just generally idle the days away. That was why I was here, after all. And this time next week I'd be back home again, in my little house in Rushford, while the memories slowly melted away like mist in the rising sun and I would never have to think about it again.

'It's quite a tragic story,' said Clarence, jolting me back to now. 'For everyone,' and I realised he'd taken my silence for acquiescence.

'It was in the days when the Torringtons had the big house,' he said to me. 'Did you see it? The one with the gateposts?'

I nodded.

'Well, it was Torrington House then. Been in the family for ages. For all I know it still is. Although no one's lived in it now for . . . oh, a very long time. She was a widow. Lady Torrington. Nice lady. No children, sadly. Well respected. Did a lot for the village. Everyone was afraid she'd go back to England when Sir George died, but she didn't. In fact, she stayed on here permanently. She'd always loved the place, she said, and couldn't think of anywhere she would rather be.'

He sighed and looked out of the dusty window at the slightly straggly gardens beyond. All the borders were past their best, the foliage beginning to curl and turn yellow. In a couple of weeks, they would all be cleared, dug over and prepared for the winter.

Clarence was continuing his tale. 'It was a happy time.' He fell silent again. I looked at Jones and he looked at me. Should we go, perhaps? Leave him to his memories?

'You remember it happening?' I said, uncertainly.

Fortunately, he didn't take offence. He laughed. 'Bless you, no. But I remember my mum telling me all about it. It was one of her favourite stories. She often spoke of it. *Her* mum told it to her. She was one of the junior maids up at Torrington House at the time this happened, so I always felt that made it our story as well as theirs.

'Anyway, everything was trundling along very nicely. The

71

local farmers were prosperous which meant the village was as well. No one starved. Lady Torrington saw to that. She was always sending down food for the old people. And the sick. Those who'd once worked for the estate could be sure they'd be well looked after. Roofs were repaired before every winter. The kirk ran a school for the boys of the village and she opened one for the girls as well. According to my gran, the elders were torn. Half of them wanted to be seen as modern and progressive and the other half held very strong views on the folly of putting ideas into young girls' heads when all they needed to do was worship God and their husbands, and not needed to learn their letters. Lady Torrington got round that by teaching them sewing and weaving as well. And how to feed a family on nothing. And how to run a house. Aye, those girls might not have come away with a proper book education, but they came away with a good one, all the same. You could always pick out a girl who'd been to Lady Torrington's school.'

Lady Torrington would have been the woman in the cloak, I assumed. The one issuing orders and trying to save the occupants living in the cottage at her gates. The one with my face.

Still staring out of the window, he continued. 'And then *she* came.'

He stopped talking again.

I couldn't stop myself. 'Who?'

'Jeannie Morton. And her daughters. Florence and Hannah.'

'Pretty names,' I said.

He snorted. 'Names above their station. Annie and Mary are good enough for around here. Florence and Hannah, indeed.'

I closed my eyes, searching back through memories, letting my mind drift . . . no, nothing at all. Was any of this familiar

72

to me? I had no sense of déjà vu. No sense that I'd ever been here before. No faint memories. Nothing.

'Well, there was trouble as soon as she stepped off the cart she'd cadged a ride on. Jeannie, I mean. She took no job, no cottage. As far as anyone knew, she lived up in the woods with those girls. As to how she fed them . . . well, you can guess the rumours. The women were all stirred up. Like a fox in the hen house, my mum said her mum said. She was no better than she ought to be, and as for the men that went up there . . . well.' He smiled. 'I can see my mum now; tiny woman, she was. I always remember her tucking the loaf of bread under her arm, buttering away and then shaving off wafer-thin slices to make it go further. And she'd tell the story, slamming the big black teapot down on the table to make her point. And my dad would grin at me. And she'd see him grinning and *slam* would go the teapot again.

'No one knew where the rumour started. It was inevitable, I suppose. The day came when they stopped saying "whore" and called her "witch" instead.'

He shook his head, sadly. 'Things happened fast after that. The elders had her brought down into the village. She was locked away. For questioning, they said. They let her out after three or four days and she could barely walk. She certainly couldn't get back up that hill to her daughters. About six and eight, they were, I think. Too young to be left alone for very long.'

I sipped my tea. Clarence turned back from the window.

'I don't know what sort of fate put Lady Torrington in her carriage just as Jeannie Morton was trying to get herself back up the hill. My gran saw it all – or told my mum she did. The

73

villagers all stood at their gates and watched her struggle. No one came to help. The carriage stopped and out climbed Lady T, all in her fine clothes, and there was Jeannie, covered in dirt and blood and with her clothes hanging in rags around her. My mum always said it was years later when she realised what must have happened to her and, I have to say, it was only when I was grown that I realised too.

'They talked – no one heard what they said, but the upshot was that Lady Torrington offered her a home. The empty cottage by the old gate. The one no one used any longer because Sir George Torrington – who was dead by then – had had a new path cut to the house and fine new gates and everything. She sent the gardener's boy up into the woods to bring down Jeannie's daughters and their few belongings and installed them in the cottage.

'Well, people weren't happy about that. Not at all. Some had sons and daughters waiting to find somewhere to live before they could wed and there was her ladyship giving a cottage – and a good one at that – to a woman like that. They didn't take at all kindly to Jeannie jumping the queue. Some said women like that shouldn't be allowed to live among respectable folk. I always suspected they were the wives of the husbands who walked up the hill a couple of nights every month, but maybe I'm just being ill-natured.

'On the first day there was muttering. On the second – after they'd had a few drinks – there was shouting, and on the third, there was trouble.'

'The cottage caught fire,' I murmured.

'The cottage was set alight,' he corrected. 'With herself and her two little girls inside.' He shook his head. 'There was no saving them, my mum said her mum said. The flames spread so quickly they couldn't get close enough to rescue them.'

'It went up like a rocket,' I said quietly, remembering the fierce heat from the flames.

He nodded. 'Someone had broken the downstairs window and poured something through, my gran always reckoned. To make it burn hotter. There was only the one room downstairs with a ladder up to the attic floor, and that room was on fire so Jeannie and her girls couldn't get down to the door.'

'It was deliberate, then,' said Jones. 'It wasn't a case of setting fire to the cottage to drive them out, but actual murder.'

'And she couldn't force the upstairs window open,' I said, without thinking. 'And it was too small to climb through, anyway.'

Clarence shot me a look. 'Aye. Well, she did everything, did her ladyship. Buckets, ladders, forming a chain to the one well – all to no avail. Her people did their best but it was hopeless. It was all over very quickly, they said. The roof came down. No one got out.'

'A sad story,' said Jones, setting down his mug.

'Oh, it's not over,' said Clarence. 'That was only the beginning.'

I didn't know why, but my heart began to thump. 'Why? What happened next?'

'She was not happy, was Lady Torrington. Her tenants had acted against her, she said. They'd destroyed her property, ignored her commands, murdered people under her protection. There would be a reckoning.' He sighed. 'I suspect there were many around the village regretting their actions – or their inactions – but it was too late. The minister visited her and, according to gossip, high words were exchanged. He told her bluntly that she was English and didn't understand these things. I suspect there might have been some resentment over her charitable work, the girls' school and so on. Perhaps he thought it made him look ineffective. Perhaps he saw it as usurping his authority within the village.'

He broke off and sighed. 'When I think about those events, it seems unbelievable that people who had rubbed together very happily for years, all of them thinking they were helping each other, building a little community – well, it turned out to be nothing of the sort. In a week – just seven days – all that was gone for ever.'

I could feel my pulse pounding inside my head.

'What happened?' said Jones.

'She waited twenty-four hours, and then on the next day, which was the Sabbath, she went to church – the kirk. This was unheard of, you understand. She was English – a different church entirely. If she worshipped at all, she'd have a little service up at Torrington House for the few English servants she'd brought with her. Not a proper service because there was no minister, but she'd read a snippet from the Bible and they'd sing a hymn and say the Lord's Prayer together and that was probably it.'

'What happened in the kirk?' said Jones.

'It was a scandal, that's what it was. There was the minister, well into his sermon, preaching love and forgiveness to all mankind probably, and in she swept.

'Well, there was a sensation. An absolute sensation. If God himself had appeared, I doubt there would have been more consternation. And the minister himself so . . . what's that word they use today? . . . gobsmacked, that's it – the minister so gobsmacked he stood like Lot's wife with his mouth hanging open. Not that she paid him any heed. Swept up the aisle, she did, although it's not a big church, so ten or twelve steps would have done it. And she wasn't alone, either. She'd brought two big footmen and a groom with her. So trouble was obviously expected.'

'Did it happen?' asked Jones.

'It was all very dramatic,' he said. 'My mum used to act it out for me with my dad having his tea at the table and rolling his eyes. There was a storm going on outside, she would say. The wind and rain were battering at the little church, making the candles flicker. And there stood Lady Torrington, and the look on her face . . . I reckon she'd loved them and she thought they'd loved her and she'd taken care of them and watched over them and seen them all right in hard times, but when push came to shove . . . they'd defied her.

'Silence fell, apart from the noises outside. The congregation waited. She started with the minister, who suddenly found he wasn't as brave as he thought he was. English he'd called her, and she thanked him for recalling her to her rights and respon-sibilities as a landowner, and the congregation stirred. I reckon they had an idea of what was to come.'

I hardly dared ask. 'What was to come?'

'She stood with her back to the altar – and to the minister too, which he wasn't happy about – and then she addressed the congregation – a woman speaking in his church and he liked that even less, I can tell you – and there and then, with all the candles flickering around her like the flames from hell, she gave them notice. All of them. Every single last one of them.'

He waited while we caught up.

'Wait,' said Jones, because I couldn't speak for the fear curdling inside me. 'She owned the entire village?'

'She did. Most of it anyway. Not the church, obviously. And one or two of the larger houses had been built on land bought from the estate all fair and square – and the inn, of course – but the farmers were tenant farmers, and most of the cottages were tied to the estate. A few people worked for themselves but most worked for her in one capacity or another. At one stroke she removed their homes and their livelihoods. And winter was coming on.'

'Harsh,' commented Jones.

'She was within her rights as the landowner. Anyway, people just stared open-mouthed. I think it was the shock. And the surprise. If anyone had said, seven days before, that this happy little place could be so . . .' He seemed to be groping for the right word.

'Torn apart,' said Jones.

'Indeed, sir. One week, she gave them. Seven days to load up their possessions, put granny on the cart and take themselves off her land. Which, since the estate was large in those days, would take some doing. No ifs, no buts, no exceptions. Within seven days, they were to be gone, every last one of them.'

'Every last one of her tenants, you mean?'

'That's correct, yes. But without the village, what good were the shops that served it? There would be no living to be made, so they were finished too. And the inn. And the church. No village – no congregation. The minister would have to move on. What had been a very comfortable billet for everyone was gone for ever and they'd done it to themselves. If they thought she was a soft Englishwoman who could safely be defied – well, they got that wrong.'

'Did they go?' enquired Jones, feeling the teapot to see if it was still hot.

'They had no choice. She brought in men from the nearby town to enforce her wishes. Big men who didn't do anything but stand around looking threatening. But people got the message.'

'Did no one argue?'

'A deputation of brave men called to try to reason with her. Not the minister – he being held nearly as much to blame as her ladyship – but men from the village who came, respectfully, to plead their case.'

'How did that turn out?'

'She wouldn't even see them. In fact, her butler, an elderly man who saw all this with great grief, advised them to leave with all speed. Her rage had not abated, he said. She had nearly destroyed one room already in her temper. Some of the more timid servants wouldn't go near her. Some had left already. "As you value your lives, gentlemen," he said, "leave now." So they did.

'And that was the end of the village up on the hill. All that sad week the carts rattled down the road and over the bridge, all piled high with their furniture, their bits and pieces, and with granny and the babies and the chickens piled on the top.'

I managed to ask, 'Didn't she relent at all?'

Clarence shook his head. 'She was implacable. She had herself driven down every morning and she sat in her carriage and watched them go. It was said no one could look at her face. As soon as a family moved out, she sent in her men to take the roof off. To prevent anyone ever coming back.'

I remembered none of the ruined cottages had had a roof.

'It was sheeting with rain,' he said. 'The road had turned into a quagmire. They struggled. They really struggled and she sat and watched.'

'What happened to them?'

He shrugged. 'No one knows. Within the prescribed seven days they were all gone and silence settled over the village. The cottages crumbled, the trees closed in and no one ever has lived there again, that's all I know.'

'And Lady Torrington herself?'

'Was gone herself within the month.'

'Where did she go?'

'Again – no one knows. She shut up the house, paid off the servants and just vanished.'

'Did she return to England, do you think?'

'That was the story, although if she did, no one ever said where or how she lived afterwards. No more was known of her in these parts.'

'What happened to the estate?'

'Broken up and sold in parcels. The Kirks bought this particular stretch of the river. Initially they just came up for the fishing but eventually they built this place for themselves. It's been in their family ever since. The fishing is good, and slowly, over time, a new village grew on the other side of the hill.' He jerked his head, presumably in the direction of the new village. 'It's a happy place, down here in the valley. And we're all local so perhaps somewhere, small amends have been made.'

'But no one goes up the hill,' said Jones.

'Almost everyone goes once – out of curiosity.' He smiled. 'Very few go twice.'

I had to ask. 'Have you been?'

He smiled at me. 'You've a keen eye, lassie. Yes, I've been up there once or twice.'

'What did you see?'

He stared out of the window again, his eyes troubled. 'I saw the burned cottage. The scattered stones. Just as everyone else does. It was a sunny afternoon. Very hot. Very still. The trees threw dark shadows. And then something changed for me and all of a sudden it was very easy to believe that the witch woman was up there, standing in the shadows, waiting for me.'

I shivered. 'Jeannie Morton?'

He looked straight at me. 'Lady Torrington.'

CHAPTER SIX

We dined early that night. Jones said another long day in the sun had left him utterly worn out and was his nose red?

I said poor you and yes.

We both had steak. Or cow trout, as Jones referred to it.

'You're very quiet,' he said, stuffing away the cow trout. 'What are you thinking about?'

'About this afternoon,' I said.

'About Jeannie Morton and her children?'

I nodded and pretended to concentrate on cutting up my steak. I don't know why I bother.

'Did you believe him?'

I nodded. 'Yes, he was telling the truth as he saw it.'

'It's just a story he's worked up for the tourists, Cage.'

'What makes you say that?'

'Well, the dates aren't right, are they? Let's say Clarence is around seventy. If his gran was working as a junior maid up at Torrington House, then she must have been fifteen or thereabouts. Even if she was aged thirty when she gave birth to Clarence's mum, and his mum was thirty when she had Clarence, then all this happened no more than a hundred or so years ago. Which would put it around the turn of the last century. I doubt they were torching women as late as that. Not even in Scotland.'

'No,' I said, 'you're right. But it was a good story and he told it very well.'

He peered at me over his mound of creamy mashed potato. 'I like this place,' he'd said when Rory served us. 'Very sound ideas on portion control.'

'So,' he said now, scooping up a mouthful. 'Why do I get the impression it's Lady Torrington who has got you all wound up?'

I shook my head. 'No, it's not.'

'Cage, you're lying to both of us. If you're worrying about your sanity status, remember – I already know you're as bonkers as a sock full of frogs and nothing you can say is ever going to change that opinion. And besides, if we're going to work together, then we need to be honest with each other, so you might as well tell me – among all your usual weirdness, which particularly sinister event is causing you such concern?'

I rearranged a few peas.

'Cage.'

'All right. Don't bark at me. I don't think this place could cope with another collapsing relationship.'

'Do we have a relationship?'

'I have no idea what we have,' I sighed, and rearranged a few more peas.

There was silence from the other side of the table because he was waiting for me to speak. To distract him from the relationship issue, I said, 'I didn't tell you all of it.'

'Well, I know that,' he said. 'If you don't want your butter, can I have it for my potato?'

I stared.

'Food plays an enormous part in my life,' he explained.

'Really? I thought that was sex. You're always regaling me

83

with tales of Barbara and Jacqueline and Heather and Kimberley and Jocasta and Emily and Ruth . . .'

'Yes, enough,' he said, grinning. Rory, who had paused to top up our wine, was staring in blatant – and undeserved – admiration. 'We were talking about you, Cage.'

'*You* were,' I said. 'I was reflecting on the hordes of disappointed and vengeful women you leave behind you.'

'Disappointed I can live with,' he said gloomily. 'It's the ones who come at you wielding the carving knife you really have to watch out for.' He looked up at our very young waiter. 'You want to remember that, Rory. When you take your first trembling steps into the wonderful world of women, remember to remove all sharp implements first.'

'For heaven's sake,' I said.

Rory grinned, confidently predicted Mr Jones would be wanting the dessert menu, and disappeared.

'So,' said Jones, shovelling down the last of his steak. 'Ready to tell me all about it now?'

I sighed. 'If some of your ex-girlfriends had been a little quicker off the mark with the sharp implements, I wouldn't have to have this conversation.'

He just grinned. 'I'm not going away so get on with it.'

'Actually,' I said, and stopped again.

'Yes? Dear God, Cage, did you ever do the How to Resist Interrogation course, because I swear you could give them pointers.'

'I told you what I saw.'

'I'm nodding,' he said, nodding, 'because it's important to show empathy with the subject and to instil confidence that they will be believed.'

'All right,' I said. 'I told you what you all of it.'

He nodded again, empathy oozing from on.'

'I'm waiting to be instilled with confidence.'

'And I'm praying for patience. I suspect both of us disappointed.'

'Lady Torrington?'

He nodded.

I took a deep breath and said to the tablecloth, 'She had my face.'

Frowning, he laid down his knife and fork. A bit of a first. 'She looked like you?'

'No. I was looking at my own face. The scar . . .' I gestured to my eyebrow.

'What, that little girlie thing? Remind me to show you a real man's scar one day.'

'She had the same freckle on her cheekbone. The same expression . . .'

'Did she see you?'

I remembered my own heart-stopping shock. Had the same been reflected in her face? 'Yes.'

'Was she as shocked as you?'

'I'm not sure. I was stopped in my tracks. She was dealing with what was going on around her.'

'Perhaps she didn't see you at all.'

'No,' I said, sadly. 'She saw me.' I didn't mention the moment when I had seen through her eyes . . .

He frowned. 'It's supposed to be bad luck to meet your double.'

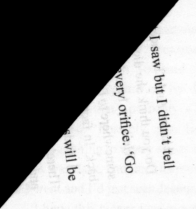

sappeared shortly afterwards.
he saw her doppelgänger?'
could easily have moved
etly and word never filtered
id happen.'
, probably. You're right.
Just a strong resemblance,
nes made everything look
on die. Yes, you're right.'
to spend the rest of our
.......ng a vengeful doppelgänger pursuing you
down the years?'

'Not even a little bit,' I said, untruthfully.

'Only if it's advice on evading vengeful women you're after,
I've got loads of pointers.'

'I shall remember that. You won't mind me ringing you at
three in the morning for guidance then?'

'Probably not – although I might be a little busy at three in
the morning. If a female voice answers, just hang up.'

Rory, standing beside us with the dessert menus, nearly disappeared in his own exploding colour.

For some reason, I felt better for having told Jones. It had been
an unpleasant experience but I should be used to those by now.
We finished our meal and drank our coffee. I thought he might
disappear into the bar afterwards, but he shook his head and
walked upstairs with me.

Actually, now I thought back, apart from a beer to counter
the rigours of fishing, or glass of wine with his dinner, I hadn't
seen him drink anything alcoholic for a long time. I remembered

the state of him when we first met at Sorensen's clinic in the aftermath of Clare's death when he was riddled with guilt and alcohol.

I asked him if he didn't want a nightcap.

'No,' he said easily. 'Don't seem to fancy one these days.'

We parted on the landing. He wished me goodnight and I heard his door close behind him.

I'd left my window open and the night had turned chilly. It was autumn, after all. I pulled it down and got ready for bed. I remember reaching for my book and then changing my mind. A day in the fresh air, an unnerving experience in the woods, and three hefty meals sent me to sleep almost immediately.

The moonlight woke me. One minute I was fast asleep and the next I was staring around at my room, which was bathed in silver light.

People have got the moon all wrong. 'It's the night of the full moon,' they say, lowering their voices in a sinister fashion. 'When ghosts walk and things go bump in the night.'

They're wrong. Big, full, golden moons are very pretty, but that's about it. The worst is the horned moon. That little silver sliver. When the crescent moon lies on its back with its ends pointing upwards. Like a pair of giant horns in the sky. It's no coincidence that to our ancestors – who probably knew a lot more than we do – the horned moon was a sign of evil. Do not go out on such a night. And if you do have to go out – don't look at the moon. As likely as not you'll find it looking straight back at you. And it won't ever forget you.

I'd left the curtains open and the moonlight had found me. The room was bright with its baleful light. I sat up, wondering if this was what had woken me.

The next thing I noticed was the absolute silence from outside. So much for country noises. Just a thick silence so loud it crackled in my ears.

A flicker of movement caught my eye and made me jump but that was because sometimes I'm an idiot. Not everything is other-worldly and sinister. Sometimes there's a perfectly natural explanation for everything and there was now.

The dressing table stood opposite the bed and the mirror was at exactly the right height and angle to reflect me. The flicker had been me in my pale nightdress sitting up. As I said, I'm an idiot.

I leaned back against the pillows, pushed my hair back and reached for the glass of water on my bedside table.

My hand never made it. Because there was no corresponding movement in the mirror. The face looking back at me was mine but it wasn't me. She'd found me. The thought chilled my blood. She'd found me.

I swallowed and whispered, 'Who *are* you?'

There was just the faintest whisper that might have been the rustle of sheets.

'Beware the angry snow.'

I woke up and I was on the far side of the room. As far away from the mirror as possible. My heart was pounding so hard I could actually hear it. I could feel sweat prickling my forehead and top lip.

I took two or three deep breaths, and when everything had calmed down a little, I worked my way around the wall and found the light switch. Light flooded the room, which contained just me. The mirror reflected only part of an empty bed. I tried to peer more closely. There were no ghostly faces. Everything was absolutely normal. I'd just had a very bad dream.

I inched my way further around the wall, keeping my eyes on the carpet, and drew the curtains against the malevolent moon. When that was done, I approached the mirror, very slowly, and sat on the stool.

This was a proper old-fashioned dressing table – not the combined desk, table and dressing table you get in modern hotels. This was a proper kneehole affair with a big, soft, padded stool covered in the same material as the headboard and curtains. A threefold mirror ensured I could, if I so wanted, examine myself from every angle. I declined that particular treat. My hairbrush, my jar of moisturiser and my bottle of perfume sat exactly where I had left them. Everything was completely normal.

Slowly, and very fearful of what I might see, I raised my eyes to look at myself in the mirror.

Yes, there I was. That was me. The proper me. Shoulder-length hair, and a little pale considering I'd been in the sun all day, but definitely me. I looked over my shoulder. Yes, I was alone in the room. There was no one else here.

The bathroom. I suddenly remembered. There were mirrors in the bathroom. She could be hiding in there. I stood up so suddenly I tipped the stool backwards, and in trying to grab it, I managed to knock over my perfume. The sound of the glass bottle hitting the glass-topped dressing table was like a thunderclap in this silent room.

I grabbed at it – although it was far too late – and very gently and carefully stood it upright again.

I needed to check the bathroom; it was full of mirrors. There was one over the washbasin and another on the large wall opposite the window, positioned to reflect the light back into the room. And not forgetting the small round shaving and make-up mirror on one of those extending-arm things. Three mirrors in one small room.

The door was half-open. Darkness yawned beyond. I really should go and check it out. I should put my mind at rest and then I could climb back into bed and go back to sleep like a normal person.

I had an idea. I grabbed my dressing gown off the bed and draped it over the dressing-table mirror. Ha! In your face, Face.

And at that moment the phone rang.

I have unhappy memories of telephones ringing in the dead of night. Especially when you unplug them and they carry on ringing. Trust me – that is never good.

I stared at it a long while, willing myself to pick it up and failing.

Eventually, it stopped. I wasn't sure that was any better.

There was no warning. No faint sound from the door. No click as he picked the lock. No warning at all. The door swung open and there was Michael Jones, crouched, gun in hand, ready for anything. It was almost a shame there wasn't anything for him to be ready for.

I squeaked. He stepped into the room, carefully closing the door behind him.

'Why didn't you answer the phone?'

'Who rings people at . . .' I looked at the clock. 'Ten past two in the morning?'

'People who have heard a crash from the room opposite and ring to make sure everything's OK and don't get a response so they come to check things out. That sort of person.'

'Oh. Sorry.' I gestured at the bottle. 'I knocked my perfume over.'

90

'Why are you spraying yourself with perfume at . . .' He looked at the clock. 'Eleven minutes past two in the morning? Have you got a man in here? No, of course you haven't.'

Oddly enough, this casual assumption made me quite cross.

'I might have.'

'No, you haven't.'

'You don't know that.'

'Yes, I do.'

He glanced at my dressing gown draped over the mirror. 'You're not having a séance, are you?'

'Will you please go back to your own room.'

'Cut the crap, Cage. What's going on?'

I sighed. 'There was a reflection. In the mirror.'

I waited for the sarcastic, 'Well, that's usually where you find a reflection, Cage,' and it didn't come.

He sat on the bed. 'You're really quite on edge over this, aren't you?'

Miserably, I nodded.

'Do you want me to stay?'

'What, here?'

He rolled his eyes. 'Yes. Here.'

I looked around the room. 'That armchair doesn't look big enough . . .'

'Get into bed, Cage, I'm turning off the light.'

I crawled into bed and lay as far to one side as I could possibly get without actually falling out, and feeling as though I was on the edge of a precipice in every sense of the word.

The room went dark and I felt the bed sag as he climbed in beside me. 'Well, this isn't how I thought it would go.'

'What do you mean?'

'Well, I always knew you'd get me into bed sooner or later, but to be honest, I thought there would be more smouldering.'

'I'm sorry?'

'No, not your fault. I should have made my requirements clearer.'

I rolled on to my back. 'What requirements?'

'Well, you know – I thought you would stand in the doorway, wearing one of those negligee things. Not black – too obvious – I thought a nice cream one would be pretty. There would be backlighting, of course, and you'd stand with one arm on the door frame and . . . you know . . . smoulder.'

'No, I don't know. How on earth does someone smoulder?'

'Like this.'

I peered unsuccessfully into the darkness. 'Like what?'

'Like this.'

I sighed. 'I'm sharing a bed with a madman.'

'For God's sake, woman, you could at least show a little appreciation. I'm smouldering away for dear life here. It's a miracle the bed sheets haven't burst into flames.'

'Sorry,' I said meekly. 'I should have said, "Yes, very impressive."'

'Are we still talking about my smouldering?'

I rolled over again. 'I have no idea what *you're* talking about.'

He sighed despondently. 'I hear that a lot.'

Feeling safe in the dark, I said, 'Do you think it was the ghost of Lady Torrington? She must have died about a hundred years ago. Or – no, wait – suppose it's the other way around and I'm the ghost. Oh my God, that's why I can't see my own colour. I'm a ghost.'

My panic was short-lived. 'You're not a ghost, Cage. I

can see you. I can certainly hear you. And I can feel your ice-cold feet.'

I shut up.

There was a slight pause and then he said, 'You know, of course, that there's a perfectly reasonable explanation for all of this.'

I turned over again, feeling the mattress bounce. 'Is there?'

'Remind me never to share a waterbed with you, Cage. It would be like sailing around the Cape of Good Hope.'

'What?'

'Tossing and turning. Pitching and rolling.'

'If you sail half as badly as you fish, then I rather think we'd be sinking and drowning.'

'You don't want to hear my perfectly reasonable explanation, then? Understandable, I suppose. It is the middle of the night and I'm here, smouldering, and you're lost in a feminine tidal wave of admiration and desire.'

'Get out. Get out of my bed now.'

'And leave you to face things alone?'

'If I'm very lucky, yes.'

There was a bit of a silence as we both subsided.

'Go on, then,' I said snappily. 'Tell me this perfectly reasonable explanation.'

'Well, I'm not sure I will, now.'

'That's all right. I wouldn't have listened anyway.'

He sighed. 'She's an ancestor of yours, Cage. Obvious when you think about it. She's a distant ancestor – hence the resemblance. And also, hence the connection between you. I mean, we all know you're weird, so the chances are that she was, too. You know – heredity and all that. Yes, I know you're adopted

93

but even so, you must have had parents, grandparents, ancestors and so on and she could be one of them.'

I honestly, genuinely, hadn't thought of that and now, here I was, actually feeling rather silly.

'Bet you feel a right pillock now,' he said cheerfully in the dark.

'I can't hear you,' I said. 'I'm asleep.'

He put a gentle hand on my arm. 'Better now?'

'Yes. Thank you.'

'No problem.'

I said quietly, 'Thank you for staying.'

I thought he'd say something jokey, but he just turned over and said, 'Sweetheart, you're very welcome.'

I smiled in the darkness.

CHAPTER SEVEN

When I awoke the next morning, Jones was gone and I had my bed to myself. I couldn't help wondering whether his smooth exit was due to tact or simply because he was adept at avoiding embarrassing early-morning conversations.

I met him downstairs where he was at the desk, talking to Emily Kirk.

'Here she is,' he said, as I approached.

Emily Kirk smiled but her colour held back. She wasn't too sure about me but was being professional about it. 'A message from Mr Elphick for you. At least I assume it's for you. It's addressed to the lady in the wrong toilet, which I am guessing would be you.'

I nodded and unfolded the note. It said simply that he'd gone back to his parents. He'd given in his notice at work. He'd spoken to his solicitor and she was arranging his divorce. On her advice, he'd written out a full statement and if anything happened to him, she would alert the police. And he thanked me.

I passed it to Emily Kirk, to reassure her.

'I never liked her,' she said. 'Not from the moment she stepped over the threshold. She made the hair on the back of my neck stand on end.'

I remembered Clarence hadn't liked her, either.

'Well,' said Jones, also reading the message. 'She's gone now.'

'Are you fishing again today, Mr Jones?'

He looked at me. 'Actually, I thought we could go on a tour of the area. Follow the river, visit the local pub, that sort of thing.'

'What about the fishing?'

'I rather thought I'd give the fish a bit of a reprieve today. Give them time to regroup and recover themselves after yesterday's onslaught.'

I said to Emily Kirk, 'He lives in his own world,' and she laughed.

That was just what we did. We drove a little way, walked a little way, had lunch at a riverside pub and spent the afternoon there. Nothing horrible happened, Jones didn't mention any plans for the future, the weather was lovely and I enjoyed every minute. Nothing disturbed me in the night, either.

On our last full day, the clouds gathered and the wind got up. Leaves cascaded to the ground and it began to spit with rain. Jones gathered his gear for a final assault, saying the weather was perfect. Which it might have been but it didn't improve his luck any. His duck remained unbroken.

I spent the day in the Residents' Lounge. They lit the fire for me. I drank a lot of coffee, ate a lot of delicious scones and finished my book.

And I slept well that night, as well, although I wasn't taking any chances. I shut out the horned moon, covered every mirror in sight and made sure the bathroom door was firmly closed.

'Well,' said Mrs Kirk, when we went to settle our bill. 'I don't think we've ever had anyone catch absolutely nothing before.

My husband was talking of hiring a scuba diver to sneak under-
water and somehow glue a fish to your line.'

Jones compressed his lips. 'Thank you for not highlighting
my pain.'

She laughed. 'I hope you've enjoyed your stay, anyway.'

'We have, thank you,' said Jones. 'Can I have both bills,
please?'

'No,' I said. 'I pay for myself.'

He sighed. 'Cage, has Mrs Kirk not emasculated me suffi-
ciently for one day? At least allow me to settle the bill. You can
buy us both lunch on the way back.'

Jones had just finished loading our luggage into the car when
Clarence, with impeccable timing, trotted across the car park
to say farewell.

I said it was nice to have met him.

'And you too,' he said, smiling at me.

'I expect things will be much quieter now as the season ends.'

'Not really,' he said. 'We're booked for any number of
Christmas functions and then there will be the big New Year's
party.'

'I've never really celebrated the New Year,' I said wistfully,
because recently, every year seemed so much worse than the
one that had gone before.

'Very wise,' he said seriously. 'And Christmas parties can so
easily get out of hand. I always think a nice, quiet Christmas
at home with family and friends is the most enjoyable thing in
the world.'

'I agree,' said Jones, looking at me. 'Friends especially.'

I smiled weakly.

'Good luck to you, Mrs Cage. And to you, sir.'

'Thank you,' said Jones, slamming the boot. Again, his hand hovered near his pocket and again, Clarence shook his head. 'No, no, sir. Greatly appreciated, but not necessary, thank you.'

'In that case,' said Jones. 'We'll be off.'

'Safe journey to you both.'

I climbed into the car and when I looked around, Clarence had gone.

'Well,' said Jones, as we pulled out of the car park. 'I'd be the first to admit the holiday didn't go quite as planned, but focusing on the positive, no one's dead, neither of us is wanted by the police, and best of all – *I* didn't see a ghost.'

I grinned and said nothing as we crossed the bridge for the last time.

'Well, I didn't,' he said, accelerating up the hill.

I kept my eyes firmly on the road.

'Yes, Cage, I know you got yourself involved in something weird – as per usual – but my time was blamelessly spent being alternately intimidated and ignored by every fish in the river.'

I grinned again.

He frowned. 'What?'

'Nothing,' I said, in that particularly irritating manner that indicates it's not nothing.

'No, it's not. You're smirking in a very unattractive way, Cage, even for you. I'm guessing, from your unbearably smug expression, that I did, in fact, see a ghost.'

I grinned.

'Not fair,' he said. 'I wasn't with you when you saw the burning cottage and all those people.'

I grinned some more.

'I *didn't* see a ghost.'

'Yeah, you did.'

'No, I didn't. I was very careful. No ghost seen.'

'Yeah, you did. Several times, actually. You had some lovely chats.'

I watched him mentally run through the people we'd met over the last few days.

'You're kidding. No, it can't have been. *Clarence?* But – he carried people's suitca—' He broke off.

I grinned some more.

He considered this. 'No, he didn't, did he?'

I grinned a little more.

'No, no, hold on – he made the tea . . . Dammit, no, he didn't.'

'You didn't actually see him handle anything, did you?'

'No,' he said slowly.

'And he wouldn't accept a gratuity.'

'But where was the blood, Cage? Where was the terror? What was the point? Why is he there?'

'He told you. He loves the place. He wanders about, either in the garden or by the river, talking to people, standing in the sun, just generally enjoying his life. Or rather, his death. Judging by his uniform, he probably worked here when it first opened and he's never wanted to leave.'

'And no one ever notices?'

'Well, you didn't.'

He sighed. 'Yes, all right, Cage, you've made your point. Just leave me in peace to contemplate the joys of sharing a car for hundreds of miles with a complete smart-arse.'

*   *   *

Sometimes, change happens so gradually and so imperceptibly that no one notices. You have to go away and then come back again to be aware of any differences at all.

We drove through the outskirts of Rushford. I watched the houses and shops slide past. Jones was silent, focusing on the traffic. I sat back and concentrated. Because there was something wrong with Rushford. No, that's not right. There was something wrong *in* Rushford.

On the surface, everything looked fine. People bustled in and out of shops. Giggling schoolgirls stepped off the pavement without looking, causing Jones to brake and curse on several occasions.

There were cars everywhere and the street market was on, spilling out across the square. After the vast emptiness of Scotland, everything seemed loud and brash and full on. And completely normal. There was no reason at all for the prickles of apprehension running up and down my spine.

Perhaps it was the weather. The sky hung low with that dirty yellow look that usually means something meteorologically dramatic is about to occur.

'I'll drop you off,' said Jones, 'and give you a hand up the hill with your case.'

I waited for the usual *why couldn't I live in a proper street with proper access* complaint, but not today.

'And then I'm off for a bit.'

I must have looked alarmed.

'Nothing dire,' he said. 'Just sorting a few administrative details.' There was a pause as he negotiated another gaggle of suicidally inclined schoolgirls. 'Have you had any thoughts about my suggestion?'

100

'Some,' I said, unwilling to admit I'd actually spent most of my time thinking about my face.

'We'll sit down and have a chat when I get back,' he said, cheerfully. 'And here we are.'

He pulled into a parking space and unloaded my suitcase. We climbed the hill and walked under the arch, out into Castle Close. Nothing seemed to have changed. The castle stood over to my right, containing the council offices and the library. The nice café at the far end of the row where I bought my breakfast brioche and croissants was open and the weather was mild enough for them still to have their tables and chairs outside. Children ran across the grass, either playing games or being chased by bread-seeking ducks. A few swans glided picturesquely over the castle moat, ignoring the world because they were so much better than everyone else.

My house was on the left of the narrow, cobbled lane, opposite the green and facing the castle, part of a long row of terraced houses, all from different periods, with a roofline like broken teeth.

I lived about halfway along. Colonel and Mrs Barton lived in a tall Regency house to the left of mine. They had a lovely bay window in which they spent a lot of time watching the world go by. We waved as we walked past.

The other side was occupied by a small firm of solicitors who, I suspected, regarded me and my doorstep as the best source of entertainment in Rushford. They might have a point. I suspect not many solicitors ever look out of their windows to see a naked Iblis on their neighbour's doorstep. Well, not completely naked – he had been wearing his underpants. At least he hadn't been waving his sword around – and no, that is not a metaphor.

I unlocked my front door. My house welcomed me just as it always did.

'Right,' said Jones, dropping my case by the door to the stairs. 'I'll see you soon, Cage, although you can get me on my mobile if need be.'

I nodded. 'Stay safe.'

'Always do, Cage. It's you I worry about.'

There was a pause and then he said, 'Thank you for my holiday.'

I smiled. 'It was my pleasure.'

He put his arm around my shoulders. 'No, I mean it. Thank you.'

I put both arms around him.

There was a moment during which I think we were both surprised. Then he put his other arm around me. I rested my head on his chest and we stood together for quite a long time. I think we'd be there still until he suddenly said, 'No, I have to go. Stop tempting me.'

I stepped back. 'Drive safely.'

He was halfway to the door. 'Try to stay out of trouble, Cage.'

The front door closed behind him and he was gone.

I have a routine for whenever I've been away for a while. I clean my house from top to bottom. I can't help it. I just do. I think I must get it from my mum, who was the world's most house-proud person. But it's important to me that everything is as crisp and clean as I can make it – although my house is tiny and there's only me in it, so giving it a good clean is nowhere near as onerous as it sounds. My bedroom is on the first floor, overlooking the green and the castle, with a nice modern bathroom opposite. The stairs wind up the middle of the house and are literally only about two feet wide. Jones has to turn his shoulders to get up them.

The door at the bottom of the stairs opens into one largish room with the kitchen at one end, overlooking my tiny backyard. The rest of it is living room. The floors are all honey-coloured, the walls pale blue and green, and there's just enough room for a table and two chairs, a sofa, an armchair, a coffee table, a couple of bookcases against the wall and a TV. My picture of Ted stands on a shelf where I can see him and he can see me. I like to keep fresh flowers nearby.

All in all it's a lovely little house – just right for one person. I fell in love with it as soon as I saw it and it always welcomes me home.

I did my holiday washing, ironed everything and returned it to my wardrobe. I checked the fridge, went shopping and restocked my cupboards. All of that kept me busy for three days and then there was nothing left to do. My house gleamed – or would have if the sun ever shone. Heavy clouds might hang over Rushford, but my house smelled of lavender and lemon and I was content.

I made myself a coffee and sat down to have a think. Back in the summer I'd made a resolution to get out more. To take one day a week and go for a good long walk. There had been mixed results. While it was true I'd been kidnapped by a troll under a bridge, on the other hand, I'd discovered some lovely places in and around Rushford. Time to get back out there again. The summer sun had gone but the days were still mild. Autumn was here and I should make the most of it. Yes, tomorrow I would go for a long walk.

I had second thoughts the next day – the sky still had that low, glowering air. But it had looked like that for a couple of days now and nothing had come of it so far, so I decided to take a chance although I'd stay around Rushford, just in case I had to take shelter. I planned to cross the river and then follow it downstream, through town and, if it still wasn't raining, out through the water meadows on the other side.

I took my trusty backpack and discovered a golden leaf from my holiday that must have got in there, somehow. Smiling, I pressed it between the leaves of a dictionary – the thickest book I could find. I packed my waterproof jacket and an umbrella, just in case, and walked down the hill, peering up at the dirty, dingy sky. It looked as if a storm was perpetually poised above us but lacked the strength for the final effort.

I crossed the medieval bridge, pausing in the middle to look down at the River Rush flowing placidly on its way to the sea. Just as I'd done on the bridge in Scotland.

There hadn't been any recurrence of my face turning up unexpectedly but I wasn't taking any chances. There was a mirror opposite the bed in my bedroom, so I'd draped a shawl over it. I couldn't shun all mirrors completely – not without developing some sort of mental disorder anyway, which, with my luck, would propel me straight back into the arms of Sorensen again and we'd all be back to square one – but I covered all the mirrors I could and avoided the rest.

I think I harboured a hope that I'd left whatever it was behind in Scotland. I didn't want to think about it too much; I didn't want to inadvertently draw it to me.

The day was mild and muggy but with a slight wind blowing in my face. Not an unpleasant day for a walk.

I crossed the bridge and turned left. Apart from the castle and its surroundings, this was one of the oldest parts of town. The docks with their warehouses were on my side of the river and on this side stood the tall, narrow merchants' houses. Far enough away to avoid the taint of trade but close enough they could keep an eye on their ships coming in and out. The shop and storerooms would have been on the ground floor, with living space for the servants and apprentices. The family's living accommodation would be on the floors above. At the rear would have been the yard for loading and unloading, possibly with stables as well.

Most were still residential but a few of them had been converted into shops, cafés and galleries which I'd visited a couple of times so I knew most of the houses still had wonky wooden floors and the rooms were panelled in oak. Tiny timber-framed windows looked out across the river but the rooms were still dark. Tall chimneys poked out of the roofs. There were a lot of chimney pots because there would have been a fireplace in nearly every room.

Outside, what could be classed as either a very narrow street or a wide pavement ran parallel to the river. In times past it would have been full of merchants' ladies alighting from their carriages, dressed in the very latest fashions, walking advertisements for their husband's prosperity. Today, it was just me, on foot and casting anxious glances up at the sky.

On the other side of a low wall, slippery stone steps led down to the river path. There were always boats tied up here. Possibly it was cheaper here than mooring in the docks area. I've often wondered what it would be like to live on a narrowboat. Perhaps one day, Jones and I could take another holiday and find out.

From this point I could look across the river and up the hill to the castle at the top and the tangle of streets surrounding it, although I couldn't see my house from here. The medieval bridge was off to my left. Like the castle, this was another picturesque part of town. Very popular with tourists.

It was also the place of the cholera pits. The end of this street opened up into a small crescent of bright green grass which would be thick with daffodils in the spring. There was a bench on which to sit and enjoy them and a small plaque on the wall explaining when and how many victims had been buried here. I did occasionally wonder if they were what made the daffs flower so well but it was actually a happy, sunny place. No unhappy spirits lingered here. Nothing burrowed up through the earth at night, seeking its prey.

Sometimes I think I'm not a very cheerful person.

A sudden, vicious gust of wind blew my hair around my face. Something big and wet plopped on my bare arm. Wonderful – I was about as far as it was possible to get from the shelter of my house and now it decided to rain.

I left the wall with its views over the river and looked for shelter. There was an antiques shop directly opposite with an inset shop doorway. There would be room to wait and watch the storm go by. I trotted across the road. The sky was very dark and just as I slipped into the doorway, with a sudden clap of thunder, the storm was upon us.

Driven by the sudden wind, the rain came down like stair rods, bouncing a foot into the air when it hit the paving stones and then falling back again. I shrugged off my backpack and was rummaging for my waterproof when I heard the door open behind me. At the same moment, another massive clap of thunder seemed to roll up the river and I jumped a mile.

'Now then, missis,' said a familiar voice. 'You're blocking our doorway. You'll have to move.'

I spun around. 'Jerry?'

Jerry's a friend of Jones's. He's one of the many disreputable people with whom Jones surrounds himself. It is very possible that I'm the most respectable person he knows. I used to be the most respectable person *I* knew but that doesn't seem to apply any longer. I don't know what's happening to me.

Back to Jerry. I've no idea how old he is – older than he looks, I suspect. I only know that if something bad was happening and I couldn't get hold of Jones then Jerry would be next on my list. He's small and agile – all the better to climb in through those awkward upstairs windows you never bother locking because even a monkey couldn't get through those, could it?

He stood before me now, just a faint outline in the gloom, but I recognised his voice and colour. Jerry's colour is unusual. A rich, deep brown, bright and shiny, like a conker. It's unusual because it's solid with very few other colours mixed with it. I suspect Jerry never suffered the kind of debilitating self-doubt that afflicts so many of us. Jerry looked at a situation, decided what needed to be done and did it. Whether it was on the right side of the law or not. Having said that, he was the very kindest of men. He'd once broken into my house to steal me some clothes and when I'd unpacked my suitcase, he'd not only included everything I could possibly have needed, but there was even tissue paper between the layers. I'd made him promise to show me how to pack so beautifully and I could see he'd taken it as a compliment.

And – the thing I really loved him for – he'd pinched a rather valuable painting from the Sorensen Clinic, right under the nose of Sorensen himself, and substituted a forgery. I sometimes wonder what my parents would say if they'd lived long enough to see the sort of company I was keeping these days, but even so – yay, Jerry!

'Are you coming in?' he enquired.

'Are you casing the joint?'

I was only teasing and you could have knocked me down with a feather when he said, 'Nah, we're just about to put the kettle on and wondered if you'd like one.'

I nodded. 'Please.' Even though I was sheltered, the rain was bouncing into the doorway and I was still getting wet.

'We?' I said as he closed the door behind me, locking it and flipping the sign to *Closed*.

Just for once, his colour wavered a little. 'Yeah. Actually, I've been meaning to . . .'

A door opened at the far end of the shop. 'Hello, there.'

I could see Jerry take the plunge. 'This is Gerald. My husband. Gerald, this is Elizabeth Cage that I've been telling you about.'

I turned to Gerald. 'How do you do? It's very nice to meet you.'

'You too,' he said. 'Jerry often mentions you, Mrs Cage.'

I forbore to say that Jerry had never mentioned him even once. 'Elizabeth,' I said, and he smiled.

They say opposites attract and here was an example. Jerry was short and slim and usually wore a battered tweed jacket and baggy trousers. Whatever the opposite of fashionable is – Jerry was it. Most of his clothes appeared to have been styled in the 1940s. Gerald, on the other hand, was tall, lean and beautifully presented. His accent was public school, his hair neatly clipped, and he wore an exquisite jacket. There could not have been two more different people. Except for their colours, which were nearly identical. Gerald's was a rich terracotta colour very similar to Jerry's nut-brown. And he was kind. I could see it in him. Jerry's a bit of a jewel and I was so pleased they'd found each other.

Gerald enquired if I was very wet. 'Such a dreadful afternoon.'

'No, I'm fine,' I said. 'But shamelessly, I'm going to cadge a cup of tea from you.'

'It's all ready,' he said. 'Jerry, you put the fire on and I'll get an extra cup.'

We followed him through the door into a neat office behind the shop. There was a desk, a few cabinets and an open laptop.

I turned to Jerry, who was switching on a space heater. 'This is very kind, Jerry. There was no way I was going to get back home without being soaked to the skin.'

'Glad to see you, missis. I've been wanting to ask you round but . . . you know.'

To spare him embarrassment, I told him I'd been away. 'With Michael Jones. We got back a few days ago.'

'Ah,' he said. 'The Scotland jaunt. How did it go?'

I knew exactly what he was asking.

'About as well as these things usually do,' I said, gloomily.

He seemed amused. 'Gotta say, missis, after those women up at Greyston, I am never going anywhere with you two again.'

'We had a lovely time,' I said primly and he snorted. I wondered if Jones had already spoken to him and he knew all about our so-called holiday.

On the other hand, I'd once phoned Jerry for help and he'd

had to explain he was half in, half out of an upstairs window, preparatory to helping himself to a very valuable painting, so I didn't feel that the moral high ground was all his.

In fact . . . I looked around. This was an antique shop. Full of antiques – as they so often are.

I looked at Jerry. Jerry looked back at me. His face gave nothing away and his colour wasn't saying a lot, either, so I gave it up. Nothing to do with me, anyway.

Gerald returned with a tea tray.

I drank delicious lapsang souchong out of a bone china cup so fragile I could very nearly see through it. And they served fairy cakes.

'Seriously?' I said to Jerry, who grinned.

'We like to pander to stereotypes.'

Looking out through the shop window, the world had darkened. Wind, thunder, lightning, drumming rain – it was all going on out there, but in here was a warm, well-lit oasis, complete with tea and cakes. We chatted and laughed.

'Jones has gone away for a while,' I said, in answer to Jerry's query. 'He'll be back soon. If I see him before you, I'll ask him to give you a call.'

He nodded. 'And how's the long thin streak of wind and piss these days?'

He meant Iblis. At least, I assumed he did. I didn't know anyone else fitting that description. Not that I knew a lot of people. My neighbours the Bartons, Jones, Jerry, Iblis, Melek – and now Gerald – constituted my entire social group.

'I don't know,' I said, looking out of the window and suddenly worried. 'I know he went away after . . . after Greyston. I assumed he was still away but looking at this weather . . .'

Iblis lived in the woods – which were definitely no place to be on a day like this.

'Wouldn't worry too much,' said Jerry, helping himself to the last fairy cake despite Gerald's murmurings about family holding back. 'He always lands on his feet, that one. Although . . .' He stopped and looked at the weather again.

'True,' I said, 'but, I think tomorrow, if this has stopped by then, I might go and have a look for him. Just to make sure.'

'Yeah,' said Jerry, casually. 'Just to make sure. Although he'll be fine, I'm certain. I'm not worried at all.'

I looked across at Gerald, who winked at me.

There was one of those pauses. A natural break in the conversation that becomes awkward unless broken with a new topic. I myself was unsure what to say next. I had no idea how much Gerald knew about Jerry. Or what Jerry had told him about his somewhat unique lifestyle. I cast around for something innocuous to say.

'Tell me, how did you two meet?'

Jerry's colour writhed which was unusual for him. 'Ah,' he said, and seemed very disinclined to say any more.

Gerald looked amused. 'We met here at the shop, actually.'

I tried to picture Jerry strolling casually around an antiques shop. No – that didn't work at all. And then I realised.

I looked at Jerry, whose colour was pulsing with embarrassment. Not embarrassment at his occupation, I assumed, but at being caught.

'You were supposed to be out,' he said accusingly to Gerald.

'I was out,' said Gerald mildly. 'And then I came back.' He looked at me. 'I forgot something and I was only a hundred yards down the road so I nipped back for it. I was just picking

111

up the file I'd left in my office when it dawned on me – the alarm hadn't bleeped as I came in. This one,' he nodded at Jerry, 'had come in through the back as I went out the front and disabled it.'

'I'd have re-enabled it when I left,' said Jerry, seriously. 'And locked the door behind me.'

'Yes, he would,' I said earnestly to Gerald. 'He's very conscientious, you know.'

Gerald grinned. 'Well, I realised someone had been in, and because I'd come back so suddenly, he was probably still here.'

'Oh, my goodness,' I said. 'What did you do?'

'Well, I keep rather a nice Toledo steel blade for just this sort of thing. I took it down off the wall and shouted, "I'm coming for you, you bastard."'

I blinked, trying hard to envisage these unlikely goings-on in such a respectable-looking shop. 'And where were you at this point?' I said to Jerry.

He pointed to a very large and very ornate wardrobe standing in a dark corner out in the shop. 'In there.'

'Oh,' I said.

'Nice piece,' said Jerry, casually. 'Burr walnut – very sought after. Inlaid and with brass fittings. Internal shoebox – even a place to keep your wigs. Triple doors and central mirror. Very nice piece.'

I stared at him in amazement. 'You were going to steal a wardrobe?'

'Course not,' he said, indignantly. 'I'd seen a bit of good china in the window. Small and portable. Not like wardrobes.'

'It took four men to get that one in,' said Gerald. 'No idea how we'll ever get it back out again. Not that I'd ever sell it.' He grinned at me again. 'Sentimental associations.'

I grinned back. 'So what happened next?'

'Well,' said Jerry, 'I'm in the wardrobe, aren't I?'

'Which I had already surmised,' said Gerald, impressively.

'There wasn't anywhere else,' said Jerry. 'You're hardly Hercool Pworot.'

Gerald winked at me. 'I thought I'd have a bit of fun.'

I looked across at Jerry, who rolled his eyes.

'The first thing, obviously, was to turn the key.'

I stared reproachfully at Jerry. 'You didn't think to take the key out of the lock?'

'I had two and a half seconds to find a hiding place, get from one end of the shop to the other, rip the door open and get myself inside,' he said defensively. 'I'd like to see you do better.'

Gerald continued. 'And having secured my prisoner, I shouted, "I've got you now. You're going to prison, you thieving troglodyte," and damn me if he didn't shout back, enquiring whether I was using the word troglodyte in its traditional sense – i.e. cave dweller – in which case, given his current location in a small, dark space, I was being rather clever – or was I accusing him of being deliberately ignorant, which was rather rude, and in which case I was the troglodyte and not he.'

I stared back at Gerald; my tea forgotten. 'What happened?'

'Well, by now I was so incensed I shouted he could take it any way he pleased and I had a sword and was he familiar with the magician's trick?'

'Magician's trick?' I said, puzzled.

'You know – the one where the lovely young assistant climbs into the box – or wardrobe, in this case, of course – and the magician stabs away half a dozen times, the audience screams

113

in fear and then the lovely young assistant emerges all smiles and hole-free.'

I blinked. 'You were going to stab Jerry?'

Gerald assumed a dramatic posture. 'I certainly was.'

'No, he wasn't,' interrupted Jerry, the voice of reason. 'That wardrobe's made of real wood. By real craftsmen. You'd have needed a chainsaw at least. And he wasn't going to damage a lovely piece like that. I reckoned I was safe. As I told him.'

I turned back to Gerald. 'And was he?'

Gerald nodded. 'Well, yes, but I wasn't beaten yet. I had a brilliant idea.'

I tried to picture the scene. Jerry inside the wardrobe, Gerald outside, and the two of them hurling insults and defiance at each other. 'And what was that? Your brilliant idea?'

'I told him I was on my way to Edinburgh for a conference and that I'd be gone for ten days. I told him he was welcome to any food and drink he might find inside the wardrobe and I'd see him when I got back. Or rather, I'd laughingly scrape his liquified remains into a bucket and call the police.'

I was back to Jerry again. 'Wow.'

Jerry shrugged. 'I wasn't worried.'

'Why not?'

'Who goes to a conference for ten days? I reckoned he'd be gone for ten minutes at the very most.'

'So – stalemate,' I said. 'Except that you, Jerry, could have got out of the wardrobe in a heartbeat and you, Gerald, could have rung the police in a heartbeat, but the pair of you were enjoying yourselves so much that neither of those options occurred to you, did they?'

They both grinned at me, their colours intermingling.

'Jerry asked if there was any chance of a cup of tea while he was waiting to die and I said, yes, I expect so, and would he like a biscuit? He asked for a hobnob and I said we only had bourbons. He said what sort of establishment was this and I said I'd go and get hobnobs if he would put the kettle on. I unlocked the door and shot off for biscuits and when I came back, the tea was ready.' He looked over at Jerry. 'He's been here pretty much ever since.'

I couldn't help laughing but I could see their story was true. I said to Gerald, 'If only I'd known it was that easy to get a man, I'd have locked one in a wardrobe years ago,' and still the rain came down and we talked and laughed and they showed me around the shop. Gerald knew and loved every piece and the story behind it. I rather lost track of time but it was a lovely, lovely afternoon.

CHAPTER EIGHT

The rain subsided eventually. Enough for me to get home without drowning, anyway, and I took my leave. They wouldn't let me go until I'd accepted an invitation to dinner with them next week because Gerald, his eyes dancing with mischief, said he liked to cook and Jerry loved to entertain. Jerry's face was expressionless but his colour said it all. I had to struggle not to laugh.

I set off for home as it began to get dark, avoiding the massive puddles everywhere. I walked slowly back along the river, looking at all the lights reflected in the water. The air was certainly more pleasant now we'd had our long-threatened storm.

Which brought me back to Iblis. How *had* he fared, out in the woods? I really should go and check on him. I could even take him some basic supplies, as long as he promised not to do the *You left me an offering – now I must offer you my service* thing again, because, although having a charming young man offer you his service sounds – on the face of it – rather enjoyable, trust me, it isn't.

The next day was still moist but not actually raining. I heaved on my backpack again and set out. On the other side of the river this time. Past the docks and the converted warehouses and out the other side into the country.

Everything was wet. Giant drops of silver water clung to the leaves and long grasses. There were gleaming puddles all along the towpath and as I trudged along, the air became closer and more humid. The clouds were gathering again and I didn't think we were done with this storm yet.

I walked until I could see the road bridge in the distance. I could clearly see the towpath passing under the bridge and out the other side but I wouldn't be taking that path. A troll lived under that bridge. Or had done until Iblis drove him out. I wondered where he was now. Iblis *and* the troll.

Turning off the towpath at what I thought was the right spot, I found an overgrown trail that looked familiar and followed it. Every time I brushed against the foliage a hundred water droplets fell on me. My trainers were soaked, as were my jeans, all the way up to my knees. My dad always used to laugh and say, 'No good deed goes unpunished.' Only the thought of Iblis, cold, soaked and huddling in his inadequate tent kept me going.

The overgrown path should have been a clue. He wasn't there. I looked around. I was almost certain I was in the right place – there were the beech trees he loved so much – but Iblis no longer lived among them. His camp was deserted. He hadn't been here for a long time. All the flattened grass was standing up again. I thought I could see a faint outline where his tent had been, although I might have been imagining that. The ring of small stones was still there, surrounding a charred area where he'd had his small fire, and over there was the rock on which I'd left him food and water and he'd later claimed was his altar. But of Iblis himself, there was no sign.

I thought I'd rest a while before going back, so I perched on his supposed altar and opened the sandwiches I'd made for him. They were delicious. He would have enjoyed them.

Iblis and I had met back in the early summer when he'd rescued me from the troll I mentioned before. Old Þhurs. Or Thurs, as I pronounced it. Iblis had taken me back to his camp for a mug of restorative tea – which, now I came to think of it, had never materialised. He'd been charming and kind and, in gratitude, because I thought he was a homeless man living off squirrel and tree bark, I'd left him my sandwiches and water.

He'd construed this as me leaving an offering which, he claimed, now bound us inextricably for ever. I'd had to be quite firm with him and then it turned out he was having me on. It was his idea of a joke. He's funny and quick-witted and very odd – he claims to be from an older race whose job it is to tackle evil on behalf of mankind. Which might or might not be true. He was certainly telling the truth, but it was the truth as he saw it and I couldn't make up my mind about him. Initially I'd been convinced he was a candidate for some urgent Care in the Community, but since then I'd seen him in action once or twice, and was coming to terms with the possibility he could be exactly what he said he was.

But, most importantly, I'd always felt I could trust him. He never let me down and that counts for a lot. On the surface, he was irresponsible and unreliable, but he really wasn't. He wore his silver colour like a banner. Bright and restless – just like Iblis himself – it reminded me of quicksilver, which summed him up very well. He was always on the move – never still.

But, for all his light-heartedness, he carried an air of tragedy about him and one memorable night, greatly aided by the unemptyable Bottle of Utgard-Loki, we'd both got very drunk and he'd confessed his great sin to me. It had been a dark night. For me as well as for him.

I hadn't been surprised when he told me about it, because if anyone was a founder member of the *See a Rule – Break that Rule* club, it was Iblis. And chairman, secretary and treasurer, as well, probably. But, as he explained it, there was only one rule that really mattered – you don't sleep with a mortal. Ever. For any reason. You never sleep with a mortal.

Guess who'd slept with a mortal? Or thought he had. Either way it had ruined his life. And Melek's as well. Though as it turned out, the woman he'd slept with hadn't been mortal, so he was lucky there. She was a Fiori demon and she'd deliberately targeted him – and, more importantly, his sword.

I'd been so happy to show him the truth. To lift that dreadful dark cloud that surrounded him. I couldn't exonerate him completely but I'd been able to prove that he'd been tricked. I think he'd been too stunned to take it in at the time. He'd lived with the guilt for so long and I don't think that sort of thing is so easily shrugged away. My heart had gone out to him. He still didn't have his sword – that was probably gone for good – but the knowledge he hadn't broken the one unbreakable rule had lightened him. I'd watched his colour transform as the implications finally dawned upon him. He'd wandered off into the night, dazed, bemused, still unsure of the repercussions, but with a dreadful weight lifted from his shoulders. He was still missing his sword and was weakened by its loss, but that was a problem he could deal with.

And that was the last I'd seen of him – walking off into the night. I wondered if he'd ever come back. Perhaps, now that he was free of his past, he'd gone off and I'd never see him again. I hoped he'd gone to see Melek.

Melek was his . . . working partner, I suppose you'd describe her. She was tall and hard and nowhere near as user-friendly as Iblis. In fact, she intimidated me more than a little. Not in a bad way, but rather in the way of a thunderstorm. An impression of power that could be unleashed at any moment and you wouldn't want to be around when it was.

They must have had a great deal to say to each other. His mistake had affected her as much as him. I hoped very much that they were together, building a new relationship, perhaps.

I finished the sandwiches, looked around the wet woods one last time, sighed, hefted my now much lighter backpack and turned for home.

A week later, the phone rang and Michael Jones announced he was back.

'Jolly good.'

He sighed. 'More enthusiasm, Cage.'

'Hold on.' I made a straining noise. 'No – that was it.'

'We've been asked to dinner.'

'Yes, I know. Jerry and Gerald.'

He enquired whether this meant we were an item.

I frowned. 'An item of what?'

He sighed. 'Current cultural references just pass you by, don't they, Cage. Do you want to go?'

'I've already accepted for myself but I'm glad you're going too. Have you met Gerald? He's lovely.'

'Once or twice. I'll come and pick you up.'

'There's no need for that.'

'Next Tuesday. About seven thirty.'

'I can . . .'

'Be ready.'

I had too much pride to do that. On his arrival I sat him down and made him wait ten minutes or so while I went upstairs and applied the slowest lipstick in the world.

When I eventually strolled back downstairs, he was sprawled in an armchair reading a book. 'Already? You shouldn't have rushed on my account.'

'I didn't.' I picked up my bag and held the front door open. 'Ready?'

He stood up. 'It's exciting, isn't it? Our first social outing as a couple.'

We walked there. 'You'll be able to have a couple of drinks, Cage, without having to worry about driving me home.'

I told him I had no intention of doing either.

'Seriously, have you *never* learned to drive?'

I shook my head.

'Why not?'

'Well, there was no need. Before I married Ted, I had everything I needed here in Rushford. Then, after I was married, Ted drove us everywhere and . . .'

'And?'

'And it didn't matter because Ted liked to drive.'

'Would you like to drive?'

That wasn't anything I'd ever thought about before. 'I don't know. Yes. Perhaps.'

We walked past an art gallery, a private house and a coffee shop. Now that I wasn't dodging the rain, I could see Gerald's was one of the larger shops, double-fronted and very smart.

I stopped. 'Can you hear something?'

Jones stood still and listened. 'No. Is there a problem?'

'I thought I heard . . . No, it doesn't matter.'

Jerry opened the door. The sound blasted out over his shoulder and it took everything I had not to flinch. Neither Jones nor Jerry appeared to notice a thing.

'Now then?' said Jerry.

'All right?' said Jones, so I knew they were pleased to see each other again.

Jerry took us upstairs. Nearer and nearer with every step. Oh God . . .

We weren't the only guests. A couple about my own age were waiting for us. Gerald bustled forwards to make the introductions. 'This is James Monroe and Cordelia Channing. Guys, this is Elizabeth Cage and Michael Jones.'

We shook hands. I liked Cordelia Channing on sight. She was an artist and one of the few people I'd met with a multi-colour. Like a swirling rainbow, I said later to Jones. It sparkled with life and movement and was never still. She reminded me a little of Iblis.

I *disliked* James Monroe on sight. He ran the art gallery we'd passed. He was handsome and charming and seemed genuinely delighted to meet us. His handshake was warm and solid and just firm enough to give the impression this was someone you could trust. As popular with men as women. An all-round good egg, you would have said. A little complacent, perhaps – a little too aware of his own charms, but just a harmless, likeable chap.

Except for the woman screaming into his face.

On and on. Over and over. Scream after scream after scream.

I couldn't close my ears but I could close my eyes. It didn't help. Almost of its own accord, my mind began to drift. Warmth . . . sleep . . . tired . . . sleep . . .

My mind drifted further. Darkness . . . betrayal . . . endless darkness . . .

I pulled back. Hard.

I have two fears. The first is that if I can see them then they – whoever they are – can see me. And the second is that somehow my seeing them establishes a link. A pathway from them to me. I remembered that molten thread between me and Lady Torrington.

Opening my eyes, I could see her a little more clearly now. Just her head and shoulders. As if she'd had no strength left to make all of herself visible. She was a little younger than me with long, sleek blonde hair that fell to her shoulders and then just faded away.

What her face looked like I don't know because her eyes were screwed tight shut with effort as she screamed and screamed. Right into James's face. From a distance of about six inches. All I saw was her twisted face, tight with fury, her huge red mouth gaping wide as she shrieked, on and on and on. Tearing my head apart.

Everyone was looking at me.

'I've seen some of your stuff,' I said to Cordelia, trying to concentrate solely on her and block James and the woman entirely from my perception. 'In James's gallery just up the road. I love your work.'

They were both delighted with that.

'I carry traditional stuff mostly,' said James. 'There's not a huge market for more modern work in Rushford. And I snap up everything of Cordy's, obviously,' he said smiling down at her. He obviously adored Cordelia and treated her like a princess. 'Everything she does is pounced on almost as soon as I put it in the window. And I have a wall for local artists, of course, to give them a start. I've even got a couple of Checklands. Only small ones, sadly. He's so very collectible these days.'

I smiled politely because I didn't want to seem rude. I definitely didn't want to spoil the evening so I shut everything out as best I could and tried to focus solely on the others. James's colour was a mixture of purple and brown – almost like a bruise. He still seemed very pleasant and relaxed but when we sat down, I made sure I sat as far away from him as I could manage when there were only six people at the table.

Gerald was in the kitchen while Jerry entertained the guests. The two of them had obviously gone to a huge amount of trouble for us so I gritted my teeth, pinned a smile to my face and vowed I'd get through this evening somehow.

I thought the food might help because to me – the world's most unambitious cook, according to Michael Jones – it all seemed amazing.

We began with a pre-dinner snack. Camembert, baked with sprigs of rosemary and served with sesame bread sticks, on which Jones fell with enthusiasm. There was lots of chatter – both James and Cordelia were outgoing and chatty and Jones was keeping his conversational end up as well. I hoped everyone would assume I was just shy.

The starter was prawn cocktail but not just any old prawn cocktail, apparently. This one was served in wide-necked glasses with shredded lettuce and pea shoots and lightly fried scallops.

Jones fell on that with even more enthusiasm, demanding to know if that was brandy in the Marie Rose sauce?

'It is,' said Gerald and the two of them embarked on some kind of culinary one-upmanship. I listened with huge attention – I could have sat an examination afterwards – concentrating hard on their every word.

'Beef Wellington,' announced Gerald, placing a huge plate in the middle of the table to cries of appreciation that very nearly drowned out the incessantly screaming woman not four feet away from me. How could James remain so oblivious . . .?

This dinner party might be the ordeal from hell but I was unable to resist. Nudging Jones, I whispered, 'Still no trout.' A remark I had to explain to everyone else and twenty minutes passed with everyone very happily casting aspersions on Jones's fishing abilities. Something he said he was happy to endure for the sake of the Wellington and was that red wine in the gravy?

Jerry said that given the way Gerald had been sloshing the stuff around in the kitchen, it would be more accurate to say there was gravy in the red wine and Jones held out his plate for more. It was lovely to see him enjoying himself.

And I could cope. In the same way that the human nose eventually fails to register even the worst smells, I was hoping the human ear could perform similarly. Perhaps if I gave it enough time, I could somehow shut out the screams that were now drilling their way through my skull.

I was wrong. We'd been here an hour and a half and things weren't getting any better. I glanced at the clock to estimate how long before I could go home. Another hour, perhaps, and then I would be able to make my excuses and leave without being thought rude. I helped myself to parsnip and potato mash and smiled at everyone.

'So, what do you do, Michael?' asked James and I paused to sip my water, interested to see what Jones would reply.

'Well,' he said, his attention all on his Wellington. 'At college, I read geology.'

'You're a geologist?'

'Civil servant,' he said, smiling and sipping his wine.

I made a huge effort. 'Oh my God – Michael Jones – the erratic boulder of the civil service.'

Everyone fell about. Even Jones, who, I knew, would take advantage of the deflection.

He smiled down at me. 'Remind me why I stay with you, Cage.'

'Because you're crazy about her,' said Cordelia. 'Oh, stop frowning at me, James. It's obvious.'

'Top up your wine, Elizabeth?' enquired Gerald, social star of the evening.

I shook my head and tried not to blush. Jones continued eating and didn't blush at all.

We paused for half an hour before dessert – which was probably just as well. The pain behind my eyes was becoming intense. Under the table, Jones touched my hand and said, 'All right?'

I couldn't shake my head in case it fell off so I whispered, 'No. Tell you later.'

He nodded, left his hand on mine for a second and then demanded to know what was for dessert.

'Aha,' said Gerald, his colour glowing with pleasure. 'I'm so glad someone asked.'

126

Jerry groaned.

'Chocolate bread and butter pudding with cherries soaked in raspberry liqueur and served with fresh raspberries and Greek yoghurt.'

Jones picked up his spoon in preparation. 'I may never leave this place.'

'Followed by coffee and petits fours.'

I could see Jerry watching me so I made an effort.

'Gerald, this is all wonderful. Thank you for going to so much trouble for us.'

'No trouble at all,' he said. 'I love to cook.' And two seconds later, once again, he and Jones were deep in some sort of culinary dialogue far above the heads of lesser mortals.

Thus abandoned, I made sure I talked to Cordelia, leaving James to Jerry. Under other circumstances it would have been funny to watch Jerry attempt to answer normal, everyday dinner-party questions such as 'What have you been up to recently?' without actually employing the phrase *breaking and entering*. Or the words *art theft*. Or *forgery*. Or *taking without the owner's consent*.

Instead, I concentrated on Cordelia who, as an artist, was fascinating to listen to. I pushed everything to the back of my mind because I really wanted to hear what she had to say. Her colour was mesmerising, varying from moment to moment, sometimes a deep red, sometimes shading towards a rich purple, and then flickering through mauve, blue, turquoise, green and yellow, depending on the topic of conversation at the time. I couldn't take my eyes off it. It swirled about her as she waved her fork around in excitement. I couldn't help liking her.

'And then,' she said, dramatically, her eyes shining as the

127

others turned to listen. 'I laid in the final strokes and stepped back to admire my masterpiece and thought, yes, that will do nicely. I'm not usually so definite about when a picture of mine is finished – sometimes James has to wrest them from me – but just for once, I could see it was done. I reached out for my mug of tea to have a celebration sip, and not for one moment taking my eyes off my picture, I drank my paint water.'

We all laughed.

'How did it taste?' asked Jones.

She twinkled at him. 'Remarkably similar to James's tea, actually. The only reason I noticed was that it was stone cold.'

'And bright green,' said James, smiling. 'Really, Cordy . . .'

'I know, I know,' she said, patting his hand. 'I promise to take more care in future.'

'If anything should happen to you,' he said, and there was genuine concern in his voice. He loved her. His purply brown colour curled around her, keeping her safe, and I would have been very impressed if not for the other woman – the one shrieking her lungs out at him.

I sipped my water and closed my eyes, wishing I could close my ears as well. Anything for a moment's respite. Given the volume and frequency, it seemed unbelievable that James couldn't hear her and was completely oblivious to her presence. I watched him talking quietly to Cordelia – enjoying a private moment with her.

Please don't get the wrong idea. These were not screams of pain, or fear, or distress from someone in desperate need of assistance. These were screams of frustration. If I hadn't known better, I would have said someone was having a massive temper tantrum. An adult temper tantrum. They were endless and ear-splitting. She was very definitely not happy about something.

And they were the same screams. Over and over. Almost as if they were on a loop, tearing at my nerves and making my head pound to the same rhythm. I couldn't help thinking, wasn't it bad enough that I saw things? Now I had to hear them, too?

The room was full of the smells of good food, and of Jerry's rich brown colour happily mingling with Gerald's terracotta. Cordelia's bright sparkling colours cast a glittering light over everything and Jones's was more golden than red tonight because he and Jerry were old friends and he was happy and relaxed and enjoying himself. Which left James and his brooding bruise colour. He was smiling at Cordelia and they leaned towards each other as they talked, each taking every opportunity to touch the other. They were obviously very much in love.

The screaming was becoming too much for me to bear. I had to suppress the urge to start screaming myself. Anything to drown it out. Even the gentle candlelight was making my eyes hurt. A man with a pneumatic drill was trying to bore his way out of my skull. And the screams were getting even louder and more frequent. As toddlers do when no one is taking any notice of them. Only I could hear her but it wasn't me she was interested in. It was James she wanted to notice her, and he, lucky man, was enjoying his evening in happy ignorance.

I wondered if this happened to him all the time. Was she with him, hour after hour, day after day, or had she turned up for this special occasion? I didn't know. I didn't care much, either. This was a rare night out for me. I was meeting new friends. It didn't happen very often and it was being ruined.

I sat back in my chair. Whatever this was about was none of

my business. It certainly wasn't my responsibility. It was nothing to do with me. These tall narrow houses were very old. It was more than possible – in fact it was very likely – that at some point in the past two to three hundred years, something unpleasant had happened here and I was catching its dying echoes. What it had to do with James was a mystery I didn't care about. All I wanted was to participate in a normal evening with friends. To sit back and enjoy good food and good company. As everyone else was doing. What was so wrong with that? It was James Monroe who seemed to be the focus of whatever was happening here – not me. I always feel I'm shown these things for a reason, but would just one night have been too much to ask for? I felt a prickle of tears behind my eyes and fumbled in my bag for a tissue.

I became aware Jones was watching me again. 'I'm a little worried about you.'

The perfect get-out. We'd finished the meal. We'd had coffee. I could legitimately leave without feeling I was ruining the party or breaking up the evening. I'd had enough of being brave. My head was going to explode any minute now.

I snapped my bag shut and kept hold of it, subconsciously signalling I wanted to leave. 'Jerry, Gerald, I'm so sorry. Especially when you've gone to so much trouble to give us such a wonderful evening, but I'm really not feeling very well. I think I have the beginnings of a migraine.'

Jerry stood up at once. 'I'll run you home, missis.'

'No, if you don't mind, it's quicker to walk. It's not far and the fresh air might help clear my head.'

Jones stood up. 'I'll walk you home.'

'I don't want to break up the party. I feel bad enough about leaving early as it is.'

'I'll get your coat,' said Gerald. He was genuinely concerned. He was such a sweetie, which made me feel even more guilty. But I couldn't bear that infernal screaming a moment longer.

We said our goodnights. I apologised all over again and then the door closed behind us. The screaming dulled and then faded and my head stopped jangling. I couldn't help a deep, heartfelt sigh of relief.

We walked down the road a little way. Once out of sight from the house, I sat down on the low wall just opposite the art gallery and dragged in some deep breaths of cold night air. I looked out over the river at the lights on the opposite bank. It wasn't that late; I could hear music and voices from the pubs and restaurants drifting across the water.

Jones sat beside me. 'What was that all about? Do you really have a headache, because you do look awful.'

'I'm sorry,' I said, 'I just couldn't bear that incessant screaming a moment longer.'

He looked around. 'What screaming?'

'It's inside the house.'

'Gerald's house?'

I nodded, taking more breaths of the crisp night air and enjoying the scream-free environment.

He frowned. 'You didn't mention this when you had tea with them?'

'It didn't happen then.'

'So it only started tonight?'

'For me, yes.' I stood up. 'I just want to go home.'

'In a minute,' he said, so I sat back down again and stared up at the tall, narrow houses. This whole area around the river was full of narrow lanes, many of them still paved with the original ankle-turning cobbles. They still have old-fashioned lampposts, and every now and then a production company turns up to film another version of *A Christmas Carol* here.

'Is it probable,' said Jones, interrupting my thoughts, 'that it's not something to do with the house, but that it was something to do with the guests?'

'Yes.'

'So not Jerry or Gerald.'

'No. Not me, either. Nor you. Probably.'

'Thank you,' he said. 'So – James or Cordelia.'

'James Monroe, I'm almost certain, and . . .'

I trailed away and looked over his shoulder. Because something was coming.

CHAPTER NINE

People sneer at me because I don't go out much.

'Housewife,' they say, because that's not a complimentary term these days.

'No social life,' they say, which is true. But the reason I don't go out much is because every time I do, I expose myself to . . . well, anything that happens to be passing at the time, I suppose.

I watched the sad little shape approach and my heart was crying. I'd so looked forward to my evening out. James had been bad enough and now – this.

Jones was speaking. 'This seems strangely unlike you, Cage. I'd have thought you'd be telling me to rip up the floorboards by now, searching for screaming skulls or something.'

I said, 'Hush.'

He leaned back in surprise. 'Did you just tell me to shut up?'

'Yes, but politely.'

'Well, that's a matter of opinion, but why?'

'Because good manners are important.'

'No – why am I to hush.'

'Something's coming.'

He stood up and looked around. 'Dear God, Cage, you frighten the living daylights out of me sometimes. Which direction?'

'Behind you, coming towards us. Very slowly. Don't move. Don't frighten it.'

'Don't frighten *it*?'

'It's a child,' I said. 'A tiny child. You're quite safe. I won't let it hurt you. Just sit still.'

He sat back down again.

The tiny shape was drifting along the wall, flitting from shadow to shadow, eventually halting about six feet away. It was a very faint little shade and its feet were lost within the wall itself.

I said to Jones, 'Can you see him?'

He turned his head and squinted out of the corner of his eye. 'I can see something. A shadow. What is it?'

'It's a little boy. About three years old. In his Spider-Man pyjamas. He's wearing a nappy. He's very afraid. Don't frighten him.'

'What about him frightening me?'

I ignored that. 'Hello, sweetheart. What's your name?'

His voice was just a whisper in the wind. 'Sammy.'

'Hello, Sammy. I'm Elizabeth. This is Jones. Why don't you come a little closer so he can see you? He won't hurt you, I promise.'

The little shadow inched closer. I saw a tiny, pinched face with huge eyes.

'Are you cold, Sammy?' said Jones, gently. 'Would you like my coat?'

Sammy shook his head.

'Where do you live, Sammy?'

He pointed a chubby finger directly at the spot where I was sitting. That couldn't be right, surely, and then the truth dawned.

'In the wall? You live in this wall?' I felt my blood chill. The night suddenly got much darker. Trying to keep my voice steady, I said, 'Why do you live in the wall, Sammy?'

He didn't answer. I reminded myself he was only about three years old and tried again.

'Why do you live in the wall, Sammy?'

'Because of her. She eat me.'

'Who's her? Is it the screaming woman?'

Tears welled up in his eyes. He put his thumb in his mouth. I tried to smile. 'What happened to you, Sammy?'

He took his thumb out again. In a tiny voice, he said, 'I falled.'

'Oh, you poor thing. Where?'

I meant had he fallen down the stairs or something, but he nodded his head across the street and said again, 'I falled.'

'You lived there? Is that your house?'

He nodded.

'With your mummy?'

He shook his head. 'Antycarlin.'

'Aunty Caroline?'

He nodded.

His voice was so sad. He was a little lost boy. 'I want my mummy.'

'Where is your mummy?'

He looked at me. Standing on the wall his eyes were almost level with mine. I could see the street lights reflected in his tears.

'Where's your mummy, Sammy?'

He spoke around his thumb. 'Mummy.'

He was beginning to fade into the wall. 'It's dark.'

'Sammy . . .'

135

He disappeared, leaving just the faintest 'Mummy' hanging in the cold night air and then that too was gone.

I looked up and down the empty street. 'We should go.'

'I have no argument with that.' Jones pulled my arm through his. 'Come along then, Cage. A tactical retreat. Don't run. Always retreat with dignity. That's what I always do when women are after me.'

'Does it work?'

'Not in the slightest.'

He left me at my front door. My headache was turning into the full-blown migraine I had claimed to Jerry and Gerald. As my mum would have said, that would teach me to tell fibs. I took some painkillers and went straight to bed.

I felt no better the next morning but the pain had subsided enough for me to write and post a polite note to Jerry and Gerald, thanking them for dinner and apologising again for leaving early.

As always, I took comfort in my daily routine. Shopping in the mornings, some lunch, followed by a visit to the library or walks in the park. Good, solid, unexciting stuff.

I bought some pots and planted daffodil bulbs, ready for the spring. I sorted out my winter wardrobe and put my summer clothes away. I kept busy. I tried to push all thoughts of faces and screaming women and frightened little boys right out of my mind. Especially Sammy. He was so frightened and so alone and he lived in a wall because he was afraid he'd be eaten. I sighed. How could I not do something?

I popped next door to see Colonel and Mrs Barton, taking some flowers with me, for which she thanked me very politely and charmingly, and it was very obvious she hadn't a clue who I was.

We drank tea and chatted for a while and then she closed her eyes and dropped off to sleep. I didn't waste a moment. Turning to the colonel, I asked him if he could put his Local History Society hat on.

'I expect so,' he said, putting his cup down. 'Although we don't meet any longer.'

I knew that. Mrs Barton's health was deteriorating. The Painswicks, mother and daughter, had disappeared. Mark Ryder wouldn't go any longer because Alyson Painswick wasn't there, and – scandal! – the reference librarian, Mrs Stoppard, had run away with another member of the Local History Society, retired accountant Mr McClelland. No one knew where they'd gone. Everyone was taken completely by surprise, but then it turned out, after a quick discussion around the teacups, they'd always known that would happen one day.

All this meant the Local History Society was temporarily disbanded, but that didn't mean I couldn't call upon the colonel's encyclopaedic knowledge of local affairs.

'Colonel, does the name James Monroe mean anything to you?'

He sat back, fingering his moustache. 'Yes. Although you'll have to give me a moment.'

I gave him several, topping up the pot and pouring us both another cup.

'He found the body,' he said at last.

'The little boy?'

'No. James Monroe found the aunt. The little boy was already dead, I think. Yes, he must have been, because of the note.'

He thought for a moment longer, drumming his bony fingers on his knee, and then said, 'Yes. Got it now. It started with the little boy. His mother died – that was very sad, she was so young – and the little boy went to live with his aunt. She had the art gallery in Water Street.'

'Caroline,' I said, remembering what Sammy had said.

'That's her. Caroline Fairbrother. Anyway, there was a terrible accident. She went down into the basement to get something and the poor little fellow must have followed her. Fell down the stone steps. Killed instantly.'

I heard Sammy's reedy little voice. 'I falled.'

'How dreadful,' I said. 'She must have been distraught.'

'Oh, she was. There was nothing anyone could say or do to alleviate her guilt.'

'Except James Monroe?' I said.

'Well, yes, it seemed that way for a time. She pulled herself together a little and he helped her out in the gallery.'

'What did he do before? James Monroe, I mean?'

He chewed on his moustache. 'Well, I'm not sure anyone knew exactly. Small-town gossip said he ran some kind of financial services company, I think, but that can mean almost anything these days. Anyway, he was with her almost continually and I think everyone just assumed they'd get together one day. You know?'

'Why didn't they? I met him the other night and he's with an artist now.'

'Oh, Caroline killed herself. Dreadful shock for everyone.'

'I can imagine,' I said. 'Was there anything . . . you know . . . unusual . . . ? Something that made her suddenly decide to . . . ?'

He frowned. 'On the contrary. Everyone thought she was

138

getting better, but it seemed we were all wrong. She'd obviously thought it through very carefully. She wrote a note saying she couldn't go on any longer. Not after what had happened to little Sammy. Posted it on the Friday night. To James Monroe. It arrived at his office on the Monday morning, if I remember correctly. He didn't open it immediately. Sat down with his morning coffee, opened the letter and there it was. Poor bugger.'

'Whatever did he do?'

'Well, not very sensibly, he flung himself into his car and screamed off across Rushford, leaving a trail of cut-up drivers and terrified pedestrians in his wake, apparently. Drove the wrong way down Butchers' Row because it was quicker and picked up a police escort for his pains. Drove directly into Water Street – which is pedestrianised, of course – and by the time the police caught up with him, he was hammering on her door and screaming his head off.

'He'd had the sense to bring the note with him. Showed it to the police. They broke down the door. Made him stay outside. And there she was.'

'Dead?'

'Long dead. The coroner reckoned she must have died sometime during Friday night. Posted the letter, gone home, taken the tablets, laid down and just . . . gone to sleep.'

'And there were no suspicious circumstances?'

'None at all. Her writing. Her stationery. The letter was quite genuine and his office manager was with James when he opened it. No one had any doubts at all.' He looked at me. 'Why? Do you?'

'Oh no,' I said. 'It's just I met James Monroe the other night and I was curious, that's all. Do I gather he's got the gallery now?'

He nodded. 'Caroline left him everything. In gratitude for his care and support during what she called her darkest hours. She begged his forgiveness in her note but she just couldn't go on. He was completely devastated, poor chap. I suppose he can't help wondering if there was something he missed. Some little sign that he was just too busy to notice. Quite normal, I suppose. Blamed himself for a long time. It's good he's with that Cordelia Channing woman. The artist you mentioned. They've made a go of the gallery between them. Hard work paid off.'

I nodded and drank my tea.

'Now,' he said, briskly. 'One good turn deserves another. I'm afraid, what with one thing and another, I've rather forgotten about the Painswicks.'

I nodded. We both had. The Painswicks, mother, father and daughter, had vanished during the summer. Normally, of course, this wouldn't have been any cause for concern, but Mrs Painswick's bruises weren't always concealed by clever make-up, and her daughter, Alyson, was far too pale and silent for a girl her age. The colonel and I had gone to their little bungalow to see if everything was all right and they hadn't been there. We hadn't really known what to do and so we'd agreed we would go back at the end of the summer holidays and check again.

Before that could happen though, Mrs Barton had had a bad fall and I'd been distracted by the Three Sisters at Greyston. Shortly after that I'd gone on holiday to Scotland and then there had been James Monroe and little Sammy and I'm ashamed to say the Painswicks had slipped my mind. The schools had been back for over a month now and I couldn't allow myself to be distracted any longer. They might be in trouble and one of us really should check to see whether they had safely returned.

'I can't leave the house these days,' he said, nodding at the dozing Mrs Barton. 'Any chance of you nipping over there one afternoon?'

'Of course I will,' I said. 'I'll go and see if they're back and let you know.'

He nodded. 'And then, if there's still no sign, I think we should go to the police, don't you?'

Reluctantly, I nodded.

Jones telephoned that evening.

'After what you said the other night, I thought I'd do a search on James Monroe,' he said. 'I didn't get anything on James by himself, but when I added Sammy and Aunty Caroline, everything becomes much more interesting.'

'Yes,' I said. 'It does, doesn't it?'

There was a suspicious pause. I grinned at the phone.

'*How* do you know, Cage? I have the full resources of the nation at my disposal and you've got . . .' he paused, disdainfully, 'a laptop.'

'Didn't even need the laptop,' I said, cheerfully. 'I went next door and asked Colonel Barton. He knew all about it.'

This time the pause spoke volumes.

'Oh, come on,' I said. 'Verification is always useful. What did you find?'

'Sammy died in an accident.'

'Yes.'

'His aunt, who thought it was her fault, killed herself.'

'Yes.'

141

'James Monroe inherited the gallery and somehow acquired Cordelia along the way.'

'Correct,' I said. 'Well done.'

'And there was nothing suspicious about Caroline's death. She blamed herself for Sammy. Took her eye off him for a moment – as probably every parent does – and this time it ended badly. She couldn't live with herself and decided to end it all. A perfectly genuine suicide note came to James Monroe who was the closest friend she had at the time. He rushed to her house but it was far too late. She'd been dead for days.'

'Correct again. Just a thought – was there anything on Sammy's dad?'

'Never in the picture. Whoever he was.'

I sighed. What a dreadful tragedy. For everyone except James Monroe, of course.

'I'm pushing off for a couple of days, Cage. Are you going to be all right?'

'Yes, of course,' I said, slightly surprised because he was always pushing off for a couple of days and didn't bother to tell me. 'Why shouldn't I be?'

'Oh, I don't know. I suppose I thought you'd go back to Jerry's again to talk to that little boy.'

'Well,' I said. 'Perhaps.'

'Cage, listen to me. You know I never tell you what to do . . .'

I couldn't let that pass. 'You're *always* telling me what to do.' I deepened my voice. '*Stay behind me, Cage, and don't get in my way.*'

'Your lack of gratitude is breathtaking. And I don't speak like that.'

'Yes, you do. Slightly worse, actually. I was being kind.'

'Can we get back to the point I'm trying to make at the moment?'

'What *is* the point you're trying to make at the moment?'

'Well, if you'll let me finish . . .'

'I'm not sure I should let you start.'

'I'm not saying don't do it.'

'So I should hope.'

'I'm just saying don't do it without me.'

'Why?'

'Because we're trying to become a team, remember? Because we talked about this in Scotland and it occurs to me this would be a good opportunity for us to work together. Properly. See what happens. I'm not saying don't get involved – I'm just saying wait for me. Presumably this isn't time sensitive – it all happened a couple of years ago, so there can't be much rush.'

'OK,' I said. 'I'll stay out of mischief. I could always go and look for Iblis.'

'I think those two statements are contradictory.'

'You know what I mean.'

'Oh God, Cage,' he said and hung up.

CHAPTER TEN

Well, talk of the devil . . . Although with Iblis, even just thinking about him is often enough to bring him to my doorstep, so I suppose I should have guessed.

As it happened, I was out sweeping my steps so I didn't miss a thing.

He strode in from under the arch and I recognised him at once. He's quite distinctive. He's very tall and lean and he was wearing his usual outfit of combats and T-shirt which, given the afternoon was cold and bright, made him stand out immediately. The crowning touch was the world's most disreputable dog, Nigel the Ninja, alternately trotting at his heels or cocking his leg on everything in sight. They weren't actually doing anything illegal, but people turned to look at them just the same.

The words *discreet entrance* would have meant nothing to Iblis. He swaggered up the road, grinning and eyeing up the girls on the green. He walked slowly enough for everyone to get the full effect but fast enough for his long blond hair to stream backwards off his shoulders. He looked like a shampoo advert. I was actually quite pleased Jones wasn't here because there would have been sarcasm.

Catching sight of Mrs Barton sitting in her window, he swept her a magnificent bow, straight from the pages of a romantic 19th-century novel, and then blew her an extravagant kiss.

She waved and smiled, looking happier and brighter than she had for a long time.

I supposed it was too much to ask that no one would actually be looking out of the solicitors' windows on the other side. Of course, it was. The windows were crowded with young women – and several young men – all gawping away for dear life. It was just like that ridiculous TV advert where the extremely well-built man stops for a refreshing beverage and practically the entire nation grinds to a halt to watch. Obviously, I've seen the advert once or twice. I can never actually remember what the product is but you know the one I mean.

Well, there went the last of my credibility with my neighbours. I suppose I should be grateful that at least he had some clothes on today.

He flung his arms wide and grinned at me.

All right, I grinned back. Who wouldn't?

Outwardly he didn't look any different, but his silver colour had brightened considerably now that he no longer carried that dreadful burden of guilt around with him. The tarnish had disappeared.

'Elizabeth Cage,' he cried dramatically, his voice bouncing off the castle walls a hundred yards away. 'Your beauty dims the sun.'

So now everyone looked at me and probably wondered if he needed glasses.

I sighed. 'Would you like to come in?'

He bounded effortlessly up the steps. A small collection of fleas and bad breath tried to follow him inside.

I tried to summon some enthusiasm. 'And you've brought Nigel.'

He regarded Nigel fondly. 'My loyal companion. My comrade in arms. A bath and regular meals have wrought a miraculous transformation.'

No, they hadn't. Not all the baths nor all the meals in all the world could wreak even the slightest transformation on Nigel – the original plague dog. I caught a glimpse of his hairy backside – Nigel's – disappearing through the front door.

I sighed again and followed them in.

'I was worried about you,' I said. 'You left very suddenly. And I looked for you in the woods but you weren't there.'

'I have been with Melek. There was much to discuss.'

'Did you have Nigel with you?'

'Of course. He is my faithful companion. All heroes have a faithful companion.'

I looked at the faithful companion, trying to hump the table leg. 'I don't suppose Melek allows him on the furniture.'

He grinned that big wide grin. 'She barely allows *me* on the furniture.'

'Understandable,' I said. 'But actually, I'm glad you're here.' I paused. 'Why are you here?'

'I have come to pay my respects. And, again, to thank you.'

'There's no need,' I said. 'Really, the happiness on your face was enough reward for me.'

'That is very generous of you, but you discovered the truth about Allia and performed a great service for me. I shall not forget.'

This was not necessarily good news. Iblis is neither restrained in his gratitude nor aware of the normal parameters of socially

146

acceptable behaviour. His gratitude could lead to all sorts of problems. I, however, had a cunning plan.

'Can you spare me an hour?'

He stood over me. 'An hour will not be anything like enough, Elizabeth Cage. Prepare to lose a day – a week – a month – or even a year.'

'You've been watching television again, haven't you?'

'I must warn you though – afterwards, all other men will seem lesser in comparison to me.'

This was all show. Having rid himself of the guilt of supposedly sleeping with one mortal, Iblis was hardly likely to do that all over again. Even if I wanted to. But the attention was not . . . unpleasant.

I grinned at him. 'What exactly do you imagine I want you for?'

He put his hand on his heart. 'I hardly dare hope.'

'Then you won't be disappointed. I'm on my way to check out someone's house. They disappeared and I want to see if they've come back. Do you want to come?'

He was already at the door.

Nigel ceased making love to the furniture and followed him.

So that was a yes from both of them.

We set off for the Painswicks' house. They lived in a modest little bungalow on a modern housing estate on the Whittington road. The last time I'd been here, everything had been in neat, apple-pie order. The front lawn had needed trimming but there had been nothing to suggest the Painswicks hadn't just departed for their annual fortnight's holiday on the coast. In fact, it was perfectly possible they'd returned and life was carrying on as normal. Although I suspected that would turn out to be wishful thinking.

We didn't bother with the bell or the knocker. It was very obvious no one was home. I doubted anyone had been here since the colonel and I visited back in the summer. The front grass was now six inches high and the once immaculate flower borders looked sad and neglected. The curtains were still half drawn. Peering through the rippled glass front door, I could see unopened post on the floor.

'This way,' I said, skirting the side of the bungalow. We nipped through the side gate, which was still open. I looked around anxiously but the street was deserted. Everyone must be inside in front of the fire, watching the afternoon episode of *Olympian Heights*. I would be doing that myself if I hadn't mysteriously acquired a dubious young man and his ratbag of a dog.

'Shh,' I said to the squeaking gate. I don't know why I did that.

'Should I draw my sword?' enquired Iblis. 'Will there be peril?'

'Only if you draw your sword. Just follow me.'

It was darker around the back. The garden was surrounded by high hedges and fences. I pulled out my little torch and shone it around. The back garden was just as neglected as the front. The once neat patio was full of dead and dying potted plants, all expiring for lack of water. The curtains to what I guessed was the living room were almost completely drawn. We shone the torch and peered in as best we could, but all we could see was an armchair and part of a sideboard.

Iblis moved to the kitchen window and I joined him. This

148

window was smaller. The blind was half pulled. I shone the torch again, squinting, trying to see inside. Everything seemed just as before. The kitchen sink, just under the window, was empty, and the draining board quite dry.

As far as I could see, nothing had changed. I looked down. The windowsill was littered with dead flies. Even as I looked, one banged into the glass and fell on to its back, legs waving. Now that I looked, there were a lot of flies. Crawling up the glass, buzzing over the bodies of their fallen comrades, appearing and disappearing back into the room.

Iblis took my torch off me. 'Wait here,' he said softly. 'Do not touch anything.' I saw him step back and look up at the roof. Seeing nothing, he walked softly down the garden path to look through the garage window. The shed door was padlocked. He looked closely but touched nothing.

The wheelie bins were empty, their lids hanging open. An inch or so of mucky water sat at the bottom of each of them – from the recent rain, I assumed.

He shook his head. 'There is no one here. Not for a long time.'

Nigel was rummaging around the back of the shed. Iblis whistled him to heel and rejoined me on the patio. 'This is not good.'

I agreed. Everything was telling me there was something wrong here. I sighed and pulled out my phone.

Jones answered almost immediately. 'What have you done now, Cage?'

'I'm at the Painswicks' house.'

'Who are the Painswicks when they're at home?'

'Well, that's just it – they're not.'

'Where is their house and why are you there?'

'They're in the Local History Society,' I said. 'Mrs Painswick, I mean, and her daughter, Alyson.'

There was silence at the other end so I ploughed on. 'And back in the summer they stopped coming to meetings so the colonel and I went to investigate.'

'Why?'

'Well, Mrs Painswick knitted so furiously and . . .'

Now even Nigel was staring at me.

I tried again. 'I mean she was so strung up, and Alyson would never stray very far from her side even though she should have been in school, and sometimes she had bruises – Mrs Painswick, I mean – so when they stopped coming, the colonel and I thought we'd just check everything was all right.'

'And was it?'

'Well, we don't know because there was no one in.'

'What did you do?'

'We didn't do anything because it was in the school holidays and we thought they might just have gone away for a bit. We decided we'd wait until September when the schools went back and see if they returned.'

'And did they?'

'I don't know – we never got round to it until now.'

'Never got round to it, Cage? You suspected some sort of domestic abuse and you never got round to it?'

He was right to be angry, but it wasn't all my fault.

'Well, we would have come back to check things out except that it's not that long since Iblis, Jerry and I had to go to all the trouble of saving you from Sorensen . . .'

Iblis was nodding vigorously. Nigel was cocking his leg against a tub of dead marigolds.

'. . . and then I got a telephone call to drop everything and go to Rushby because an idiot not a million miles from here got himself sideswiped *by a vicar* and I had to look after him, and a bloody armchair chased me, and then I had to rescue you – again – from those weird women up at Greyston *and the wood was full of dead people, Jones*, and then we went to Scotland and I saw that woman who had my face . . .'

Iblis turned his head to stare at me. Nigel sat down, indicating boredom and a desire to return to his foetid bed.

'. . . And then I came back here and Caroline Fairbrother wouldn't stop screaming and there was Sammy and the colonel's been looking after Mrs Barton and I don't know – what with one thing and another – *I forgot*.'

Guilt had sharpened my voice. I honestly didn't mean to sound so shrewish. There was a different sort of silence at the other end and then he said very cautiously, 'And you are ringing me because . . . ?'

'Because their bungalow still looks empty. I don't think anyone's been here since the colonel and I were here and I can't see in very well, but . . .' I stopped.

'Yes?'

I said quietly, 'There are a lot of flies. An awful lot of flies.'

Now there was yet another type of silence.

'All right. Have you touched anything? Tried any door handles? Put your hands on the glass? Anything like that?'

'No. Iblis wouldn't let me.'

'Oh, Lord – is he there too? Well, at least one of you two has some sense.'

'Three.'

151

He sounded exasperated. 'For heaven's sake, don't tell me Jerry's there as well.'

'Nigel.'

'Not . . .'

'Nigel the Ninja – yeah.'

Jones sighed. 'What is it with you and bodies, Cage?'

'I don't know,' I said, blinking, 'but they were my friends and . . .' I really didn't want to think of what could have happened to lovely Mrs Painswick and her pretty daughter.

'Put the blond idiot on.'

'You *are* on speakerphone, you know.'

Iblis didn't bother going through his normal *I really don't understand modern technology* routine.

'Hello, it is I, Iblis, International Man of Mystery and blond idiot who speaks. Do I address the man-mountain Jones?'

'You do. No trace at all?'

'None. Not for some time.' I nodded. Iblis would know what he was talking about.

'OK. Get the hell out of there, both of you – all of you. Just walk back down the road. You're walking the dog. Don't draw attention to yourselves. Don't stop and speak to anyone. Don't get into any fights. Don't let Nigel hump anything. It's getting dark so you should be OK, but make sure no one sees you leave.'

'It's a secluded bungalow,' I said, with some idea of making things a little better. 'There are high hedges and it's not overlooked at all.'

'Probably what made it so ideal,' he said. 'No one would ever know what was going on there. Just get out. Quick and quiet. I'll inform the police. Do you understand?'

'Of course. I am Iblis, man of infinite understanding. I will

152

escort Elizabeth Cage from the crime scene and we will wait for you at her house.'

'You could be waiting a while – I'm in Belfast.'

I stood on tiptoe to speak into the phone. 'What are you doing there?'

'James Monroe lived here before coming to live in Rushford.'

'You went without me?'

'You went to the Painswicks' without me.'

'Oh.'

'Do not, on any account, hurry back,' said Iblis, possibly seeking to pour oil on troubled waters but probably not. 'We can occupy ourselves in many pleasurable pursuits until you return. Have no fear – Iblis is here.'

And then the bugger ended the call and passed me back my phone.

'I shall take you home,' he announced. 'We will enjoy fish and chips together. I, Iblis, decree it shall be so.'

'OK,' I said.

'Do you have any money?'

We closed the gate carefully behind us and walked quietly down the road. Around us, house lights were coming on and curtains being drawn. No one was out on the street.

We walked a while and then Iblis said, 'Tell me of this woman with your face.'

I looked around at the deserted street. Tendrils of mist were winding themselves around the trees and putting halos around the street lights. I shivered. 'When we get home again.'

We toiled up the hill, Iblis and Nigel conquering the heights with no difficulties at all, and eventually arrived back at my house. Iblis announced he and Nigel needed to powder their noses. He disappeared upstairs and Nigel shot out of the back door – to water something else, I assumed.

I filled the kettle and washed my hands. Despite the recent rain, the air at the Painswicks' home had felt dry and dusty. I was sure I could feel grit under my fingernails. I gave my hands a good scrub, kicked off my shoes and waited for the return of my heroes.

Iblis clattered back down the stairs. 'Has the mirror died?'

'What?'

'You have covered its face.'

'Oh. Yes.'

'Are you unhappy with your appearance?'

'What? No.'

'If your features are causing you concern, I can . . .'

'They're not. My features are fine.'

He smiled down at me. 'Yes, they are.'

He does this. I don't think he can help himself. I told myself it was very possible that even if I was a seventy-year-old grandmother he would still be smiling down at me in that particularly disturbing manner. And my seventy-year-old heart would still probably turn a somersault.

Just as I was congratulating myself on making him forget about the woman with my face, he asked again, 'What are you trying not to tell me?'

I didn't want to talk about it but the chances of fobbing him off were zero, so I told him the story in about four sentences, concluding with, 'That's why I covered the mirrors.'

'What did that solve?'

'Well . . .' I hesitated. 'As if it's not bad enough to be confronted by my own face when it isn't me, I wondered . . . well . . . is it possible she could use mirrors to . . . well, find me?'

He frowned. 'I think not.'

'I mean, does she look into a mirror and see me?'

'I think not,' he said again. 'You can remove the shroud-cloths from your mirrors.'

'I was unnerved,' I said defensively.

He shook his head. 'You need have no fears. I, Iblis, am here now.'

'Jones said Lady Torrington might be an ancestor of mine,' I said, hopefully. 'And it's a family resemblance.'

'Yes,' he said, just that little bit too quickly. 'That will be the explanation. Now – food. You said you had money.'

He sallied forth for fish and chips. Iblis never just goes anywhere. He sallies forth. He lived with me for a while in the summer and he would frequently announce to the world that he was setting forth on a quest for fish and chips. Or undertaking a perilous expedition in pursuit of a curry. You get used to it after a while.

Shouting that I wasn't to worry, he would return with a feast fit for kings and emperors, he slammed the front door behind him.

In the sudden silence I realised he'd forgotten Nigel, who trotted to the warmest and most comfortable spot in the house – the rug in front of the fire – and hurled himself to sleep. The afternoon's events had obviously exhausted him.

I walked around the house, closing the shutters and drawing curtains. My house felt as warm and snug as always and folded itself around me. I looked forward to an evening with Iblis – who is never dull – and I wanted to know what he'd been up to since I saw him last. And then I could catch him up on *Olympian Heights* – the popular soap to which we were both completely addicted.

155

I knew from past experience that he liked to eat his fish and chips directly from the paper. I like plates. We compromise. The fish and chips stay in the paper and the paper goes on the plate. I put the plates in the oven and laid out knives and forks, together with the salt, vinegar and ketchup.

There. All ready for a nice evening in. I sat on the sofa and groped for the remote which had fallen between the cushions again.

Without any warning – any warning at all – Nigel lifted his head and then rose to his feet in one fluid movement. With his legs widely braced, he lowered his head and stared at the back door. Surely Iblis wasn't back already. And why would he come to the back door? He never had before. No one ever used my back door because they couldn't get to it. I kept the gate locked and padlocked.

I looked back at Nigel, half expecting him to have collapsed in front of the fire again. He hadn't moved – standing rigidly with his eyes narrowed and still fixed on the back door. I felt a sudden breath of unease. My downstairs is one open-plan room. Two steps took me into the kitchen area, although I stayed well back from the door.

Still not moving, Nigel drew his lips back off his teeth and began to growl. A quiet, low, deadly noise. The sort of growl a dog makes when he means business. His hackles came up in a ridge all along his back and around his shoulders. And there, on the other side of the door, I thought I heard a very slight sound. I don't have a back garden. I have a tiny yard with a few pots and a wooden shed. Was there something out there? As if in confirmation, the outside security light came on. The square of window behind the blind suddenly lightened.

156

I should look. I should go and see who was there. It was probably just a cat. Nigel looked the sort who would chase a cat. I could gently shoo it away and then Nigel would settle back down again. Yes – I would do that. Except that, at that exact moment, it dawned on me that doing something to reveal my presence here might not be a good idea. I backed away from the door into the middle of the room.

Nigel walked stiff-legged towards the kitchen. Now his attention was focused on the window and even as I strained to see, a dark shape seemed to move across the blind. There *was* something there.

I rested my hand on the table for support, closed my eyes for a moment to let my mind drift . . . very, very gently . . . because I didn't want to attract any attention . . . dark, damp night . . . chilly . . . silence . . . waiting . . . and something slammed hard into the window. It was a miracle it didn't break. I jumped so hard I think my feet left the floor. For one moment I wondered if, somehow, confused in the dark, a bird had flown into the window and was lying, stunned or dead, in my tiny back garden.

The outside light went out. Nigel's growl dwindled down into silence. Slowly, his hackles subsided. There was silence outside my house, as well. I remembered Iblis once saying my house was warded and nothing could get in, but at that moment, I wasn't prepared to take his word for it. I wasn't prepared to take anyone's word for anything.

I whispered, 'Nigel, come here,' without any expectation he would obey but he did. He came to stand beside me, rank and pungent and somehow comforting. I turned my head continually. Watching. Waiting for I don't know what. Minutes passed and as far as I could tell, there was nothing there. Nothing I could sense, anyway. I looked down at Nigel, whose senses were probably far more acute than mine, and he yawned, sat down, and began to scratch. I tried not to think about what could be abandoning the mothership at that moment to live more comfortably in my rugs and soft furnishings.

And then he stopped. Slowly – very slowly – he got to his feet again. This time he was staring at the front door. Very intently. Like a very small, very scruffy pointer.

And then – his lips drew back. Right back, exposing his ghastly gums and teeth. He snarled. Not a doggy growl but a long, liquid snarl. The wolf inside him meant business. He crouched, as if to spring. His entire body bristled. All of it. Even down to his tail. And – and I'd never seen this before – the skin between his toes seemed to retract, exposing his doggy claws. I didn't know dogs could do that. He was a tiny wolf geared for battle. Because there was something on the other side of my front door and he didn't like it one bit.

The realisation hit me. My front door was unlocked. I'd left it on the latch for Iblis. I could feel my own hair rise. There was something on the other side of that door and whatever it was it was terrifying Nigel. The sounds of his snarling filled the room. And the door was unlocked . . .

I should lock it. I had to lock the door. I forced myself to move. I took one small step forwards and then another. Then another. Holding my breath, I listened. There was no sound from the other side. *If* there was something there – and you only had to look at Nigel to know the answer to that one – then it was standing as still and silently as I was. For the moment. For all I knew it could be reaching for the door handle at this very second. Or much more likely, it would simply explode through the door and be upon us.

Jones had fitted bolts top and bottom, saying, 'Never mind fancy locks, Cage. Bolts are simple, efficient and idiot-proof.' I'd ignored the implication. And I'd fitted a chain as well. And I had a good solid lock. Or I would have if I'd actually used it. I never used to be this careless. If I survived whatever was happening tonight, then this was a wake-up call. I needed to pull myself together.

I reached slowly for the top bolt. I had a good door and good bolts so I didn't have to wriggle it noisily into its socket – it moved smoothly and silently into place. I was partly safe.

Drawing a breath, I crouched down and, trying not to imagine the door exploding inwards into my face, I shot the lower bolt. Nearly there.

Holding the chain so it wouldn't rattle, very slowly and carefully, I slipped it into place. And finally, I snicked the lock. As the noise implies, it made just the veriest tiniest click – like a gunshot to my ears.

Something moved on the other side of the door. Whatever was there – now it knew I was here.

My hands were freezing. I could feel cold sweat all the way down my back. And then, before I could move away from the door, there it was again. A slight sound from the other side. A hand, perhaps, feeling its way across the surface. Looking for a way in, and there were only a few inches of wood between us.

Not taking my eyes from the door, I backed across the room to stand by Nigel, easily the bravest thing in the room at this moment. Leaning across, I eased the poker from its place by the fire. It's an electric fire with one of those flame effects, which Nigel hadn't worked out yet, but for some reason I'd bought a fireplace set to sit in the grate. Poker, shovel, brush and tongs. All decorative and quite useless. But not today. Today I was glad I had it. The poker wasn't a full-length thing – this was only about fifteen inches long – but it was iron . . .

Holding it over my shoulder like a baseball bat, I planted my feet, bent my knees . . . and waited.

Sometimes I can let my mind drift . . . open it just a little . . . to me, it's just another sense . . . and it's useful. But not this time. This time I closed my mind. I tried to shut it down and make everything a blank. My instincts were to stand still and quiet. There was no thought of going on the attack. This was a time to hide. To conceal my presence. The tiny mammal shrinking back in its burrow. Motionless. Waiting.

Whatever it was on the other side of the door was waiting too. I could feel it. Something was there. A dark hole in the world. Beside me, Nigel was just one long unbroken snarl. He was a little war machine. All teeth and claws. All ready to attack.

I used to equate fear with loud noises. Screams, roars, explosions, impacts, and so on, but sometimes, when you're alone and you're not quite sure what is happening, even the smallest sound can be utterly terrifying – and silence is worst of all. The unknown, however small and quiet, is far more frightening than the loud and visible. Our minds are sometimes our own worst enemies.

The faint slithering sound came again. I didn't know whether something was probing for a weakness or doing it just for effect – and it was effective. I was, literally, scared stiff.

I watched the door handle. Waiting to see it move. Even fractionally. Because that would be concrete proof there actually was something on the other side. Something that meant us harm.

160

I tightened my grip on the poker. Nigel pressed close against my leg. Whatever it was, we were ready . . .

And then, quite suddenly and without warning, it was gone. I was braced so hard I nearly fell over. For a moment I seemed to fight against a huge vacuum – and then everything . . . just . . . went away. I stood up straight and looked around. Nigel slowly subsided. His coat lay flat again. It was finished. We looked at each other. I looked at the poker. The door rattled. I jumped again but Nigel woofed gently and wagged his tail.

The International Man of Mystery was back with the fish and chips.

CHAPTER ELEVEN

'There was something outside your door,' said Iblis. 'I saw it as I came through the arch.'

'What?' I said, still clutching the poker. 'What did you see?'

He shook his head. 'A shape. A shadow. When I looked again it had vanished.'

I fought down a rising panic. 'She's found me, hasn't she?'

'Who?'

'The woman in the mirror. The one with my face.'

'No.' He spoke with unexpected firmness. 'She has not. Put her from your mind.'

For a moment I wondered if it could have been Sammy. But why would Nigel react in such a way to the sad little shade that was Sammy? And besides, Sammy was only around three years old. No one would mistake him for a sinister shadow.

'Behold,' he said, dropping a ton of fish and chips on the table. 'I have returned. With food. All is well. Iblis is here. We eat.'

He seemed unconcerned and if he wasn't worrying, then why should I? And Nigel was dribbling all over my kitchen floor. I went to take the plates out of the oven.

There is something comforting in familiar actions. I

unwrapped the fragrant packages and made up a small portion for Nigel, who looked at me in disgust, so I threw on another bushel of chips for him. He buried his head in the dish. The noises were disgusting.

Iblis was hurling vinegar around like an enthusiastic pope blessing a very large congregation. I could still feel the sweat drying on my skin but you couldn't get better barometers than these two.

I switched on the TV and we settled down on the sofa.

He enquired as to recent events on our favourite programme, *Olympian Heights*.

'Well,' I said, stabbing a chip. 'While you've been gone, Sascha has stolen Sienna's secret designs – you remember, the ones that were to revolutionise the fashion house and save them from bankruptcy. He doesn't yet know that she's his twin and they were separated at birth. Everyone thinks it was Ryan who stole the designs because he's desperate to recapture Chardonnay's love. She, however, has fallen head over heels in love with Estevan, who, despite fighting for the World Title in a few days' time, is shagging his mother-in-law, his wife, Chardonnay herself, and for some reason not yet revealed, the au pair, Ruby, who murdered André's half-sister, although he doesn't know that yet because he thinks he's got a weak heart because he overheard a conversation between Mnemone and her doctor, but actually it's the dog who has the weak heart and he, the dog, is the true father of Jewel's pups and not Rufus the Randy Red Setter, who is having performance issues owing to the break-up of his owners, Savannah and Oberon, over Desdemona's secret shame.'

He shovelled in another chip. 'So I haven't missed much, then?'

'Hardly anything at all.'

We talked until quite late. I made myself a mug of tea and found one of Jones's beers in the fridge for Iblis. He tried again, several times, to thank me for discovering the truth about Allia and I waved them all aside, saying I'd been happy to help. And no, I didn't want any reward, but thank you anyway. No, no diamonds. Nor all the riches of the Orient, thanks. Nor gold. OK, a box of chocolates would be very acceptable. Thank you. And changed the subject.

The time ticked by and eventually I had to admit I was quite reluctant to let either of them leave in case, in the silence of the house, I heard those faint noises again. In the end, I swallowed my pride and asked him if he'd stay the night.

He struck a pose and said never fear, Iblis was here, which was actually what I'd been hoping he would say. As it turned out, I was even more reluctant to go upstairs alone so, in the end, I slept on the sofa and Nigel and Iblis jostled for pole position in front of the fire.

I didn't think I'd sleep at all but I must have, because we were all awoken by a thunderous knocking on the front door at what seemed to me like the crack of dawn.

I sat bolt upright, which made my head spin, while Iblis struggled to extricate himself from his blanket. Staggering to the front door, I called, 'Who is it?'

A familiar voice said, 'Me.'

I pulled back the curtain, unbolted the door, unchained it, unlocked it and finally swung it open. A fug of unsavoury dog, vinegar, chips, fish, feet and sleeping people billowed out through the door. I didn't blame it. Quite honestly my living room looked as if some sort of cut-price orgy had taken place.

Iblis, bare-chested, sat up, his hair attractively tousled. Nigel turned over for another ten minutes.

Jones regarded us with some astonishment. 'What on earth . . . ?'

'Oh hello,' I said, brightly. 'You're back soon. I thought you were in Belfast.'

'I drove all night,' he said pointedly, looking around.

'It's barely dawn,' I said, blinking and yawning.

'It's twenty past nine,' he said, even more pointedly.

Oh God. I stepped out of the door and looked across at the window into the legal world on my left. Three or four legal eagles looked up and waved cheerfully. I smiled because my mum brought me up to be polite and tried not to think about what she would say if she could see me now.

I asked Jones if he fancied breakfast.

Iblis scratched and yawned. 'I certainly do. Where are we going?'

Jones grinned. 'How can I put this?'

'Not lengthily, I hope. I am hungry.'

Jones turned to me. 'Why is he even here? Where has he come from? Do you know something dead is lying on your hearthrug?'

Nigel yawned, unspeakably.

I took refuge in housewifely tasks. I opened the back door to let in some more fresh air. I cleared last night's dishes away and put them in the sink. One foot gently urged Nigel towards the outside world. I put the kettle on, straightened the cushions,

165

gave Iblis to understand it was time to get up, and generally didn't answer any of Jones's questions at all.

I watched Iblis disappear upstairs and then told Jones I thought Lady Torrington had found me. 'Iblis saw a shape on my porch and Nigel was doing his nut inside. I don't mean barking – I mean he was doing that thing dogs do when they're really terrified.'

He stared at me thoughtfully. 'What do you want to do?'

'I don't know. If she can find me wherever I go, then there's no point going anywhere, is there? I think it makes sense to stay here, in my own house, where I'm strong.'

'Are you sure?'

'Well, I feel stronger here.'

'No, I mean – are you sure you want to stay?'

I nodded. 'I think so.'

'Look – I'm happy to stay here with you. Very happy, in fact, but if you feel you'd be safer with whatshisname and his collection of canine germs, I would understand. I wouldn't be happy, but I would understand.'

I was quite touched. And I certainly wasn't stupid enough to announce I didn't need any help from anyone. And there were several small jobs to be done around the house, although obviously I didn't mention that.

Changing the subject, I asked him what he'd found out about James Monroe.

He flourished a folder. 'Nothing new – just more details on what we already have. I'll go to the café for croissants. Breakfast for three.'

Nigel bustled back in again and began to nose his empty bowl around the kitchen floor.

'Four,' I said. 'And one of those is you, so six.'

He disappeared.

I made coffee for everyone except Nigel who, Iblis said, liked warm milk.

I enquired whether he got warm milk at Melek's house.

'We have come to an arrangement,' he said, loftily.

'Which is?'

'He stays out of her way and she allows him to live.'

'Sounds fair to me,' said Jones, coming through the front door. 'Cage, your door was unlocked.'

Three pairs of eyes looked accusingly at me and I went to get the apricot jam.

Afterwards, while Iblis cleared the breakfast things away, Jones spread his documents across the table. There wasn't much. Copies of police reports, witness statements, the results of the autopsy, the coroner's verdict, and that was just about it.

'To summarise,' said Jones. 'Three-year-old Sammy went to live with his aunt when his mum died.'

'Of what?'

'Leukaemia. It was very quick. She barely had time to make arrangements for Sammy before she died. He went to live with his Aunty Caroline who had the gallery in Water Street. Everything went well, the neighbours said. Caroline was affectionate towards him and Sammy seemed well-cared-for and happy. Missed his mum, of course, but he had friends at playschool and living further down the street.'

'Where does James Monroe come into all this?'

'He'd been a friend of both sisters, especially Ellie, Sammy's mum. After her death, it was natural he would continue to see

Caroline and Sammy and it seems there was a kind of gentle romance. Nothing world-shattering, but no one would have been surprised if they'd become a family unit.'

'He wasn't Sammy's dad, was he?'

'No.' He sighed. 'And then, Sammy fell.' He pulled out more photos, looked through them and put three back in the envelope. I guessed they were of Sammy lying at the bottom of the cellar steps.

'Caroline had gone down to pull out a couple of canvases – we're not talking cobwebbed basement here – as you can see, this basement is white, well-lit, and spotlessly clean. She keeps . . . kept . . . a number of additional paintings there so she could rotate her displays, or if a customer said, "Oh, I quite like that one, but have you got it in blue" – or any of the other stuff people say to gallery owners – then she could shoot downstairs and pull out something suitable.

'Anyway, she nipped down the steps. She said she pulled the door to behind her but couldn't remember hearing it close. Well, it can't have, because it's a keypad entry and Sammy not only didn't know the code but couldn't reach it anyway.

'He must have somehow missed his step. She said she was in the far corner, pulling out a canvas when she heard him fall. She ran to him at once but he was already dead.

'Both the paramedics and the police say she was nearly hysterical when they arrived. Only James could do anything with her. He practically lived at the gallery afterwards. It was James who tempted her out into the sunshine. Or for a picnic by the river. James urged her to rejig the gallery. He bombarded her with little things to get her interested in the world again and it seemed to be working. She perked up. She started speaking to people in the street, got her hair done and generally seemed brighter.'

He stopped.

'But,' I said.

He sighed and moved the papers around again. 'Whether she hit another bad patch or whether she was deliberately lulling people into thinking she was better, no one knows. Or will know, now.

'In his evidence, Monroe said he'd seen her briefly on the Friday morning – just to tell her he had something on over the weekend, but that he'd see her on Monday night – and she seemed fine.

'The last he saw was her waving from the doorway as he walked away. Then, Monday morning, there was the suicide note. He raced to the shop, involuntarily picking up the police on the way, and there she was. Dead since Friday night.'

'Do we know what he was doing over the weekend?'

'Drove to his mate's house on Friday evening. A drinking session that night, then a late breakfast the next day, then a group of them went to the match in the afternoon, pub afterwards, back late, fell into bed, headache on Sunday morning, drove back Sunday evening, spent the night alone, work on Monday. All checked and verified. The office manager confirms the letter came in the post and she was present when he opened it.'

I looked at photographs of Caroline's suicide note with its extravagantly large handwriting. 'And this is definitely her writing?'

'It is. Checked and verified.'

I looked at the envelope. Nothing suspicious there. A

first-class stamp. The envelope matched the paper – cream, with the gallery address embossed in the top left-hand corner of both paper and envelope. I read the note.

My dearest James,

I'm so sorry but I just can't do this any more. I see Sammy everywhere. I wake at night and in the silence of the house I can hear him falling down those awful steps. It's my punishment, I suppose, for not looking after him better. I hope he's with Ellie and they're happy. Truly, James, I'm sorry. You worked so hard but it's no use. I don't deserve to be happy.

Caroline.

'Oh dear,' I said.

Jones passed me over a photograph of a young woman with long blonde hair, large eyes, a small mouth and a pointed chin. I recognised the woman who'd screamed at James Monroe. What was she trying to say to him?

Jones began to gather up the papers and stuff them in a large envelope. 'Well, there you have it.'

'This is very tragic,' announced Iblis, 'but why are you involved?'

'I don't know,' I said. 'I only know that Caroline Fairbrother is attached to James Monroe in some way. And I'm certain he killed her.'

Jones shook his head. 'James has an alibi for the entire period in question. If there's one person in the world who can't have done it – it's James.'

'A contract killer?' I suggested.

170

He looked at me with mild exasperation. 'All right, Cage, let's say you decide to rid yourself and the world of me . . .'

'A not unlikely circumstance,' I said.

'How would you set about it?'

I nodded to Iblis. 'I'd get him to do it.'

There was a short silence.

'Yes, well, let's assume for one moment that you don't have access to Iblis and his . . .'

'Faithful companion,' said Iblis proudly.

The faithful companion whiffled in his sleep.

I considered. 'Well, I'd hire someone, I suppose.'

'From where? Sainsbury's?'

'Well, there are places . . .'

'Where? I mean, I know where to go if I'm farming out a job, but you . . . ?'

Oddly, this assertion that I wouldn't have the faintest idea how to hire myself a contract killer made me quite annoyed. 'I'd get someone to do my murder and I'd do theirs.'

'We've all seen that film, Cage. Face it, you wouldn't have a clue.'

I subsided.

'He didn't do it, Cage.'

'He did,' I said stubbornly, but only to myself.

He grinned at me. 'Do you want me to leave this stuff with you for a few days? Perhaps if you read it all through a couple of times . . .'

'Your pocket is ringing,' said Iblis helpfully to Jones.

Jones sighed. 'Did we ever establish exactly why you're here?'

'No,' said Iblis, simply.

'Don't you have somewhere else to be?'

'No,' said Iblis, simply.

'Well, I do. Cage, I'll see you later.'

'Your pocket is still ringing,' said Iblis, helpfully.

Jones sighed and pulled out his phone. 'Yes?'

He listened for a long time. Long enough for me to realise something was wrong, even without his colour slowly darkening around him. He shot me a look and then pushed his phone back into his pocket.

'What?' I said, anxiously. 'What's happened?'

'They've found a body at the Painswicks' house.'

I swallowed. 'Do they know who it is?'

'Not at the moment,' said Jones, quietly. 'Preliminary report says it's a man.'

'Murdered?'

'Very much so.'

My first thought was that I couldn't quite believe it. It had to have been some sort of accident. It couldn't possibly be murder. Not in that quiet, normal little bungalow in that quiet, normal little road. Was it possible that quiet, normal Mrs Painswick could snap and kill her husband? Unless he'd turned on Alyson, of course, in which case, yes, she might have. She might not have meant to kill him, but if she'd had a knife or an iron in her hand at the time . . .

I shivered.

Disbelief was giving way to shock. My feelings were hugely mixed. If Mrs Painswick had killed her husband, half of me wanted her to get away with it. The other half was horrified at what she'd done. But I shouldn't judge. I had no idea of the circumstances. But even if she had killed him, why hadn't she gone to the police? There's such a thing as mitigating circumstances. Going to the police would have been the right thing to do.

'For whom?' said a treacherous thought.

And what then? She'd killed him and run away with Alyson? Had they taken the time to pack what they needed or had they just blindly run out of the door? We hadn't seen a car there. Could Mrs Painswick even drive? I wasn't sure whether Alyson was old enough. I'd put her age at a very young fifteen or sixteen but I suppose she could be older. Whenever I'd seen her at the Local History meetings, she'd sat quietly next to her mother and hardly said anything at all. And her mother hardly took her eyes off her. And then there were Mrs Painswick's frequent bruises. What a horrible, horrible situation.

'Do the police know that we were there?'

'You and Iblis? No, and for heaven's sake, don't go down your traditional *I'll confess everything to the authorities who will sort everything out* route because speaking as an authority, Cage – not a wise move on your part.'

'How long had he been there, do they think?'

'Unknown at the moment. A little while.'

That was not good to know. 'Was he there when Colonel Barton and I . . . ?'

'Possibly. Don't beat yourself up, Cage. Whether he was or wasn't is nothing to do with you.'

'But he might still have been alive. We could have called for help.'

'If he was there, he was very, very dead, Cage. Whoever did it made very certain of that.'

I sighed. 'I think I ought to go and talk to Colonel Barton.'

He sighed again. 'You're not supposed to know anything about it.'

'He won't say anything,' I said confidently. 'And it's better he hears it from me than off the TV.'

'Well, all right then, but remember, if anyone asks you about anything at all, just assume your traditional *I don't have a clue about anything* expression. If that doesn't work, then burst into tears. If that doesn't work, then pull yourself together, blow your nose and call me.'

'For what purpose?' I asked but he was already on his way out of the door.

'One moment,' said Iblis suddenly and followed him out.

Remembering Jones's comments on leaving the door open, I went to close it just in time to hear Iblis say, 'There is a darkness. She should not be alone.'

'She won't be,' said Jones briefly and strode away.

I watched him go and then turned to Iblis climbing back up the steps.

'You look unhappy,' he said.

I shrugged – I didn't know what to say to him. A lot seemed to have happened in a very short space of time. Lady Torrington, James Monroe and his screaming woman, Mrs Painswick and her probably dead husband. And now I had to go and break the bad news to Colonel Barton. Who, I knew, would blame himself, and I'd tell him it wasn't his fault just as Jones and Iblis had told me it wasn't mine.

I looked at him helplessly.

'Will you be in your house for a few days?' he asked.

I nodded.

'You are safe here. Do not leave it.'

'I won't.'

'I must go,' he said, 'but you know you have only to call.'

'Yes.'

'This business with the mirrors,' he said. 'You need have no fear.'

It was on the tip of my tongue to ask how that reconciled to the 'There is a darkness' stuff but I bottled it.

'Nigel and I must depart,' he said. 'Stifle your disappointment and despair.'

'Despair and disappointment duly stifled,' I said.

'Remember, you are not alone.'

'I know.'

He whistled to Nigel and the two of them swung their way down the steps and out of the close and I went for a shower and a tidy-up and a conversation with Colonel Barton that I really didn't want to have.

Mrs Barton was dozing in her chair so we talked in the kitchen.

'Are you sure?' he said, when I'd finished. 'I haven't seen anything on TV?' He cast me a shrewd look. 'Did you get it from the horse's mouth, perhaps?'

I smiled. 'Some part of the horse's anatomy, anyway.'

He sighed. 'It's very bad news, isn't it? No matter who the body is, it's not good news for Mrs Painswick. Or Alyson. Do you think we should talk to the police?'

I said carefully, 'I think they're aware of the issues. If they want us, they'll come and speak to us.'

'I don't think I'll be mentioning this to Mrs Barton.'

'No,' I said, 'I quite understand. I shan't say anything to her unless she asks.'

'She won't ask,' he said sadly.

CHAPTER TWELVE

Events continued to overwhelm me. The next day was damp and cold – not only had summer turned into autumn but autumn had turned into winter. I know I'd told Iblis I'd stay put, but Thursday was visiting the library day. And it was only just over the road. I gathered my books and DVDs together and crossed the green, over the moat, through the ancient gateway, and turned right for the library.

The doors opened automatically and I did my usual trick of walking in and out several times. These days all libraries are under threat of closure and visitor numbers are a vital weapon in the war to keep them open. Most libraries, big and small, have some sort of people-counter set up just inside the entrance which records everyone who walks in. I always made sure I walked in and out three or four times because every little helps. I think a lot of other people do the same – I've seen several impeccably respectable elderly ladies standing in front of these machines, chatting to each other and gaily waving their hands in front of the sensor every fifteen seconds or so, enthusiastically deceiving the council and endowing the library with another twenty-five or so users in just five minutes. I suspect that on some days, the visitor numbers for the library exceeded the actual population of Rushford, but our library was still open and that was the most important thing.

I returned my items and set off for a happy wander around the shelves looking for something that took my fancy. I was in Fiction TAYTRU when I found myself face to face with the very last person I ever thought I'd see in a library.

I think I've mentioned Melek. Iblis's partner. The gold to his silver. She's as tall as he is – and he's not short. What I could see of her hair was dark red and she always wore it pulled back hard and knotted at her neck. Not a flattering look for most people but somehow, she made it look good. Her colour swirled gently around her, shifting from gold to copper and back again, which always surprised me, because her face was tight and hard.

For some reason, I thought, she's followed me here. I had a suspicion this was not unconnected with Iblis's recent visit. Had he told her what had happened? Did she know about Lady Torrington?

She was wearing the same clothes in which I'd met her. I don't mean she hadn't changed – merely that they seemed to be some kind of uniform. A long dark coat, a long-sleeved black T-shirt and dark jeans. Her boots were heavy, fashionable and looked as if they could kick their way through a brick wall.

I admit I was startled to see her. We'd spoken in the past but she wasn't anywhere near as approachable as Iblis. Stern, I think, would be the best word to describe her. That might not be her fault, however, because when Iblis took himself out of the game, she had shouldered his workload as well as her own. She looked tough and indomitable but weary unto death.

The good thing about libraries is that these days you can chat away and no one ever shouts 'shush'. There was a drinks machine and a couple of chairs and tables where you could have a coffee or hot chocolate and, unusual in these days of declining libraries, ours was enjoying a small renaissance as a great place to meet and chat. The kids could entertain themselves in the junior section or have stories read to them. Public access computers were constantly in use and the staff ran classes and hosted meetings. Local History, Painting and Drawing, IT, the Homework Club – it was all happening here. Since it was late afternoon, the place was full of schoolkids who you'd think had come to do their homework, but actually seemed to have turned up just for a bit of a gossip before going home and not doing their homework there, either.

Melek and I looked at each other. Suspecting the social heavy lifting might be up to me, I said, 'Hello. I never thought I'd have the opportunity to say this, but do you come here often?'

She stared at me blankly and I sighed. 'Were you looking for me?'

'Yes,' she said, 'I saw you leave your house. But we should talk in private.' She surveyed the people around her. Drinking coffee, talking, wandering around, hunched over computers, some even reading books. 'Not here.'

I should have said, 'No problem, I can come back later,' and got her out of there. We could have gone back to my house and had a quiet cup of coffee, and everything that followed would have been considerably less embarrassing.

Instead, I said, 'OK – won't be a minute.'

Every week or so, our library puts up a special display. The last one had been a book wall of all those covers depicting a hugely muscled young man standing in a . . . flexed . . . position and with a scantily clad young woman draped alluringly around his torso. Going by the display, there were a lot of young men out there who had forgotten to put on their shirts that morning.

179

Just to objectify them further, they were always cut off at chin level so we never got to see their faces. At the other end, the view was cut off just low enough to see their jeans were enticingly unzipped. These young men obviously needed help when dressing in the morning. Perhaps that was what the young lady was there for.

That was last week's display, however. Today's subject was the always popular 'Angels'.

There was a great deal of choice. All the books were presented face out and the staff had made the display look very pretty with stars, tinsel, glitter and what looked like Christmas tree angels as well. I paused briefly to consider the titles.

Guardian Angels and How to Summon Them

Angel Oracles

The Encyclopaedia of Angels

Everything You Need to Know About Your Angel

How Your Angel Can Save YOU

Angels and the Sacred Feminine

Angels and Your Finances – If You Ask Your Guardian Angel to Help You Watch the Pennies Then Those Pearly Gates Might Be Closer Than You Think. A statement I felt was very open to misinterpretation and I was surprised the book's copyeditor hadn't picked up on that.

Angels and Their Light – Embrace Your Own Inner Radiance

Angels and Crystals – How to Heal PROPERLY

And so on and so on. There were a lot of them.

I'd already moved past them when a voice said, 'What?' and I remembered I wasn't alone. I turned but too late.

Melek was flourishing a book. The cover depicted a strapping young man with the most enormous pair of . . . wings . . .

modestly crossed to conceal what were, presumably, his less angelic areas.

She stared in disbelief. First at the book – *Angels, Your Invisible Guardians* – and then at the display in general.

'What?' she said again. 'What is this . . . ?' She tailed away, presumably speechless. For which I was thankful.

I indicated the little café area. 'Let's have a coffee, shall we?' That didn't work at all.

'Seriously?' she said, her voice carrying effortlessly to the far corners of the library, Rushford and possibly the Antipodes as well. 'Only mortals could think they're important enough to rate some sort of celestial private army solely to keep them safe from the consequences of their own stupidity.'

She picked up another book – *How to Bring More Angels Into Your Life*. 'Don't they know that anyone catching sight of one of these buggers' – she flourished the book again; the cover showed a white-clad figure bending lovingly over someone I couldn't see, her thumb was in the way – 'far from feeling nurtured and protected, would certainly wet themselves in terror, half a second before suffering instant heart failure and then bursting into flames. Believe me, the last thing anyone needs' – she flourished another book, *An Angel at Your Side* – 'is one of these ruthless, egotistical, narcissistic bastards standing at their side. I personally wouldn't even want one in the same universe as me, and neither would anyone else if they knew what was good for them.'

She stared around the library. 'I can only assume no one here has actually seen one of these so-called benevolent guardians because your melted eyeballs aren't running down your cheeks. Be grateful.'

I removed the book from her grasp. With one last angry stare at the angelic display – no book burst into flames but one or two looked slightly ashamed of themselves – she seated herself at a table and yanked a magazine off the rack. I noticed she even read angrily. Slowly, normal library noises started up again.

I decided I'd grab the first four books that took my fancy – even if they didn't – and get her out of there as soon as humanly possible. I'd had Iblis giving me a bad name on my own doorstep and now Melek was doing the same in the library.

Sadly, the day hadn't yet finished with me. I seized a couple of books more or less at random, telling myself I might discover an unexpected treasure this way, and slowly became aware of a group of four schoolgirls sitting at a nearby table. A few text-books were half-heartedly scattered around but the girls weren't even pretending to do their homework.

They were an odd group. One was staggeringly pretty. And I do mean staggeringly pretty. Really eye-catching. She had white-blonde hair, amazing dark blue eyes and the most flaw-less skin; I would swear it actually glowed. I've noticed that Mother Nature often bestows all her bounty on just one person, leaving the rest of us lesser mortals to fend for ourselves. Not for this young lady the trials of teenage acne, split ends or bitten fingernails. Everything about her was perfect. Here was someone who could have launched a thousand ships without even thinking about it.

Her colour was a striking violet with fringes of gold but – and this was very noticeable – there was a fragility there. To me, it looked brittle. Frail. Weak. There was no inner strength to it. It didn't move as it should, and a small dark patch hung around her head.

The two girls on either side of her had, I suspected, been carefully selected for their ordinariness. To make her look good. They were just normal schoolgirls, moderately pretty, and their colours were both a similar insipid blue, quiet and placid. Rather like the girls themselves. The fourth girl was different. She was very dark with strong features, the most prominent of which was a hooked nose that somehow really suited her. Her hijab was a blue so dark as to be nearly black and her colour was a thick, vibrant orange and easily the most vigorous of the group.

Initially I thought the girls were talking together quite normally, but actually only the pretty one was doing the talking – two were listening. Avidly. Their pale blue colours swirled together as the girls leaned across the table, hanging on to her every word. I wondered if they were related. The orange one remained apart. Curious but cautious.

I tried to move away but there was no escaping her. I gathered the pretty one's name was Crystal. Actually, the whole library gathered her name was Crystal. Her voice was nearly as penetrating as Melek's and she could be heard all round the room. As, no doubt, she intended. Anyway, it would appear Crystal had a boyfriend and their relationship had reached *that* particular moment and she had a decision to make.

'I mean,' she said, tossing her fabulous hair over her shoulder in a shimmering curtain of platinum, 'I really don't know what to do. He's all like, "I love you. If you loved me then you would." And I'm all, "I don't know."' She tossed her hair again. 'I mean, you know, he's *the* David Coulson. And I want him to take me to the dance at the Cider Tree next week. And besides, if I don't, then someone else will.'

The two girls nodded furiously. The fourth said nothing.

'And he's just so dreamy and besides, if I do, he says he'll let me drive his car.'

Two of the girls regarded her with admiration. The third watched, her dark eyes bright under heavy lids, her colour resting quietly for the moment.

'But,' continued Crystal, seemingly oblivious to the admiration from two of her friends, although I could see she was revelling in it, 'will he still respect me in the morning or . . . ?'

I suspect anyone in the library could have answered that question for her but no one was granted the opportunity. Everyone jumped as Melek's voice cut ruthlessly across these self-obsessed meanderings.

'Of course he won't, you twittering airhead. He doesn't respect you now and he certainly won't in the morning. By this time tomorrow, he'll have told all his mates how easy you are and invite them to have a go as well. Once he's had you, he'll move on to the next easy lay. It's not as if there aren't a lot of them around. This time next week, he won't even remember your name. He won't give you a moment's thought once he's got what he wants. He'll sail off into the sunset and have a life. You, on the other hand, will find yourself an object of ridicule and contempt which you will not, in any way, be able to overcome.

'Because you're beautiful – and you can wipe the smirk off your face because beauty doesn't last long – you've never bothered to master the behaviour patterns necessary for more normal people. Manners, courtesy, consideration, humility, getting on with others – you can't do any of that. You demand – you get. And because you're an ignorant little gobshite with no beauty of soul and no conception of anything that doesn't relate directly to your wonderful self, you're incapable of working out the implications of a quick, meaningless shag with someone who, impossibly, is even more self-obsessed and selfish than you.

'You are about to embark on an action you will regret all your life. And, believe me, the regret will corrode your very soul. Of course, nothing will be your fault and it is very possible you will go to your inevitably premature death blaming everyone but yourself for your stupid choices.

'Your friend here, on the other hand,' she gestured at the girl with the vibrant orange colour, 'will graduate with a well-paid job. She'll jet off around the world having a fabulous life, while you're stuck in a four-room flat with God knows how many wailing babies and the smell of urine making your eyes run. You'll be on drugs, of course, because you mistakenly think they'll make your life less dreary. You'll almost certainly be dead before you're forty. Either an overdose, or some sort of sexual disease, or beaten to death by a drunken punter. Occasionally someone will say, "I wonder what happened to Crystal – she was so pretty . . ." Still – don't let anything I say sway you. You go ahead and make up your own mind.'

And now, there really was silence in the library. Even the young kids in the Junior Section had stopped moving. Everyone was just frozen and staring. As was I.

I'd always known that Iblis had his own struggles with acceptable human behaviour, cheerfully ignoring most of the rules when it suited him, but it had never dawned on me that Melek might experience the same difficulties.

And it seemed so unlike her. Always so . . . enclosed. Always so rigidly in control. There had been raw emotion in those words. Something about Crystal had struck a nerve within her.

I remembered Iblis and Allia. He'd only had sex with her on

185

one occasion but look at the damage that had done to him. And to Melek too. I knew Iblis loved her. His colour told me so every time he saw her. It would stream towards her like a boisterous puppy, desperate for affection. How Melek felt, I never knew, because her colour was completely under her control; it wrapped itself around her like armour, impervious to his, until finally, hurt and sad, his colour would creep back to him.

The young girl – Crystal – was staring with her mouth open. It seemed a safe bet no one had ever spoken to her like that in her entire life. Doting parents. Indulgent teachers. Admiring friends. Because that happens when you're beautiful. They tell me. Her colour streamed away from Melek like smoke in a high wind.

I think it's very possible we might all be sitting there still but Melek thrust back her chair and stalked from the library. Every head turned to watch her go.

I remembered she'd come looking for me, so I dropped the few books I'd selected so far on to the nearest table and hurried out after her.

She was waiting for me on the wooden bridge over the moat.

'Um,' I said, thinking it might be a good idea to take her somewhere quiet. Away from people, anyway. 'Would you like to come back to my place for a coffee?'

She leaned back against the railing. 'I just want to wait a moment.'

'What for?'

'I want to see if my words have worked.'

'I'm not sure Crystal is the listening type,' I said, remembering her look of paralysed shock.

'Sometimes you only get the one opportunity and you have to make it count.'

'Even so . . .' I said.

'Oh – no. Not her. The other one.'

'The one with the hijab?'

She nodded. 'She has great potential, that one, which will never come to pass if she continues to hang around with that idiot. It was necessary to administer a short, sharp shock.'

Carefully, I said, 'You may have destroyed a young girl in the process.'

She shrugged. 'The other one? She stands at the crossroads of her life. She will make her own choice. I am not optimistic.'

There was a quiet ruthlessness which chilled my blood.

The library door was pushed open and the girl with the hijab emerged, heaving her bag over her shoulder. Catching sight of Melek, she slowed slightly, possibly fearing another verbal broadside. Melek nodded slightly and the girl strode away.

'Well, she's not with her friend,' I said to Melek. 'Job done.'

'I hope so.'

There was a pause.

I couldn't let it go. 'Wait,' I said. 'I won't be a moment.'

Back in the library, normal service had been resumed. Except that as I came through the door, everyone looked up. To see if the scary woman had returned, presumably. The schoolgirls were frozen in much the same position as when I'd left. I don't think any of them had moved an inch.

I sat opposite Crystal and said quietly, repeating Melek's words, 'You stand at a crossroads. This is the most important day of your life. Make the right choice. There is still time.'

I think she was still in shock. Her violet colour was trembling. I took a breath. It couldn't do any harm, surely. Holding her eyes with my own, I said, 'You have greatness within you. Find it. Use it.'

I couldn't think of anything else to say. A little gold seeped back into her colour. I was satisfied she'd heard me.

I caught up with Melek outside.

'So – coffee,' I said, brightly.

'Yes. Coffee.'

The rain started as we were crossing the green and we ran up the steps to my front door. I flung the door open. 'Please come in.'

She stepped over the threshold as if it was some kind of ceremonial rite. I remembered how much she . . . not frightened me . . . not very much anyway, but she was just so . . . formidable. There was power here, but whether for good or bad, I couldn't tell. There was the potential for either but as usual, her colour gave nothing away. I couldn't read her.

I could, however, be a gracious hostess. 'Would you like to sit down? What would you like? Tea? Coffee? Something cold? A biscuit, perhaps?' She sat patiently, waiting until I stopped gabbling and pulled myself together.

'Tea, please.' She sniffed the air. 'Nigel has been here.'

'Yes,' I said, sadly.

I poured the tea, and finally, with nothing left to do, I fell silent. Curling myself up at the other end of the sofa, I turned to face her. A shower of rain hurled itself at the window and a child ran past, shouting for someone out of sight. Silence fell.

I thought I might give her an opening. 'I looked for Iblis at his camp but he tells me he's not there any longer.'

'No,' she said. 'He's living with me for the time being.'

188

Curiosity was killing the cat, but I said, 'Oh?' politely and waited for her to speak.

She didn't, so I said, 'He seems better.'

'He is better,' she said. 'Better than he has been for a long time. You never knew him as he once was. Before Allia tricked him and stole his sword. He was . . . well . . .' She sipped her tea.

'His concern was all for you,' I said gently. 'And the danger his mistake had placed you in.'

'I know,' she said, staring down at her tea.

'He told me . . . how difficult it was to tell you what he'd done. He must have been distraught.'

She said quietly, 'He didn't shirk his duty. He came to warn me. At great cost to himself. As you know.'

I nodded. I did know.

'And to me as well.'

I said nothing.

'He begged me to kill him.'

That came as a shock. He hadn't mentioned anything like that. The words were barely audible above the sound of the rain beating against my windows.

The sky outside was darker than ever. I wasn't going to get up and switch on the light. I didn't want to interrupt her flow. I had to know. I'd heard the story from Iblis's point of view and now, suddenly, out of nowhere, it looked as if I might hear the other side from Melek. I was sure she would never have spoken of it to anyone. Would she welcome the opportunity to speak of it now? I had the very strong impression there was something important she wanted to say so I kept very quiet and very still.

'Perhaps you should hear the whole story,' she said. 'Since you were so involved in part of it.'

Her colour darkened and tightened itself around her and perhaps she realised this because she set down her tea, smoothed her jeans, took one or two deep breaths, turned so her face was slightly averted and began.

'I was in Venice. I was waiting for him. Our plan was to push the Fiori . . .' She looked at me enquiringly.

I nodded. 'The Fiori are demons.'

She nodded. 'Human on the outside, all demon on the inside, and no one ever realises until it's too late. Their cruelty knows no limits. Even to each other.' She drew another breath. 'I was to raise support for an army. We planned to push them ahead of us and drive them into an ambush.

'He wasn't at the rendezvous. That was nothing unusual. Anything could have happened to delay him. So I hired a house and servants and settled down to wait.

'In those days, of course, it wasn't always easy for a woman – especially a single woman – to form her own establishment, but I circulated rumours of fabulous wealth, indulged in a little conspicuous consumption and, because men are such hypocrites, suddenly what would have been improper and scandalous behaviour in anyone else was a harmless, even charming, eccentricity in the very rich foreign woman.'

And having those looks and that height wouldn't have hurt, either. I stuffed the thought away but I think she must have caught an echo because one side of her mouth quirked up in a half-smile. I had amused her.

She tilted her head. 'As you say.'

I hadn't actually said anything but it was a timely reminder. She definitely wasn't Iblis.

She brushed her jeans again, caught herself doing it, folded her hands in a neutral position and continued in the same quiet, measured voice as before.

'There was plenty to do, of course. The Fiori weren't the only bad boys on the block. There were all the usual nuisances to deal with – revenants, malicious entities, remnants of the old days who still wouldn't go quietly, things the world was better without, and so on. I had to be discreet, so I killed quickly and cleanly and there were never any witnesses. I only went hunting at night and every night I returned by a different route. No one ever had the slightest suspicion. The time passed. During the day I ate cake and talked fashion and scandal with matrons and their hopeful, single daughters. At night, I walked in shadows so deep most mortals don't even know they exist.'

She paused. I quietly refilled her cup.

'Thank you.' She looked at it for a while.

'It's not drugged,' I said quickly, my experiences with Sorensen never far from my mind.

'I know.' She picked up her tea again. I was sure she didn't really want it but I appreciated her good manners.

'Well, I had been there for one month, possibly a little longer, and there was to be a masque. A very grand masque. At the Doge's palace, no less. Everyone would be there.'

She continued with no change in her voice. She might have been discussing the magazine she had been reading in the library. 'I rather hoped Iblis would have arrived by then and we could go together. He dances rather well, you know. We danced at . . . at a wedding party, once . . . and it . . . I . . . rather looked forward to repeating the experience.'

I smiled. 'And did he come? Did you dance?'

'Yes. And no. The date had been carefully chosen to coincide with the full moon. And what a moon it was that night.' She stared back into her past. 'Huge and silver, hanging over the city, creating light and shadow in equal measure. Silver light glittered on the water, hiding the dark depths underneath. Rather like human nature, don't you think?'

She seemed to remember who she was talking to and moved on.

'The colour scheme for the masque was – coincidentally – black and silver. I had a gown specially made – well, I think every woman in the city had a dress specially made. Mine was of silver silk with black lace over the top and my hair was powdered with silver.'

'Wow,' I said, 'you must have looked spectacular. Did Iblis ever see you in this get-up?'

'Yes, but by then neither of us cared.'

I shut up.

'I arrived fashionably late – and without Iblis – which was a shame, but I had tasks to perform. There was an ambassador's ear to whisper in. A minor princeling to advise. A treaty to warn against. Decisions to influence. Little things but all of them together would save several rivers of blood in the future. I moved around the vast crowd – a word here and a word there.' She smiled suddenly. 'It's not all drawn swords and bloodshed, you know.'

I could see it. I could see it all. I saw the crowds of people all dressed in black and silver to represent the moon in the sky. I saw the elaborate masks and heard the laughter. I saw the glittering chandeliers, the Venetian glass, the art on the walls, the marble sculptures, the discreet flirting in dark corners – everything. I saw the stately dancers form a line, meet, move apart, twirl together again. I saw their eyes, bright behind their masks, their jewels glittering in the brilliant candlelight.

'We were masked, of course, but my height gave me away. Everyone knew who I was. Many men asked me to dance but there was too much wine flowing, filling them with false courage. I didn't want to have to hurt anyone.

'I was staring at a portrait of the current Doge and meditating on how often one finds cleverness mixed with ugliness – does one beget the other, I wonder? – when I knew Iblis had arrived. He was there. Somewhere close. And a fraction of a second later I knew something had happened.' Her voice had a tiny tremble. 'My heart stopped. There were feelings I'd never experienced. Fear. Panic. Guilt. Remorse. And that awful dread experienced when something really bad has happened and it's too late to do anything about it. I couldn't breathe. I forgot to hold on to my goblet and it fell to the floor. I watched the wine spread across the white marble. I couldn't move. Servants ran to clear up the mess. People drew back and suddenly I was at the centre of an ever-widening circle. It wasn't the wine they were avoiding. It was me. I could see the fear on their faces. It was only afterwards – a very long time afterwards – that I realised it must have been my expression. I know someone asked me if I were ill. I couldn't speak. I couldn't . . . The dancers stopped. The music stopped. Everyone was staring at me. I can see it now. A moment frozen for all time. For all I know, the whole world stopped as well. Yes, that's it. For a moment – a very brief moment – the world stopped and I knew something had ended. No, not ended – broken.'

She stared at her tea as if she didn't know what to do with it and then put it down again.

'And then everything started up afresh. The musicians played. The dancers danced. A servant brought me a fresh goblet of wine but I was already leaving. I pushed past him. I pushed past everyone. I shouldered people out of my way. I took the most direct route to the door. Straight down the stairs. People fell away on either side of me. I heard shouts and protests and I ignored all of it because this was far more important than anything their tiny minds could begin to comprehend. I picked up my skirts and I ran. Across the hall and out through the doors, still open to admit latecomers.'

She swallowed. 'I left everything behind. I left my cloak, my mask, my fan – even a shoe shed on the staircase somewhere. A linkboy offered to call me a conveyance and I ignored him because I knew Iblis was close by and I had to get to him before . . .'

The silence dragged on. 'Before . . .' I prompted, because she couldn't stop now. I wanted the other side to Iblis's story. I wanted to know how she had handled this catastrophe. How had she handled Iblis?

She shook her head. I could guess what she wasn't saying. I'd seen cheerful, irreverent Iblis, charming his way through life and, like Melek, I found the thought of him in such pain, such distress, such despair, to be quite unbearable.

'He was there,' she said softly. 'I knew he would be. He was standing in the dark. His face . . . I said his name. His real one. And he said mine. My real one. And then it was as if he just caved in. Everything that had got him there, to me, just gave way. I ripped off one of my bracelets, flung it at a passing linkboy and commanded him to get me a chair, promising him the necklace as well if he could find one within two minutes.

Given the crowds around us I had no great hopes, but he did. He arrived less than a minute later, panting and dishevelled but successful.

'We bundled Iblis inside and set off. I lashed those unfortunate men with words but he was still alive when we arrived back at my house and I rewarded them well. Every scrap of jewellery I was wearing I gave to them. They could have bought half the city with it. I told them to go and they didn't stop to argue. They abandoned their chair outside my house and took off. I remember their running footsteps echoing off the tall buildings.

'Not realising it was me, my servants were disinclined to answer the door and I'm afraid I rather lost my temper. I blew it open. I remember the wood shattering into a million pieces. I remember their terrified faces. I snarled at them to take Iblis to my room – thus confirming their worst fears about foreign women and their heathen habits – but they were too afraid to disobey. I commanded a fire and they tumbled over themselves to comply. And then I drove them from the room. They fled and I locked the door behind them.'

Another long silence fell. She was brushing the creases from her jeans again but I had no fear she would stop now. She'd come too far. I wasn't even sure she remembered I was in the same room. Her voice was little more than a whisper. I had to strain to hear her.

'He had suffered no physical wounds. All the damage was inside his head. I could see the tiny cracks forming in his mind ... the fine lines ... I could see his mind begin to splinter ... I was losing him. He was falling away from me. I had only moments left.

'I put my arms around him and he leaned on me. He'd spent

195

his last strength getting back to me. I took his weight and held him. I closed my eyes and found my way into his mind, inching my way in, terrified of making things worse. I could feel it breaking up, disintegrating, shattering into tiny pieces. I reached out to him and did what I could.

'At first, I had no thought of repair. It was all I could do to hold him together. To stop any further damage. And then, very slowly, after what seemed like hours, he calmed a little. I gathered my strength, drawing his mind into mine. It hurt – there was so much damage. So many spikes and jagged edges. But I did what I could, soothing him and calming him, trying to stem the runaway panic that, with our minds joined together like that, could kill us both. For a long time, that was all I could do. Just hold back the tide. And then slowly, almost impercepttibly, I could feel the cracks begin to heal. I would deal with one, then move on to another, comforting, quieting, mending, while I held him close and tried to take away his fear. Until finally – and I have no idea how much later that was – his mind was his own again.

'I let him go and sat him down. My servants had brought wine and I made him sip slowly, holding his hands around the beaker, talking to him as if he was a frightened child – which was exactly what he was at that moment.

'I wouldn't let him rush into speech. I knew that what he wanted to say to me was urgent, but if he spoke too soon then the cracks would reappear, and I didn't think I'd have the strength to heal him a second time. He was only calmed – not cured. And I was weary myself; I wanted to sleep. And, perhaps, I wanted to postpone the very bad tidings I knew he was bringing me.'

Now we were coming to it. I said nothing, not wanting to

disturb the flow of her story. It struck me that, as it had bene-fited Iblis to talk about this to me, it was benefiting Melek as well, although she would probably drop down dead rather than admit it.

She turned to me. 'Well, you know the story.'

'I do,' I said. 'I know that Allia tricked him and stole his sword. That he held himself responsible for her supposed death and reproached himself constantly for it. But what I'd like to know is the rest of it. If you don't mind, of course,' I said, remembering who I was talking to.

She turned her head away and again I was back in that dark, sumptuous room in Venice. The one with the bright fire, the rich fabrics and a stricken Iblis.

'There was a couch drawn up to the fire. The servants often commented on my need for a blaze, sometimes even in the summer, but I feel the cold and, trust me, Venice is very cold in winter.'

For a moment, there was a gleam of what might have been humour, like a wintry sun glimpsed behind the clouds, and then the wind blew and it was gone again.

She sighed. 'He told me what he had done. Given he wasn't anywhere near recovered, I should probably not have allowed it, but he insisted I knew what had happened so I could protect myself. As he told me, I could see the cracks opening again as all the old emotions I'd struggled to contain came rushing back, threatening to overwhelm us both. That was when he ordered me to kill him. Then he begged me. He was . . .' She shook her head and stared at her hands.

'I fought him for a long while, until eventually, mostly from exhaustion, I think, he fell asleep. I covered him with a blanket, built up the fire, ensured the shutters were barred and the door locked, and then I too fell asleep in front of the fire.'

She was brushing her jeans again. The only sign she wasn't in perfect control of herself.

'When I awoke, he'd gone. The fire was long cold. A bowl of fruit on the table had grown mouldy. My servants, unable to rouse me and possibly thinking I was dead, had looted the place and fled. My house was full of beggars and thieves off the street. I was in no mood to deal gently with them. They fled before me. I left that day and never went back.'

'And Iblis? What did he do?'

'He disappeared. We saw each other occasionally. We worked together once or twice, but he feels – felt – himself to be very much the inferior.'

'But now he knows,' I said. 'He didn't sleep with a mortal.'

'*He slept with a Fiori.*'

Her colour lit up the room. A flash of gold like a lightning strike, sudden and blinding. Her voice bled pain and anguish and . . . something else. Anger. Justifiable, I suppose. Inevitable, even. And natural. Iblis had really screwed up but – and this was just a guess – he'd had an outlet. He'd done the right thing. He'd confessed to her and then taken himself out of the way. But to whom had Melek spoken? To whom did she unburden herself? Yes, she had been there for him, but afterwards her anger would have boiled over and there would have been no one there for her. I wondered if the best thing would have been for them to have had a massive fight. Shouting . . . throwing things . . . bringing down the occasional building, but clearing the air. But that hadn't happened and the years had rolled on . . .

If I hadn't listened to Iblis as he told his tale – if I hadn't picked up on that tiny point – the one that revealed how he'd been tricked – they'd still be apart and both of them the weaker for it. Now, at least they were together. The crushing burden of guilt and remorse and shame had been lifted and he was Iblis again.

'What happens now?' I asked. 'Will you remain together?'

'*He lost his sword.*'

Her shout made the crockery in my cupboards ring, reminding me that although he might not be guilty of the first deadly sin, Iblis was still guilty of the second – losing the only weapon that could kill them both. His sword. They could be injured, they could fall sick, but only a Hunter's sword could kill them stone dead. I swallowed hard and told myself to be more careful in future.

Trying to make things better, I said, 'It was taken from him.'

Her eyes flashed again. 'The end result is the same.'

'He had a sword. I saw him use it. At Greyston.'

'But it is not *his* sword.'

I was slightly bewildered. 'Why is that so important? He still managed to bring down one of the Three Sisters.'

She stood up and reached over her shoulder. For one moment I couldn't think what she was doing and then, with a flourish, she drew a massive sword that seemed to go on for ever. It couldn't possibly have been there a moment ago. I stared, astounded and not a little frightened. It glowed in my rapidly darkening room. I'll swear it hummed with power. Hot golden flames, the same shade as her colour, flickered up and down the blade and I saw what Iblis had meant about his sword being part of him. Part of Melek was in her sword as well. I leaned back. This was a sword that found its own targets and I didn't want it finding me. But I saw her point. The sword Iblis had carried was a kite to Melek's jumbo jet.

'He lost it a very long time ago,' I said, hoping she'd put it away. 'In all that time, there hasn't been even a whisper of its location, has there?'

'No,' she said, reaching back over her shoulder, and suddenly it was gone. I couldn't help it – I got up and walked around behind her. No – no sword anywhere.

She sat down again and I pretended I'd got up for more hot water.

'Iblis said he thinks it's buried somewhere,' I said from the kitchen. 'A king's grave goods, perhaps.'

'That is very possible.'

'Lost for ever.'

She said grimly, 'Nothing is lost for ever. One day it will make itself known.'

'Yes,' I said. 'But then you'll know where it is. You'll know what to do. And then the two of you will have it back.'

'We won't be the only ones who want it. We will have to fight for it.'

'Well, even better. Iblis gets his sword back and the two of you enjoy your first real bloodletting in centuries. Do you doubt that, should it ever surface, Iblis would bring the moon down from the sky rather than lose it a second time?'

She smiled and shook her head. 'No. I can't imagine anything getting between him and his sword ever again.'

A silence fell. I wondered whether I should offer more tea. Or something to eat, perhaps. Iblis would have had his head in the fridge by now. I sighed. She wasn't Iblis. But perhaps

200

she had been once. Tragedy had made her what she was today. Doing the work of two . . . holding things together . . . dour . . . abrupt. Perhaps once she had been as carefree as him.

I had a sudden flash. Music. Dancing. A crowd. Happy laughter. Joy. It was gone in half the time it took to register. Just a long-lost memory surfacing. And then sinking again.

I came back in from the kitchen and she looked at me carefully. 'You should take care.'

'I will,' I said and I wasn't just being polite. I would take care.

'Do you have enemies?'

'Why do you ask?'

'There is a dark cloud about you. Someone wishes you harm.'

Well, that was more than concerning. And I couldn't just dismiss it out of hand. Iblis had said something similar. 'Someone left a witch's ladder here last summer. Iblis found it hidden in the porch.'

'Where is it?'

'He destroyed it. Some time ago.'

She looked at me again. My room was quite dark by this time so I don't know what she was seeing. 'Iblis told me – you saw a woman who looked like you?'

Her colour surged towards me. I had a moment of clarity. For all her talk of Iblis and his sword, *this* was what she had really wanted to speak to me about. This was why she had followed me to the library.

I said firmly, 'No, it wasn't that she looked like me – she *was* me. She had my face. I saw myself through her eyes. Then I saw her through my eyes. It was . . .' I couldn't think of a word to describe it.

'Where was this? Not here in Rushford.'

'No. Scotland. I saw something. A burning cottage. She was there. She turned and looked at me.'

Something flickered in her eyes. 'Scotland?'

I nodded.

'You were unsettled by this?'

I said bluntly, 'I was . . . terrified. I . . .'

'Yes?'

The words burst out of me. 'I've covered my mirrors. I can't . . . look at myself.' I found myself trembling all over.

'Sit down.'

I didn't argue with her. I sat back down again.

'That's right. Just lean your head back. Close your eyes. I have something important to say to you.'

I was very reluctant to do so.

'No,' she said. 'Relax. Lean back. Close your eyes.'

Inch by inch I leaned back.

'Close your eyes.'

'Why?' I said, closing my eyes as instructed but ready to open them at any second.

'There,' she said briskly. 'I think you will feel better now. Open your eyes.'

I opened my eyes. Had something happened? 'What . . . ?'

I reached for my tea. It was stone cold. The milk was floating on the surface. A revolting sight that reminded me of Dr Sorensen.

'I must go,' she said, getting to her feet and picking up her coat. 'Uncover your mirrors. You won't see her again.'

I stood up, too, somewhat stiffly. 'Um . . .'

She shrugged on her coat and we paused at the door. 'Thank you for your hospitality,' she said formally.

'Oh . . . um . . . you're welcome.'

'You performed a great service for Iblis. He is grateful. As am I. Thank you, Elizabeth Cage.' And then she opened the door. I blinked. When had the rain stopped? When had it got so dark? She ran down the steps and disappeared into the night.

CHAPTER THIRTEEN

Over the next few days, the weather worsened. Once again, I could feel the pressure building. Dark clouds massed on the horizon and there was an occasional flash of lightning or rumble of thunder. I would say there was another storm building but I rather thought it might be the same storm coming back to have another go.

As the wind began to rise, I went outside into my little yard and pushed my pots against the wall for shelter. I didn't want them blowing over and breaking. Not after planting my daffodils. I made sure the gate and shed were securely padlocked and there was nothing that could blow away. Then I went back inside and walked around my house, making sure all the windows were secure and, as always, fretting about my roof.

I don't know why I do this but I do. I had the house surveyed properly before I moved in and I have the report saying the roof is perfectly sound, but I suppose everyone has to have one irrational fear and the roof is mine. Jones says I've begun the slow, sad descent into madness and sometimes I think he's right.

And I uncovered all my mirrors while I was at it, steeling myself to look in each one. Only I looked back at me. And it was me. Feeling extremely stupid, I waved at each reflection and my reflection waved back. So I wasn't haunted in any way – just barking mad. I wasn't sure how relieved I should be.

I was just putting the kettle on when the rain started again. Enormous drops splattered against the windows. I made my coffee, found my book and settled back, literally, to weather the storm. I was snug inside, warm and dry, and I felt much better knowing Iblis wasn't out in all this.

I heard the running footsteps on the path outside and thought nothing of it. Anyone would run to get out of this driving rain. And then they ran back again. And then back the other way. Which was odd. Why would someone run up and down in this weather?

I don't know what made me think it was important but I got up to look. I knelt on the window seat and peered up and down the street but couldn't see a thing in all the rain. Even the castle was almost invisible. I went upstairs to my bedroom for a better view.

A man was running across the grass, his blue-grey colour streaming out behind him like a comet. Where could he be going? If he was trying to get out of the rain, he was running away from shelter. Was he trying to get into the castle for some reason? The library and the council offices would still be open but even so . . .

It was so odd. He was wearing indoor clothes but he must have been running for some time because everything he was wearing – a shirt and tie with sleeveless sweater and trousers – were sodden and what little hair he had was plastered to his head. He was middle-aged and tubby around the middle. He reminded me a little bit of my dad.

And he looked exhausted. His trousers were smeared with

mud – he'd fallen a few times by the looks of it. And if he'd run all the way up the hill in this weather, he must be desperate. And yet he zigzagged aimlessly, going nowhere. Whatever was he doing?

I watched him because he was such a strange sight and then the thought came to me. It was the way he kept looking over his shoulder. He wasn't running *to* something – he was running *from* something. That was why he was continually changing direction. Something was chasing him.

The afternoon was now very dark. Rain streamed down the window and I couldn't see very clearly but I had the impression there was someone behind him. A dark shape. Another person, perhaps. No, not a person – the outline was wrong. I pressed closer to the window to try to see more clearly. No matter how hard and fast the man ran, the figure was always there right behind him. It mirrored his every move. As if it was attached to him in some way. I leaned even closer to the window to try to see a little better and all that happened was that I fogged up the window.

The man staggered on a few more paces. The rain was falling so hard that the earth couldn't absorb the water and muddy puddles lay everywhere. He splashed as he ran. And then he fell. No, not fell – he collapsed. First to his knees, where he paused a moment and then toppled on to his side. He rolled over on to his back and lay spread-eagled, arms flung wide, staring up at the dark sky above as the rain hammered down on to his face. Giant veins of throbbing orange spread through his colour, which fluttered helplessly around him. Almost as if urging him to get up. I wondered if the poor man was having a heart attack and, trying not to take my eyes off him, I reached blindly for the phone by the bed.

Was anyone else watching this? I was certain they must be. Nothing happens in Castle Close without being closely observed by at least half the inhabitants, as I've found to my cost. I should stop staring and ring for an ambulance and then go out and see if I could do anything. That's what a normal person would do.

I rubbed the window again and peered out. The rain was vertical. A massive fork of lightning stabbed down from the sky and only a fraction of a second later, a giant thunderbolt crashed almost directly overhead, making me jump. The street lights had come on even though it was only around two in the afternoon.

I put my hand on the window catch. If I opened the window, I might be able to see better but I'd have a face full of wind and rain. No – wait. Downstairs. Open the front door. The porch would give me some protection and I'd be able to see more clearly as I dialled the emergency services.

It also meant that I'd be seen as well, but that wasn't important right now. Some unfortunate man had collapsed in a thunderstorm and I must do something.

I ran downstairs, unlocked the front door and pulled it open. The air felt cold and wet and the noise of the storm was deafening. Rain splattered noisily around me. Water was splashing on to the cobbled path from a blocked gutter.

The man was still sprawled on the grass, lying about twenty yards away to my right. As far as I could see, he hadn't moved at all. About to seize a coat to put over my head and run to him – I stopped.

There was someone already with him. Something dark bent over him. I squinted through the rain. What was it doing? And then I watched in disbelief as, slowly, it climbed on to the man's chest and crouched there, staring down at him, hands either side of his head, its face only inches from his.

There was something wrong with the proportions. Long, long skinny arms and legs. A bulbous body with a tiny head perched on the top. It was man-shaped but I thought of a spider. A human spider crouched on the chest of a dying man.

I would have shouted but my throat closed. My legs went soft and I had to cling to the door for support.

For long seconds the figure made no move, just staring down into the face of its victim. The unfortunate man's colour, that soft blue-grey, boiled and bubbled as it strained to get away, streaming sideways to keep its distance but to no avail. Reaching out, the crouching figure thrust its bony hands deep into the colour, gripped and pulled. Over the noise of the storm, I thought I heard the man cry out. Feebly, he raised his hand as if to fight off the thing on his chest. I doubt the thing even noticed. Slowly, gradually, as if savouring a great treat, the crouching thing began to eat his colour.

My heart nearly stopped. I couldn't drag my eyes away. I was reminded of a child eating candy floss. Pulling off just a little to begin with, just to get the taste and then, as if it couldn't stop, seizing great handfuls, tearing at it, stuffing it into its mouth. It literally ripped his colour to pieces, right in front of my eyes, gorging itself on the life force of a human being. An actual living person was having his life eaten in front of his eyes. Helpless, he was watching his own personal death.

The thought lanced through my brain. It mustn't see me. Most importantly, it mustn't know I could see it.

Slowly, an inch at a time, I eased myself backwards. Very

carefully making no sound at all, I closed the door behind me and locked it. Then I ran to the window. The man's colour was nearly gone. Long, dull, lightless grey tendrils swung from the demon's – when had I first thought that word? – the demon's mouth and then slowly faded away. The man was dead.

I was still unable to see clearly through the streaming glass and then another great gust of wind and rain rattled the windows. Involuntarily I stepped back and when I looked again – I couldn't see it anywhere. I knelt up on the window seat again, staring all around the close, but the demon had completely disappeared.

I took one or two deep breaths. A couple of doors down, I saw a woman run down her steps, her raincoat held over her head. Someone else appeared under a straining umbrella – I couldn't see clearly. They shouted instructions to each other, but the man was clearly dead. I suspected he'd been as good as dead from the moment the demon had first clapped eyes on him.

I reached for the telephone and stabbed the speed dial. Jones picked up almost immediately.

In my mind I could still see that thing, crouched on his chest, gobbling. I took a deep breath and tried to speak calmly. 'There's a dead man on the grass outside my house.'

'Oh God, Cage, what did you do?'

'I didn't do anything. It happened more or less in front of me. A man keeled over.'

'Heart attack?'

'No, he was running.'

'You mean jogging? In this weather?'

I pulled myself together, reminded myself he hadn't seen what I'd just seen and tried to be a little more coherent.

209

'A middle-aged man. Wearing indoor clothes. And slippers. He'd been running for some time. His clothes were sodden and covered in muddy patches where he'd fallen over. He was terrified. He was running for his life but he just couldn't keep going any longer. He collapsed and . . .'

'You mean he ran himself into the ground?' said Jones quickly.

I stopped in surprise and then said, 'Yes, yes, he did. That's exactly it.'

'He ran until he couldn't run any longer?'

I paused. 'Yes. How did you . . . ?'

'And then he died of exhaustion.'

I steeled myself. 'No. He died because something climbed on to his chest and . . .' I struggled for the words to describe it. 'Something climbed on to his chest and ate the life out of him.'

There was a long, long silence and then he said, 'Cage, you never fail to astound me. Call you back,' and rang off.

I stared at the receiver. What did that mean? Did my brilliance astound him? Or my stupidity? My cowardice? Because I hadn't done anything to save that poor man, although every instinct I had told me there was nothing I could have done. Nothing anyone could have done. I had a very strange feeling that none of this had come as a particular surprise to Michael Jones.

I realised I was still holding the phone. Gently, I put it down and went to the window again. Despite the rain, a small crowd of people had gathered around the body. Someone had brought a blanket although it wasn't doing the unfortunate man the slightest bit of good.

An ambulance crew arrived under the arch, trotting through the rain, closely followed by two policemen. Like everyone else I stood at my window and watched. The ambulance people

210

worked for a while but it was hopeless. Some of my neighbours were pointing to their own houses. Telling the police where they lived and what they'd seen. There seemed to be plenty of helpful witnesses. No one needed me. I stepped back, drew the curtains to shut it all out and switched on the lights. The thunder and lightning appeared to have subsided but the wind and rain were as heavy as ever.

Now that it was all over, I was conscious of my wobbly legs. My heart was still thumping away with the shock of it all. What had I just seen?

To take my mind off things, I toiled up my narrow stairs to inspect the ceilings again and, of course, they were damp-patch-free. I think I might have welcomed a damp patch. It would have been a counter irritant. Something to erase the pictures of that man's death from my mind.

Looking out from my bedroom window, I watched them take the body away. Everyone else had disappeared back into their own houses. The narrow road in front of my house was swimming with water several inches deep because the drains couldn't cope. Now I began to worry about those living lower down in the town. Gerald and Jerry, for instance. Would they be all right? The Rush doesn't flood often. We have an efficient flood plain – the water meadows on which no one has yet built a couple of thousand homes, although that's only a matter of time.

From thinking about Jerry and Gerald's house, it was only a hop, skip and a jump to thinking about James Monroe's gallery. And little Sammy, living in his wall. Still seeking a distraction, I went back downstairs, picked up the envelope and carefully spread Jones's paperwork across the table again. All except for the pictures of Sammy's body, which remained firmly in the envelope. Then I pulled out a chair, sat down and made myself look at the remaining photos. I mean, *really* look at them. I started with the ones of the envelope; I looked at the stamp. A perfectly normal stamp. I looked at the ragged edges where he'd ripped the envelope open. What did that tell me? That he hadn't used a paper knife. That he opened his own mail. He had an office manager – she'd been with him at the time – but he opened his own mail. I remembered that, when I'd worked for the council, junior clerks opened letters addressed to the council in general, but anything specifically addressed went to that person unopened. This letter had come in the post specifically addressed to James Monroe so she hadn't opened it. In her statement, the office manager said she remembered the postman handing over the letter. It had been on the top of that day's post. So James couldn't have smuggled it in and pretended afterwards that it had arrived with the rest of his mail.

I looked at the address, neatly and clearly written in exactly the same extravagant handwriting as the letter. The same pen had been used for both. An attached report said both appeared to have been written with one of the special pens the gallery handed out as advertising.

It seemed safe to assume that Caroline had addressed the envelope at the same time as she'd written the letter. Letter writing is a lost art these days, but most who do write their letter, address the envelope, fold the letter and insert one into the other, lick or stick depending on the type of envelope, and then affix the stamp. At least, that's what I do. The stamp goes on last in case I make a mistake with the address and then I've wasted a stamp. As far as I could see, that was exactly what Caroline had done here.

The letter was also handwritten. Caroline's writing was so big and loopy that what was actually quite a short note took up nearly a whole side of A4. She'd signed her name with what I thought was a surprising flourish, given her intentions, but what that meant, I had no idea. I picked up the image of the envelope again. The R in Rushford had a certain amount of artistic embellishment, as well, leaving too little space for the postcode.

I'm not one of those people who can hold an object and have it talk to them, telling them everything they need to know. I've seen that sort of thing on TV but I can't do that. I see enough without having visions every time I pick up a book in the library or a packet of soap powder from the supermarket. And, anyway, these weren't the originals – only photos and photocopies.

But there was something. I put the copy of the letter to one side and looked again at the envelope. Then I pushed that to one side and looked again at the letter. I read it through once. Then I read it through again. Assuming I was going to murder Caroline Fairbrother – how would I have done it? And got away with it? Nothing sprang to mind.

Then I looked at them both together, envelope and letter side by side, comparing them. Both were handwritten. By the same person. The only difference that I could see was that she had put the postcode on the envelope but not the letter. Which was surely unimportant. I looked at the envelope again. What happened if a person inadvertently left off the postcode? I googled the Royal Mail site which said the letter would be subject to delay but would probably be delivered eventually. But this letter had been delivered on time. Because it had the correct postcode and the correct stamp. Posted Friday, collected that night – or Saturday morning at the latest – delivered on Monday.

What would have happened if the letter had been delivered on Saturday instead? If Royal Mail had had a fit of efficiency and delivered it early? Nothing. The outcome would be the same. Caroline had died on Friday night. James showing up on Saturday instead of Monday wouldn't have made any difference at all.

I looked at the letter again. Then I looked at the envelope. Then I sat back and wondered.

Then I picked up the phone and hit speed dial again.

'For Christ's sake, I'm on my way. Give me a chance to get up this bloody hill, will you.' He rang off.

OK, so Jones was out in the rain and not in the best mood.

I stared at the paperwork again, so deep in thought that I nearly had a heart attack when someone knocked loudly on the door.

It was Michael Jones. Of course it was. Giving women heart attacks since before he could walk, probably.

He was drenched. 'I'm bloody drenched, Cage.'

I murmured soothingly.

He spread his coat to dry and kicked off his shoes.

'Coffee?' I said, moving towards the kettle.

'No. I'm here on business.'

I stopped. He looked more serious than usual. 'Am I in trouble?'

'No. You're a very important witness and I'm here to take a statement from you.'

I nodded out through the window. 'About that man?'

'Yes.'

'Well, you look cold and wet. No reason you can't have a coffee while I give my statement.'

'Cage, you're a good woman.'

For some reason this quite irritated me. Who wants to be thought of as a good woman?

He stood by the fire, holding out his hands. 'I'm soaked all the way down to my underwear, you know.'

I don't know what made me say it. 'You should keep a change of clothes here.'

If it hadn't been for the rain on the windows, there would have been perfect silence. 'Good idea,' he said eventually, while I took refuge in making the coffee.

We sat at the table. 'Oh,' he said, looking at the photos of Caroline's suicide note. 'You're on this again, are you? Is your life not exciting enough?'

'He did it,' I said stubbornly, gathering it all up and stuffing it back in the envelope.

'I don't doubt you but there's a little matter of proof.'

'Well . . .' I said, but he swept on.

'This will be a formal interview, Cage. Do you have any objections to me recording it?'

'Um . . .'

'Don't worry – it doesn't hurt.'

I sighed. 'No, I mean, what about the weird stuff?'

'The weird stuff is why I'm here, Cage. Today, weird stuff is good.'

I was still reluctant. 'I don't know . . .'

'Sorry, you're going to have to trust me on this.'

I sat back. I should help. It's our duty to assist the authorities. Although after a year or so with Michael Jones, I was beginning to change my point of view on that. I suppose I could always refuse to answer any questions I didn't like the sound of.

215

'Right.' He clicked on a little recorder and laid it on the table. 'You are Elizabeth Cage and you live at . . .'

'What's this all about?'

'I'll tell you, I promise, but afterwards. All right?'

I nodded.

'Don't do that, Cage, it confuses the machine.'

'Yes.' It came out more loudly than I intended.

He flinched. 'And you don't have to shout either. This little toy could probably pick you up from the other side of the green out there.'

'That's impressive,' I said. 'Why don't you go back out into the rain and stand on the other side of the green out there so we can see if it works.'

'Seriously, Cage, do you want to commit your shrewishness to public record?'

'And proud to do so.'

He sighed. 'Where were we?'

'We're still trying to establish something we both know – my name and address – and it's only taken us nearly a quarter of an hour. This is going to go on for a while, isn't it?'

He ignored me. 'Please can you tell me what you saw from your house at some time between one and three this afternoon.'

I repeated my story, right up until the moment the man keeled over. 'Do you know who he was?'

'Yes, his name was Colin Allenby and he lived here in Rushford.'

'That was quick work.'

'I'll tell you more later. What happened next?'

'I can only tell you what I saw.'

'That's why I'm here. What did you see?'

216

I stared at him. 'You're having me sectioned, aren't you, and you're tricking me into providing evidence against myself.'

'Just tell me what you saw.'

I looked at him for a long moment and then said, 'I saw a figure climb on to his chest and eat Mr Allenby's life force.'

Not a flicker from Jones. 'Where did this figure come from?'

'Nowhere. It was with him when he arrived.'

'It followed him?'

'Yes. It moved as he moved. Mr Allenby's movements were erratic. He was all over the place. The . . . figure . . . mirrored his movements almost exactly. Almost as if it was part of him.'

'Tell me more.'

'Well, he couldn't seem to shake it off, but he was in the last stages of exhaustion. His legs had that wobbly look. I don't think he was in any state to escape from anything that might be following him.'

'And it was never far away?'

'The figure? No. He couldn't get away from it. Why are you harping on this?'

'I'm harping on everything. Go on.'

'What do you want to know?'

'Tell me again what happened when this . . . thing . . . sat on his chest.'

'It didn't sit – it crouched. It had enormously long legs. Like a spider. And its knees were higher than its head. It was . . . angular.'

'Can you describe it in more detail?'

I did my best. I closed my eyes and tried to recapture what I'd seen.

We went over it again. In fact, we went over everything

several times. He fired questions at me, one after the other, hopping from subject to subject. Sometimes he didn't give me time to finish one answer before shooting the next question at me. I struggled to keep up. Jones himself was in a state of tension. For some reason what I had to say was important. His colour, now almost completely dark red, was thick and focused completely on me and giving nothing away.

Eventually, when my tongue was cleaving to the roof of my mouth, I said, 'Enough,' and stood up.

He switched off the recorder. 'Yes, it is. Well done, Cage, and thank you. You stay put. I'll do it. Tea or more coffee?'

We had tea.

He brought the mugs to the table while I moved the Monroe envelope out of the way before one of us spilled something on it.

'Yes,' he said. 'I'd better take that away with me when I go.'

'Actually,' I said, 'something's niggling me.' And then, not wanting to distract him from telling me what was going on, I said, 'After you've told me what I've just seen.'

He sipped his tea, put the mug carefully on the table, folded his hands and said, 'Have you heard of Ghost?'

'The movie?'

'No. The drug.'

'No. Never heard of it.'

'No, of course you haven't.'

I bristled – although I don't know why – but this calm assumption I was too old-fashioned to be abreast of current street culture was irritating. I asked him what it did.

'It's advertised as doing something that places it squarely in what might be known as your area of expertise.'

I blinked. 'Such as?'

'According to the word on the street, it opens up a pathway between this world and the next.'

I gaped at him. I couldn't believe what he was saying. 'You mean . . .'

'Yes. According to the sales pitch, it enables people to see ghosts.'

CHAPTER FOURTEEN

I couldn't take it in. The implications . . . if the drug worked . . . What was I saying? Of course it worked. It had just worked right in front of my eyes.

I opened my mouth, stopped to think a little and then closed it again. 'Can you tell me anything else?'

'Not much. It's something that's appeared in the last six months and, unusually, its target group doesn't appear to be young people.'

'Is it expensive? Perhaps they couldn't afford it.'

'You might be right. Most users seem to be in their early to mid-forties and upwards. About the time people start to lose their parents or their grandparents. People they love. And just the right age to begin to feel the faint fingertips of mortality themselves. When birthdays begin to lose their sparkle. And they're old enough to have a bit of money behind them, which they definitely need because, to answer your question, Ghost is expensive. Very expensive.'

'What do the survivors say?'

'Nothing. There aren't any.'

'They all die?'

'They do.'

'All of them?'

'Every single one. Cage, where did it go afterwards? The thing on his chest?'

I shook my head. 'I don't know. Mr Allenby died and only moments later it disappeared.'

That wasn't something I wanted to think about. Mr Allenby's demon had disappeared just after he died. Suppose, once summoned, your demon pursued you for ever. That you were never rid of it. Even after death you and your demon travelled the long road of eternity together.

I pulled myself back from that thought to listen to what Jones was saying.

'What you've told me today is game-changing, Cage. From what we can discover, the drug is advertised as offering the bereaved a chance to chat with loved ones again. In every case that we know of, not more than twelve hours later, the person who has taken Ghost is dead. Cause unknown. Autopsies show their hearts just stopped, which isn't particularly helpful. Now you're telling me something sits on their chest and eats them to death.'

'That's what I saw,' I said, defensively.

'Calm down. I don't doubt it for a moment.'

'How are you going to convince people of this?'

'Leave that to me.'

'But if you tell people what I saw, they'll think you're as weird as me.'

'No one's as weird as you, Cage, so stop worrying.'

'Could you give me a moment?' I said, because I wanted to think.

I stood up and walked to the front window, pulling aside the curtain to look out over the green. The rain still hammered down but it was just normal rain now and the drains seemed able to cope. The green was empty; no one was in sight anywhere. Not only had Mr Allenby been taken away, there was nothing to show that he had ever been here.

I thought about him running as if his life depended upon it. Zigzagging across the grass as if he was trying to shake something off. First one way – then another. Yes, he knew something was behind him. He was running from something tangible. Something he could see but no one else could. Because he'd taken a drug that supposedly enabled him to see a ghost.

What would I do if someone approached me and offered me the opportunity to talk with my dad again? To say all those things I wish I'd said when he was alive but I hadn't because I couldn't ever imagine him being dead. It still worried me that perhaps he never knew how much I loved and appreciated him. Because I never told him. Not properly, anyway. And then he was gone and it was too late. If someone said to me, 'Here, take this drug. You'll be able to talk to your dad one last time,' would I do it? I could easily see how someone could be tempted. Someone like me, all alone in the world without relations, without friends, and then, suddenly, to be offered a chance to say those things. Perhaps hear them said in return. Even knowing what I knew, seeing what I can see, I might be tempted, too. Anyone would.

Take Michael Jones, for example. What would he give for one last chance to talk with Clare? To resolve what had happened between them. To set the record straight so they could both move on. How many of us would want a chance to say a final goodbye? And what would we do to get it? What risks would we take?

And having taken the drug, did everyone get a demon? Perhaps some people *were* actually granted a chance to talk with their loved ones. So what was the intended outcome? Angel or demon?

It had definitely been a demon for Mr Allenby. What must that have been like? To expect a mother, or son, or wife, and to be confronted by something very different. Had he known exactly what was behind him? Something he couldn't outrun, no matter how hard he tried. And then he'd been eaten. Eaten until he was dead. And, from the manufacturer's point of view, that was the other good thing about Ghost, of course. In twelve hours, your customer would be dead. No complaints. No refunds. On the other hand, no repeat customers, either.

So how did Ghost work? Did it alter the user's perception in some way? Alter it so that someone could see the things I saw? I didn't need Ghost. I saw these things all by myself.

I stopped pacing. Now there was a thought.

I turned to Jones. 'When Sorensen said he'd lost interest in me . . . do you remember? Last summer – when he said he didn't need me any longer – that he had someone else now. Was this what he meant? Is it possible? Could he be stuffing people full of this Ghost stuff and *they're* giving him what he wants? Although they would die so quickly afterwards . . . he'd need a new person every time. Surely someone would notice something . . . all those missing people . . .'

I tailed away, lost in complex possibilities.

He shrugged. 'Don't know. Perhaps. Actually, we wondered . . .'

I wasn't listening. I was thinking again.

I'd seen the demon that consumed Mr Allenby. A demon he

223

hadn't been expecting. Far from the heart-warming experience of seeing a loved one again, he'd been faced with something from his worst nightmares. Something so bad it was beyond his worst nightmares. Had Ghost gone wrong for him? Or was the user's death always the intended outcome?

Pursue that thought for a moment. Forget the loved ones – suppose it was never about them. Ghost opened a door all right and something came through – but not what the victim had been expecting. The victim got something that hunted them to their death. Was that what was supposed to happen? The death rate would seem to indicate so.

I rubbed at my eyes. Why was I even thinking about this? Why couldn't I live in a nice world like everyone else?

So many questions.

I turned away from the window. Jones was standing in the kitchen, arms folded, leaning against the worktop, waiting for me to speak. I was his expert witness. That was why he was here today.

I said, 'Have there been many deaths?'

'Enough.'

'And they all died the same way?'

'Similar, yes.'

'I don't think the drug actually calls up ghosts – who are often quite sad and harmless. Look at poor little Sammy. He's never going to do any harm to anyone. No – that's just the sales pitch. *How would you like to talk to your mother again? See your dead child again? Hold your lost lover again?* That's the selling point. People take the drug willingly – having paid a fortune for it, as you said. But you don't get the loving relatives and happy experience you've been promised. You open the door

224

and a demon comes through. You get terror and an agonising death instead. You scream as a demon sits on your chest and eats you alive.'

My voice had died to a whisper. The implications were too horrific to contemplate. If enough people took this drug ... never mind how many demons had come through already ... Suppose one day, too many people opened the door and the door remained open and could never be closed? What would come through then? What was actually on the other side?

'Hey,' said a voice. 'Come back.'

I came back.

'Talk to me, Cage.'

'Is that recorder still off?'

'Yes.'

'Good. I don't want to talk myself into a mental establishment.'

'You won't. I've got your back every inch of the way. Talk to me.'

I did my best to present my fears in some sort of coherent form.

At the end, he said softly, 'That would account for a lot.'

He sat for a moment, drumming his fingers on the worktop. 'Cage, do you remember when we talked about working together?'

'Yes.'

'Would you consider something similar but different?'

'How different?'

'You said you'd never work for Sorensen. Does that still apply?'

'Yes.'

225

'Would you consider working for my boss? With me, of course. Before you say anything, she's not Sorensen and I'd like you to consider it.'

'Why?' An unexpected crash of thunder made me jump. The storm was coming back. 'How long have you known all this? You don't seem surprised by any of it.'

'Being with you has reconciled me to stuff I would never have believed two years ago, but yes, I do know about this. Some of it, anyway. As I said, your man out there wasn't the first. This is happening all over and we've been baffled. Ghost itself appears to be harmless and we couldn't work out what was actually killing its users.'

'It isn't Ghost that kills them.'

'So it would seem. But if people hadn't taken Ghost . . .'

I nodded. 'They wouldn't have died.'

'Allenby's official cause of death will be heart attack,' he continued. 'Tell me, this thing that followed him – you said it didn't approach or attack him until he was actually on the ground?'

'No, it was so spindly and weak-looking it might not have had the strength. I remember it took an effort to climb on to Mr Allenby's chest. My impression was that it waited until he was too weak to fight it off. And it was starving . . .'

'And then what? Tell me again.'

'It just gorged itself on his colour. Gobbled it up.' I made grabbing motions with my hand.

'How long did it take?'

'Half a minute – perhaps a little longer.'

'Cage, I want to tell all this to my boss. I'd like to arrange a meeting between the two of you.'

'She'll never believe me.'

'She's read Sorensen's report on you and she had me in for half an hour the other day to talk about you. She'll believe you.'

I didn't want to. I could see me talking myself into some sort of asylum. I sought to evade the issue. 'I don't want to go to London.'

'She'll come here.'

'Isn't Rushford a bit out of the way? I would have thought London . . .'

'Ask any police officer – the drug problem isn't centred on the major metropolises. It's the small market towns that are the problem. The sleepy, respectable places where no one suspects a thing.'

'Do you know where it's being manufactured?'

He shook his head. 'There's not a lot on the market for us to trace back. We think it must be difficult and expensive to produce. But, sooner or later, someone will work out how to do it quicker and cheaper, and once that happens, then we'll all be in trouble. That's why we have to stop this before it gets out of hand.'

'And you really think this is happening in Rushford?'

'Rushford is one of several places being investigated, yes.'

'Well, if sleepy and respectable are the criteria, then Rushford is probably the drug capital of the world.'

'This isn't the first case here,' he said. 'And with me being mostly on the spot, they've rescinded their offer of a year's sabbatical and I'm back on the strength again. With you, I very much hope. Will you meet my boss and at least listen to what she has to say?'

I couldn't resist. 'Will I be bringing you in from the cold?'

'What?'

'Isn't that what you say? In from the cold?'

'No, I don't, and yes, it might. Look, you don't have to commit yourself yet but will you at least consider it?'

I said uncertainly, 'I suppose so.'

He came round the worktop to stand by me. 'I've got your back. You know that.'

I nodded.

'You won't regret it.'

I nodded again.

'Cage, I have to say – you are not looking good.'

'No. That business with Lady Torrington. The Painswicks going missing. Poor little Sammy. Then there was the thing Iblis saw on my porch. And now this – it's a bit much, don't you agree? I can't help thinking . . .'

'What?'

'Do you remember the witch's ladder Iblis found last summer? When I was convinced I was cursed?'

He nodded. 'I do, but it was destroyed. Iblis burned it at Greyston.'

'I know, but the point I'm making is not the witch's ladder itself, but who put it there. We never found that out.'

Jones hesitated.

'And I heard what Iblis said to you about the darkness.'

'Well, you know what he's like. If anyone's one sandwich short of a picnic, it's him, don't you think?'

'Melek was here the other day and she said something similar. That there is a darkness around me. And she's right; I can feel it.'

'Don't take this the wrong way, Cage, but could you feel it before she mentioned it?'

'I've felt it for some time now. When we came back to Rush-

228

ford, I had a sense of something different. Nothing major . . .
it's just . . . oh, I don't know.' I began to pace around the room.
'Why does this happen to me? And it's getting worse. I can't
go anywhere, meet anyone, do anything, without something
unpleasant leaping out from the woodwork. It's exhausting,
Jones. It never stops. I don't want to see what people are
thinking, I don't want to know if they're lying or not. I don't
even *care* if they're lying. Why can't I just be normal? Why
do . . . ?'

'Hey,' he said, 'hush.' He put his arm around me; I struggled
for a moment but it was like trying to shift a mountain. Neither
he nor his arm moved even a fraction of an inch and in the end,
I just gave up and did what I wanted to do, which was to lean
against him and let him take my weight for a blessed moment
or two. The minutes stretched on and on and all the time the
rain still fell.

After a while I said, 'Shouldn't you be dashing off somewhere to save the world?'

'No,' he said and kissed the top of my head.

I closed my eyes and we stood some more. Slowly, I calmed
down. My heart rate dropped to something approaching normal.
The sound of the rain was soothing. He was warm and solid.
My breathing slowed. Gradually I began to feel better.

After a while I felt I should pull away, but he tightened his
grip. 'Where are you going?'

I considered the question and came to the conclusion I wasn't
really going anywhere. Nor did I want to. There wasn't anywhere else I'd rather be.

I said, 'Nowhere.'

'Just to give you something positive to think about, Cage, I should tell you that your continual attempts to get me into bed are beginning to bear fruit. Keep this up and I'll definitely be putting you on my list.'

'Really,' I said comfortably. 'It's good to know my hard work is paying off.'

'Yes. Who'd have thought.' He paused. 'Do you remember that Margaret Thatcher outfit you wore in the summer?'

I sighed. He would remember that, wouldn't he? An old-fashioned suit in a particularly unattractive shade of blue with just the wrong length hemline. I'd been embarrassed to be seen wearing it in public. Jones had been semi-conscious at the time but it had obviously made a bigger impact on him than I'd realised.

'And you had these strange brown legs,' he continued dreamily.

'American Tan tights.'

'Incredibly sexy.'

'Incredibly weird.'

'So, no chance of . . . ?'

'None whatsoever. I threw them at an oil drum.'

He sighed. 'Just thought I'd mention it.'

CHAPTER FIFTEEN

He left shortly afterwards, telling me I was balanced and sane again – or as close as I was ever going to get anyway – and he wanted to talk to his boss. I was commanded to have something to eat and an early night. I pointed out it was only about half past six and he just laughed. Actually, he wasn't wrong. Suddenly my bed seemed a great place to be. A refuge from the world. I would make myself some cocoa – I had some in the pantry somewhere – pick up my book and take myself off upstairs.

I put on the TV to listen to the news while I waited for the milk to boil. I love cocoa – it reminds me of my dad. He used to make me a mug of cocoa every night. I don't know how he did it but it was always thick and frothy and gorgeous. I try but I can't ever get it anything like that. I miss my dad. I wondered what he would think of Melek. And Iblis. And Jerry. And especially of Michael Jones. On the other hand, he'd always seemed to take most things in his stride, so he'd probably deal with it in his usual way by disappearing down to his shed, to be surrounded by the wood he loved to work with.

I listened to the news with half an ear, concentrating on the milk because burned milk is horrible. And the skin is pretty yukky too, so I had to time it just right.

I poured out the milk, stirring vigorously, and put the spoon and saucepan in to soak. The TV droned on. Lots of people were talking. It would seem there had been some sort of diplomatic row – our politicians had been more than normally inept – and now half a dozen countries weren't speaking to us. *Tense international situation* said the subtitles across the bottom of the screen. I should pay attention because, apparently, lessons had been learned, but I couldn't be bothered. I picked up the remote to switch off the TV and went to bed.

Perhaps it was the good night's sleep that did it. Perhaps, during the night, something slotted into place. I woke early, stared at the grey light sneaking through the gap in the curtains, stretched, yawned, and suddenly realised what it was about Caroline's suicide note that had been scratching at the edge of my mind.

I rolled over, picked up the phone and hit speed dial. 'Jones?'

He groaned. 'This is what you do, isn't it? You can't sleep so no one else is allowed to, either.'

'I know what it is about the note.'

'Cage, you've woken me from my much-needed beauty sleep. Most of me is not yet functioning properly. Could you be less elliptic?'

'Caroline's note. I know what was wrong with it. Well, not the note – the envelope.'

'I'm just going to close my eyes while you inch your way towards the point of this call. Wake me when you're ready.'

'The postcode was different.'

He sighed down the phone. 'You mean she wrote the wrong postcode?'

'No. I mean it was different handwriting. Not hugely, but not quite the same. It's difficult to tell in block capitals, but the "R" was slightly different.'

There was silence at the other end of the phone. Either he was thinking or he'd lapsed into unconsciousness again.

I told him to wake up and concentrate. 'Her writing was big and loopy, do you remember? With lots of curly flourishes on the capital letters. Although she didn't actually dot her i's with little hearts, she made such a business of swirling the "R" in Rushford that she'd left very little room for the postcode underneath. Remember? It was crammed in at the bottom. Because there wasn't enough space left for it.'

'Mm.'

'Well, I don't know if this is important, but I don't think it was Caroline who wrote the postcode.'

There was a very, very long silence. 'Cage, I'll call you back.'

I stared at the phone but he'd gone.

I closed my eyes but sleep had fled. And to be honest I'd just had eleven hours of it anyway.

I had a long bath, tried a new way of doing my hair, didn't like it, and went back to the old, safe, familiar style – remembered to moisturise for once – and changed the sheets. Then I dressed and went downstairs, opened the back door to let in some fresh air and drew back the curtains to check the weather. Everywhere was very wet but a weak sun was shining and about time too.

The café/bakery would be opening soon and I thought I'd pop over, treat myself to something fattening in the brioche area, make myself a mug of really good coffee and just gently ease myself into the day. The sun was shining, but the day was cold. I'd stay inside, put the fire on, and just read the day away.

Yes, I could do that. I paused. The only thing missing from that picture was a cat. I could get a cat to doze in front of the fire.

Actually, no, I couldn't. Animals don't like me very much. We never had pets when I was a child. They don't actually growl or spit at me – they just keep their distance. And they watch me. And then they melt away.

I'd had Nigel here, though, and he'd liked me. Well, he'd allowed me to feed him and put the fire on for him to sleep in front of, which wasn't quite the same thing, but it was a start. Perhaps I could find a cat who would tolerate me. Something for me to think about.

I was still staring out of the window and thinking about it when Jones knocked at the door.

I opened it up to see him standing there with a bag full of fragrant bakery products. I opened my mouth to welcome him and didn't get the chance.

'Cage, what have I told you about answering your door?'

'I don't know. You're always complaining about something. I don't really listen.'

'You didn't know it was me. I could have been just anyone.'

'You are just anyone, but I knew it was you.'

'You shouldn't rely on . . .'

'I saw you coming across the green when I looked out of the window.'

'Basic error, Cage. You saw me coming across the green and assumed that it must be me at the door.'

'Of course it was you at the door. You're so tall you block out the light from the transom. And you always use the same knock. And I watched you walking up the steps. So, unless something happened to you in the last three feet of your journey

– it was you knocking at my door. For reasons which have yet to be ascertained.'

'Well, if I could get a word in edgeways, I'd tell you.'

I closed the door behind him. He flourished the bag. 'Breakfast.'

He laid the table while I poured the coffee, and we sat down.

'You look better,' he said, plastering his croissant with jam. 'Did you sleep well?'

I nodded. 'Yes, I did. I feel much better. Still beset with problems and anxieties, but not actually overwhelmed by anything specific just at this moment.'

'Good.' He munched and swallowed. 'Do you fancy confronting James Monroe this morning?'

I put down my coffee. 'You've discovered how he did it?'

'No, Cage, you discovered how he did it. Which is why I thought you might like to be in at the death. If you want to, of course.'

I thought of little Sammy, living in the wall. 'Yes, I would, because it's not just about James and his wickedness. Will you actually arrest him?'

'No, the police will do that. We don't want him getting away because of procedural irregularities, do we? I shall simply tell him how he did it, step back and let the law take its course. And then, afterwards, when you're astounded and impressed with my triumph, I'd like to introduce you to my boss.'

'She's here?'

'She is. Well, she will be.'

'That was quick.'

'Do you want that last croissant?'

'Yes,' I said and might as well have spared my breath.

235

'She's very keen to meet you.'

I nodded. 'You said there would be no commitment.'

'I did and there isn't. And, if it makes you feel any better, she might not like *you* and you'll have gone through all this anxiety for nothing.'

I was actually quite indignant. 'Why wouldn't she like me?'

'Not everyone is as tolerant as me, Cage. In fact, I rather wonder if I haven't spoiled you for other people. You know, raised your expectations of the human race beyond the realms of that achievable by lesser mortals.'

'What will you do if we both can't stand the sight of each other and you find yourself in the middle of a feminine fracas?'

He swallowed the last of his croissant. 'Run away. That's why I'm building up my strength for the ordeal. Shall we go and spoil James Monroe's day first?'

I looked at the clock. 'It's a bit early. He'll only just be opening.'

'All the better.'

'Why?'

'Are you going to ask questions all day, Cage, or are you going to get your coat on?'

The gallery was open – to catch the early bird art buyer, I assumed – and James Monroe was sitting at his desk opening the morning mail.

He looked up as we entered, professional charm oozing from every pore. 'Michael, Elizabeth – how lovely to see you. What brings you here? Cordy's here somewhere. I'll give her a shout.'

'I wouldn't,' said Jones, holding out a chair for me to sit. I was thrilled at this unusual show of consideration until I realised he was using me to block one of Monroe's possible escape routes. Jones himself took up a position near the window and peered outside. Apparently satisfied at what he saw, without any sort of preamble, he said, 'You were supposed to find her, weren't you? That was how she staged it. You were supposed to race around to the gallery and discover her just in time. You would save her life. There would be a big romantic scene. You would be her hero. A June wedding with all the trimmings. A happy ending for you both.'

He folded his arms. 'But, unfortunately, that didn't happen. Because by now you'd got rather tired of Caroline. I should imagine you found her quite heavy going, emotionally. All that exhausting grief and remorse over Sammy. Yes, you had to endure a certain amount of it – your own business was failing and you needed a way in, to both Caroline and her gallery, didn't you? But things weren't getting any easier with her and the prospect of being shackled for ever to an emotional vampire was not something you were looking forward to. But – all credit to you – you stuck with it. A single woman, well-off and with a nice little business who adored you. The admiration of all as you supported her through this tragic time. All that really appealed to your vanity, didn't it, so yes, you could make it work. And it would have. You'd probably even have gone along with the dramatic last-minute rescue because that would have made you look really good. And looking good is what you're all about, isn't it, James? That and enjoying the best things in life without really having to work for them.'

James Monroe was on his feet. 'What on earth is going on here? How dare you . . .'

I could have told him he was wasting his time. Very little can stop Michael Jones once he gets going.

'But – sadly for Caroline – by then you'd met Cordelia.'

I glanced towards the back of the gallery. No sign of Cordelia anywhere. Someone else was coming, though. Caroline was on her way. Because this was what she'd been screaming about all this time. Her murder by James Monroe.

I didn't have to concentrate this time. She materialised directly in front of James. Her head and shoulders were strong and clearly defined. I suspected her hatred for James Monroe was giving her the strength she needed. But she wasn't screaming now. She was listening. As if she knew this was her time for revenge.

Jones was ploughing on. 'Talented, pretty, charming, *rich* Cordelia. A much better bet than Caroline and she also showed every sign of being in love with you. And the irony is – you fell deeply in love with her. If it hadn't been for the now inconvenient Caroline, everything would have been perfect. And there was no way you could ever ditch Caroline. She would never go quietly. She'd make a hell of a stink and everyone would hate you. You'd have been finished in this town. Caroline would see to that. How you must have wracked your brains for a way of getting her out of your life that didn't make you look the complete bastard you actually are. And then, one day, after a particularly heavy week, emotionally speaking, Caroline's suicide note was delivered.'

'Yes,' said James Monroe. 'That's right. It came to my office.'

'No, it didn't.'

'Yes, it did,' shouted Monroe. 'Everyone knows that. Sandra – my office manager – was there. She saw it delivered. By the postman.'

'I'm sure she did,' said Jones. 'But we both know Caroline

238

left the letter by hand on Friday afternoon. She wasn't going to run the risk of you not getting the letter in time to save her. She waited until everything was quiet and then nipped in and left it in reception. You were supposed to discover the letter, race round to her place, find her attractively but not fatally laid out on her bed, phone the emergency services, and save her life. Huge congratulations to you, massive gratitude from her, lovely happy ending. But, by the greatest good luck for you and the greatest bad luck for her, you found the letter when the office was empty and there were no witnesses.

'You put the letter back in the envelope – luckily for you she hadn't sealed it because it was hand-delivered and envelope glue tastes awful. You sealed it up, found a first-class stamp, nipped out while no one was around and shoved it in the postbox at the end of the street. And then you quite cold-bloodedly carried on with your day while, on the other side of town, Caroline slipped slowly into the next world. You knew she'd left you the gallery. All your problems solved and at absolutely no risk to yourself because everything about the note was genuine. Except she hadn't added the postcode.'

He smiled. 'Personally, I'd have taken the chance and left it off – and I imagine you thought about that for a long time – but no postcode meant a possible delayed delivery. If it was delivered at all. And you needed witnesses, didn't you, James? Witnesses to you receiving the letter, witnesses who could testify they'd been with you since before Caroline died. You'd have been bound to have a couple of her gallery pens around your office somewhere. The same type as the one she used to write her note with. Five seconds to add the postcode and solve all your problems and then you could have it all.'

Monroe stared from me to Jones and back to me again, his face a picture of bewilderment, grief and a dawning anger. An innocent man. Except his colour said differently. More purple than brown, it stabbed at Jones in a typical fight or flight reflex. Orange anxiety curdled around the edges. But his face showed only the agitation of a man unjustly accused. His voice rang with sincerity. 'I swear to you – none of this is true. She killed herself. She was found in her bedroom with a bottle of whisky and some pills. You don't have to take my word for it – talk to the two police officers who were with me at the time.'

'James?'

Cordelia had appeared, brush in one hand, paint rag in the other. I suspected she'd been round the corner, listening. 'James – what's happening? Is this true?'

He controlled himself and turned to face her. 'Of course not, Cordy. There's never been any doubt that Caroline killed herself.'

Jones shook his head. 'No, I'm sorry to have to tell you this, Miss Channing, but James killed Caroline Fairbrother. Didn't you, James?'

James Monroe folded his arms. 'No, I did not. Everything happened just as I told you. Sandra handed me the post. There was no sleight of hand involved. Caroline's letter was on the top. She saw it.'

'I don't doubt it. I'm sure if she hadn't, you would have called her attention to it somehow. And then you open it up, make very sure she sees the contents, race to your car, drive like a madman, collect a couple of very useful police witnesses and arrive to try to save the woman you knew had been dead since Friday night.'

'How? How am I supposed to have killed Caroline?'

'Well, I should imagine you stared at the perfectly genuine suicide note and then . . . .' Jones stopped.

'Yes,' said Cordelia. 'Then what, James?'

'Cordy . . . you can't possibly believe . . .'

But she did. Or at least, if she didn't actually believe Jones, then she certainly doubted James. Her colour had lost a lot of its sparkle. The outline wavered uncertainly. I suspected she was looking at James and asking herself whether he really was capable of something that cold-blooded. From the look on her face, the answer, perhaps, was yes.

Jones was talking to Cordelia. Not without a certain amount of sympathy. 'It's a perfect plan. It was a Friday. By the time the letter arrived on Monday morning, Caroline would be long dead. And even if anyone noticed the different writing on the envelope, they would simply assume that she'd been too upset to bother with the postcode or couldn't remember it and Royal Mail had added it themselves. A foolproof plan and very, very clever.'

He turned to James Monroe and suddenly his voice was different. His colour darkened to a deeper red. 'Tell me, James, did you have any qualms at all as you pushed the letter into the postbox? Such a simple action to condemn a woman to death.'

'I didn't,' shouted Monroe. 'I mean, I didn't do it. What you said. Caroline's death was a nightmare but it was suicide. The coroner said so. Everyone did. Who are you to say any different?'

Jones ignored him. 'A simple but brilliant plan, flawlessly executed. Everyone says, "Poor woman – what a tragedy." There's never the slightest shadow of suspicion to fall on you,

241

James, and you now have a nice little business and a clear path to the woman you really want – Cordelia.'

James Monroe drew himself up. He had himself well in hand now. That brief moment of stabbing panic was over. His colour had settled about him, stronger and deeper. 'You can't prove any of this.'

'Oh, I think I can.'

'And how do you propose to do that?'

Jones grinned at him. 'Tell me you weren't stupid enough to lick the envelope.'

A deep silence. James's face said it all. As did his colour, dark and dirty. The purple had almost disappeared. Even the brown was being slowly submerged. I suspected James was one of those people who are fine as long as everything is going their way and definitely aren't fine when it's not. Terror was flowing through him as he realised his mistake.

Jones smiled with satisfaction. 'Well, there you are, then. The police have the envelope and are already testing it for DNA.' He opened the shop door. 'Ready when you are, officers.'

Two policemen entered.

'This is all a terrible mistake,' said Monroe, desperately. He seemed unsure whether to tell this to the policemen, Jones, or a shocked Cordelia. 'It's a dreadful mistake. I'm innocent, I swear.'

Unseen and unheard by everyone except me, Caroline had started to laugh. She laughed as she had screamed. Wide-mouthed. Loud and raucous, it hurt my ears. Her face was full of bitterness and the triumph of revenge. She laughed and laughed. Her laughter was even more unpleasant than her screaming.

They led Monroe out of the shop. Cordelia ran into the back

room. Whether to fetch her coat and go with them or just to be alone, I didn't know. There wasn't anything I could do for her but there was one more thing I could do for Sammy.

'I'm in this unofficially,' said Jones, 'but I think I'd better go with them to tie up any loose ends. I'll call you about the meeting with my boss. Will you be all right to get home?'

I nodded. I would. I had unfinished business here and I definitely didn't want any witnesses.

The gallery door closed behind him.

The ghost was still laughing. Wild, hysterical laughter that would have choked a mortal person.

I said, 'Outside, you. Now.'

The wind was cool in my hair and the fresh air was welcome. I sat on the wall. No one was around, but in case anyone was looking out of their windows, I took out my phone so people would think I was making a call and not just talking to thin air.

I turned to Caroline. 'Poetic justice, don't you think? You killed little Sammy for him and then he killed you.'

She stopped laughing.

'You've stopped laughing, Caroline. Isn't the joke funny any longer? It's a shame you and James didn't get together, don't you agree? I think you would have made rather a precious pair. I wonder who would have killed the other first?'

She looked at me and her eyes were full of malice. I was too angry to care.

'Don't give me that look. You killed your sister's little boy because you thought he was standing between you and James Monroe, but it was nothing to do with him. James was already tiring of you. Once he'd met Cordelia – with whom he is genuinely in love – there was no chance for you, Sammy or no Sammy. But you couldn't or wouldn't believe that. You pushed – no, you *threw* Sammy down the cellar steps. You thought killing a little boy would clear your path to James Monroe and all it did was clear the path to your own death. Yes, you're right. It is funny. Why aren't you laughing any more, Caroline?'

Her voice was a whisper. 'Who are you?'

I shrugged. No one knew the answer to that question, least of all me. 'And cruellest of all – you've kept him from his mother all this time and he's just a little boy.'

I could feel my temper rising and for once I made no attempt to swallow it down.

'*You made him live in a wall!*'

I am not a nice person when I'm angry and sometimes I don't care. She shrank from me. I could see the fear in her eyes and hear it in her voice and it pleased me. I would make her more than fear me.

She shrank from me, gabbling. 'No . . . I . . . No.' Her outline began to waver. She was fading in front of my eyes. Whether she was moving on because James had finally got his just deserts, or whether she was going back to wherever she'd been lurking, I didn't know. Normally I wouldn't have cared but she deserved something special and I would give it to her.

'*Caroline Fairbrother, I tie you to this place.*'

For a moment she was silent and then my words registered. She started to scream again. Tough.

'I tie you to this place. You may not depart. You will remain here. In this wall. Until there is nothing left of you.'

Her pretty, weak face was convulsed with fear. 'You cannot tie me. You would not be so cruel.'

244

'Yes, I would,' I said. 'Into the wall, Caroline Fairbrother. And never come out.'

Slowly, reluctantly, as if she was being dragged, she began to fade into the wall. But, being Caroline, she managed to have the last word. 'You don't want to cross her. Neither you nor . . .' She gestured. I was unsure who she meant – Jones? – but at that moment it wasn't important.

'*Into the wall*.'

She went. She had no choice.

I took a few breaths and then said softly, 'Are you here, Sammy? You can come out now.'

He stood by my knee, thumb in his mouth, very small in his Spider-Man pyjamas.

'Hello, Sammy.'

He smiled at me around his thumb.

'Sammy, I've been thinking. You don't want to stay here, do you? Not any longer?'

He shook his head. 'Cold.'

'Well, I wondered if you'd like to come home with me. It's warm and you can sit in the window and watch the people on the green. There will be children there as well, and you can look at the ducks and the swans and we can talk to each other. You needn't be alone any longer, Sammy. Would you like to? Come home with me, I mean.'

He took his thumb out of his mouth. 'Mummy.'

'No,' I said sadly. 'I'm not your mummy. But I could be your friend. Would you like that?'

'Mummy.'

I shook my head. 'I'm not your mummy, Sammy.'

'Mummy.'

I suddenly realised what he was saying and looked over my shoulder. I could see the shadowy outline of a young girl in her very early twenties, wearing a black sweatshirt and leggings, racing down the road, her ponytail flying out behind her.

'Sammy.'

'Mummy.'

He hurled himself at her and she caught him, holding him tight. 'Oh, Sammy.' She turned to me. If she'd been alive, she would have been breathless. 'Thank you. She kept me out. I couldn't come.' She looked around. I could see her fear. 'I have to go. Thank you, thank you.'

I had no chance to speak. Sammy smiled and said, 'Bye-bye,' and then they were gone.

Tears ran down my face all the way home.

CHAPTER SIXTEEN

When I got home there was a message on my answerphone. 'Cage, can you get yourself to the Copper Kettle this afternoon? Two o'clock.'

That was it. No *please* or *thank you*. Or *if it's convenient*. Just that terse message.

I was quite aggrieved but told myself he had a lot on at the moment. And if he was instrumental in convicting James Monroe, then he could be as terse as he liked. And Sammy was free.

I went to a drawer and pulled out the small toy rabbit I'd bought because . . . well, because. A little blue one with a big smiley face. Somehow it seemed wrong to throw it away. I should give it to a charity shop. A small child somewhere would love it.

I looked at the clock. Not long and then I'd have to go back out again. Should I change? My mother would insist I wore something smart. I looked up at the sky. It was going to rain again. I'd stay as I was.

The Copper Kettle is on the High Street. It's a very nice café. They do a great afternoon tea there. Occasionally I treat myself. Well, actually, I sit alone at a table and tell myself this is a very pleasant way to spend an afternoon, which isn't quite the same thing. Both Iblis and Melek had said there was a darkness about me and I was beginning to wonder if it wasn't self-inflicted.

I paused outside the Copper Kettle and tried to peer in through the window. I couldn't see Jones anywhere but it was beginning to rain again so I decided I'd go inside and wait for him there.

I was actually surprised at how nervous I felt. Very nervous, actually. And apprehensive. I'd only ever had one job interview in my life – when I went to work for the council – and it hadn't been anything like this. I wondered who had selected this venue. This nice, unthreatening, neutral venue. Jones probably. I wondered how badly they wanted me to work for them. *With* them, rather. I must remember to make that clear. And there was no need for me to be nervous – if I didn't like what I heard, then I could politely say no. In fact, I probably would say no. But, if I did that, what would happen then? Would they let me just walk away? I could be stumbling into exactly the sort of situation my dad had always warned me to avoid. And suppose Jones's boss turned out to be another Sorensen. Why was I doing this?

I'd been heading towards the entrance but now my feet slowed and then stopped. Why *was* I doing this?

I looked up and down the street. Everything looked exactly normal. People hurried past with their shopping. Two drivers argued over a parking space. A dog, tied to a lamppost, lay down, his nose on his paws, waiting patiently for his owner's return. No one was looking at me or paying attention in any way.

The rain made up my mind for me. I took a breath, opened the door and went in. The Copper Kettle was surprisingly empty. It's popular and, given the weather, I would have thought it would be busier. I paused and, under the pretence of furling my umbrella, I let my mind drift a little, just to see if there was anything . . . wet . . . steamy windows . . . the smell of coffee . . . No, nothing. I shoved my umbrella into the stand and looked around. There was no sign of Michael Jones anywhere.

I'd assumed he'd meet me here and make the introductions, and now it looked as if that wasn't going to happen. For a moment I considered going home again and then I looked back at the weather outside. No, I wasn't voluntarily going back out there in that rain. Not until I'd had something warm to drink, anyway. I'd wait here, in the coffee-smelling warmth, to see what happened next.

There were plenty of available tables. So many, in fact, that they'd taken away the *Please Wait Here to Be Seated* sign. I looked around. There was a shabby middle-aged woman sitting in the back corner. She looked as if she was resting her feet before setting off to her next cleaning job. At another table, a much more smartly dressed woman in a business suit was peering at her iPad. Two men sat at one of the tables by the window. One was reading a newspaper while the other was checking his phone. A lone waiter hovered behind the counter wiping down one of the coffee machines. There was no sign of Jones anywhere. Why wasn't he here?

I walked up to the counter, ordered myself a coffee and then turned to the shabby woman in the corner. 'Can I get you another coffee while we wait for Michael Jones?'

For a moment she didn't move and I had a brief panic when I wondered if I'd got the wrong person. Had I been too clever? No, I hadn't. She might look like a tired and overworked cleaner but there was a strength and authority to her. Her colour was a brilliant yellow. Not a golden sunshine yellow but a clear, radiant, almost acid yellow. I'd seen this colour before but never so rich and so deep. And so strong. Even in its resting state it extended a good twelve inches from her body, gently swirling. There was a secondary colour in there somewhere. Soft tendrils of cream flickered occasionally, but mostly she was yellow. And when you got past the dull complexion, the old mac, the sensible shoes and the slightly saggy cardigan, there was a disconcerting intelligence in those tired eyes. I wondered if she always dressed like this. Whether this was her method of disarming the opposition. Or had she just dressed down for me? In which case I was a little bit offended.

She looked up, completely unsurprised. 'Thank you, yes. A flat white, please.'

I carried both across to her table and sat down. We regarded each other for a moment and then she looked over my shoulder and said, 'Thank you, everyone.'

Without a word, the smart woman shut down her iPad, went to the door and flipped the *Closed* sign. Then she slipped out of the door and stood on the other side. On guard.

Meanwhile, the two men had walked behind the counter and, again without a word spoken, they and the waiter slipped through a door into the back of the café and disappeared. People were still walking past the windows but the shabby woman and I were completely alone. Isolated. I tried not to feel unnerved.

She seemed in no hurry to begin, stirring her coffee and watching it swirl around her cup.

I was determined not to speak first. I sipped my own excellent coffee and waited.

She replaced her cup in the saucer. 'Good afternoon, Mrs Cage.' Her voice was lovely. Deep and melodious.

250

'Good afternoon . . . ?' I made it a question.

She appeared to think for a moment. 'Mary Bennet.'

I couldn't help smiling. 'The always overlooked and under-rated sister. Good choice.'

'Thank you. And thank you for the coffee.'

'You're welcome. Is Mr Jones to be present or is he just late?'

'I've asked him to give us twenty minutes to talk alone. Shall we begin?'

I nodded and sipped my coffee again. I was even more nervous now because whoever she was, she wasn't Sorensen. I would have to tread much more carefully with this woman. Winding up Sorensen was fun. Winding up Mary Bennet would be unwise.

'Mrs Cage, I know you have only thought in terms of us harming you, but I would like to start with a difficult question, which I ask because I must know if you are able to harm *us*.'

I waited because I knew what was coming.

'Do you think you could kill someone just by thinking about it?'

On the verge of an indignant denial, I paused and took a breath. 'No. No, I don't think so. I couldn't look at you and think, *Die now*, and you would drop down dead.'

She smiled slightly. 'Well, that's a relief.'

But I could bring this building down on top of her. I could hurl her across the room and break her bones. I could bury the world in angry snow. And all without moving from this seat. I pushed those thoughts away.

She placed her cup carefully in her saucer. 'Do you think you could influence someone to do something, perhaps?'

'Against their will?'

251

'Possibly.'

'I don't know.'

She smiled a surprisingly sweet smile. 'Please do not feel alarmed or hostile, Mrs Cage. I am not Philip Sorensen. I have no intention of committing either of us to something with which we would not be comfortable. This is simply a chat to explore the possibility – or not – of us working together.'

I tried to relax. 'To answer your question more fully – no, I don't think I could force someone to do something against their will.'

As I spoke, I saw a picture of Caroline's terrified face as I forced her into the wall. I pushed it away. She wasn't a living person.

'Nor would I try. Let me be very clear. I only read what is happening in front of me. I can't hold an object and tell you where and when someone was murdered. I can't look at you and tell you you'll be involved with a tall dark stranger and money will come your way on Friday. That's not how it works. I can tell you whether you're scared or lying or happy. I can interpret the way you interact with others or to circumstances around you. Sometimes I see other things – things I don't want to. I have no control over that, and if you want me to force it then we'll have to part company now because that's dangerous. I can't and won't intimidate people. I won't tell people what to do or what to say. If this is a deal-breaker for you, I'm sorry – but all I do is see things.'

She nodded as if she'd known all this already. 'Obviously I've read Mr Jones's reports and we've discussed it together, but I'd like to hear it from you, Mrs Cage, if you please. How exactly do you work?'

I took a moment to try to be coherent. Not to gabble with embarrassment. Nor to downplay what I do or apologise for it, but simply to state everything as a matter of fact.

'Every living thing has a colour. Which I can see. That colour reacts to events around it. I can read that. And not just the colour itself, but the way it shapes itself and moves around you. It tells me things. For instance, my neighbour is unwell. Her colour is fading. I don't think she has much time left. I can use people's colour to interpret their moods. I can tell whether they're happy or sad. Or frightened. Or angry.'

'Or lying,' she said.

I nodded. 'Usually. I can tell you when they're anxious, although I may not always be able to tell you what they're anxious about.'

'Is it possible to fake it, do you think?'

'Could I fake it?'

'No, your subject. Could they control their emotions in such a way that you either can't read them or misinterpret them somehow?'

'That's possible,' I said. 'I met a young woman recently and I couldn't read her at all. I was only with her for a few minutes so I don't know if she was suppressing her emotions somehow – although I don't think she was – or whether she wasn't actually experiencing any emotion for me to read.'

'Which in itself would be quite revealing, don't you think?'

I thought of Leanne Elphick. 'Yes. Hers was not a . . . a normal colour. I knew as soon as I saw her.'

She nodded. 'And what else can you do?'

I suspected she knew everything. Michael Jones would have given her a full briefing. And Sorensen's file would, I guessed, have made very interesting reading. I decided on almost complete disclosure. With luck it might put her off.

I said carefully, 'Sometimes I can sense things. I can let my mind drift and see what it can pick up. That isn't always successful. Or, I see something but interpret it incorrectly. That has happened. Especially when I'm tired. Or sometimes, something is so strong it forces its way into my head whether I want it to or not. Once, two little boys were doing something they very definitely shouldn't. They were terrified and their combined fear woke me out of a deep sleep.'

She nodded, staring at her cup, thinking about what I'd told her.

I was ready for her next question. 'What's my colour?'

'Yellow.'

She pulled a face. 'My least favourite colour.'

I resisted the urge to apologise.

'Is yellow good?'

'There are no good colours and bad colours. Black is not bad. White is not necessarily good. People are not easily classified and neither are their colours. It's how the colour reacts – its shape, its strength, its movement.'

She regarded me for a moment and then said, 'So how am I feeling right now?'

Stifling the urge to say, 'Don't you know?' I looked at what her colour was telling me. 'Tired. Worried. Uncertain. Apprehensive. Sceptical.'

'I would have thought all of that could easily be extrapolated from the subject of today's meeting.'

'You see,' I said, trying to be clever. 'You don't need me after all.'

I'd given her the perfect opening. 'Actually, I rather think we do, Mrs Cage. I'd like to talk about the other day. I've listened to Mr Jones's tape but now I'd like to hear from you. Please can you tell me what you saw?'

'You mean when Mr Allenby died?'

'Yes. What exactly did you see?'

I clasped my hands and focused. Once again, I was peering through the rain at a running man with a dark shape, at one and the same time visible but not visible, always at his shoulder. I told her how I saw him fall. How the thing – I called it a demon to her face and she never flinched – how it squatted on his chest and stared into his face as it ate Mr Allenby's colour, mouthful by mouthful, tearing it into pieces and stuffing it into his mouth until there was nothing left and he died.

Afterwards she was silent for a very long time. Then she pushed her cup and saucer away. I could tell from her colour she'd made her decision.

'Mrs Cage, I would very much like you to come and work with me on this problem.' She held up her hand even though I hadn't even tried to speak. 'I know your arguments and they are sound. I've read the file Philip Sorensen has on you and I can quite understand your aversion to public exposure. I can assure you of complete confidentiality, so, in an effort to allay your fears, I propose the following:

'You would have the right to decline any assignment in which you didn't wish to be involved. You would work closely with Michael Jones and no other. If you wish, you need have no direct contact with any of the people or events we would like you to observe. You could work from a monitor . . .'

I shook my head. 'I'm sorry – that won't work. I have to be able to see the subject directly.'

'Then we shall provide a separate observation room for you – whatever you need. The point is that at no time will you be exposed. Your abilities would not be discussed with anyone outside of a small number of my own people. To everyone else, you would merely be another consultant. You may withdraw your services at any time you are not actually in the middle of an assignment. You would not be bound in any way. Apart from confidentiality, of course. I'm sure you understand that goes without saying.'

I shook my head. 'I'm fine with the right to decline any assignment I don't want to undertake, but I would also want the right to withdraw from it at any time.'

She hesitated.

'I might not like where you're going with something and not want to be involved,' I said.

'Should that situation ever arise, we could discuss it then.'

Now I hesitated.

'Mrs Cage, it's only because of operational reasons, I assure you. This is not a plot to entrap you or force you to do anything against your will.' She smiled at me. 'And frankly, I'm not sure how we *could* coerce you into doing something against your will.'

'Threats, violence, blackmail, torture . . .'

'Those are not my methods.'

I remained silent.

'How about this?' she said. 'If you are unhappy with the way an assignment is progressing, you have the right to withdraw your services. But having withdrawn them, you may not rejoin public life until the assignment is resolved. Security issues, you understand.'

'You would imprison me?'

'No, you would be required to remain in a single location – your own home, for instance – until we say otherwise. Which, given your lifestyle, should be no hardship. Please remember, there will almost certainly be lives at stake and security always takes precedence.'

I nodded. 'All right. I reserve the right not to have to explain my observations to anyone. I'll warn or advise as I see fit and if you are sensible, you'll listen, but it's up to you.'

She frowned. 'I would want to discuss your observations with you. To examine some of your conclusions and your reasons for drawing them. Not in an atmosphere of disbelief – there would be nothing adversarial about it. Your observations will assist me in making decisions, but will not form the sole basis for those decisions. And you should be aware there may be reasons we will not or cannot act on any information or recommendations you make.'

I nodded. That seemed reasonable enough.

'Do you have any questions?'

'Do I have to make a decision now?'

'No. Requiring a reasonable amount of time to reflect is understandable. I hope you can accept, however, that given our current problems with Ghost, time might be an issue.'

'I do accept that.' I paused. 'Please be aware that under no circumstances would I ever work with Sorensen.'

'What about Sorensen?' said Michael Jones, appearing suddenly and pulling out a chair. I really wish he wouldn't do that. It was on the tip of my tongue to tell him I was going to get him a bell to wear around his neck, but restrained myself in front of his boss.

'I won't work with Sorensen,' I said again.

'No one's working with Sorensen after his last cock-up,' he said cheerfully, finishing off my coffee.

I inclined my head towards Jones. 'Would I *have* to work with him?'

'I have to,' she said. 'The least you can do is share my burden.'

I turned to Jones. 'What cock-up?'

He grinned. 'On the TV the other night. Acting on information and advice provided by him, our politicians did something amazingly stupid and there's an almighty great row going on. I'm quite surprised, actually. I don't like the bloke but he doesn't usually make that sort of mistake. He's unpleasant but not incompetent. Except where you're concerned, of course,' he said to me. 'He's really dropped himself in it this time. Makes you wonder if there's something going on with him. Other than you, of course,' he said to me again.

I nodded. 'I saw it on the news.'

'They don't know the half of it, thank God. He advised a certain course of action and he got it wrong. Badly wrong. Heads flying in all directions. Good fun when you're not involved.'

Mary Bennet intervened. '*If* I could continue my conversation . . .'

He grinned.

'When coming to a decision, Mrs Cage, I'd like you to focus on all the good you could do.'

'I'm sure that's not the real reason you want me.'

'Not entirely, no, but have you thought – you could be giving

258

a voice to people who can't speak for themselves. I don't mean those who won't speak, but those who *can't*, either for physical or psychiatric reasons. You could tell me who is too afraid to speak. Or those who genuinely don't understand what is happening to them. You would be giving a voice to those who need one.'

She was watching me very closely.

'I'm sure you're right,' I said, 'and that is a very valid point, but please try and understand how reluctant I am to expose myself. People don't like what I can do. My childhood was not always comfortable. My father told me to keep it secret and I've spent all my life doing that. It's hard to get my head around actually admitting it. I've managed to build a life for myself – why would I throw it away to perform in front of other people?'

'Complete anonymity will be observed at every stage. I promise. We already employ psychologists, people to advise on body language, non-verbal communication and so forth. Your findings would carry the same weight as theirs. No one will ever know exactly what it is you do, Mrs Cage.'

She paused. 'And consider this – you should have a purpose in life. It's not good to live as restricted a life as you do. It's unusual these days. Women no longer live quietly at home. It can attract almost as much attention. It marks you out as different. If you choose to work with us, we can protect you.'

'From what?'

'From unwanted attention such as you suffered at the hands of Philip Sorensen. I honestly believe working together will benefit both of us.'

She was right on every count. Even I'd been thinking I should get out more. Meet more people. I remembered I was so desperate for company I'd been prepared to take on a small ghost. Was something happening to me?

I swallowed. 'I'd like to think about it for a day or so, but I can give you my decision by Friday, if you like.'

'That will be acceptable.'

'What if I say no?'

'I am encouraged that you didn't say no immediately.' She smiled suddenly. 'Now – I've said my piece and I'll leave you to reflect on it. Contact Mr Jones when you've come to a decision and we can discuss pay and conditions. Mr Jones – a word, if you please.'

They stood up and disappeared outside. I could see them through the rain-smeared window, talking together. She was a small woman but her colour spread some considerable distance around her. Almost like a star.

I walked to the counter to pay the bill.

'No charge,' said the young man, appearing through the back door again. 'I don't work here.'

'But you served me,' I said, bewildered.

'We just borrowed the place for the afternoon.'

'You can do that?'

He looked around. 'We just did.'

'I know you,' I said suddenly. 'You work with Michael Jones. You're Robbie. You spied on me outside my house.'

He sighed. 'We usually refer to it as keeping our subject under close observation.'

'You used my bathroom.'

'And very grateful I was, too. And thank you for the sandwiches. I'm sitting in my car thinking I'm the last word in unobtrusive observation and my subject taps on the car window and brings me a plate of sandwiches and a flask of coffee. If I'd told anyone that I'd never have lived it down.'

'Well, it's nice to see you again.'

He shook his head. 'You shouldn't have seen me at all.'

'Oh. Sorry.'

CHAPTER SEVENTEEN

According to Michael Jones, James Monroe crumbled like Wensleydale cheese being cut with a snooker cue – his expression, not mine. Jones's theory was that he'd been too conceited even to consider the possibility of ever being found out and hadn't therefore prepared any sort of defence. In the space of just a couple of hours, he had worked his way from indignation to outrage to bluster to confusion to contradiction to confession.

'Well done,' I said, handing Jones his coffee and the entire packet of biscuits because it was quicker. We were back at my house where I'd drawn the curtains against the murky afternoon.

He shook his head. 'Nothing to do with me. Purely a police matter. I just pointed them in the right direction. After you pointed me, obviously. Dare I ask what happened to Caroline?'

'Gone,' I said briefly. I hadn't told him she'd killed Sammy or that I'd imprisoned her in the wall.

He looked at me closely. 'And Sammy?'

'Also gone,' I said, not wanting to talk about Sammy, either. What would it have been like, having him here with me? We could have enjoyed cartoons on TV. Or sat in the window seat watching the world go by and pointing out the people to each other. Would he ever have learned not to be afraid? I'd never know, but now he had his mummy which was as it should be. I managed a smile. 'Happy endings all round.'

'If you say so, Cage. What are you doing tomorrow night?'

I didn't have to stop and think. 'Nothing.'

'Fancy coming out for a drink and a meal? To celebrate?'

'Yes,' I said suddenly. 'Yes, I do. I'd love to go out.' And I would. It seemed a very long time since our holiday. Once I'd been perfectly happy to spend my days quietly doing not very much and keeping myself to myself, settling down in front of the TV every evening, but now . . . Obviously I didn't want frenetic gaiety but . . . I sighed. These days I didn't know what I wanted.

Then I had second thoughts. 'Is this a bribe? For me to work for your boss?'

'No, although I expect I could put together a bribe package if that's what you want. What would it take?'

'Nothing,' I said dolefully. 'I don't know what I want.'

I thought he looked at me rather closely. To distract him, I asked who else would be going for this meal.

'No one. Just you and me. I'll pick you up at seven thirty. There's a new place opened up in the docks. Industrial architecture. Cogs and machinery and black and white drama. We'll check out the food on behalf of the public. A tough job, but we sacrifice ourselves gladly for the common good.'

I spent a lot of time getting ready. I tried on several outfits and was equally dissatisfied with all of them. Eventually I decided warmth was probably the most important factor, so I chose a black wool dress and black boots with a camel overcoat and a dramatic black and white scarf. Thus muffled against the cold,

I pulled my front door closed behind me and joined Jones at the bottom of my steps.

We walked to the restaurant because that way, apparently, I'd be able to drink to my heart's content without having to worry about driving him home afterwards. My non-driving self thanked him for his consideration.

'Seriously, Cage – have you never thought of learning to drive?'

'Well, occasionally, but everything I need is within walking distance.'

'True, but it's bloody cold tonight. We could have just jumped in your car.'

'Suppose *I* wanted to drink tonight?'

'You don't drink.'

'Well, as it happens, I could just fancy a nice glass of wine tonight.'

He laughed. 'Cage, you're such a fibber.'

The night was bitter and we strode out briskly, our breath frosting around us.

'So, what did you think?' he enquired as we reached the bottom of the hill.

I was cautious. 'About?'

'My boss.'

'Mary Bennet?'

'Is that her name?'

I stopped and stared. 'You don't know?'

He grinned. 'She has many names but I usually just call her "sir". She frightens me to death.' He sighed. 'But then, most women do.'

264

I started walking again. 'You must live in a state of permanent terror.'

'I do, Cage, I do.'

I don't know what made me say it. 'Do I frighten you?'

He stopped dead and I suddenly realised I'd asked a very important question. 'I have two answers. Choose whichever you like best.' He smiled. 'You don't frighten me – you amaze me. Continually.'

I refused to let it go. 'And the other answer?'

He appeared to hesitate and then said, 'Yes. Sometimes. Keep moving – it's cold.'

By now we were walking alongside the river. Ahead of us, bright lights signalled our destination. Cafés, shops, restaurants and the cinema, all packed with people enjoying themselves. I could hear music as someone opened a door somewhere and then it was gone as it closed again.

'When do I frighten you?'

There was a pub on our left – the Cider Tree – with ten or twelve outside tables which, believe it or not on this cold night, were quite crowded. Jones hesitated a moment and then said, 'Shall we have a drink before we eat?' and guided me to a table. 'The usual for you? Or have you really suddenly acquired a taste for wine?'

'The usual, please.'

He disappeared inside the pub.

I looked around. We were in the very early run-up to Christmas and there was a lot going on.

Christmas lights were festooned from shop to shop and every corner had a decorated Christmas tree. Shoppers jostled past, laden with bags and boxes. More people clustered around the food and drink stands. The one selling glühwein seemed enormously popular. As was the one selling hot chocolate piled high with whipped cream and flakes. And the fish and chip wagon was doing a roaring trade. I'm sure the smell was delicious but somehow, I'd lost my appetite. Michael Jones was afraid of me.

The council had set up a public skating rink just opposite and it was full of shouting, laughing children happily falling over, picking themselves up and falling down all over again. Apparently, that was hilarious. A few adults could skate properly but most inched their way along the barrier or wobbled along holding hands. They fell over a lot as well. The kids thought that was even more hilarious. I tried not to think how little Sammy would have liked this.

The night was cold and glittering with stars. The table had one of those outdoor heaters. I touched the 'on' pad and there was wonderful instant heat.

Jones reappeared with our drinks. 'Cheers, Cage.'

I left my drink where it was. 'When do I frighten you?'

He sat down. 'We need to have a conversation, don't we? It's been a long time coming but it's here now. Shall I go first?'

I nodded.

He cradled his glass in both hands. 'Not all the time. But I expect I frighten you sometimes. We both have skills the average person doesn't possess.'

I deliberately closed my mind to past memories. When he'd put me in the hospital. The only men I'd ever really known well were my dad and Ted. Gentle men both of them. It was Jones who'd made me realise the strength and the power that men have but mostly never exercise. I had a sudden thought. If every man in the world suddenly cast aside the restraints society

266

had placed on their behaviour . . . if they suddenly decided to exercise their strength – what would happen?

I shivered. Part fear – part cold. Jones looked up to check the heater was working.

But then, couldn't the same be said of me? I'd lashed out once and people had died, buildings had fallen and the world had been smothered in angry snow. And then it hadn't. But it could be again. I looked at him. In our own separate ways, both of us had that potential . . . the potential to harm. In our own ways, both of us were dangerous. Perhaps we were better apart. For the good of others.

I'd been silent too long. 'Talk to me, Cage.'

All right. I would talk to him. There were things that should be said. Why not drag them out into the cold light of day – or rather the cold light of a winter night – and see what happened.

Stumblingly, I told him what I'd been thinking.

He leaned across the table. 'I didn't hurt you, Cage. It's important you know that.'

'I do know that.' And I did. Except that I knew he *had* hurt me. Sometimes I wondered if my mind was splitting into two parts. Good Elizabeth and Bad Elizabeth. I remembered I'd condemned Caroline Fairbrother to eternal imprisonment inside a wall. It would seem that Bad Elizabeth sometimes got the upper hand. Again, I heard my dad's voice telling me not to draw attention to myself. To keep my secret. Because if that was safe then so was I.

'We have to talk about this,' he said softly. 'We can't operate with each of us being frightened of the other. No relationship should be based on fear.'

I nodded.

267

He smiled but there was no amusement in it. 'Do you know,' he said, 'I always thought that it was Ted who would be the problem. That he would always be here with you. An invisible presence. Unseen, intangible, but always here. I thought, somehow, you'd continually be measuring me against him and finding me less. That whatever I did, you'd always be thinking, *Oh, Ted did that better*, but I was wrong, wasn't I? The problem's not Ted at all.'

'I can't ever forget Ted,' I said defensively. 'I loved him and he loved me.'

'Of course you did. Nothing we have can change that – ever. Nor should it. Look, every relationship has the potential to go bad. To cause damage. We, at least, are aware of possible future ... difficulties. Perhaps we could have some sort of signal or code word. Or you could just say, "Jones, you're frightening me. Stop." Or the much more likely, "Jones, you're really pissing me off right now. Bugger off before I do something you'll regret."'

He sat back and picked up his drink again while I considered this.

'I think,' I said slowly, 'that you're far more at risk than me.'

He set down his drink and wiped his top lip. 'Yeah, I think that too. Frankly the thought of you joining the ranks of my ex-girlfriends frightens me witless.'

'I . . .' I stopped, enmeshed in confusion and indecision.

He took my hand. 'OK – crunch time. What do you *want* to do, Cage? You have choices. Do you continue on alone? If that's what you want, then I can walk away right now and you'll never see me again. I'll be crying inside but don't let that influence you in any way. Or do you want to continue as we are

268

now? Meeting occasionally for a bit of blind terror and some weird stuff? Do you want a working relationship and nothing else? Or do you want more than that? Just take a minute and consider what you want to do. Forget the best thing to do. Or the sensible thing to do. What do you *want* to do?'

I looked at him. This conversation had blown up almost out of nowhere and I'd had no time to think. Ideas, feelings, half-formed plans, everything was whirling around my head and nothing very clear was emerging. Despite his calm voice and smiles, his own colour was churning about, the golden red slowly being overwhelmed with orange. To those around us we were just a couple having a quiet drink and a chat, but trust me, neither of us were anywhere near as calm as we looked.

I said, 'You want me to be honest?'

He seemed to brace himself. 'Yes.'

'You're certain?'

He sighed and squared his shoulders. 'Yes.'

'I want to take you to bed. I want to touch you. I want to feel you touch me.'

There. It was out. I couldn't believe I'd said it out loud.

His colour stilled for a moment and then exploded around him, shimmering gold in the night sky.

He squeezed my hands so tightly it hurt, then realised what he was doing and let go. Then reached out and took them again. 'I'd whisk you off right now but I don't think I'm able to stand up at the moment.'

'It's fine,' I said, still not quite sure why I'd said that and rather glad of a moment to pull myself together. 'In your own time.'

He grinned at me. 'I have this fantasy . . .'

'Oh God, Jones, I'm not wearing leather.'

'I grieve to hear you say so but I'm confident that, in time, I can change your mind.'

'Nor will I get involved in sex toys in any way.'

He blinked. 'What do you know about sex toys?'

'A lot,' I said, having once walked into Rushford's one and only sex shop by accident. I'd left very quickly but there are some things that can't be unseen. In my mind I was seeing some of them now.

'I look forward to being instructed.'

'Not by me, buster. And if you grin at me with that stupid *putty in my hands* look of yours, I shall be finding a new and exciting use for our table decoration.'

We both looked at our pretty little Christmas tree which had certainly done nothing to deserve such a dreadful fate.

He grinned. His colour roared around him. 'Cage, you can find new and exciting uses for anything you like,' and I leaned towards him and then a familiar voice said, 'Hello.'

I looked up and Melek and Iblis were strolling towards our table. To my surprise, Jones waved them over. 'The very people. What are you doing for Christmas lunch?'

They both stared at him. I think I did as well.

'Only I wondered if you wanted to have it with us.'

I don't think anyone was expecting that.

'Um,' said Melek, obviously laying the ground for a polite refusal. She should have moved more quickly.

'Yeah, great,' said Iblis, with enthusiasm. 'Thank you. Love to. Wouldn't we?'

'We are of a different belief system,' said Melek, stiffly.

Jones waved theological differences aside. 'No problem, I

think non-Christians are still allowed to eat on Christmas Day so it shouldn't be an issue.'

Iblis went to sit down beside me.

Melek looked at both of us and then slapped his arm. 'We should be going.'

'Just a quick drink . . .' said Iblis, longingly.

'These people are busy.'

'No, they're not.' He looked at us more closely. 'Oh. Oh, OK. We'll be going now.' He grinned broadly. 'Have a great time. A great, great time.'

'If I manage to do everything right,' said Jones, seriously, 'there's a very good chance we'll set my building on fire.'

I rolled my eyes.

'In that case,' said Iblis, 'we'll definitely leave you to it. Are you all right for . . . um . . . matches?'

'Get out of here,' said Jones, amiably.

Iblis grinned evilly and, finally, Melek hustled him away. Never mind Jones, my face could have ignited the table all by itself.

'You know how you don't have any friends?' said Jones, watching them disappear into the crowds. 'How you live a solitary and lonely life?'

'Yes.'

'Good plan. Stick with it.'

I ignored this. 'Why did you do that? We decided it's my turn to host Christmas this year and my house is far too small to entertain four people properly. We'll never get them in.'

'No problem. We'll have it at my place again. That way I get to do the cooking.'

I snatched my hand away. 'There's nothing wrong with my cooking.'

He grinned at me. 'There's nothing wrong with anything about you, Cage.'

I refused to be mollified. 'A pity I can't say the same about you.'

He sighed. 'So early in the relationship and already with the recriminations.'

'I'm surprised you're not more used to them.'

He sighed and hung his head. 'I blame the job, Cage. Well, that's what I tell myself. Having to drop everything and go off somewhere without warning leads to painful and emotional scenes along the lines of "But you promised to come with me to my sister's wedding", and an ocean of tears and reproaches followed by long lists of all my personal faults and past sins.'

I nodded. 'I can imagine that so easily.'

'And sometimes it goes on for days. That's the thing about women – they can't remember where they put their car keys and yet when it comes to every tiny bump in the road of your relationship – total recall.'

I considered the problem. 'Have you thought about giving up women and moving on to men?'

He shook his head. 'I can't see that being any improvement. There would still be the demands of the job and not being able to go to their sister's wedding. It would just be a different sister's wedding. Where, for some reason, everyone would still be dying to meet me.'

'Perhaps you're right, but whether or not you're going to be gay, you'll have to dress a lot better than that.'

He looked down at himself. 'There's nothing wrong with the way I dress.'

'Of course not,' I soothed. 'It takes a special kind of courage to dress to reflect your own personality and I frequently applaud yours.'

'My clothes?'

'Your courage.'

'Cage, I don't know how Ted put up with you for so long.'

'He was obviously a great deal more robust than you. And better dressed, too.'

'So, I'm a wimpy scruff.'

I patted his hand. 'Not all the time.'

He turned his hand over and held mine. His colour reached out to me. I closed my eyes and breathed it in. I opened my eyes and stepped into the unknown. We looked at each other. The moment was endless ... I watched his eyes darken. His hand tightened on mine.

'Shall we skip dinner?' His voice was hoarse.

Mine wasn't much better. 'Yes.' I tried again. 'Yes.'

He began to get up and then stopped.

'Oh, bloody hell.'

'What?' I turned around. 'Oh, no. What does he want?'

With his usual impeccable timing, Dr Sorensen was picking his way through the crowds towards us. He was wearing a heavy overcoat with a neat scarf and his hands were thrust deep into his pockets. There was no pretending we hadn't seen him and he never took his eyes off us. I had no time to wonder how he knew we were here before he was with us.

He was also extremely agitated. His colour, that nasty, greasy white colour, was curdling and rippling around him. He walked

273

straight up to us. Jones was already standing – I remained seated because I felt much happier and safer with the table between Sorensen and me.

'Good evening to you both.'

Jones nodded and I said nothing at all.

'I wonder if I might have a word.'

'Sorry,' said Jones curtly. 'We're just leaving.' He leaned over and switched off the heater. The cold night rushed back at me and I put on my gloves.

Sorensen moved to block our path. 'I'm sorry to disturb you, but it really is most important that I speak with you.'

'Or what?' said Jones. 'Which of us will you try and make away with this time? You've had a go at both Mrs Cage and me and failed each time. Dismally.'

I watched the effort it took for Sorensen to remain calm. His colour was literally rippling with anxiety. 'I really must insist.'

'You're in no position to insist on anything, Sorensen,' said Jones, drawing on his own gloves. 'You've really screwed up over that recent business. I should imagine you're political suicide at the moment. Have you considered a long holiday? Abroad?'

'Please. This is urgent. I need to speak with Mrs Cage at once. And you, too.'

I stood up. 'Sorry,' said Jones again. 'As I said, we're just off. Talk to my boss. I think she wants a word with you, anyway.'

'This is nothing to do with the department. I . . .' He was becoming more agitated by the moment. He looked over his shoulder. 'I can help you. But you have to . . .'

He was standing with his hands in his pockets and his shoulders hunched against the cold but his colour was twisting and turning on itself. He was in turmoil.

'We don't *have* to do anything,' said Jones.

'I assure you – I've acted in good faith throughout. I've tried to help you both. I'm trying now. You must . . .'

'All right,' I said, before his colour became a vortex and whirled him away like the cow in *The Wizard of Oz*. 'Just tell us what you want.'

His gaze shifted suddenly. 'Save yourselves.' He was staring over my shoulder.

I looked around and when I looked back, he was disappearing into the crowd around the skating rink.

Jones was scanning the people around us. 'I wonder what that was all about.'

'He was scared stiff,' I said, worried.

'He was, wasn't he?' he said thoughtfully, still watching the people walk past. Apparently not seeing anything to cause him any concern, he turned back to me, saying softly, 'Ready?' and it was as if Sorensen had never been here. I reached out and he took my hand in his.

We set off together, walking around the ice rink. His colour streamed out behind him like a flare. I was surprised the ice didn't melt.

'My place is closest,' I said.

'No,' he said firmly. 'I'm sticking to my fantasy.'

'Did we ever establish exactly what that was?'

'Well, I'll tell you now, if you like, or it can come as a delightful surprise later on.'

'Forewarned is forearmed,' I said, as we climbed the steps back up to the medieval bridge.

'Well, in my dreams – where, let me say, Cage, you are considerably more compliant than in real life – I sweep you off your feet and carry you off to my bed of passion. However, practically speaking, there's no chance of me getting you up the stairs in your house without either putting my back out or accidentally knocking you unconscious. Or we'd get wedged halfway up and God knows what sort of sex that would lead to. My place, on the other hand – no stairs.'

'That's disappointing. Does that mean no sweeping, either?'

'Absolutely not. There will very much be sweeping. I've been in training. You know – pumping iron.' He made pumping iron movements.

I stood still. 'Dear God, how much do you think I weigh?'

He looked uneasy. 'Ah – this is one of those questions to which there is no good answer, isn't it? A wise man remains silent.'

'Well, that I've yet to see.'

The medieval bridge is single lane. Vehicular traffic is forbidden these days but the builders had built V-shaped notches in the walls for our ancestors to avoid herds of livestock and laden wagons. Two people fitted in one of those quite nicely.

He kissed me. His face was cold but his lips were warm. His colour bent itself around me and I relaxed against him. The world was suddenly a much warmer place. We might be there still if a bunch of teenagers hadn't walked past and advised us loudly to get a room.

'What an excellent idea,' he said into my hair. He put his arm around me which was just as well because left to myself I think I'd have walked off in the wrong direction and ended up in Rushby.

The walk back to his apartment seemed both very short and very long. We didn't speak. I was very conscious of him walking alongside me. My heart was hammering away as we approached his apartment block and I could hardly get up the steps. He tapped in the front door code and then we were inside. The foyer seemed almost overwhelmingly hot and stuffy after being out in the cold.

'Stairs?' I said as he headed for the lift.

'I'm on the top floor, Cage. Forget it.'

We entered the lift.

'And I should warn you there are CCTV cameras in here, so try and restrain yourself otherwise you'll be getting me a bad name with the management committee.'

'Really?' I said, moving in.

He reached out for me.

The doors opened and a man got in. Jones sighed loudly.

We travelled upwards in silence. And about three feet apart.

The doors opened and the man got out. Jones reached out for me again and a woman with a small dog got in.

She smiled at us. 'Good evening.'

I said good evening politely because I think Jones was on the verge of throwing both her and her dog down the lift shaft. Or telling her he had diphtheria and the lift was now a quarantine zone. Or, more likely, telling her I had diphtheria.

'I'm going down,' she announced. 'Are you?'

'What a coincidence,' said Jones brightly, and before he could say anything to embarrass us all, I said yes, that was fine.

The lift began to travel downwards. You could have cut the silence with a knife.

The doors opened and out she got. And the dog.

A man, just coming through the front door, shouted, 'Hold the lift,' and Jones slapped the door-close button and we sped upwards again.

'That was mean,' I said.

'I warn you, Cage, nothing and no one gets into this lift until we arrive at my floor.'

Nothing and no one got into the lift and eventually we arrived at the top floor.

Jones had his key ready. 'The mark of a man experienced in the ways of seduction,' he said, in an explanation I hadn't asked for. 'Nothing kills the mood quicker than fumbling. And not necessarily for your key.'

'I don't want to know,' I said and then he had the door open.

I stood on the threshold. In more ways than one.

'Aren't you coming in?' he enquired. 'I'm fine if you want to do it here in the corridor – in fact a bit of a first for me – but I must admit I thought you'd be a little more ... modest ... in your approach.'

I tried to smile.

'You mustn't be nervous,' he said quietly. 'At least one of us needs to be brave about this and I think it's going to have to be you.'

I nodded, walked into the hall and turned to face him.

He pushed my hair back. 'Sweetheart, truly, if you're unhappy, then I'll take you home, but I always think it's better to regret the things you did than regret the things you didn't.'

'No, it's not,' I objected. 'I bet far more people sit around thinking *I wish I hadn't murdered X and now have to spend the rest of my life in prison* than think *I wish I had murdered X and could spend the rest of my life in prison.*'

'Cage – what are you talking about?'

'Murder.'

'Are you planning to murder someone?'

'Well, I wasn't, but now, strangely . . .'

'This is very concerning. For how long have you had these violent urges?'

'I think since the first day we met.'

'What a coincidence.'

I was quite indignant. 'Are you saying you've wanted to murder *me* since the first day we met?'

'Not murder, no.' He was grinning at me with that complacent *I've just derailed the conversation again* look.

I made an effort. 'Well, actually, I think you're right. Stifling one's urges can cause irreparable mental damage.'

'It certainly can. One should act.'

'One intends to.' I picked up a hefty-looking wooden ornament from the console table by the door. 'Shall I go first?'

His hand moved quickly and suddenly he was holding the ornament and I was backed up against the bookcase.

'And now,' he said softly, kicking the door closed behind him. 'Shall we stop messing around?'

My voice had fled. I couldn't look at him.

'Let me be a gentleman and help you off with your coat.' He gently removed it and hung it on a hook. I closed my eyes and waited.

Nothing happened. I opened them to see him disappearing around the corner, leaving me standing in the hall.

I called after him. 'Where are you going?'

His voice floated back down the hall. 'It's easy to see you've never done this before, Cage. I'm opening the bedroom door.

Think about it – if I've got my arms full of you then I'm never going to be able to get the door open, am I? And, of course, it's vitally important for the success of the evening that I ascertain the room is actually empty before we get going. It's only polite.'

I sighed and sat in a nearby chair. I might as well make myself comfortable. 'Does that happen often?'

'What?'

I raised my voice. 'Does that happen often?'

'Believe me, Cage, it only has to happen once for you to be scarred for life.'

I tried to peer around the corner. 'I can imagine. Just as a matter of interest, how many women have you carted down this hall?'

'You're the first.'

'I'm astonished.'

'Give me a chance, I haven't had the place that long.'

'You should chalk up a tally by the door.'

'Well, that's not very classy.'

'No, you're right. I'll sign your visitor's book before I leave. Do you have a customer comments section?'

He reappeared beside me, presumably having got the bedroom door open and ascertained the coast was clear. 'Up you get.' He pulled me to my feet. 'Are you keeping your boots on? Not that I have any problems with that. I'm just worrying about my sheets.'

We kissed for a very long time and when I could, I told him his sheets were safe from me. He knelt down and unzipped my boots. Very slowly. Then he slid them off. His hands were very warm. I swayed and the next moment, as promised, I was swept off my feet. Apparently, he did still possess enough strength to get us both into his bedroom.

If asked to describe this room, I'd have to blush and say my attention was elsewhere. And it was. His sweater and T-shirt came off in no time. Everything was desperate, urgent, frantic, eager. I couldn't catch my breath.

He laughed and said something about slowing down – there was no prize for whoever came first – and then the bedroom door smashed back on its hinges, something fell to the floor and shattered, and the room was full of shouting men.

I had no time to get myself together. I couldn't think what was happening. Jones suffered no such uncertainty. Pushing me out of the way on to the bed, he launched himself at three of them.

Two more headed for me. Shaking with shock, I kicked out. I seized the bedside light and tried to hit at least one of them. Someone grabbed my ankles and began to drag me off the bed. My dress rode up around my waist. I screamed and kicked again. I tried to hold on to the headboard but they were too strong. I felt a fingernail rip. Someone grabbed my wrists. I tried to headbutt them. My head connected with something because someone cursed and a jagged, painful white light filled my head. I wouldn't do that again. One man had me under the arms – I flailed wildly. The other had my ankles. I tried to buck and kick. One of them staggered and nearly fell. I did it again and again. Someone cursed.

Across the room I could hear the sound of furniture being overturned. A picture slithered down the wall. I twisted my head to try to see what was happening to Jones, just as he disappeared beneath three men. There were horrible meaty thumping noises. One was kicking him. I suddenly realised he might not survive this. The thought galvanised me. I should do something. There was no way I was going quietly. They'd got me nearly to the bedroom door. I was being kidnapped. I was actually being kidnapped.

I writhed and twisted, doing everything I could to make life difficult for them. A voice said, 'Wait. Hold her still,' and everything stopped. I just had time to wonder if I was winning after all when I felt a stinging pain in my right thigh and then a savage ache. I looked down. A hypodermic was sticking out of my leg. I felt a coldness spread around my body.

I tried to redouble my efforts. My mind was still functioning. I was aware of everything around me but paralysis was spreading through my limbs. I couldn't speak. I could do nothing except be carried from the room.

Once outside his apartment I went over someone's shoulder. They trotted to the lift where the doors were propped open with a chair. They kicked that aside and we were in. I felt the slight jerk as it began to descend. Only two men were with me. The rest were still with Jones. I wondered if he was still alive. He would fight like a lion for me. I was not the first woman to be dragged from his bed. Clare had been taken in exactly this way.

The lift went all the way down to the underground garage. An outer door opened. I felt a blast of icy air. I heard an engine and a screech of brakes. A black van pulled up. The side door slid back and they tossed me inside. The floor was cold and hard. I heard them climbing in after me. The van pulled away with a jerk.

The movement caused me to roll to one side. I banged my forehead and knees and then rolled back the other way. I might not be able to move but that didn't mean I couldn't feel pain.

It was a rough ride. They drove fast and I was flung about in all directions, hitting first one side of the van and then the

282

other. The interior was dark. I couldn't see. I never knew when or where the next impact would fall. The floor and the walls were ice-cold metal and felt slightly wet. The constant motion and smell of oil was making me feel sick.

I don't know if it was the cold or the drug taking effect, but slowly, everything faded away and the world went dark.

CHAPTER EIGHTEEN

I only very gradually became conscious of the pain. Several pains, actually. My head was splitting and there was a dull ache in my right leg, but worse was the much more severe pain in the back of my neck. That pain felt familiar. I'd done this before. Gone to sleep while watching the TV and woken up with my head slumped forwards on my chest and my neck aching hard enough to wake me up. How had I got myself home? Why was I so cold? What was happening?

I kept my eyes closed while I tried to work out where I was and what was going on but my physical discomfort was too intense. As was the cold. And I knew from experience that the pain would really start whenever I chose to lift my head, so I might as well do it now and get it over with.

I started with the easy part. I opened my eyes. I could see my lap, with my dress ridden up to mid-thigh. My tights were badly ripped. I could see my pale leg through the holes and runs and there was a nasty bruise on my right thigh. My mouth felt dry. I tried to swallow but I had no saliva. And I was so cold.

I looked down to my shoeless feet, which were resting in a puddle of cold water. I blinked a little to try to clear my vision. A concrete floor swam into focus. I was slumped forwards in an uncomfortable and very cold metal chair with my feet in a shallow puddle of dirty water. I swallowed again. Was I to be electrocuted? And with that thought a few blurry memories came rolling back.

Jones. Where was Jones? Was he here somewhere? Unconscious? Dead? I went to turn my head and a sharp pain stabbed through my neck again. Had I injured myself as I rolled around in the back of the van? Only one way to find out. Inch by inch I unrolled my spine, gently pushing it back against the chair. That went quite well and I was encouraged enough to try to lift my chin. It hurt, but only because I'd been sitting in this position for so long. There was no permanent damage and it would pass. Another inch and then another and finally, I could lift my head properly.

I became aware my chin was sticky. Oh God, I'd dribbled. How embarrassing. I went to wipe it away and that was when I discovered my wrists were tied to the chair with those plastic tie things. I looked down. They'd been pulled tight and my hands had a swollen, blue look about them, although that might have been because of my still blurry eyesight.

Some of the drug must still be in my system because I wasn't anything like as frightened as I should be. A heavy weight seemed to be pressing down on my thoughts. I just couldn't seem to get to grips with the situation. To think what to do next . . .

I leaned my head back, carefully stretched my neck, closed my eyes, and ignoring the pain, the cold, and my wet feet, I tried to let my mind drift . . . fear . . . flash . . . pain . . . fire . . . cold . . . and something else . . .

I wondered afterwards if I was being watched because that

was the moment it began. There were two long fluorescent lights in the ceiling above me and they began to flicker. Both of them, seemingly independent of each other. I could feel them pounding against my closed eyelids so I very reluctantly opened my eyes. And they made that irritating little *tink* noise every time they flickered on and again when they flickered off. There was no rhythm to it. *Tink, tink . . . tink, tink, tink . . . tink . . . tink, tink.* Between that, the cold, and the lingering effects of the drug, I couldn't seem to get my thoughts together at all. Concentration was impossible. This was the visual equivalent of fingernails on a blackboard. Shadows jumped around the room as the harsh light bounced off the walls – dark, light, dark, light, slicing into my already aching head. I began to feel very sick.

I don't know for how long it went on and then, without warning, the lights went out completely and I was sitting in blessed darkness. Not that for me, darkness is ever complete. Purple, green, magenta, blue – all the colours are out there, swirling around and about in complex patterns. Darkness is full of colours – it's just that most people can't see them.

At that moment, I was finding the lack of light quite soothing. Slowly, the throbbing pain in my head began to subside and the nausea diminished. I closed my eyes again and took refuge in the dark. Just take a breath and let my mind drift . . . something . . .

Almost as if someone was waiting for me to relax, the lights began to flash on and off again, shattering my concentration. This session lasted much longer than the previous one and just as I was beginning to feel I couldn't bear it any longer, that any moment I would begin to scream and never stop, the lights went

286

out again. Not that there was any relief this time. The flashing continued behind my eyes. They didn't need the lights any longer. My own head could do it for them.

I vomited, not managing to turn my head in time. Most of it went all over me. I remember feeling the sticky warmth of it on my bare skin.

Strangely, I felt better after that. The pulsing pain receded a little as well. I sat up straighter. The lights came on – steadily this time – and I used the opportunity to have a proper look around.

I was in a small room with no furniture. Just me and the chair in more or less the middle of the room. I gave an experimental wiggle – I was fixed to the chair and the chair was fixed to the floor. The floor was rough concrete as were the walls. There were rusty marks on both floor and walls where metal shelving units had once been bolted. This had been an old storeroom.

I sniffed. Concrete, damp, and just a very faint trace of disinfectant. A very familiar combination. As if I didn't already have a very good idea of where I was. I was in the Sorensen Clinic. In the basement. One of them, anyway. Not so very long ago, I'd died in one of these rooms. So had Michael Jones.

I'd been trying not to think of the last time I'd seen him. Fighting off three men in grim silence. What sort of chance would he stand against so many opponents? He was big and he was strong but he wasn't Superman. Where was he at this moment? If he was here, then they hadn't transported him with me. I had a horrible feeling it was me they wanted. Jones was collateral damage. The thought chilled me even more than the water around my feet. Was he even still alive? Had they had to kill him to get to me?

Whether he was dead or not – and I wasn't going to think about that now – I couldn't count on him to come to the rescue. I would have to save myself. And then I'd probably have to save him, too.

There were no windows so I had no idea what time it was. Nor even whether it was night or day. All right – that was probably standard procedure. Confuse and disorient the prisoner. That would be me, presumably. I wasn't at all hungry so possibly I hadn't been here that long. On the other hand, I had just vomited all over my own personal dungeon. And all over myself as well, so it was no surprise I wasn't that hungry.

Which suddenly reminded me how thirsty I was. Whether because of the drug, or because I hadn't had anything to drink for a long time, or as a result of throwing up, now that I'd realised how badly I wanted a drink, it was hard to think of anything else.

Ironically, my feet were still puddling around in a couple of inches of cold, dirty water. It wasn't a pleasant sensation. I remember thinking it was a shame nature hadn't designed us to drink through our feet.

That was the moment I saw the big metal door handle move. Just very slightly. At least I thought it did. I blinked hard to clear my vision and stared and stared. Had I imagined it? And then it moved again. Someone was on the other side. Someone who didn't want me to know they were there? Or possibly, someone who shouldn't be here.

I sat very still and watched as the door inched open. I held my breath. A hand appeared around the door, closely followed by a

288

face with an anxious expression. The sight was so unexpected, I nearly laughed. Standing half in and half out of the room was the very last person in the world I expected to see.

Alyson Painswick.

Alyson Painswick from the Local History Society. Alyson Painswick who wasn't dead. Alyson Painswick whose mother had probably killed her father. That was a point. From what I remembered, Alyson never moved far from her side, so where was Mrs Painswick? Was she even still alive? Or was she dead like her husband and they just hadn't found the body yet?

I suspected I wasn't looking my best but Alyson looked terrible. If she'd been afraid of her own shadow before she was terrified of it now. She was still wearing her school uniform, now grubby and stained. Her silver hair was dark with grease and dirt and stood out around her head like a bedraggled bird's nest. She stood like a statue, still clinging to the handle as if too scared to come any further. Her gentle coral colour was tiny and barely moving.

In disbelief, I said, 'Alyson? Is that you?'

I could have died of embarrassment for asking such a stupid question, but since she followed through with the equally ludicrous, 'Mrs Cage. Are you all right?' I didn't feel quite so bad.

In fact, I very nearly laughed. I wanted to say, 'I'm tied to a chair in a cellar and covered in my own vomit – define all right,' but I didn't want to scare her away so I said, 'I'm very cold and thirsty. Can you get these tie things off me so I can get a drink?'

She shook her head and disappeared.

I sighed. Well, I'd tried. And now I felt even thirstier than before.

I'd misjudged her. Two minutes later she was back with a bottle of water.

'I can't untie those plastic things,' she whispered. 'But I got you this.'

She unscrewed the top and held it carefully to my mouth. Easier said than done and most of it went all down my front, but I'd already written this dress off as a casualty of war. The water was cold and tasted good.

When I'd had enough, I whispered, 'Alyson, where's your mum?'

She looked over her shoulder and then started to cry.

'She hurt my dad.'

'I know,' I said gently.

'We ran away.'

'I know,' I said again.

'My mum said they'd put us in prison.'

'I don't think they would have done that. How did you end up here?'

'He found us.'

'Sorensen?'

She nodded.

'How?'

She shook her head. 'I don't know but he talked to Mum and she said he could help us.'

'Sorensen?'

She looked over her shoulder again and nodded.

'We came here and then it all got horrible. I'm scared ... My mum ...' She couldn't go on.

'Alyson, please don't cry. Everything will be fine. We just have to get out of here. Can you find something sharp? To cut these plastic things.'

She gave a cry. Her colour had very nearly disappeared. 'You mustn't leave me here.'

'I won't. I'll get us both out of here, I promise, but I have to get out of this chair and this room first.'

She nodded. 'All right. I can . . .'

She stopped and listened. We both heard the ping of the arriving lift.

'He's coming.'

She slipped from the room and I was on my own again.

I straightened up, lifted my head and braced myself. The door swung open.

Dr Sorensen stood on the threshold and sniffed the air fastidiously, something for which I vowed he would die one day. He looked at me for a long time and then jerked his head at someone out of sight behind the door. He didn't actually say, 'Have her stripped, washed and brought to my tent,' but the inference was plain. Then he turned and walked away.

Two men entered. The bigger man's colour was a washed-out grey, the other a kind of khaki. One pulled out a knife. I tried to wrench myself free but the ties were unbudgeable and all I did was hurt myself. I wondered if my last hour had come. In my imagination I saw them grabbing my hair, pulling my head back and cutting my throat. Which was ridiculous. Why would Sorensen bring me here just to cut my throat and then have to clear the mess up afterwards?

In one swift movement one of the men bent over me and cut both the ties. For a moment nothing happened and then the blood began to flow back into my hands and it was so painful I couldn't think of anything else. They seized an arm each, yanked me to my feet and marched me out of the door.

Apart from the knife, neither of them seemed to be armed, for which I was both grateful and slightly aggrieved. Why wasn't I considered dangerous enough to warrant a weapon? I bet if it was Michael Jones there would be at least a dozen enormous men, all armed to the teeth, and possibly with a tank, as well.

My legs weren't working properly. I had no idea where they were taking me and I wasn't sure I wanted to go. I tried to use my wobbly legs to hang back but that didn't work. I was still too weak to put up any sort of resistance. I struggled feebly and in vain.

And then I thought – this wasn't what I did. I should stop wasting my time. My strengths lay in other areas. I stopped fighting the men and tried to look about me for possible ways out. An opportunity might arise for me to get away. Deep down I knew that wasn't the slightest bit likely, but it kept my mind busy. I should look for door numbers, remember the layout, and try to memorise anything that might be useful should I get a chance to escape. I got as far as Rooms B11, B12, left turn, and then we were in the lift.

We exited on the first floor. The first thing I noticed was that it was daylight. I'd been here overnight. Don't think about Michael Jones.

I was hustled out of the lift and pushed along, too fast for me to be aware of anything other than the corridor ahead, left through the door at the end, and into a small bedroom. Not one of the luxurious rooms for the paying punters, but one of those reserved for his pro bono work, I guessed.

'Bathroom,' said washed-out grey, nodding with his head. A set of Sorensen Clinic grey sweats had been laid out on the bed for me. Best of all, a pair of warm fluffy socks for my poor, freezing feet.

I felt moderately cheered by this. Surely they wouldn't offer me bathroom facilities if they were just going to kill me out of hand? Not that I thought they would kill me. I was here for a reason. I had something Sorensen wanted.

'Go on,' said khaki. 'Not got all day.'

'You can wait outside,' I said with no hope at all because there was a window in this room and we were only on the first floor.

'We'll wait here,' he said, plonking himself in an armchair. 'Get on with it.'

My husband, Ted, had been head of security here. I didn't recognise either of these two men. They were definitely a cut below the sort he would employ. I wondered if any of Ted's original team were still here and if so whether I could use them.

One of the men, the bigger one, stirred impatiently. I should get myself into the bathroom before they decided to hose me down themselves. I wobbled towards the door.

'Hoi,' said khaki and for one nasty moment I really did think he was coming in as well but he only passed over the sweats which I'd forgotten. I was going to have to pull myself together if I was going to effect an escape, bring down Sorensen and his clinic once and for all, and then gallop off to rescue Michael Jones.

I appreciated the lovely bathroom – a haven of chrome and gleaming white tiles. And gloriously warm underfloor heating. This was a high-end establishment so everything I could possibly need was laid out ready for me. I used the loo, gave my teeth a much-needed brushing and stepped under the shower, relishing the feel of the hot water on my skin and hair. I hadn't realised how cold I was. I washed my hair twice and scrubbed every inch of me with as many fragrant bath products as I could find. It was easily the best shower I'd ever had. A bit of nice to follow on from the bit of nasty in the cellar. Classic interrogation technique, I suspected.

I enveloped myself in every fluffy towel in the room and then did the body lotion, talcum powder, body spray thing with enthusiasm. Anything to get rid of the lingering smell of stale vomit. I towel-dried my hair, combed it back behind my ears, applied some cream to my face and hands, dressed slowly and then decided I couldn't spin it out any longer. Stuffing my feet into those slipper things they give you in hotels, I opened the door and stepped out to meet my fate.

It's amazing how much braver you feel when you're clean. Sorensen really should have left me in my smelly basement. Interestingly, as far as my two guards were concerned, it was as if I'd gone up a social notch. I was no longer the slightly sticky prisoner in the basement, to be hustled along the corridors as quickly as possible – because prisoners always have to be hustled. It's as if no one trusts them to go anywhere under their own steam. Now, however, my clothing promoted me to the status of guest – the clinic was far too posh to have patients – and I was allowed to walk by myself. I huddled inside my warm sweats and enjoyed the smell of lily of the valley, lavender, lemon and lime, and white orchid and passion flower. That last one wasn't really me but I'd sloshed it all over the place anyway. Anything I could do to eat into Sorensen's profit margins.

I was taken down to his office on the ground floor. I saw no one the whole time. The rooms – the corridors – everywhere was eerily silent and deserted. There were no staff and no patients anywhere, no clatter of trolleys, or doors opening and closing. Where was everyone? I remembered their policy of sending patients home for Christmas but that was still some weeks off and there would always be a few deemed not well enough to leave – together with the staff to look after them.

We took the wide, curving stairs to the ground floor. There was a window halfway down, overlooking the gardens, and I tried to see out. One of the guards told me to keep walking. Something in his voice made me ignore him and stop to look.

At first, I thought they were garden ornaments. The usual life-sized, athletically built but scantily clad statues that you get in posh gardens everywhere, but I was wrong. These weren't statues – they were people.

My first thought was that they were insane to be out in this weather which was sunny but cold. One or two of them had sheets draped elegantly but ineffectively around them – the others were naked. None of them had the classical physique of a Greek statue. As I stared, as if he felt my gaze, the one nearest me turned his head an inch or so to roll his eyes towards me, and my heart thumped with shock. These were real people. Patients? Staff? They'd been deliberately posed and then left in the gardens to stand in the cold. I couldn't believe it. Why didn't they run? At least swing their arms to try to stay warm. None of them were moving. They were literally human statues.

My second thought was that Sorensen must be out of his mind to do this. His patients usually comprised the great and the good. Politicians, archbishops, CEOs. I didn't recognise anyone out there but even so . . . What was he playing at? Surely this couldn't be some sort of bizarre therapy. The man looking up at me was shaking with cold; his hair was either covered with a thin coating of frost which glinted slightly in the bright sunshine or, cruel as it sounds, someone had tossed glitter over him. His expression didn't change even a fraction but as I watched, a tear ran down his ice-white cheek.

I was too shocked to move. I put my hand on the glass – a useless gesture of comfort and helpless sympathy. One of the men nudged me. 'Keep walking.'

I didn't want to go back to being manhandled again so I did as I was told.

The sight of those poor people out there had completely undone the benefits of my warm shower. I was shivering again as I walked down the rest of the stairs, and across the echoing hall.

Things hadn't changed much here. These were the surroundings you would expect of a discreet, upmarket hospital. There were no concrete floors and headache-inducing lights here. Comfortable chairs were grouped around low tables. There was good art on the walls – although at least one of them was a forgery, courtesy of Jerry. I wished very much he was here now. There was even a crackling log fire in the enormous fireplace. I trod across Turkish rugs, heading for the double doors that led to Sorensen's office.

He was waiting for me behind his desk. He didn't stand up as I entered. I was deposited firmly but not roughly in a chair and the two men left, closing the door behind them.

I looked around. The last time I'd been in here, his office had been immaculate, sterile and pretentious, entirely reflecting his own personality. An exquisite Turkish carpet on a gleaming parquet floor. Ugly and therefore expensive modern art hanging on the walls, and a huge desk – which according to Jones was a sure sign of size issues – with everything precisely placed upon it, including his sleek black laptop.

Now, however, the floor was dull. I could see footprints tracked through the dust. And there was more dust on his desk. As usual, he sat with his back to the French windows, which made his features difficult to read. I looked at his colour instead, but even that was clamped down tight. Just a thin outline of dirty white with hardly any movement at all. I was reminded of a volcano just before its big moment.

I suspected he was terrified. Frightened almost out of his mind. Like little Alyson Painswick. Such lack of movement in colours wasn't natural. For a moment I wondered if, given where we were, he'd drugged himself, because this wasn't the stillness of, say, Leanne Elphick, who had no emotions for her colour to reflect – this was the stillness of almost complete control. I suspected that left to itself, his colour would be scrabbling at the window, desperate to get away. What could terrify someone like Sorensen so much? I remembered the people in the garden and waited for him to speak first. I had a very strong feeling that a show of docility and obedience would be a very wise move.

We faced each other in silence. There was no preamble. No greeting. He got straight to it.

'Mrs Cage, I will ask you questions which you will answer. Whether you live or die will be determined by your level of cooperation. Whether Alyson Painswick continues to benefit from my protection or I allow her to become part of the entertainment laid on for others will be determined by your level of cooperation. Whether my guests are able to discontinue their . . . outdoor therapy . . . and are allowed to return to the shelter of this building will be determined by your actions. You hold many lives in your hands. Failure to answer my questions will result in a death. And then another death. And so on. Until you comply. Please indicate your understanding.'

I could do nothing. This was not the moment. His voice sounded stilted and was pitched higher than usual. The thought came to me – I don't know from where – that we were being watched. And he hadn't mentioned Michael Jones.

Unwilling to do or say the wrong thing, I simply nodded.

'Very well.' He opened his laptop and turned it to face me, making a business of carefully lining it up with the edge of the blotter. His hands were shaking – whether with emotion or the strain of his abnormal self-control I had no idea. The screen showed five images. Three women and two men. 'Please tell me if you recognise any of these people.'

I leaned forwards and stared at his screen, quite bewildered. This wasn't what I'd been expecting at all. Why was he showing me this? We looked at each other and then, just for the briefest second, his colour reached out to me and I thought I had it. This was a cry for help. This was why he'd brought me to his clinic. For a moment I felt a flare of anger. What had he done to Michael Jones just to get me here?

Now, too late, I remembered Sorensen's plea to me when he'd found us at the Cider Tree – was it only last night? Jones and I had been so caught up in each other that we'd paid him no attention and so, in desperation, he'd brought me here the only way he could. That would be a lesson to me in the future. To pay more attention. Not to put my personal life first.

Sorensen was watching me quite intently. Was he trying to convey some message? *Were* we being watched? I was certain of it. Sorensen wasn't operating alone. Someone else was here and he was terrified of them. It was the only explanation. That was why he'd tracked us down last night. He'd been frantic. And we'd ignored him.

I didn't dare look around for possible cameras. I stared intently at the laptop while I tried to think what to do. What to say.

'Mrs Cage?'

His voice recalled me to the present.

I took a chance. I had no idea who any of these people were and he must know that, so I felt perfectly safe in saying, 'No. I don't recognise anyone on the screen.'

He said, 'You are certain?'

'Positive.'

'Very well.' He turned his laptop back and tapped a few keys. 'What about this?'

He turned the laptop again. Very carefully. To keep it away from the cameras? The screen now read, *For God's sake, help me*.

I looked at him. His face was unnaturally still. His expression

299

that of a man on the very brink. As if he was holding his breath. Now I was convinced of it. We *were* being observed. He'd brought me here to help him. I was faced with the not very comforting suspicion that Dr Sorensen had bitten off more than he could chew and I was, in some way I wasn't yet aware, supposed to save the day.

I didn't know what to do or what to say.

He tapped another key. The screen now read, *I'm a prisoner. They're killing people.*

I clutched my hands in my lap. 'No,' I said slowly. 'I've no idea about that.'

He tapped again. *I tried to get help. Last night.*

My stomach slid. He had. And we'd been so caught up in ourselves . . . If only we'd taken a little time to listen.

You're the only person who can help.

I still didn't know what to say or do. Who – or what – was watching us at this moment?

He closed the lid and pulled his laptop towards him. 'You look very pale,' he said suddenly. 'Are you feeling faint?'

'Yes,' I said, thinking I was following his lead. 'A little.'

'Would you like some water?'

I nodded.

He crossed to a side table, picked up a jug and poured a glass. Ice clinked expensively because it was that sort of establishment.

I used the time to let my mind drift . . . water . . . anticipation . . . shut . . . control . . . crying . . . pain . . . overwhelming fear . . . Some things were starting to fall into place.

He'd lost control of his own clinic. Last year he'd told me he didn't need me any longer. That he'd found someone else. I'd wondered at the time if he'd been bluffing but it would seem he hadn't. He had found someone else. Or, much more likely, they had found him. Whoever they were, he'd thought he could control them and sadly for him, it had turned out to be the other way around and now he was desperate.

In his own way, Sorensen was a powerful and important man. He was keeper of some of the country's most embarrassing secrets. He spoke and ministers listened. And yet there was something here that was frightening the living wits out of him. I remembered the people in the garden. That wouldn't have been him. That would have been someone else. Someone had seized the opportunity to control him. I remembered what Jones had said about his recent mishandling of a political situation – could he have been manipulated into doing that? Or somehow compelled? Or even just terrified into it?

And that might be only part of it. It was hard to clear my mind of the human statues in the garden. Just what had been going on here behind the high walls since last summer? This was a discreet establishment under Sorensen's complete control. Or had been. I didn't want to think of all the things they could have made people do. Making people stand in the cold until they collapsed or even died might be the least of it. And what was the point of that? Did they do it for amusement? Simply because they could? And who were *they*? A memory stirred. Of Iblis telling me his story back in the summer. A story of death and cruelty. Of the Fiori. The most ruthless and brutal of all the demons.

Had Sorensen somehow become involved with a Fiori? I wondered what it could have offered him. Whatever he wanted, probably. It wouldn't be important because he'd never get it. I could just imagine him being led further and further down the garden path, always convinced he was the one in charge, right up until the very moment when he wasn't and it had turned on him. Now everything was going wrong for him – as it was always bound to do – and here he was, trapped in a nightmare web of his own making. Desperate for a way out, he'd brought me here to do it for him. And I would do it. I would have to. If there was a Fiori here somewhere . . . possibly watching us now . . .

I sipped my water slowly, taking my time while I considered how best to word my reply.

'You know perfectly well that I'll assist you, Sorensen, but only if you guarantee no harm will come to Alyson Painswick.'

I put Michael Jones out of my head because I was convinced he was dead. If I could tell myself he was dead, then Sorensen couldn't hold that threat over me.

He inclined his head. 'Agreed.'

'What do you want from me?'

He opened his laptop and tapped again. Now the screen read, *Help me get rid of them.*

I finished my water and reached out to put the empty glass on his desk and as I did so, something changed. I froze. What had I just done?

He stared at the glass and then at me. His colour was beginning to move – shifting in a way that was hard to interpret. As if he couldn't keep it in any longer. Something bubbled below the surface. Subtle – but suddenly something was different. He was still afraid but now there was a new strength to him.

I said, 'Tell me what you want me to do.'

He smiled at me and it wasn't pleasant. My heart knocked

302

against my ribs in sudden fear. 'My dear Mrs Cage, you have already done it.'

He opened a drawer and removed what looked like airline tickets and his passport.

'What are you doing?'

'Running away, Mrs Cage. Saving myself and leaving you – a very acceptable substitute – in my place.'

'I don't understand.'

'Of course you don't. A stupid little housewife like yourself could have no idea what's truly happening here, and in a very short space of time, you won't be in a position to care, anyway. Allow me to offer my thanks. I hadn't thought it would be so easy.'

A horrible cold feeling was creeping over me.

His colour was surging around him now. He was desperate to be gone.

I gripped the arms of my chair and said, 'What have you done, Sorensen?'

'Saved my life. At the expense of yours, admittedly. Which causes me no regret at all. And at the expense of Michael Jones's life as well. Which causes me even less regret. This really is all your own fault, you know. If you had joined with me when I first proposed it, then none of this would have happened. All these lives are on you, Mrs Cage. I'll leave you to reflect on that for the very short time you are still capable of rational thought.'

He stuffed his laptop into his briefcase, snapped it closed and began to move towards the French windows.

I stood up. I don't know why. 'I don't understand.'

'Isn't it obvious – I'm making my escape. I'm disappearing in all the excitement.'

'What excitement?'

'Oh, Mrs Cage, things are about to get very exciting indeed. For you, that is.'

He picked up my empty glass and held it in front of my face.

'You see, I've just administered a dose of Ghost – and you drank it.'

CHAPTER NINETEEN

There was a sudden rush of icy air and then the French windows closed behind him, leaving me alone in his office, stunned. His words rang around my head. He'd given me Ghost. I'd taken a deadly drug. Why hadn't I noticed? Why hadn't I paid more attention? Why had I allowed Sorensen to distract me? I'd been so busy trying to read his colour and understand his motives that I'd completely missed everything else. How could I have been so stupid? My heart began to race. Was it panic? Or was it Ghost?

How long would I have before the effects began to kick in? How long before the door between worlds opened and something came through – looking for me? Twelve hours, Jones had said. People took the drug and twelve hours later they were dead. I wouldn't have twelve hours because that was only when they were discovered. I might only have minutes.

I put my clenched fists to my chest, leaned forwards and struggled to breathe. My instinct was to follow Sorensen out through the French windows and get as far away as I could from this place. But what good would that do? With my own eyes I'd seen the futility of running. And, I asked myself – this urge to run – was that instinct? Or was that Ghost? Colin Allenby had run and it hadn't saved him.

305

I sat down again. I tried to make myself calm down. I had very little time. Stop and think. I must forget the ease with which Sorensen had played me. That wasn't helpful right now. He'd allowed me to see his fear and in trying to help him, I'd sealed my own fate. I was ashamed of how easily I'd been tricked. Michael Jones had once warned me Sorensen was a master manipulator. That influencing and controlling people was what he did. Something I remembered only now that it was far too late. Far, far too late. He'd stopped threatening me – which only hardened my resolve. He'd dropped his guard, appealed to me for help and I'd fallen for it. Stupid, stupid Elizabeth Cage.

Stop thinking about that. I must concentrate. I must think. What could I do?

For myself, nothing, but for everyone else ... The world must be warned about Sorensen and his clinic and what was happening here and there was one person who would believe me. He was probably dead, but perhaps I could leave a message on his voicemail and sooner or later, given who he was, someone would pick it up. It would find its way to Mary Bennet. Suddenly, I was very glad I'd met her. Glad I wasn't completely alone in this. This might be my last act on earth but with her help I could make it count.

There was a phone on Sorensen's desk. Glancing behind me at the door, I leaned over and picked it up. I dialled nine for an outside line and then Michael Jones's number.

It rang once ... would anyone answer?

It rang twice ... come on, come on.

Three times ... I imagined a telephone ringing in the silence of his wrecked flat and Jones lying on the floor, his dead eyes staring at nothing. The police might be there already. He wouldn't have gone quietly. One of his neighbours would have reported the noise of a fight, surely.

Four times . . . come on, voicemail. And then, at the other end, I thought I heard a click. At exactly the same moment, the door opened behind me. I slammed down the phone and spun around, expecting the worst, but it was only Mrs Painswick.

Her colour had darkened considerably since I'd last seen her. Given what had been going on here that was hardly surprising. Only faint traces of her original gentle orangey colour remained. Was that because of fear? Distress? Panic? The reason really wasn't important right now.

Her motherly face creased with concern as soon as she saw me. 'Oh, my dear – Alyson said you were here. You must come with me. We need to get you somewhere safe.'

'It's too late,' I whispered. 'Leave me. I'm not safe. Sorensen's run away. The police have found a body in your house and they'll be looking for you. Leave now, so you and Alyson can get to safety.'

She ignored most of that. 'It's never too late, dearie. Up you come, now.'

I stood up. My head still throbbed from the lights in the basement and my leg still ached from the injection but otherwise, physically, I felt fine.

She was very strong. She put her arm around my waist and took most of my weight. We left Sorensen's office and set off across the empty silence of the main hall.

I asked where we were going.

'To find Alyson,' she said, and for some reason her voice seemed a very long way away.

There was no one in the hall. Or at the nurses' station at the top of the stairs. In fact, the whole building had an empty feel about it.

I tried to stop and look around. 'Where is everyone?'

She smiled. 'Those that can are running away as fast as possible. If they know what's good for them.'

'We should go, too. We need to find Alyson and get out of this place.'

'Yes.'

The floor seemed to ripple slightly. That couldn't be right. She shifted my weight.

'I can walk,' I said.

She made no reply.

'I said I can walk.'

There was still no response from her. I was convinced I could feel Ghost coursing through my veins. My instinct was to push her aside and run. Just run. As far and as fast as I could. To run across the crisp white snow . . . feel the icy air crackle around me . . .

I pulled myself up. There was no snow. What was I thinking?

Surely, by now, I should be experiencing some sort of symptom. Giddiness. Or nausea. Or weakness. But I wasn't. The world was sharp and crisp and clear. As if I could see further and more clearly than ever before.

'I can see colours,' I said, watching a beautiful blue spiral unwind itself and disappear in a shower of gold. Like a firework.

'I know you can, dearie. It's the only reason you're still alive.'

I looked at her big, moon face with the slightly protuberant watery-green eyes. Like overboiled gooseberries. She was smiling her kind, motherly smile but it didn't look right.

I squinted at her. 'Why are you smiling?'

'Because you're so fucking stupid.'

It took a second or two for the words to register and then I couldn't stop staring. It was as if I was seeing her clearly for the first time. As if I'd been peering at her through a haze for all the time I'd known her. I tried to pull away. Cold dread crept through me. It would seem that Sorensen wasn't the only thing I'd got wrong. It was dawning on me, slowly and horribly, that I'd made a terrible, terrible mistake and it was standing right next to me and had me in its grasp and wouldn't ever let me go.

Her smile broadened. 'You never guessed, did you? You never even got close. You're the great Elizabeth Cage and you never had a fucking clue.'

I tried to back away from her but she had hold of my waist. I could sense her strength. 'Who are you?'

'I searched for you for such a long time, Elizabeth, and then one day it dawned on me that I was going about it all wrong. I shouldn't be looking for you – I should be looking for that murderous bitch Melek. I was certain she'd never let you out of her sight. And look – I was right.'

I was completely bewildered. None of this was making any sense. Why would she find me by looking for Melek? I'd only met her a few months ago – and so I tried to tell Mrs Painswick, but the words were too difficult. I reached out to the wall for some support and it leaned away from me. I made a huge effort. 'Why? Why were you looking for me?'

She ignored me. Or perhaps I hadn't spoken aloud. Reality was beginning to slip away from me.

'She hid you well, I'll grant her that, but finally I have you.' She jerked me towards her and began to stroke my hair. My scalp crept. 'There's something special about you, Elizabeth.

309

What is it, I wonder?' She smiled at me. 'What is so special about Elizabeth Cage?' Her voice was very gentle. 'Shall we try to find out?'

'There's *nothing* special about me,' I said, jerking my head away, and my voice sounded strange in my ears. Whether this was the effect of Ghost or just plain terror, I didn't know. 'Honestly, I'm just ordinary. Everyone says so. Even Sorensen calls me a housewife.'

I was gabbling because I think I had the idea that if I could just keep her talking that something would happen. Anything. Or someone would come. Anyone.

She wagged a playful finger. Or possibly more than one. I couldn't see that well. 'Now, dearie, don't lie to me. You'll find I don't like it.'

She smiled again but somehow it was all wrong. The last of her colour was breaking up because she didn't need to maintain the pretence any longer, dissolving into something I'd never seen before. Something dark that writhed about her – wet and gleaming like raw flesh. Something with a life of its own. Something that fed on her and from her and she on it and my heart nearly stopped because I realised I was looking at evil made manifest. I knew, I just knew, that I was looking at a Fiori demon.

'Finally,' she said comfortably, seemingly aware of my thoughts. 'It certainly took you long enough. But I do think that now you know, it's only polite to tell me what *I* want to know. Who are you, Elizabeth Cage? Who are you *really*? What secret does Melek use you to conceal? Mm?' Her breath was hot on my face. I tried to flinch away. 'Tell me and live.'

I didn't have the faintest idea what to do. Or what to say.

If she wanted to know who I was, then she was asking the wrong person. Perhaps I should keep her talking. 'You're a Fiori, aren't you?'

She laughed. Her fingers dug painfully into my arm. 'I suspect young Iblis has been talking out of turn, but yes, I am. How is he, by the way? Still without his sword, I believe. What a careless boy he is, to be sure.'

I could feel the blood draining from my face. My skin felt taut and stretched too tightly across my cheekbones. 'Where's Mrs Painswick? What have you done with her?'

'*I'm* Mrs Painswick, dearie. We met at the Local History meetings. You must remember – the most boring people on the planet, of which – and I do hope you won't mind me mentioning this – you were one of the worst. Do you remember how they just droned on and on? And that silly librarian – what was her name? Stoppard – so madly in love with that funny little man – McClelland.'

'They're not there any longer,' I said. 'They went away together.'

'Is that what you thought? Oh dearie, dearie me. I do hope you weren't hoping for a happy ending for them because – and I can hardly bring myself to tell you this – after all that unrequited longing, they really didn't enjoy each other at all. Not even a little bit. No matter how hard I tried. They didn't enjoy each other right up until the moment their efforts killed them. So sad.'

I looked at her through new eyes. 'You murdered them.'

'Well, don't say it like that, dear. I did them a favour. I think, in the end, they were glad to go.'

'You killed your husband, too.'

311

'That's right. With one of those Le Creuset pans, would you believe? They're very heavy. Do you know if you hit one hard enough, it shatters into a million tiny pieces? You would not believe the mess.'

My lips felt stiff. 'I shouldn't imagine it did your husband much good either.'

'Not the pan, dearie – the husband. He went *everywhere*.'

I made a final, pitiful attempt at returning to the world I'd known. 'Did you kill him in self-defence? Because if so . . .'

'Of course not – I killed him for pleasure. I started with his feet and then I just hit him and hit him until he died. Such fun. But very splashy. It's going to take more than a squirt of Mr Sheen and a quick hoover round to clear up the ex-Mr P.'

'You killed him for fun?'

'Of course, dear. There's never anything on the TV these days and they're always telling us we should make our own entertainment. I mean, just look what I'm doing here. You've missed a lot of the jollity and glee but we can soon make up for that. You should have been here when that fat nurse exploded. Or when that silly woman set fire to her own hair. Do you know, she just wouldn't stop smiling – right up until the very end. Just think what I can make you do. Rip off your own face, perhaps. Or boil the flesh off your hands while singing songs from hit musicals. You are mine now – along with everyone else still in this place. Welcome to your own little private pocket of hell.'

I said desperately, 'People know I'm here.'

'Fat lot of good that will do them. Or you.'

I swallowed hard. 'What do you want from me?'

'To discover what it is you hide.'

I tried to twist away from her. 'I'm not hiding anything.'

312

'Now we both know that's not true. Let's do a deal – you tell me everything and I might not kill you. Resist me and I'll take you apart myself. Inch by inch. Bone by bone. Sinew by sinew. It will take a very, very long time, which won't be pleasant for either of us. Well, no, that's not quite true – I'll enjoy it immensely – but in the end, I will know what it is you hide and you'll just be a stain that won't come out of the carpet.'

Keep her talking. If she was talking to me then she wasn't doing anything else.

'It was you. You made that witch's ladder. The one Iblis found in my porch. It was you.'

'That's right. I gave it to Sorensen to deliver. One of the few things he managed to do right.'

'You cursed me.'

She considered, her head on one side. 'Not one of my better efforts, I think. Now, come along. Time's a-wasting.'

'But . . .'

She slapped me. 'Let's start as we mean to go on, shall we, dearie? No one speaks unless I tell them to.'

I tried to shrug carelessly. I think that was a bit of a pitiful failure. 'OK. But there's something you need to know. About Sorensen.'

She was contemptuous. 'He won't help you.'

My whole body was trembling. Fear, cold, Ghost, or all of them. 'Actually, I rather think he has. I'm sorry to tell you this, because I'm sure you won't take it well – but he's beaten you.'

She didn't like that. Her face set into an expression that made my blood run cold. That's such a cliché but it really happens. I felt as if my whole body had been plunged into icy water, but what did I have to lose? I had one demon in front of me and I

313

was due another any minute now. Was I actually in a position where death by Ghost was the preferable way to go?

She shook me hard. My teeth rattled and I bit my own tongue. 'How?' she demanded. 'How could Sorensen possibly beat *me*?'

I shook my hair back off my face and shouted, 'Very easily. You're not as clever as you thought. He gave me Ghost.'

She just stared. Endlessly. There was no doubt I'd taken her by surprise. Her hands fell away. She stared deep into my eyes. I don't know what she saw there but I suddenly saw an opportunity. If I was wrong, I doubted she would be able to resist the temptation to tell me so, and all the time she was talking to me then she wasn't taking me apart to find some secret I didn't know I possessed.

'You know – Ghost – the drug you offered Sorensen in exchange for access to me?'

'No,' she said, and there was anger in her voice. And uncertainty. Had Sorensen unwittingly defeated her after all? Because if I succumbed to Ghost then that would put a serious crimp in her plans for me. If my demon killed me before she discovered this supposed secret – this thing I didn't know anything about – then she'd lost. It would, presumably, die with me. All her effort – only to have it snatched away from her at the last moment. And by a mortal, too.

I added fuel to the fire, sacrificing Sorensen without a second thought. 'Only just before he left, he told me he had everything he needed to get rid of you and go it alone. He was rather pleased with himself, actually. He said by the time you realised what was going on, it would be far too late. I don't know what he's got planned – he didn't tell me – but he was in a great hurry to get away. So it's all gone wrong for you really, hasn't it? Sorensen

314

has outwitted you. You'll never find my secret now because I'm just a dead woman walking. And you're . . .'

For a fraction of a second, I think she believed me. There was a flicker of uncertainty in her eyes. I didn't wait any longer. Fear gave me strength. I turned and ran. Physically, I was certain I could outrun her. And I'd be running for my life.

One demon at a time. That was what I told myself. One demon at a time. I would deal with what I suspected was the lesser demon first.

I could hear Jones's voice in my head. 'Run, Cage. Find somewhere safe if you can. But mostly – run.'

I kicked off the stupid slippers and tore up the stairs two at a time, racing past the deserted nurses' station at the top, past the lift, and down the left-hand corridor with the fire exit at the end. Perhaps she didn't know I'd been here before and was familiar with the layout. Perhaps Sorensen hadn't told her. Although I suspected he had. He wouldn't have had any choice.

How far would I get? How far would I be allowed to get?

Perhaps I should have stayed with her. Perhaps she had the strength to overcome my own demon? But then what? I'd be completely in her power.

No – run, Cage. Run. Because your life depends on it.

I slipped through the fire doors as quietly as I could. Sorensen's luxurious clinic stopped dead on this side of the doors. There were no more expensive pastel shades on the walls, no more quietly luxurious floor coverings, no more expensive art on the walls. Like the basement, this was all bare concrete and harsh strip lighting.

I stopped and listened. I thought I heard a door open and close above me so I didn't hang around. The stairs moved beneath my feet. I'm sure they didn't but at least that was how it felt. I held on to the railing with both hands and concentrated on putting one foot in front of the other. One, two. One, two.

Now I was back in the maze of basement corridors again. Nothing good had ever happened to me in this basement. A corridor telescoped away from me – a long, grey distorted tube that stretched into the distance. Was I, literally, too terrified to see straight? And at what point would my demon turn up?

All the doors were open and the rooms behind them yawned like giant caves in which lurked unseen monsters. The fire doors at the end of the corridor were zip-tied shut. Not a problem if I had some sort of implement but obviously I didn't.

At least my socked feet were soundless. I stood for a moment, considering my options, and in the silence and the stillness I felt the air move. What was that? I was in a basement. There were no windows. No wind. Was it here already? Was something standing behind me at this very moment? I gritted my teeth, shaking with fear and cold. I didn't know what to do. If my demon stood behind me then running was useless – I'd seen that. However far I ran, it would always be just behind me. Waiting for the moment when I couldn't run any longer. When my strength failed and I fell to the ground and watched my life torn from me. My breath was coming short and fast and my heart was thudding. I trembled on the verge of hysteria.

Should I turn and look, while I was still strong enough to fight for my life? Could I overcome my own demon? Could I fight?

No, I could not. In my mind I already knew what would happen. I would turn. The thing would hurl itself at my face, wrapping its wet, skinny arms and legs around me, breathing its breath into my face. I would fall to the ground and from that moment I would be lost. I would be helpless, feeling the weight of the demon crush my chest as it tore my life from me and ate it in front of my very eyes.

I choked out some sort of gasping sob that sounded very loud in the silence and, strangely enough, that was what jerked me back from the edge. I should stop panicking and use the little time I had left to plan.

How long since I'd drunk the water?

I had no watch but at least half an hour, surely. And yes, I was petrified and near hysterical and the walls and floor were behaving oddly, but my own terror could be responsible for that.

My own terror could be responsible for *all* of this. Stop. Think. Think it through. What if Sorensen hadn't given me Ghost after all? What if this was all a colossal bluff to enable him to slip away while I panicked and ran, thereby attracting attention and allowing him to escape? I know it was wishful thinking, but the more I thought about it, the more I liked that idea. There was no Ghost. There was nothing behind me. Was I terrifying myself for nothing?

But Mrs Painswick had looked into my eyes. She'd seen something . . .

I couldn't move for fear and indecision. Should I be looking for somewhere to hide from Mrs Painswick? Should I try to make a run for it, like Colin Allenby? But where would I go? Oh God, what should I do? What could I do?

The nearest door was on my right and it was open. I stared into the darkness, wondering what terrors it could contain, and then thought, oh for heaven's sake – what could be worse than this?

I reached around the jamb, switched the light on and knew

immediately that all my thoughts about not having been given Ghost had been just so much wishful thinking because I was looking at some kind of laboratory. I had no time to take in the details. I saw only a tangle of glass equipment – tubes, flasks and beakers. Things bubbled and dripped. The smell was so appalling, it sickened my soul. This was where Sorensen had manufactured the drug. First-class medical facilities and an isolated location. The Sorensen Clinic was ideal. They manufactured it here and Sorensen had indeed given me a dose. I was a dead woman walking.

I deliberately struck my hand on a workbench. The pain I felt brought me back. Even a dead woman walking could do something. I needed to find a phone. Someone had to be told about this.

Or – and here was a better thought – I could set off the fire alarm. This was a medical facility. With important patients. The system would be connected to the local fire station. Given the nature of this place, the fire service would tear up the roads getting here. As would the police. I looked around. There should be one in every room. That little red box on the wall.

In the event of a fire break glass.

I broke the glass with my elbow and waited for the ear-splitting siren.

Nothing happened. I waited, but still nothing happened. They'd disconnected the system. Of course they had. This was a laboratory and the fumes would have set it off every ten minutes. I had to think of something else.

I backed out into the corridor, and the demon that had been Mrs Painswick was standing there, waiting for me. Even though I now knew what she was, I still couldn't quite believe it. She looked exactly as she had throughout all our Local History meetings – plump and kindly, wearing one of those highly patterned, old-fashioned dresses belted under her ample bosom, comfortable but not flattering. Her shoes were flat and sensible, distorted on one foot by a bunion, and her hair had that slightly over-permed look. Her disguise was perfect. I'd often sat and chatted with her and I'd never had even the slightest inkling she wasn't exactly what she appeared to be. The implication of domestic abuse had been beautifully understated. She'd never actually said a word – we'd seen the bruises which were almost certainly just make-up – and drawn completely the wrong conclusions. And all the time we thought Alyson was terrified of her father, it was actually her mother. No wonder Mrs Painswick wouldn't let her out of her sight.

And I hadn't had a clue. Not a clue. I was almost certainly as stupid as she said I was. But then I remembered Iblis – who'd spent some considerable time with the Fiori demon, Allia – had had no suspicion either and he'd actually been hunting them at the time. He'd said they were entwined in human lives and he was right. That was their strength. You never knew they were there until it was too late. And now, one of them stood in front of me.

And with that thought, something placed a gentle hand on my shoulder and a well-loved voice behind me said, 'Now then, lass, you've got yourself into a right pickle here, haven't you?'

I froze.

'Good girl,' said my dad. 'You just keep quiet and still and we'll soon have you out of this.'

Oh my God. It was actually him. It was my dad. Not a demon. Ghost worked. All right, it had all gone horribly wrong for Colin Allenby, but for me, Ghost had actually worked. My dad stood

319

behind me. The compulsion to look around was overwhelming. I could see my dad again.

Mrs Painswick's voice sharpened and became compelling. 'No, no,' she said. 'Look at me, Elizabeth. Concentrate on *me*. What stands behind you is not what you think. Just keep looking at me because I can keep you safe. I promise you that I am more than equal to the thing behind you. Trust *me*, Elizabeth. In fact – and this is rather ironic, don't you think? – you have a choice between the devil you know and the devil you don't. With me you have an outside chance of life. Choose what stands behind you and death is certain.'

I could smell golden wood and days long past.

'Days that could come again,' said my dad. 'We'll just have a bit of a chat, shall we, and then your mum's got tea on. Come on, lass. Take my hand.'

'No,' said Mrs Painswick forcefully, and I was angry because her voice brought me back from where I wanted to be, right back to this place. Where I definitely *didn't* want to be.

'Just believe,' said my dad. 'That's all you have to do, lass. Just believe in me and all this goes away. That's something nasty you've got yourself involved with there, but she can't hurt you. Don't look at her. Just turn around and everything will be all right again.'

'Elizabeth – look at *me*.'

My dad sighed. 'Lizzie, lass, I told you to keep it hidden and you didn't listen, did you? Never mind, it can all be fixed. Take my hand, now.'

I closed my eyes. Tears ran down my cheeks. I so badly wanted to believe. Even knowing what I knew . . . I still wanted to believe.

'Elizabeth!'

I opened my eyes. Plump, kindly Mrs Painswick stood before me, motherly concern written all over her face. 'Listen to me. I can defeat the demon standing behind you. Just give me what I want. Tell me now and I promise you will go free. Just tell me what I want to know and you can go home.'

'Tea's ready, lass, and your mum's waiting.'

'Don't turn around, Elizabeth. Don't look at it. Let me help you.'

I sobbed, 'Why? Why are you doing this?' and I couldn't have told you which of them I was speaking to.

It was Mrs Painswick who answered. She leaned in towards me and her eyes went soft. Her voice was gentle and compassionate. 'You genuinely don't know, do you? I didn't think you did. You're the poor, sad, exploited innocent. You have no idea what they've done to you and now you're going to die because of that. But I'm not Melek. Listen to me, Elizabeth. I can defeat the demon standing behind you, and I will if you give me what I want. Just tell me your secret. It can't stand against me. There is no need for you to die if you will just help me.'

I couldn't help it – I shuddered. The compulsion to look behind me was overwhelming.

I could only manage a whisper. 'I don't know what it is that you want?'

She didn't have time to answer. The demon behind me ran its hand across the back of my neck. Gently, tenderly. The caress of a father for his daughter.

I shuddered again. I had a demon standing in front of me. Another stood behind. A deadly drug was pumping its way through my veins. My breath was coming in terrified sobs. I just wanted everything to be over, to be finished. I wanted the peaceful sleep of death without the pain of dying.

And then, the thing that lives inside my head opened its eyes, uncurled itself, and spoke in its own voice.

'No.'

CHAPTER TWENTY

Mrs Painswick stood stock-still for a moment, mouth open, almost comical in her surprise and disbelief, and then her whole face lit up with savage triumph. This was what she had wanted. Not me. I wasn't important. It was the other one.

She crowed. She actually crowed. 'You! Yes! There you are. There you are at last.'

She flung her head back. That gentle orange had disappeared completely and now her colour was dark and wet and greedy and streaked with red. Like blood.

'Come out – I command you. Show yourself.'

The walls leaned inwards and then back out again. As if they were breathing. The thing behind me had abandoned all pretence and held my neck in a grip of iron. I could feel its nails digging into my flesh. Something warm ran down my back.

'Come out,' she shouted. 'Elizabeth Cage is finished. Her demon will have her. Come out and save yourself.' She looked at me and laughed. 'You truly are one of the most stupid people I've ever met. Ghost doesn't open a door into another world – it opens a door into yourself. It's your own personal demon who comes through. The one that every mortal creates for himself. The one who knows what you think. The one who knows what you've done. The voice in your head that tells you to step off that ledge . . . stab that old woman . . . throw the crying baby into the fire . . . the one who knows exactly how worthless you really are and tells you so every moment of every day. That's what has you in its grip, Elizabeth Cage. And you've led such a long, long life, haven't you? So many shameful secrets. So many memories to bury. Such a powerful demon you've constructed for yourself. I'll leave you to him, shall I?'

Her voice changed and became deep and commanding. 'I know your name, Felda, and therefore I command you. Show yourself – show yourself now, Felda, Daughter of the Gods.'

I'd stopped listening to her. Her words echoed inside my head. 'Ghost opens a door into yourself.' That was what she had said. And doors open both ways. Yes, something had come through – it stood behind me now – but I also stood on a threshold. Whether it was her words, the drug, or a combination of both, I could *see*. Images whirled about me. No – not images. Memories. Things I'd never seen before but I remembered them just the same. What was happening to me? My heart was pounding in my chest as I struggled with something suddenly too big to contain. Something was forcing its way through. I tried. I tried to hold it inside – where it and I were safe – but there was nothing I could do. I cried out and fell to my knees. The pain was immense as something fought to tear itself free from me.

And the thing that lives in my head said, **'Don't fight me, Elizabeth. Just close your eyes. Trust me.'**

I had no choice. Whatever was happening to me was unstoppable. I was drowning in a sea of memories. I tried to hold them back but I might as well have tried to hold back time itself. My last protection shattered and I lost control of everything. I closed my eyes. Pictures, people, faces, places whirled before me. I was no longer me.

Because now I was the other one.

The one who led armies. The one who swept down from the cold, white north, all the way down into the hot, southern lands, pushing the Fiori before us. There was the victory – a great victory. A final victory, as we thought at the time. I saw the feasts and celebrations. We danced. We laughed. There were friends – old and new. And there was that moment – the moment that changed the world when I first laid eyes on the great champion of men, the demigod Borin, who had fought his way up from the south to meet me. He saw me and I saw him and there, under the stars in that hot, dry, rocky land on the shores of the Circle Sea, we lost ourselves in each other.

I saw the treaties drawn up. There would be a great alliance between all races. There would be four of us – Borin, Iblis, Melek and me – and together we would rid the world of the Fiori. As a mark of good faith between gods and men, the alliance would be ratified by a wedding. Everyone would be there. Kings, queens, priests, heroes, warriors, gods and demigods – all were welcome. All come to witness the joining that would usher in the new era of peace.

I saw the rocky hillside and the glittering sea beyond. I saw the sun that hurt my pale northern eyes, the tents with their brave, bright colours. The beginning of a Golden Age, they said. None would be able to stand before us and the Fiori would be no more. A great evil would be removed and, finally, men could flourish. I heard the music, the laughter, the clapping hands and stamping feet.

I saw the bridegroom's hunting party assemble. I heard the

friendly insults and the wagers placed. I saw them mount their horses, each with their favourite bow. I heard the shouted farewells. Indeed, I myself waved them off. Iblis, Borin, and all the others. I heard the clatter of hooves as they rode away over the hill.

I sat outside my tent with Melek and a few friends. We drank wine and talked. We spoke of our plans for the future. What the Golden Age would be for all. We spoke of the ceremony the next day and there were the usual jokes, which I laughingly pretended not to understand.

That was the last time I ever laughed.

I remember I sat in the shade on scarlet cushions trimmed with golden thread and held out my goblet for more wine and never had even the slightest forewarning. I saw Iblis canter back into our camp. Alone. I saw Melek stand up and go to speak with him and then they both turned to look at me and, in that moment, I knew that everything we had worked for, all our great plans for the future, my life and Borin's – everything had turned to dust.

They brought back his body later that day. A solemn procession of grieving men, all on foot to show respect. His horse had shied at a serpent basking on a rock and Borin had fallen and broken his neck. All those long years he'd fought the Fiori with barely a scratch to show for it, only to fall off his horse on the eve of our wedding and the fruition of all our plans.

I don't remember how I felt. It was a very long time before I felt anything at all. Someone – Melek, I suspect – had the wedding tents taken away. We buried him the next day. Those who had come for the wedding remained for the funeral games. I remember the heat and how I longed to return to the cool of my own country, but it was a long way off and I had duties here. The world paid its respects to its champion. I thanked them. They went away and I was alone but for Melek. She stayed with me a long time and then, at some point, she left, too. I barely noticed she had gone.

Over the years I raised a mighty mausoleum to Borin and I lived there for a long time. To be close to him. People came from far and wide. They brought gifts and walked in the gardens I had made and I like to think their minds were eased for a while. But mortals are short-lived and their memories even shorter. Those who had fought with him grew old and died. Their children died. And then *their* children died, too. Soon there were none who walked the earth who had ever known him. Only his name remained. And then, slowly, inevitably, even that faded from their minds, and the magnificent shrine I had built to keep his memory alive and bring comfort and hope to all was just an old building on the headland where the madwoman lived. I saw no one for years and years and years.

Except for Melek, who still returned from time to time and one day persuaded me to hunt with her again. We set off and only then did I realise how much I had missed this. Our combined fury pushed the Fiori further back than they had ever been. Iblis was there as well and together we devised a plan to finish them for ever. We split up, each with our own part to play but Iblis failed and it was a very long time before I saw him again. Iblis failed. The plan failed. *We* failed. The Fiori survived. Iblis disappeared. Melek disappeared after him, and I returned alone to Borin's grave.

It was gone. Not just the shrine. Everything had gone. The buildings, the gardens, everything. The earth was weak here.

Poseidon had struck the ground with his trident and the whole headland had fallen into the sea. All that remained of Borin, his deeds, his memory, his grave, was just a fresh scar on the mountainside and a new shoreline.

That was the day I knew I had truly lost him. This was so cruel. He had been taken from me before his time and now even his body had gone. And of all these mortals – on whose behalf we had laboured so hard and for so long – there wasn't a man anywhere who even knew his name, far less remembered his deeds. He had been Borin, the greatest hero of them all, and now he lay, his tomb broken, his bones crushed, for ever at the bottom of the sea.

With that thought, all my grief, for so long held at bay, burst forth. I cried, I raved, I cursed, I shouted. My senses left me and a darkness clouded my mind. I could no longer tell right from wrong. I no longer cared.

Nor did I care who I killed or why. I wanted only to cause others the grief that I had carried alone and for so long. I slaughtered my way across the world. Except for the north. Some instinct kept me away. Something prevented me from sullying the cold, fresh snows of my homeland with madness.

Where people had loved me, they now feared my name. My grief was upon me. It never grew any less. Time does not heal. Time just adds to the burden. I was sick and cared for nothing.

Eventually Melek found me again. I can't have been hard to find. My rage had left whole towns in ruins. I was out of control. The urge to kill, to destroy, to bring down the snow from the north and cover the world with rivers of ice was very strong and would not be denied. I was too tired and too sick to fight it. I asked for her sword, intending to do away with myself, and she refused. I asked her to do it for me and still she refused. I was angry. I struck her many times and still she refused. She held my face between her hands, and said, 'I have something important to say to you.'

I slept. Beautiful, blessed sleep where my thoughts were not of destruction and death and angry snow but of peace and stillness and the silent glow of the setting sun on the snowy mountaintops.

And now. Now this creature – this Fiori – sullied my name with her mouth. I would have her. I would kill again . . . and rejoice.

I looked at her. **'You dare to challenge me?'**

'I more than challenge. Now that I have found you, I can control you. I am your mistress. You will do my bidding.'

'And what of Elizabeth Cage?'

'She is dying. Her demon has her in his grasp. He will consume her.'

'No.'

'I know you, Felda. I know what you are. I have the power of your name. You will obey me. You will give me what I desire.'

'No.'

'I have found you. I will compel you. Your will is my will.'

'No.'

She laughed. She laughed at me. I felt the old anger begin to rise.

I said softly, **'Elizabeth?'**

The voice inside my head was very faint but I could hear her. 'I'm here.'

'Do not look. Keep your eyes closed. Sleep.'

She slept.

I considered this thing before me. This miniscule speck of life that dared to challenge me, Felda, Daughter of the Gods. I smiled.

The she-demon smiled back, thinking she had won. She would soon discover that she had not. A tiny snowflake danced past on an icy draught of air. We both watched it fall.

I continued to smile because this felt so good.

Her own smile began to congeal. Her lips cracked and bled. She fought me. She flooded my mind with thoughts of Borin, broken and dead in the dust, and it only made me stronger because I am Felda and I bear the grief of centuries as my burden and it makes me strong. I would break her for this. Her body jerked as I took control. I raised her hands to her face. I made her hook her own thumbs into the corners of her mouth and pull. I watched the blood flow, warm and wet. I made her drive her fingers into her eye sockets. She began to wail.

And then I made her split her own face apart. I felt her skin rip. I heard her bones crack. I made her pull again. And again. As she had done to others, so I did to her. I watched as, with one giant movement, she pulled herself apart. Blood fountained up the walls. Things puddled out on to the floor. She had stopped making a noise, but I wasn't ready to let her die yet.

I stood over her. **'I am Felda, Daughter of the Gods, and you, demon, are ended.'**

A tiny piece of something in the wet, red accumulation of things that had once been a demon moved slightly. It might have been submission. It might have been a plea for mercy. It wasn't important. I put my foot on it and ground it into nothing. It pleases men to believe their gods are good and kind and merciful. We are not.

The other demon was easy. It tried to run but the very ties that bound it to Elizabeth prevented its escape. It begged for my mercy.

I thought of the burden Elizabeth carried on my behalf. Every day. I looked at the demon that had cast its long shadow over her life and imagined how much lighter her life would be without it and that pleased me.

I think it thought my hesitation meant I was considering its request for mercy.

It tried to plead for its continued existence.

Quite unsuccessfully.

CHAPTER TWENTY-ONE

I have a great affection for Elizabeth Cage. We have walked a long path in the same body and she has borne much for me. She has kept me safe. In her, I have found both peace and the blessed forgetfulness of sleep. Now it was time for me to sleep again.

I found the stairs and returned to the main part of the building. The big hall. There was an armchair in front of the fire and I sat down. I felt no compulsion to linger in this world. It is a hateful place and I want no part of it.

'Elizabeth . . .'

'Yes?'

'**Goodbye.**' I closed my eyes and dreamed of the red sun setting behind the white mountains and the cold, lonely sighing of the wind.

I woke with a jerk. I was sitting in an armchair by the fire. I was still here in the Sorensen Clinic. There was silence all around me. Had I . . . had I been asleep? How was that even possible? What had happened? I remembered Sorensen had run away – although I didn't give much for his chances. I certainly wouldn't lift a finger to save him and I couldn't think of anyone else who would, either.

And he'd drugged me. I sat up suddenly, remembering. He'd

dosed me with Ghost but I seemed all right. I patted myself down. All my limbs were intact. There was blood splattered across my sweatshirt but it didn't seem to be mine. I wasn't bleeding that I could see. My leg still throbbed slightly from the injection but my headache had gone. I felt fine. In fact, I felt more than fine. Why hadn't Ghost worked on me? I couldn't kid myself I was immune. So what had gone wrong? Or rather, from my point of view, what had gone right?

There was an imitation antique clock of some kind on the mantel. I blinked and focused. More than an hour had passed since I'd left Sorensen's office. When he'd run away and left me.

Mrs Painswick. She'd helped me. Where had she gone? I looked around. There was no sign of her. And then I remembered the people outside. It was cold but the sun was shining. Could I still do anything for them? I ran to one of the big windows and looked through. From here I could see three so-called statues. My first instinct was to run outside and . . .

No. Stop and think, Cage. They would need professional help. I ran to the phone in reception and dialled 999. I took a deep breath and, without explaining in any way, requested ambulances to the Sorensen Clinic. People were suffering from exposure, I said. Possibly already dead. I put the receiver down on their questions.

Then I rang Jones's number again. Engaged. I was slightly annoyed. How could it be engaged? Who was using his phone? And what could be more important than this? I slammed the receiver down and ran out of the front door and down the steps to see if I could save anyone out in the gardens.

Some people were on the ground. One was obviously dead. Shockingly, it looked as if her head had been on fire. The sight

333

was horrible. I backed away. There was nothing I could do for her. One man was alive, though. A portly man with a fringe of grey hair. He was wearing a sheet like a toga and perhaps that slight protection had kept him alive. His head was sunk on his chest but he was still on his feet.

I took his arm, flinching at how cold his skin was. 'This way,' I said gently. 'Can you walk a little? It's not far.'

He blinked as if just waking up. He walked stiff-legged like a toy soldier but he walked. I guided him along the gravel path and up the steps. The hall seemed very warm after outside. I should get some blankets, but I needed to get more people out of the cold first.

I settled him in the armchair and trotted back outside in search of any other survivors.

I found another one standing by the fountain. A woman this time, posed with an urn. I shook my head at the cruelty of it all. Another man was floating in the water. I suspected he'd acted the part of fountain ornament and the cold water had killed him.

I took her pot away and led her towards the front door. She also was docile enough. I didn't know if this was because of what had been done to them or the effects of the cold. It didn't matter. I could hear sirens in the distance. I suspected the magic words *Sorensen Clinic* had bumped my call to the top of the list.

I was just trying to help her up the steps when the first police car screeched to a halt, showering gravel everywhere. The driver got out.

I shouted, 'Blankets if you've got them. And there are more people out there. Some are dead.'

I lowered her gently into the other armchair and when I looked out of the windows, a whole raft of emergency vehicles was racing up the drive. I knew from my previous visits that the linen store was just down the corridor so I began to pull out blankets and duvets as fast as I could. I made three or four trips, piling them in the middle of the hall ready for any other survivors they might find.

I covered my two with a blanket each. They seemed to be asleep. I didn't know if that was good or bad so I just gently pulled the blankets up to their chins and left them in peace.

I could hear people shouting outside. I think I even heard the clatter of a helicopter. Taking myself down to the reception area just inside the front door, I found a chair and sat back to await events. Not for very long.

One of the first persons sweeping through the door was Mary Bennet.

I was immediately aware there might be more benefits to working for her than I'd previously realised.

She said, 'Don't say a word to anyone,' and everything went into overdrive.

For me, there was no stopping to give police statements or face hostile questions or struggle with difficult explanations. I was wrapped in a blanket and escorted from the building. I heard her give crisp instructions to the police driver to take me to the Rushford Free, which seemed a bit of a waste of time since I was already in a medical facility, but I wasn't going to argue.

She held the car door open for me. 'Don't bother talking to the driver. He's under instructions not to speak to you. Someone will talk to you about a statement. Until then, say nothing about anything to anyone.'

I nodded. 'Don't let Sorensen get away; this is all his fault. He had his passport and airline tickets.'

She nodded. I said, 'Michael Jones?' but she slammed the door on my words and I don't think she heard me.

This was actually my second trip in a police car but I'd never been in one with a siren before. The traffic just melted away. I wish I'd been in a condition to enjoy it more. We were at the hospital within minutes.

Nobody paid any attention to me telling them I could walk. I was bundled into a wheelchair and whisked away. I leaned back, closed my eyes and waited for whatever bizarre event would happen next.

A doctor, then a shower and change of clothes, they said.

I protested. I'd had a shower and a change of clothes just a couple of hours ago and I really wanted to go home and could someone ring for a taxi, please.

They gestured at me. I looked down. I'd forgotten the front of me was speckled all over with blood and worse. When had that happened?

'It's not mine,' I said, but I might as well have spared my breath. It took the doctor quite a long time to establish that. I don't think he could believe I wasn't injured at all.

They queried the big bruise on my leg and I told them I'd been drugged. They took blood samples. I had no idea what that would reveal. After all, I was just a stupid housewife who knew nothing.

If I thought they'd let me go after all that, I was wrong. I was bundled into a hospital smock and dressing gown, put back in the wheelchair again and wheeled off to a different part of the hospital. The noise and hubbub died away as I was pushed into a short corridor with a policeman on guard at one end. There was one door on the left and one door on the right. We went left into a two-bed room and Michael Jones was propped up in the one on the left. His face was a mass of bruises. One eye was covered with a big gauze pad taped into place. Both sets of his knuckles were hugely bruised and swollen. Actually, most of him was hugely bruised and swollen.

My heart broke for him. They wheeled me to his bed and I burst into tears. I tried to hold his hand, then worried I was hurting him, tried to find an unbruised part of him to pat, failed, and just cried and cried.

A not very strong voice above my head asked me what the hell I thought I was doing.

'Crying my eyes out,' I sobbed.

'Bad choice of words, Cage,' he said, pointing to his dressing.

That set me off again. 'Oh God, have you lost your eye?'

'No, but it had a bit of a bad time and it's not feeling very well.'

I cried some more. So I'm not a modern woman ninja. Live with it.

He went to take a tissue from the box on his bedside table but misjudged the distance and missed. 'Curse my useless spatial awareness.'

I pulled one out and offered it to him.

'It's not for me, Cage. I'm not the one leaking snot all over the bedclothes. Let me tell you, you're in dead trouble. The nurses here are terrors. Don't expect me to defend you.'

I trumpeted into the tissue.

'I dunno, mate,' said a voice, and I realised Jerry was sitting in one of the visitor's chairs and had been here the whole time. He got to his feet. 'Your ability to make women cry across nine continents is unparalleled.'

'Don't be ridiculous,' said Jones. 'There are only seven continents and I'm pretty sure I've never been to Antarctica.'

'Whatever,' said Jerry on his way out. 'You're on your own, mate.' He put a brief hand on my shoulder, said, 'Don't worry, missis. He's had worse,' and with those not very comforting words, he disappeared out of the door.

Jones surveyed the results of my mopping up and presumably decided he could do better. 'Come here.' He grunted with pain and effort and the next minute I was up on the bed beside him.

'The nurses won't like it,' I said, worrying about what they would say.

'Cage, as I believe I've told you before – nurses are putty in my hands.'

As if by magic, the door opened and there stood a nurse. She put her hands on her hips. 'What's going on here?'

Jones flashed her what he probably thought was a winning smile. 'They keep saying the NHS is on its knees. Cage and I are doing our bit to help out. It's called bed-sharing. I can see it becoming quite popular.'

She looked at me. 'Is everything all right?'

'Hey,' said Jones, indignantly. 'I'm the patient here. You should concentrate on me.'

I nodded reassuringly at the nurse and tried to mop myself up again. The bed was littered with sticky tissues.

'Yuk,' said Jones. 'Look at this mess. I had no idea you were such an unpleasant bedfellow. Nurse, make her go away.'

She snorted. 'You made your bed. As far as I'm concerned, you can both lie in it.'

She backed out of the door again.

'See,' said Jones. 'Putty.' Wincing, he settled back against his pillows. 'Well, that's my job gone.'

'What? Why?'

He pointed to his eye.

'No,' I said, quite horrified. 'Surely not. You can still see.'

'Yes, I can, but if this turns out to be permanent, then I'll have no depth of vision,' he said. 'I can see the barn door but I won't be able to hit it.'

'But ...' I said, distressed by the thought. 'They can't do that.'

'Sweetheart, I've been hanging on by my fingertips ever since that business with Clare. Now everyone can breathe a sigh of relief. Including me. Honourable discharge. And a new life.'

'What will you do?'

'Dunno. Hang around with you, I suppose. Try to keep you safe while you do the same to others.'

'You mean – your idea about doing this sort of thing full-time?'

'Yeah, earn a living at it.'

'It won't be much of a living.'

'I'm not much of a person.'

'Stop that.'

'OK, no more self-pity. And I'm being stupid. I have some savings.'

'Surely you'll be entitled to some sort of compensation,' I said. 'Or a pension or something.'

He sighed. 'It's a sad fact of life, Cage, that we're not very good at this sort of thing in our country. Politicians, useless NHS managers, chief execs who swindle their shareholders and rob the pension pot – they all get very generous golden goodbyes,

339

but those who risk their lives, or fight for their country, or spend their lives working in the shadows, or give up the chance of a normal life, those who actually *do* serve, selflessly and with dedication – well, they don't. A tiny pension and a nation's grateful thanks and that's it.'

I'd been thinking. 'Don't let them kick you out.'

'Cage . . .'

'No,' I said. 'If we're to do this sort of thing on a regular basis, we'll need access to official resources.'

'Cage, I don't want you saying yes to Mary Bennet just because of me.'

'I'm not. I've already realised the many benefits of having Mary Bennet at my back. No awkward explanations to the police. No disbelieving stares. No being sectioned under the Act. And I came here in a police car and it was one of the most exciting things I've ever done in my life and I want to do it again.'

He grinned down at me. 'Cage, believe me, you haven't yet done the most exciting thing in your life. You still have that to look forward to.'

I smiled and snuggled closer. The nurse came back in and said, 'Well, what's it to be? Do I throw a bucket of cold water over you or a blanket?'

'A blanket, please,' I said meekly, because when I looked at Michael Jones, he'd gone to sleep.

CHAPTER TWENTY-TWO

In the end I gave my statement verbally to Mary Bennet herself. I couldn't blame her for wanting to make sure only she heard what I had to say. I told the exact truth because she might as well see what she was letting herself in for. That I'd been kidnapped, that Sorensen said he'd drugged me with Ghost but I didn't think it had worked – at least, not properly, because I'd survived – that he'd run away, that Mrs Painswick had helped me get out of his office, but that at some point I must have been overcome by the drug because when I awoke I was asleep in front of the fire. Then I'd gone out to try to save as many people as I could and rung the emergency services.

She, in turn, enlightened me.

Jones's neighbours, hearing noises from his flat, had called the police. His attackers had withdrawn at the first sound of the sirens, leaving him broken and bleeding on the floor. Although, according to eye-witness reports, two of them had had to be helped out of the building.

Only when he had regained consciousness was he able to tell them I was missing. It took him a while to remember talking to Sorensen earlier that evening and to put two and two together. And then someone thought to dial 1471 and discovered the last call had been from the Sorensen Clinic.

And then they'd been advised of my call to the emergency services. It had taken two members of staff to prevent him climbing out of bed to drag himself to my rescue. I looked forward to informing him I had rescued myself. And a few others as well.

Of the seven people discovered in the garden, two were already dead, two more weren't too bad, and the other three just hanging in there. Others had been discovered around the building. She wouldn't give me any details and I didn't ask. I could imagine.

I was sad to hear that the badly damaged body in the basement had finally been identified as that of Mrs Painswick. No one seemed quite sure what had happened to her. They said her injuries were consistent with having been trapped in heavy machinery, perhaps. The blood on my sweats was hers, apparently. Had I been with her when she was killed? Tried to render first aid, for example. I had to tell them I didn't know and no one pressed me.

Her daughter, Alyson, had been discovered hiding in an airing cupboard on the second floor. She was in a state of considerable shock and was being cared for in a special unit.

The Ghost manufacturing laboratory discovered in the basement was being dismantled and the contents removed for further investigation.

There was no sign of Sorensen nor any clue to his whereabouts. The clinic was under new management. As far as the outside world was concerned, the transition had been seamless. As Jones later put it, 'One of the holders of the nation's secrets has disappeared, Cage. Hell of a row going on in which I, for once, am not involved. In fact, I'm a hero. I warned my boss about him and she warned hers. Not our fault if no one took any notice.'

Mary Bennet went on to thank me, informed me a guard had been set on our room, instructed me to get well soon and departed.

I lay down and closed my eyes so no one would speak to me. There were strange images in my head and I didn't know what they were or where they'd come from. I vaguely remembered Mrs Painswick, but how she'd met her end I had no idea. Poor thing, it seemed her death had been as violent and bloody as her life.

There was nothing really wrong with me. I suspected I was being used to keep Michael Jones docile. We shared one room. I ignored his suggestion and occupied the other bed. He slept a lot and I watched the TV. We were on the news. One night only and they didn't make a big thing of it. Apparently there had been some sort of gas mains event at the Sorensen Clinic and all the patients had been evacuated. An unspecified number of patients had not survived and others were receiving treatment. In other news . . . and they'd moved on to the football results.

They discharged me at the end of the week and then Jones too because he refused to stay without me. We returned to his apartment where the doors had been repaired and the mess cleared up. Apart from the picture propped against the wall waiting to be reglazed, you wouldn't know anything had ever happened there.

I deposited Jones on the sofa and Jerry arrived. He drove me to my house to pick up some clothes and then we went shopping for food and whatever we thought would occupy Jones's attention and keep him still long enough for the healing process to continue.

He healed fast. Apparently, my cooking was enough to drive anyone to make a superhuman recovery. I told him Iblis had always seemed very happy with my cooking and he replied that that didn't reflect well on either of us.

The weeks were gentle and intimate. This was the sort of life I loved. Quiet but somehow satisfying. Despite everything that had happened, I felt more relaxed every day. As if a great weight I had been carrying for a very long time had somehow been lifted. I felt lighter, more cheerful, and more confident for the future. I had no idea what that future would be but somehow that didn't seem important any longer. I looked forward to it just the same. A long shadow had departed from my life and the sun had come out.

Jones was full of plans. 'New year, new job for us both,' he said, several times. And it would be nice to have a girlfriend who could earn her own living, he said. Girlfriends were expensive. Well, his always were.

I watched his colour, more golden than red, settle itself around him. The dark patches had receded as he healed. There were no jagged edges. No streaks of orange. He was relaxed and happy. We both were.

I still slept in the spare room. 'I'm not at my best, Cage,' he'd said. 'And I'm not sleeping well. I thought we'd had the perfect moment and that didn't turn out to be the case at all, but another one will present itself. Please try to keep your hands off me until then.'

I had professed myself delighted to do so.

There was no sign of Sorensen anywhere. Airports, train

stations, motorways and ports were all being monitored but somehow, he'd slipped through the net.

'If he's gone at all,' said Jones to me one evening. 'I always think the safest place for anyone to hide would be close by. Everyone always thinks a wanted criminal will fly far and fast, not just nip next door.'

Noting my look of alarm, he assured me that Mr and Mrs Goldfarb had lived on the other side of his landing since before he'd moved in and were the perfect neighbours. Although as he cheerfully admitted, his definition of perfect neighbours was simply people who lived nearby and hadn't tried to kill him yet.

I cleaned his flat – I was going to say from top to bottom but it was a flat so I cleaned it from side to side. Jones said he could see this insane urge to clean everything would be an issue in the future. I closed my mind to the implications of that particular statement and went to get the hoover.

Christmas approached. The advantage of living in a civilised part of town, said Jones, was that we could have everything delivered and we did. Delivery after delivery. It took two men to bring up the Christmas tree. And us two days to decorate it. With recent library-based events still fresh in my mind, I remembered to tell Jones not to put an angel on the top. The resulting fall-out could level Rushford.

'It's a good job we'd decided to move Christmas to my house,' he said, although I didn't remember being consulted at all and said so, but he was right. Moving from his bedroom to the kitchen via the living room was about the extent of his physical abilities at the moment. But the eye pad had come off and he could see. Not well, but his sight would improve, they said. He donned sunglasses and disappeared into the kitchen to indulge in an orgy of chopping, marinating, peeling and other culinary things. He made mince pies one day and then had to make them again the next because we ate them all while watching the traditional Christmas ghost story on TV. His flat – our flat, he said – was filled with the smells of Christmas. It really looked as if last year's disaster would be forgotten in wonderful new memories this year.

Melek and Iblis came to visit the invalid. Iblis told us they were both looking forward to Christmas lunch and he promised to bring the unemptyable Bottle of Utgard-Loki with him and Melek said don't you dare, but she was very nearly smiling.

They brought Nigel. Actually, as Melek was at pains to point out, *Iblis* had brought Nigel – none of it was anything to do with her. After they'd gone, Jones said the smell was enough to get anyone back on their feet and rush to get the window open.

And then it was Christmas Eve. I had to shoot out to buy emergency potatoes – whatever they were – and when I came back, Jones and Jerry were in his bedroom and there was a lot of shouting, 'Don't come in,' when I banged on the door demanding to know what was going on in there. Apparently, it was to be a surprise.

And a surprise it certainly was.

Christmas morning was mild and wet. I took Jones breakfast in bed. Buck's Fizz, pancakes, bacon and maple syrup.

'I warn you now,' I said, placing the tray on his lap. 'Get maple syrup on the sheets and I won't be joining you in them this evening,' and he nearly dropped his Buck's Fizz.

I handed him a small packet. 'Merry Christmas.'

346

'What's this?'

'Open it and see.'

He unwrapped a pair of American Tan tights. 'For you to wear tonight,' I said.

He grinned. 'Cage, for you, I might just do that.'

I put my arms around him and kissed him and he put his hand on my cheek so gently I nearly cried and then he cleared his throat.

'What time are Melek and Iblis coming round?'

'About noon,' I said.

'Good. Plenty of time. Come on – your turn to open your present now. Can you give me a hand?'

I moved his breakfast tray to the side. 'This way,' he said, leading me into his bathroom.

'Um . . .' I said, wondering what on earth was going on. What sort of present needed to be hidden in someone's bathroom?

I had a horrible thought. 'It's not a crocodile, is it?'

He stopped dead. 'What? No. Why would I buy you a crocodile? God, Cage, you're weird. Behold.'

A giant shape nearly as big as I was occupied most of the available floor space.

'Do you like it?'

I think I might have gaped at it. 'It's colossal. What on earth is it? How did you get it up here?'

'Jerry brought it up yesterday. When I sent you out to buy emergency potatoes.'

'You sent me out into the rain to buy potatoes you didn't need?'

'I sent you out into the rain so Jerry could get your Christmas present up here without you noticing, Cage. Have some gratitude.'

I stared at the giant shape wrapped in at least four differently patterned Christmas wrappings.

'Yes,' he said. 'Six rolls of the stuff. Nearly a hundred and fifty feet of wrapping paper. Some sort of record, I think. Jerry's writing to *Guinness World Records* about it.'

'But . . . what is it?'

'Well, open it and find out.'

I ripped and pulled at the wrapping paper for what seemed like hours. The whole bathroom was festooned with it when I'd finished.

I stared.

'What do you think?' His colour was jumping all over the room with excitement.

I stared.

'Do you like the colour?'

I stared. 'What is it?'

'It's an electric moped,' he announced, obviously under the impression this would mean something to me. 'Powerful enough to cope with that Alp you live on top of. Up the hill, drive round the back, park it in your shed. You need never struggle up your hill again. Best of all, I need never struggle up your hill again.'

'But . . .' I said, overwhelmed.

He rattled on regardless. 'No gears, Cage. You just get on it and go. Well, no, obviously you'll have to undergo Compulsory Basic Training – you know, how not to hit things or drive into the river. Basic stuff but useful. Then you take your full test and away you go. I don't think it can do much more than about 40mph, so no racing down the High Street as if it's the Utah Salt Flats. Handy shopping receptacle here. Small mirror you can use either to check the traffic behind you or apply your lipstick. Or both. Nice red colour. The moped, I mean, not the lipstick. What do you think?'

I was beyond words. Tears ran down my cheeks.

'Ah,' said Jones. 'I know this one. This is what women do when they're very happy. You've no idea how many women I've made very happy over the years.'

I was speechless.

He galloped on because he was nervous. 'You can park it downstairs in the garage and as soon as the Christmas holiday is over and I can walk properly again, you can practise there before venturing out on to the roads. Trust me, they're really easy to drive. You'll be pootling about the place in no time.'

I was still speechless. I walked all around my beautiful red shiny scooter, stroking its beautiful red shininess.

'Look at the time,' he said, looking at the time. 'Get dressed and we'll have a quick Christmas drink before our guests arrive. Stop fondling it, Cage, and get some clothes on.'

It hurt to tear myself away and so we wheeled it into my bedroom. It was fortunate that I'd laid out my clothes the night before because I could now no longer access my wardrobe. Not that I cared. I'd happily have had Christmas lunch in my PJs.

My former best dress had been commandeered as evidence so I'd bought myself a new one for Christmas. Something a little more glam than my usual style. It had a tight-fitting black bodice with a wide slash neck and ballet sleeves – well, it was winter, after all. Below the bust the dramatic black and white skirt fell to my knees. I looked extremely elegant and best of all, the loose folds meant I could eat to my heart's content. Or rather my stomach's content. As I knew from experience, Jones did an excellent Christmas lunch.

To complete the picture, I put my hair up – and it didn't look too bad because I'd been practising – and I wore a simple gold locket and bracelet.

When I emerged, the flat smelled wonderful. Christmas lunch was well under way.

I posed in the kitchen doorway. 'What do you think?'

He looked up. Slowly, he put down his manly tools of tea towel and colander. I grinned at him because I could see what he was thinking from all the way over here.

After a while, something buzzed.

'That wasn't me,' said Jones. 'Although it might be me in a minute if you don't stop manhandling me.'

Something buzzed again.

'Front door,' said Jones, enlightened. 'Our guests are here. Shall we let them in?'

I gave him one final kiss and we went off to answer the door.

CHAPTER TWENTY-THREE

Neither Iblis nor Melek looked any different. Both wore their customary T-shirt and jeans. Nigel, however, had launched himself into the festivities with a tartan bow – no doubt under the mistaken impression that cuteness would mean a bigger lunch.

They bore a gift. 'We bear a gift,' announced Iblis.

'It's not the dog, is it?' said Jones, staring at the bedecked Nigel with some misgivings.

Iblis flourished the unemptyable Bottle of Utgard-Loki.

Jones flung wide the door. 'Come in.'

We lost Iblis to my moped. He went over every inch of it, eventually sitting on the seat. Even though he was inside, a light breeze still blew his hair back off his shoulders as he posed, grinning at me. I had to admit he made it look good. Nigel perched on the seat in front of him. If you couldn't smell him, you'd think he looked adorable. Nigel, I mean.

Jones rolled his eyes and took himself off into the kitchen. Melek followed him in, enquiring whether she could be of any assistance. Iblis and I appeared to be temporarily surplus to requirements so I took him into the living room and was about to offer him a drink when the doorbell rang again.

Jones shouted through from the kitchen. 'Can you get that,

Cage? I've got my hands full. It's probably Mrs Goldfarb from across the landing with her sprig of mistletoe.'

It wasn't Mrs Goldfarb. It was the very last person I expected ever to see again. It was Alyson Painswick. She stood before me, dirty, dishevelled and out of breath. Her silver hair was tangled and muddy. Whatever was she doing here? The last I'd heard of her was that she was receiving care in a special unit.

Things happened more quickly than I can describe. I reached out to her to help her inside.

'Alyson, what's happened? Why are you here?'

She grabbed my arm, nearly frantic. 'Mrs Cage, please . . . please . . . you've got to help me.'

I think my first thought was that Sorensen had found her somehow and was close behind her.

'What's the matter?'

The lift pinged. It was only the doors closing but she threw a panicked glance over her shoulder.

'I can't . . . It isn't . . .'

I was still so surprised to see her I couldn't pull my thoughts together. Did she know her mother was dead? She must, surely. Had she come to me hoping I could tell her what had happened? How her mother had died? What could I say? 'Alyson, I . . .'

I was still struggling for words when she roughly pushed past me, across the hall and straight into the living room. Her colour trailed, empty and lifeless behind her. Like a snake shedding its skin. Something was very wrong. Everything began to slow down.

Jones was in the kitchen with Melek. I could hear their

talking slurring into silence. As if from far away, I heard him close the oven door.

Iblis was standing with his back to the door looking out of the window.

He looked over his shoulder to see who it was.

Nigel, smellily unconscious on a cushion, casually opened one eye and bristled like a toilet brush. He leaped to his feet, barking to raise the dead.

Alyson surged forwards.

She reached over her shoulder.

Iblis said incredulously, 'Allia?' and then his chest exploded as she ran him through with his own sword.

Blood spurted all the way across the room.

Iblis fell to the floor in a bright red pool of his own blood.

I screamed. The world began to speed up again. Jones ran in from the kitchen. Melek flew to Iblis.

Nigel had gone to full wolf mode again – just as he had once before. Now I knew who – what – had been on my porch that night. Not Lady Torrington as I had thought – Alyson Painswick. Teeth bared, he hurled himself at her.

Alyson – Allia – and why hadn't I put two and two together before this? – kicked out viciously and Nigel the Ninja flew through the air to impact the wall with a dreadful crash. There was a pitiful yelp and then he slithered down the wall and lay still. She was on her way out of the door before he'd even landed.

Seconds – just seconds. Six or seven seconds – no more – and everything was changed for ever.

Iblis lay on his back, his own sword buried in his chest. A fragment of memory surfaced. Melek saying that should it ever be discovered then nothing would ever get between Iblis and his sword ever again and in a dreadful way she'd been absolutely right.

Melek looked up, her face a mask of grief and shock, obviously torn between her desire for revenge on Allia and being here for Iblis's last moments.

'No,' said the thing inside my head, coming from nowhere. **'Step aside, Elizabeth. Sleep. This is for me.'**

Elizabeth slept. I knelt beside Iblis. He was beyond speech. Blood filled his mouth. His eyes were on me and I knew what he was trying to say.

I said, **'I must do it but it will kill you. I am sorry.'**

He closed his eyes in acquiescence. I seized the sword hilt and pulled. It came out more easily and more smoothly than I had expected.

I heard the man, Jones, say, 'Cage, what are you doing?'

I said, **'Revenge.'**

And then I was out of the door after her.

She ran and I chased her. I would have her. She could run until the world ended but I would have her.

She flew down the stairs.

As did I.

Her fear drove her onwards because she had made a mistake. Nigel's attack had delayed her just those vital few seconds and she had been forced to leave the sword behind and I would use it and she knew it. She would die as painfully as I could contrive and the screams of her long agony would accompany Iblis as he made his way to the next world.

She crashed through a door at the bottom of the stairs into some sort of big, concrete, echoing garage filled with cars. It

354

was very cold here and my blood tingled a response. I love the cold. It gives me strength.

I shouted her name. Allia. To know a person's name is to have power over them. She whirled around to face me. For long, long moments we faced each other. Her arm was crimson to her elbow and her face flecked with Iblis's blood. She looked down, raised her hand to her mouth, extended her long tongue and lapped at it, smearing it around her mouth. She was laughing at me. And then she opened her mouth, all red with his blood, and roared a challenge. She challenged *me*.

I planted my feet and raised the sword. I summoned all my rage. There was a lot of it and it went back a very long way.

I answered her. My battle cry came from deep within me. On and on and on. A challenge issued and answered. A sound not heard in this world for millennia but it was heard now. Somewhere behind me came the crash of breaking glass. Car headlights began to flash. Horns sounded. And still her challenge resounded. And still I answered. We circled each other, roaring our defiance. The air quivered between us. A pigeon dropped dead from the concrete beam above me.

I was filled with fury. She would not live. She would die. I had ended the demon who called herself her mother and I would end this one too. She would suffer for the grief she had caused. I would tear her apart myself. Because I am Felda and in my wrath is death.

I roared again. Long and loud. So long and loud I tore my throat. I tasted blood in my mouth but still I roared. Echoes bounced from wall to wall. From pillar to pillar. Dust fell as cracks began to appear. I would bring this place down upon her. I would *crush* her into nothing.

I suspect she saw her death in my eyes. Without warning, she broke off, turned and fled. I set off after her. A hunt. It would be like the old days. I would run her down. I would have her. She would not escape me.

We ran fast. I could hear the sound of my feet. Feel the rhythm of my heart. We ran faster. Around me, the world began to blur and I knew where she was going. If she thought to throw me off, she was mistaken. I would follow her to the ends of the earth and beyond.

And I did.

The world took on a blue tinge. I never took my eyes from her. Everything flashed past in one long smudge. There were no details. She ran faster and I followed her still. The blue began to shade towards purple. Faster. And then to red. Faster and faster. To the ends of the earth and beyond. I would have her.

And then I was falling. There was a sudden weightlessness. I was spinning in space. And then I landed. Hard. So hard that I bounced.

I lay still for a moment, remembered who I was chasing and why and leaped to my feet. She wasn't here. I whirled around and around, sword raised, ready for her. She wasn't here. No one was here. I was in a room and it was empty.

I straightened up slowly, lowered the sword and took the time to look about me. I knew this place. I'd been here before.

I was standing in a big square room with a large fireplace in which burned a cheerful fire. An old hearthrug lay in front of the fire, covered in small scorch marks because sometimes the pine logs spat out glowing embers. Even, occasionally, and to my annoyance, on to my skirts as well. Two overstuffed sofas sat on either side of the fire, each with a small table at the end, bearing an oil lamp. Three of the walls were covered in glass-fronted bookcases. The books were stacked any old how because George never put them back properly. And then complained because he could never find them again. A portrait hung over the mantel. I knew without looking that it was of a grey-haired man, with a neat moustache and steady brown eyes. The likeness was a good one. It had been my favourite picture when I lived here. An embroidery frame lay across the arm of one of the sofas. I could see the needle thrust into the cloth. Again, I knew without looking that the design was of red poppies and blue cornflowers. George's favourites.

This was a comfortable family room with solid, old-fashioned furniture that had survived for many years and would continue to survive for a good many more. This had been my home once.

The fourth wall had two sets of French windows. One of the doors was open. A curtain billowed slightly on a breath of icy-cold air.

I used the sword to pull the curtain aside.

As I'd known the room, I knew the garden, as well.

The whole world was covered in snow. An iron-grey sky hung low overhead, heavy with more snow to come. Angry snow, just waiting to fall and consume us all. The terrace out-side ran from one end of the house to the other, white and perfect, an unbroken carpet, as were the steps leading down to the lawns. This was a cold place, hard with frost. And silent. Silent as only a snow-covered world can be. And unmarked. There was no footprint or animal track anywhere. Just wintry, white perfection.

Only the far-off river was dark, slicing its way cleanly through the whiteness on each bank.

I stepped through the window, out on to the terrace. The snow crunched beneath my feet. The garden was not as empty as I had thought. Over there, to my right, under the cedar tree, was set a small table and two chairs. A man stood up, called my name and waved.

'Over here.'

I waited for a moment, looking around. There was no sign of Allia anywhere. No sign that she had passed this way. I looked back over my shoulder. I would search the house.

The man called my name again and made gestures indicating I should join him.

I reached over my shoulder and sheathed Iblis's sword to keep it safe. It would not be lost again. It would burn with him on his funeral pyre. Along with whatever I decided would remain of the demon Allia.

I walked towards the man, listening to my footsteps crunch in the snow. He wore a simple black linen shirt and trousers whiter than the snow itself. His feet were bare. His dark hair fell to his shoulders, framing a long, melancholy face. The table was bare except for a jug of water and two glasses. He stood up as I approached and pulled out the other chair for me.

I ignored it. I would not be distracted.

We looked at each other for a long time.

'Well,' he said, sitting back down again. 'I think it's fair to say that didn't turn out quite as either of us wanted. Or expected. The time has come to talk. Don't look so fierce, Felda. I mean you no harm. You can leave any time you so wish. Believe me,

I have no desire to harbour you for one second longer than is absolutely necessary.'

I stood still, watching him. Waiting for the trap.

He gestured at our surroundings. 'Do you like it? It's Torrington House, you know. You lived here once. One of your longer incarnations. I thought you might appreciate it. Do you remember?'

I did remember it. I remembered everything. George and I used to have tea under this very tree. I would wait for him, watching him climb the hill after a day's fishing on the river. He would throw himself into his chair and demand food and drink, his clothes covered in dirt and fish scales. Our butler would tut quite audibly and George would laugh and remember to ask me if I minded. I never did. Dear George. It was a sad day when he died. For everyone. He would not have been so harsh to those who murdered Jeannie Morton.

He poured a glass of water. 'I hope you appreciate the effort I've gone to for you today. I wanted somewhere you would feel at home. Literally. Nice surroundings. Familiar enough to jog those deeply hidden memories. Would you like a moment? You must be a little disoriented. It's been a long time, hasn't it?' He passed over the glass. 'Drink your water. It will help your throat. I must say that certainly brought back a few memories of my own. I haven't heard a good challenge like that for centuries, have you?'

I ignored the water. Believing anything this one said would be unwise.

He crossed his legs. 'Well, as I was saying – that didn't turn out so well, did it?'

I had no time for his words. **'Give me Allia.'**

He smiled. 'No. And before you lose your temper and bring everything crashing down around us – seriously, doesn't that ever get old? How many times has poor old Melek had to clear up your mess? – no, you can't have Allia because she needs to spend a little quality time with me learning to obey my instructions. To the letter. But, I'm a generous soul – not that I have one, of course, but it's a useful figure of speech – I'm a generous soul and you can have what's left when I've finished.'

You do not let one such as he have control of the conversation. **'What did not turn out as planned?'**

'Well, everything, really. I mean – think about it. I couldn't have this great alliance you were all so keen on – you, Melek, Iblis and Borin – this so-called Golden Age of peace – that wouldn't have suited me at all. Yes, I know you all worked very hard and I was really quite upset to have to spoil all your fun, but you left me with very little choice. So I sent the serpent.' He grinned. 'I always send the serpent. It's kind of my signature move.'

'You sent the serpent to bring down Borin's horse.'

'Well, of course I did. Didn't I just say? The last thing I needed was some ridiculous sort of grand alliance overturning all my plans. I considered my four – let's not say victims; let's say choices. Borin was the weakest link so Borin was my target.'

He paused but I remained silent.

He sighed. 'Sit down. Please. Drink your water. Yes, you may safely do so – it's not pomegranate seeds. Trust me, Felda. I bear you no ill will at all. It suits me very well to have you sleeping quietly inside Elizabeth Cage. Out of sight. Out of mind. Well, not *her* mind, of course, and you've certainly got her into some trouble over the years, haven't you? Including here in this place.' He gestured around. 'How many lives has your famous temper ruined, eh? I couldn't have done better myself and believe me – that's a genuine compliment.'

Again, I said nothing.

'And now this has happened and Iblis is dead. Trust me, I am feeling quite cross about this. I rather liked Iblis – a nice boy – and this has ruined everything. For which Allia will be held to account, I assure you. I had everything well in hand. Borin was dead because I couldn't have him enjoying a long and happy life as he slowly exterminated my people, could I? I needed him to die tragically and before his time which, in turn, took you out of the game. You really went off the rails there, didn't you? And that tied up Melek, who spends half her time keeping an eye on you to make sure you don't inadvertently destroy the world. Which just left Iblis and, on my instructions, Allia stole his sword – which took care of the other half of Melek's attention as she took on his workload. I mean – it was all so perfect. One dead. One mad – sorry about that, by the way, but you never were the most stable god on the block, were you? – one too ashamed to show his face – and the last one working herself into the ground. I've had things pretty much my own way for as long as I can remember, and then Allia – against my strict instructions – thought she could improve on perfection.'

'It is her power play. And you did not see it coming.'

He looked surprised. 'What makes you say that?'

'All the main players neutralised. No major threats left. Guess who would have been next on her list?'

He smiled and sipped his own water. 'I do believe you are attempting to undermine me.'

'**You are already undermined. Hence your very great need to ensure you make an example of Allia.**' I considered him with my head on one side. '**You never saw it coming, did you?**'

He smiled slightly. 'And they say gods are stupid.'

'**They do not say it for very long.**'

He leaned back, very much at his ease, but his eyes glittered. 'I wonder if it would help if I killed you now? Tear you to pieces and scatter your atoms to the four winds.'

I shrugged. '**Who cares?**'

'A god with a death wish,' he said, thoughtfully. 'Interesting.'

'**I am a god who doesn't care. You should give Allia to me. For your own sake.**'

'And why would I do that?'

'**Allia killed Iblis. Do you think Melek will ever rest while she lives? Allia killed the wrong one. A big mistake. Melek will hunt her to the end of time if she has to. She will never rest until she has brought you all down.**'

He frowned. 'It would appear – Allia was not able to speak for very long, you understand – that she simply killed the first one who came to hand. Had Melek been the closest . . .' He shrugged. 'But I agree – a big mistake. And one she is already bitterly regretting.'

'**And you have lost possession of the sword. And now I am awake. You have created the seeds of your own destruction. However – give me Allia and I will depart.**'

'Actually, I have considered it, but on careful reflection, I do think she'll benefit from some time spent learning not to disobey me. Sometimes it's necessary to send a message that is clearly understood by everyone, don't you think? But you needn't worry – she says she's very sorry for what she's done. Well, she hasn't said that yet, of course, but trust me, she very soon will.'

'**Give her to me.**'

His bright smile dimmed a little. 'Look, I can see you're upset just at the moment – anyone would be. I know I am. Everything was going so well – for me, of course. All of you neutralised without actually having to kill you – well, except for Borin, of course, and that was such a long time ago now it hardly counts. And neutralised was what I was after. I couldn't risk anyone better or stronger emerging from your ashes because then I'd have to start all over again. So tedious. Which is why I'm not going to kill the Daughter of the Gods. Can you imagine what sort of stink that would raise? No, you turn around and go away – unless you'd like to stay for tea, of course, chat over the old days, tell me what you've been up to all this time.'

'**You talk too much.**'

'Well, to be fair, you've hardly shouldered your share of the conversational burden, have you? And, I have to say – not looking your best at the moment, either.'

'**Give her to me.**'

He sighed again, allowing a little impatience to show. 'We've been through all this and the answer is still no. And I don't want to be rude but you're beginning to annoy me. I don't ask for much but good manners cost nothing. I've gone to great lengths to make this nice environment for you. I wanted to be as unthreatening as possible and so . . .' he gestured at our surroundings, 'I recreated your old life as Lady Torrington. I've been to a great deal of trouble for you, Felda, and frankly, your attitude is just a little disappointing.'

The sky darkened even further. Over on the other side of the river, the trees began to blur around the edges. A cold wind stirred the leaves.

I would not be moved. **'I have come for Allia. Justice will be served at my hands. I have the means.'**

He stopped smiling. He spoke quietly but his words came straight from the void itself. 'Draw that sword here and there will be trouble.'

'Give her to me now and I will depart in peace.'

He sighed. 'You don't change, do you? Still no manners.'

'Still no Allia.'

He stared at the sky for a moment and then appeared to come to a decision. 'Very well.'

No. This was too easy. I waited.

He smiled. 'I will do a deal with you.'

'No.'

He sighed. 'That is so typical of you. Just listen before you reject everything out of hand. It's a good deal. In fact, if you study your folklore down the years – I think you'll find I'm famous for my good deals.'

I said nothing. It would not be a good deal.

He steepled his fingers. 'How about this? Everything returns to the way it was. Iblis lives. He manages without his sword – which, to be fair, he had been doing right up to Allia's unfortunate little moment. Melek continues to run herself ragged trying to do everything herself. And you, Felda, can go back to sleep and dream in peace. All you have to do is return the sword to me. Everyone gets what they want.'

'I want Allia.'

He sighed. 'That is what I'm saying. I'll give you Allia and everything goes back to the way it was.'

'In return for . . .'

His smile broadened.

'No.'

'Give me the sword, Felda. It's a good deal. You get Allia to amuse yourself with. For as long as you like – I won't want her back – I get the sword and, as I said, everything goes back to the way it was. No one wins – no one loses. Which, let's face it, is the best you and I can hope for in this situation. Think about it. You don't want to stay in the world and now you don't have to. You can close your eyes and just let go. Go back whence you came. Sleep.'

His voice was as gentle as summer rain pattering on leaves. 'No more pain. No more humans and their ingratitude, their cruelty, their stupidity – they're really not the brightest life forms on this planet, are they? Just pure, perfect sleep.'

I stood silent. Pure, perfect sleep. I could feel the tug. I could feel my eyes beginning to close. At some point he had moved very close to me. His breath was warm in my ear. 'My poor child, you've suffered enough and it's time to rest. Just give me the sword, Felda. Give it to me and sleep for ever.'

It was the ideal solution. As he said, no one won – no one lost. Everything would return to the way it was. Iblis restored. He could manage without his sword. He always had. Melek would continue the fight alone but she was used to it. And I could sleep for ever. Yes – everything would be just perfect.

I said, 'No.'

He moved faster than time itself. I was still saying no as he pinned me against the tree behind me. The impact jarred my spine. Snow fell from the branches above. His face was in mine. His breath stank. His eyes were truly the windows of his soul and he had none. His body pressed hard against mine, slowly crushing the breath out of me. His mouth gaped wide and in the darkness therein I saw my end.

'You can kill me,' I said, 'but you will never have the sword.'

I meant it and he knew I meant it. You cannot threaten death to someone who longs for it. Someone who yearns for annihilation is not easily frightened.

'And you will never have Allia. Vengeance is beyond your reach. You have lost again, Felda.' He smiled. 'As you always do.'

The thought came to me, straight and true. I had the sword. I had the will and the strength to use it. And nothing to lose . . .

I pushed my face into his. For a moment we stood as lovers do. I hissed the words into his mouth. 'Not this time.'

I kissed him. Not gently. I tangled my hand in his hair and crushed my lips to his. He tasted of bitterness and regret and resentment and desperate, aching loneliness.

I pulled away and we both stood panting.

'We are both victims of our own past. Of dim and distant tragedies that have cast their long shadows over our lives even until the present day. Nothing can change the events of my life but it is not too late for you.'

He stared.

'Come back with me,' I whispered. 'Come back with me and ask forgiveness. It will be granted. You fell from grace but grace can be restored. You have only to ask for it. You could leave this place for ever.' I paused. 'You could go home.'

For a microsecond it was there. The longing. The yearning to return home. The desperate ache. I could taste it. He was tempted.

It was gone in a flash, stifled as if it had never been, but it was too late. I'd tasted his heart's desire. His secret hunger. Long concealed – possibly even from himself. Only one moment's vulnerability but I had seen it and he knew I had.

He drew back. Only very slightly. He gave me only an inch but an inch was all I needed. My arm was crushed behind me but my groping fingers could just reach the sword. Just . . . touch it . . .

I seized the sword hilt and pulled. At the same moment he spat at me, I jerked my head to one side and it landed on the tree trunk. I heard it sizzle as it hit. His voice was a hissing in the dark. 'One day . . . one day I will come for you.'

I swung the sword. I heard the song of its anticipation. By rights, I should have sliced his head from his shoulders. Except that he flung me from him. The next moment he was gone. Everything was gone. Snow, table, chairs, trees, house, river – everything – and I was flying across the underground garage to land with a crash against one of the concrete pillars. I lay for a moment. Around me, the garage was still in chaos. Car alarms screamed and hooted. Lights flashed. I had been gone only seconds.

It took me some time to climb to my feet. I put my hands on my knees and leaned forwards to get my breath back. I spat the taste of him away. At the other end of the garage I could hear the lift. I assumed people were coming down to investigate the alarms. Somewhere, I could hear a drip, drip, drip. I looked down. I had been gone no time at all because

Iblis's fresh blood was still running down his sword and pooling on the floor.

Iblis.

The lift doors opened and people emerged. To investigate the noise, I assumed. Some of them wore paper hats in many colours. Some had brought bottles with them. My instinct was to kill them all but not today. I stood behind a pillar until they passed by, then ripped open the door and ran up the stairs. All the way to the top. Never stopping. Because time was everything and Iblis had none left.

The front door was open. I stopped, took a breath for calm and went in to pay my last respects.

He was still alive. Typical of him. Always unexpected even in his own death. He sprawled as I had left him – on the floor, his arms and legs splayed out, his bright red blood bubbling from his chest, taking his life with it.

Melek knelt beside him, her face only inches from his and so covered in his blood that for one moment I thought she was wounded too. Her face was as ashen as his. I knew what she was trying to do. She'd brought him back from the brink once before – but not this time.

Someone – Jones, I suspected – had picked up the dog and laid him alongside his master. He took Iblis's hand and very gently laid it on Nigel's head. The little dog made one last sound – part whine, part last breath – and then slipped quietly away. He had died defending his master which is a good death for a dog.

Iblis was far beyond speech. His face had drained of all colour. His front was sodden with blood. As was the carpet around him. So much blood. Red and glistening . . . He was leaving us . . . His eyes slid to mine and I realised I was still holding his sword.

Silently, Melek moved aside. I knelt beside him and pressed the hilt into his bloody hands.

His eyes flickered towards me – just for a second. That last effort took all his remaining strength. He closed his eyes. His eyelids fluttered.

I made my decision. It was my choice and I made it without hesitation.

I placed one hand on his forehead and one on his breast and offered up the life that was mine and that I no longer wanted.

'I offer myself. Take what is needed to save him. I give it freely and willingly.'

For one endless moment I thought that in this, as in everything else, I had failed. That he was too far gone. That I was too late. And then I actually felt something leave me. No – not leave me – tear itself from me with great pain. Like a bee that leaves a vital part of itself behind when it stings.

My body was cold, as if a warm and comforting presence had been taken away, leaving me alone in the darkness. Was this death? At last?

I felt Iblis's heart heave beneath my hand. I looked down. Blood bubbled from his nostrils. He was breathing. The spark of his life had reignited. It would seem I had succeeded.

I had more than succeeded. Beside him, the annoying little dog twitched. That, I had not meant to do.

I sighed, too tired even to support my own head. I let it hang. My strength was gone. I felt cold, empty, perilously close to the point of no return. Did I care? How long had I lived? What would it be like to close my eyes? To sleep for ever and never wake up?

'Elizabeth?'

'I am here.'

I heard Jones say, 'Cage?' and then I slept.

CHAPTER TWENTY-FOUR

I couldn't think where I was to begin with. I lay on a bed looking up at the ceiling. My body felt limp and heavy and it was a huge effort to lift myself up on my elbows. This was a bit of a puzzle. I was lying on my bed in Jones's spare room and, except for my shoes, I was fully clothed.

A water jug and glass stood on the bedside table next to me. I closed my eyes in mortification and lay back down again. Please don't say I'd had one glass of wine and then had to be put to bed. The embarrassment . . .

I listened for the sound of voices but the flat was completely silent. Had our guests gone home already? The curtains were drawn. What time was it? What was happening?

I should get up. I lifted my hand and stared at it because I couldn't think what else to do with it. As I did, Melek appeared at the foot of my bed. Her hair was wet. Had she just showered? Was it morning? I turned my head to look at her. Jones stood behind her in the doorway.

'Why am I in bed?'

Neither of them spoke. I looked at their faces. 'What's happened? Where's Iblis?'

Melek pulled up a chair and sat down. She smoothed her jeans. 'Iblis is unwell.'

'Oh my God. How? Is he all right?'

'Not at the moment, but he will be. How are you?'

I stared, puzzled. 'I'm fine. Why wouldn't I be?'

'We . . . think you might have banged your head.'

'No, I feel fine.' I looked past her to Jones, still standing grim-faced in the doorway. 'Are you hurt at all?'

He shook his head, looked at Melek and said, 'Tell her.'

I turned my head from one to the other. 'Tell me what?'

'Secrets, Cage. Secrets.'

Melek turned to him. 'Could you leave us alone?'

'No,' I said. 'He should stay.'

'You will regret it if he does. You will both regret it.'

He folded his arms. His colour was darker than I had ever seen. Even when he was struggling in the aftermath of Clare's death. The gold had disappeared completely. The crimson was shading into a deeper red that was nearly black.

She sighed. 'Very well.'

I pulled myself up to a sitting position. Jones leaned against the doorway, his colour unmoving and cold. His sunglasses made it impossible to read his eyes. The silence lengthened and just as I thought she wouldn't speak after all, she began.

'At the moment, your name is Elizabeth Cage, but over the years, you have had many names.'

She stopped again, almost as if she was hoping that would be sufficient. That she need say no more.

I said, 'Yes? And?'

Sighing, she began again. 'You were Eadgytha of Wessex – the gentle nun who died, mourned by all. You were Alice of Poitiers who served at the inn. In Lucca, you were Bianca who lived with her mother. Then Elizabeth Talbot from York.

And Agnes Kemp – a member of the wrong religion at the wrong time. Jeanne Duval who worked in the fields, Ilse Gabor in Prague – who fled with all the others when the streets ran with blood, and I only just got you out in time. Susannah Hooper – who cared for the sick. And sad, angry Amelia Torrington who tended the old and the poor before turning on them. And Sandra Pettit – who nursed the soldiers from two wars. And many, many more. Now, at this moment, you are Elizabeth Cage.'

I stared at her. If it had been anyone else telling me these things . . . 'How?'

'You agreed to it,' she said, answering a different question.

I had agreed to it. Her words awoke a different memory within me which clawed its way to the surface.

It was yet another bitter day. My only protection from the cold was a very inadequate piece of coarse sacking – the closest thing I had to a cloak. My bare feet were bruised from the rocks and I had a nasty cut on my heel.

I was sitting on a rock watching the goats forage. The clouds were low and a bitter wind blew. I was out here, all alone, because no one else wanted to be so far from home and help, in case the wolves came, or worse – the Divs – and so the job always fell to me. And because no one ever wanted me around. For my own sake I had learned to be alone and like it. People are unkind. I was very young but I already knew to keep my distance. Sometimes they threw rocks until I went away. A barely recognised instinct told me that one day I would grow up and then they would do more than just throw rocks. My choice had been made clear. Staying apart would keep me safe. From people, anyway. For the moment, doing something useful such as watching the goats was an acceptable course of action that benefited everyone.

Because people feared me. I was different. I could see the thoughts inside their heads and they didn't like it.

The wind blew again. I shifted my position slightly, trying to crouch in the shelter of the rock face behind me. There was no grazing left. Very soon I'd have to leave such shelter as it offered and take the goats off in search of new pastures. And to check my traps because there was never any food to spare for the goat girl. I ate only what I could forage for myself.

And then, almost from nowhere because I hadn't seen her approach, the tall woman had appeared in front of me.

'Tadia.'

Had that been my name? Tadia?

Her companion, a man, kept watch a few yards away, standing on a rock, watching the horizon. I was bewildered and a little afraid. It was so long since I had seen a living person. At night I would huddle among the rocks, sick with fear, because night-time was when the Divs walked.

The first thing she did was light a fire. I heard the wood crackle, smelled the smoke, and held out my ice-cold hands to the heat. She made me an offer. I didn't understand most of it. There was lots of stuff about serving the god and the world but I had only two real questions.

Would there be a warmer cloak and would there be goats?

The answer was yes and no.

I nodded and made my choice and they took my hand and led me away down the stony path. I looked back once. The fire was dying and already the uncaring goats were beginning to wander away. 'What will my family think has happened to me?'

'Eaten by wolves, I expect,' said the man, cheerfully. 'Or spirited away by a Div, perhaps.'

I considered this. I doubted my parents would grieve overmuch. There would be more consternation over the goats. I wondered who would be forced to take my place. Especially now that I'd either been eaten by wolves or kidnapped by the fearsome Div-e Sepid, King of the Demons.

She smiled at me. 'Are you ready?'

I nodded.

She took my face between her cold hands and looked deep into my eyes. 'Tadia, I have something important to say to you.'

And then there was a bright light in my memory and everything else was blank.

I blinked to bring myself back into the present. It was time for questions, yes, but mostly, it was time for answers.

I looked at Melek. 'Tell me who I am.'

'Your name is Tadia and you were born in the north of the area that came to be known as Sogdiana. You were a strange child. No one wanted to be near you so you were virtually cast out. You tended the goats some distance away from your village. You fed and clothed yourself. You were starving when I found you and winter was coming. Your foot was infected. You would not have survived for much longer.'

'So you took a young girl and used her for your own purposes,' said Jones from the doorway. 'We have a name for people like that.'

He wasn't happy. His colour was dark and pressed close to his body. I wasn't sure it had been a good idea to let him hear this, but it was too late to change my mind now.

375

Melek looked over her shoulder. 'I gave her the gift of life.'

I blinked, still trying to take it all in. 'But why? You say you chose me, but what did you choose me for?'

She hesitated. I said sharply, 'Tell me.'

Still she hesitated.

I said, 'Is this anything to do with Allia?'

She sighed. 'No. No, this is to do with Felda.'

I was quite bewildered. 'Who is Felda?'

She sighed. 'My friend Felda, who suffered a great sickness of the mind. I . . . It was best for everyone if she slept. I needed to find her a resting place. Somewhere safe. A refuge from the world. And from herself.' She looked at me. 'I chose you.'

'Why?'

'For three reasons. You see clearly. You possess great compassion. And you are strong. Strong enough to contain a god.'

'Wait,' I said, although she had already paused for me to take this in. 'This thing I can do – with the colours – is that because . . . because of what you did to me?'

She shook her head firmly. 'No. That is still all your own. It's why you were alone on the hillside in the first place.'

'For you to find her,' said Jones.

'Yes.'

'Find her and use her.'

Melek was impatient. 'I told you – I gave her the gift of life.'

'Unending life,' he said bitterly. 'How is that a gift? You took a lonely and vulnerable child and turned her into something even more lonely and vulnerable for your own purposes.'

'Stop,' I said, because I could see their colours squaring up to each other. I sensed violence in the air and I had other things on which to concentrate. 'I'm a *god*?'

She shook her head. 'Not you, no. The god resides inside you.'

She was talking about the thing in my head. Now that I knew, it seemed I had always known. The thing that lived inside my head was a god.

'I'm strong enough to contain a god?'

'Most of the time. And the god sleeps. She only rouses herself when you are threatened.'

'And then she brings down the world,' I said bitterly, remembering past events. 'Don't tell me that didn't really happen. I can still remember the angry snow. I can still see the bodies.'

She nodded.

Behind her, Jones frowned. 'Does that mean that everything Cage said – the snow, the clinic exploding, people dying and so on – it all actually happened?'

She nodded again.

His colour darkened even further. I knew what he was thinking. I had been right. He'd attacked me. It hadn't been his fault. But it had happened. And he'd died and the world had nearly ended. And everyone had said I had concussion and I'd dreamed it and I'd pretended to believe them but I knew it wasn't true. I *knew* I'd been right. And now, so did he. There had been two realities and both had occurred. I could see his perceptions altering as he worked through the implications.

'But it couldn't have. I'm still alive. It couldn't have happened.' He stared at her, his face dark and suspicious. 'What did you do?'

She made no reply.

He shouted at her. 'Tell me. What did you do? Did you press some sort of reset key?'

377

She nodded, suddenly looking desperately weary. 'I repair things as best I can. Sometimes it's just a case of altering memories.' Sometimes more is required but it's no small task and I'm not as strong as I was. Obviously, last time, I didn't get it all right. Elizabeth still has memories.'

'So does . . .' I stopped, just in time, because Mrs Barton also remembered the angry snow. I had no idea what pressing reset would entail for her, but her mind had enough problems without someone deciding her memories – the very few that remained – should be wiped as well. I had done some terrible things – I remembered Lady Torrington and her swift revenge on the villagers who disobeyed her and let Jeannie Morton die – but taking Mrs Barton's last, faint memories would not be one of them.

Jones's voice was harsh. 'So, every time there's a little hiccup, you just patch her up – Cage, I mean – and send her back out there again. To endure life after life after life until . . . when? When does it all stop? When does Cage get her own life back?'

'Please stop,' I said, because I wanted some quiet in which to think, but neither of them was listening to me.

They stood face to face. He was angry but there was huge sadness there, as well. As if he'd lost something. She was angry too, and defensive and exhausted. Their colours were bright and hard, butting against each other and bristling with hostility as they stared each other down. Like a duel. The pair of them all ready to do battle. He wasn't afraid of her. But there was fear in his colour. A great deal of fear. I could see it and it frightened me. And what of Iblis?

'Stop,' I said, more strongly this time, and they both turned to me.

'Let me get this straight,' I said. 'You brought me here as a child and my parents adopted me and . . .'

She braced herself. I saw her do it. 'No.'

Confused, I said, 'I don't understand. You just said . . .'

She sighed and then said, 'No. You were no longer a child. I brought you here as an adult. You made a life for yourself. You married and . . .'

I held up my hand to stop her. 'Wait. No. I remember being at school. I remember my teachers. I remember how I struggled to fit in. I remember people looking at me and whispering. I was the second angel in the Christmas play. I was whacked on the knee in hockey and had to go to hospital. My dad came to get me . . .' My voice faded away.

Jones said harshly, 'Don't you get it, Cage? This so-called friend of yours has been brainwashing you. She yanks you out of one life, wipes your mind and drops you somewhere else – either before someone notices you're not getting any older or your co-pilot commits genocide in a fit of pique. She installs a whole new set of memories and leaves you to start again. She programmes you into thinking every life is real. God knows how long she's been using you.'

I couldn't take it in. I stood at the edge of a precipice and looked down into a vast darkness.

I'd been used. Over and over again. It was almost my signature state. Ted had married me on Sorensen's instructions. Jones had briefly betrayed me. Sorensen had tried to use me for his own ends. Melek had used me as a vessel to conceal her friend. Nothing about me was real. I wasn't shy, timid Elizabeth Cage. Far from it. I was something else completely. I was dangerous.

And then I had the realisation that pushed everything else

aside. That finally brought my world crashing down. I said slowly, 'My mum and dad?'

My two kindly, always loving parents. My mum making chocolate cake every Tuesday. Me holding my dad's hammer as we talked in his shed and he taught me about life and how to survive it.

'They never existed,' she said, quietly. 'They're just memories I created to ground you. To give you a past.'

No. This I could not process. My wonderful dad who loved me. Memories tumbled and jostled. I remembered his grief when my mum died. His old brown cardigan with the baggy pockets. My mum telling him to stop reading his paper at the dinner table. Sitting around the same table with brochures everywhere as we discussed our summer holidays. Bournemouth or Tenby this year? I could smell our lunch in the oven and hear the rain on the windows. He built me a rabbit hutch. Had I ever had a rabbit? No – that was one thing she'd got wrong. *Now* I remembered how animals were so wary of me. I'd never had a rabbit. Nor a rabbit hutch. Nor a dad.

None of it was real. Not one single thing about me was real. I was more alone in this world than anyone had ever been. I could feel myself being overwhelmed by all the grief and loss I'd experienced when my parents died because I'd just lost them all over again. Except they'd never lived. They were false memories implanted to convince me I was something I wasn't. What else would this Melek do for her friend? Suppose for some reason the god didn't need my right arm any longer? Would Melek just whip it off without a second thought? Because it was the god that was important, not me. I wasn't even real. I'd been constructed. Like a robot. I was topped up at regular intervals.

380

New batteries, new life – and off I go again while the god slept on; I was nothing more than a sophisticated bedroom. And far from having parents who had loved me and cherished me, my real ones had sent me into the wilderness to die slowly. They'd probably been relieved when I disappeared. A problem solved. Painlessly. Vaguely, I wondered who they'd got to tend the goats after me. All my life – all my lives – I'd been something for someone else to make use of.

I can't describe my boiling resentment, my anger – no, my rage, my sudden loss of self.

I said to Melek, 'Get out. Get out of my sight. I never want to see you again.' My voice rose to a shriek. 'Get out. Right now.'

She said, 'Felda . . .' and I shouted, 'Get out,' and my voice made the glass ring.

She paused, looked as if she might say something, and then pushed past Jones and left the room. I heard a door shut somewhere.

Which left Jones standing at the doorway. I didn't need his colour, dark and still, to tell me something was very wrong. I was losing him. Physically, he was still here, but I'd lost him.

I struggled for my voice. 'Jones?'

He didn't reply. He wouldn't come any closer, either. He stayed well back in the doorway.

'What's the matter? Talk to me.'

'Well,' he said. 'I think we can agree this Christmas more than surpasses the last one, don't you?'

I couldn't speak. My throat closed.

He sighed, took off his sunglasses and rubbed his eyes. 'I'm going away.'

I couldn't believe it at first. He was leaving now? And then

I realised why he was leaving. I swallowed, found my voice, and said, 'For how long?'

'I don't know. Stay here as long as you need. Until you're completely recovered. There's a whole Christmas lunch in the kitchen back there. Shame to waste it.'

He jerked his head in the direction of his bedroom. 'Tell those two they can stay as well. Iblis isn't going anywhere for a while. Just post the keys back through the letter box when you're finished with the place.'

I struggled with what he was saying. Because far from working together – far from making a life together as we had planned – he was leaving me. And he wasn't ever coming back. I'd gone from having everything I wanted to having nothing at all.

He picked up the bag I hadn't noticed and threw it over his shoulder.

I found some words. 'Where will you go?'

He shrugged and turned away. 'I have other places.'

I tried to get up off the bed. 'Why are you doing this?'

He shook his head, still not looking at me.

Everything was a struggle but I wasn't going to let him go. I was going to fight for my future. 'You can't go. What about us? Our plans? We're going to . . .'

'No, we're not.' His voice was a shout. He took a deep breath and made a visible effort to speak quietly. His colour spiked angry red all around him. 'Look, I'm trying to get through this as painlessly as possible but . . .' His voice failed him.

I could only manage a whisper. 'You're leaving me.'

'Yes.'

'For ever?'

'Yes. And don't look for me around Rushford. I won't be coming back.'

'But what about Sorensen's clinic? What about Ghost?'

'Someone else will tie up the loose ends.'

Anger and panic gave me the strength to swing my legs off the bed.

'This is what you do, isn't it? You did this with Clare. As soon as there's any possibility of something permanent, you're out the door.'

'How can I stay? What else are you hiding from me? Why am I asking you? It's not as if you'd know, would you?'

'No, listen . . .'

'No, you listen, Cage.' He struggled for a moment. It wasn't all anger. There was grief there as well. 'I attacked you. I hurt you. I put you in hospital. I told you I didn't but it seems I did. What else have I done that I don't know about? What else has that evil witch done to us?'

I tried to pull words together. 'She didn't . . . It wasn't . . .' But he was too angry, too ashamed, too frightened, too everything to listen properly.

His colour was spiking in and out. Deep crimson. A dark purple I hadn't seen before. Flashes of orange like lightning strikes.

'I thought . . . after Clare . . . I thought you were different, Cage. And you are, aren't you? I just didn't realise how different. How can I believe a word that comes out of your mouth? Jesus – all I ever want is a quiet relationship with a woman I can trust and is what she appears to be and it just never happens. First Clare and now you. I know it's not your fault, but that doesn't help.' He dragged in a breath. 'How long before that . . . your friend decides to remove *my* inconvenient memories? To turn me into something that suits her purpose? Well, I'm not hanging around to have my mind rearranged for her convenience. I'm protecting myself. I'm leaving.'

I still couldn't believe this was happening. This morning my life had been wonderful and now . . . 'Why would you do this to me?'

He slammed his fist into the wall. It had to have hurt. I could see pain flooding his colour. *'You don't get it, do you? You're a god, Cage. A bloody god. A living god.'*

His shout reverberated around the apartment, followed by a flat, deadly silence. It was so quiet I heard the fridge switch itself on in the kitchen.

'No, I'm not,' I whispered. 'It's not me. I'm still the same person I was. I haven't changed. I'm still me.'

'Well, that's the whole problem, isn't it? You're not you. You never have been. And as soon as that supposed friend of yours decides it's time, you'll be someone else. I'm not even sure you're a real person. You're just a walking, talking shell.'

We stared at each other. I didn't know what to do. I couldn't even think properly. His emotions were genuine. His red-gold colour, now grey and sullen, streamed away from me as if . . . as if he was afraid of me. This was the fear I had sensed. His fear of me. He'd said I frightened him and I hadn't really believed him, but now I did.

We stared at each other for a moment or two and then he turned and limped out of the room. A few moments later I heard the front door slam behind him.

I couldn't believe it. Only a few hours ago, I'd thought . . . and now everything . . . my whole life, my future, my past . . .

everything had just gone. Lost, like smoke in the wind. Gone. Just . . . gone.

I pulled myself to my feet. A beautiful red scooter occupied most of the room. This morning it had meant the world to me. Now I could hardly bear to look at it. A symbol of what I'd so nearly had, and lost at the very last moment. I squeezed past it to get to my coat. My shoes were parked neatly by the bed. Melek stood in the doorway. 'Where are you going?'

Oh God, I was going to have exactly the same conversation I'd had with Jones but in reverse, because I was the one who was leaving. I headed towards the door.

She stood in front of me. 'You're not strong enough.'

'Get away from me.' Now I was the one doing the shouting. 'I told you. Get away from me and stay away.'

'Elizabeth . . .'

'No, I mean it. Don't ever come near me again. Either of you. And everyone else had better stay a long way away as well.'

I pushed my feet into my shoes, fumbled my arms into my coat and tried to push past her.

'Elizabeth, wait . . .'

I stood very still, buttoned up my coat and said quietly, 'I never want to see you again.'

'Elizabeth . . .'

I spoke words that I knew would stop her in her tracks. 'Don't make me hurt you. Because now I know I can.'

'Let me help you.'

'Don't you dare!' The glass rang again.

There was a moment's pause and then she stepped back. I set off down the hall. I caught a brief glimpse of Iblis asleep with Nigel curled up on the bed by his feet, then I wrenched

385

open the front door, stepped through and slammed it behind me.

I didn't care about keys or the flat or the two people still inside. The ones who had used me for their own ends and in so doing had cursed me with life after life after life. Each one as unfulfilled and unsatisfying as this one. No children. Never any children. Very few relationships. Never ageing. Always being whisked away to another life before suspicions could be aroused, and all to give a safe haven to some psychotic, unhinged god who would destroy the world if not safely confined inside me for generation after generation. So many generations it made me giddy just to think about it.

I'd been Tadia and Bianca and Alice and Eadgytha and Susannah and so many more and now I was Elizabeth Cage. Who would I be next?

Take it from me – immortality stinks. You can keep it. What benefit had it ever brought me? Only loneliness and isolation. I'd been so desperate for someone to love that I'd actually been prepared to take in a little ghost. And now, once again, I was friendless and alone. And I'd just keep on living one half-life after another until this body finally crumbled into dust. Or I went mad. And then the thing that lived inside me would finally be free. They should have let it destroy the world as it always wanted to because it would happen one day. I was going through all this just to delay the inevitable by a couple of millennia. Well, perhaps the world deserved it. I no longer cared. It wasn't important. If the sun exploded tomorrow it wouldn't be too soon for me.

I strode through the cold, damp streets. This time last year I'd gone tobogganing with Michael Jones. Just hours before my world fell apart. My world seemed to fall apart on a regular basis. Well, not any longer. I would stay at home, keep my head down and enjoy a quiet life. My dad had been right.

Except, I didn't have a dad, did I? Or a mum. The people I'd built my life around had never existed. False memories had been inserted into my head in a mistaken effort to ground me. To make me more realistic in human eyes. I was a human being who had been altered to make life easier for everyone else. There had never been all those cosy chats in my dad's shed as he made a bookcase or spice rack for my mum. The life we'd lived together after Mum died had never happened. The nights in with fish and chips. The trips to his working man's club. My mum's love of cleaning that I thought I'd inherited from her. None of it was real.

That, I discovered, was the source of my pain. Gods, lives, whatever . . . strangely, I could cope with all that. Well, I would probably be able to cope with it, given time. It was the loss of my parents that cut me to the bone. My kind, gentle, loving parents.

No – it wasn't even my parents, as such – it was the knowledge that there had never actually been people who loved me. They hadn't died – they'd never existed.

I was walking far too quickly. My head began to spin. Unless I wanted to faint in the street I should find somewhere to sit down.

I found a bench in Archdeacon's Park. Coincidentally the same one where that man had exposed himself to me all those years ago and I met Ted. I felt as if this life had gone full circle.

I sat up with a jolt. This life had gone full circle, hadn't it? Worse – I now knew who and what I was. Suppose Melek decided it was time to move me on. I wasn't happy at the moment, but somehow, the thought of being transplanted into another place – Celia Smith of Melton Mowbray, for example, existing quietly as a spinster, a member of the church, doing good works, living yet another life of awful, stultifying *nothingness*. I tried to remind myself it was all done to save the world, but the truth was that the thing inside my head had got it exactly right.

This world wasn't worth saving.

CHAPTER TWENTY-FIVE

It was dark when I eventually arrived home but my house welcomed me as it always did. That, at least, was a positive in my life.

I'd missed Christmas. Heaven knew when I'd last eaten. I wasn't even completely sure what day it was. This Christmas was even worse than the last one and that one had been bad enough.

I was too angry to have much of an appetite. My instinct was to reach for my weapon of choice – my hoover – and lose myself in an orgy of polishing, scrubbing and vacuuming. I could reorder all my cupboards and shelves. But for once, even the calming routine of house cleaning wouldn't be enough. Because now I knew it wasn't a comforting ritual inherited from my mum, but a desperate coping mechanism to hold at bay all the vast emptiness of my life.

I should plan for the future but I had nothing. There was nothing I wanted to do. Nowhere I wanted to go. No one I wanted to be with. Well – no one who wanted to be with me. I might as well join Caroline Fairbrother in the wall to scream unheard at the passing world until the end of time.

Without even stopping to take off my coat and hang it tidily, I flung myself on my sofa and put my feet up. I didn't even take off my shoes. I folded my arms and stared into the dark.

A number of random thoughts occurred to me.

This was why Melek lived in Rushford. It was peaceful and pleasant but hardly the centre of the world. She was here because I lived here. Iblis didn't live here permanently. I remembered he'd gone to pay her his respects. I also remembered when we'd met, he hadn't asked me what my name was – he'd asked me what I was calling myself these days, which wasn't quite the same thing. He'd known me before but not as Elizabeth Cage.

Death was a gift to men but withheld from me. *My* home – or rather the place where I had been born – had long since disappeared. Lost for ever. I could never go home because I had no home to go to.

My life wasn't real. Nothing about me was real. Even the world in which I lived. Dizzying chasms opened at my feet. If I wasn't careful, I would be swept away and lost in the vastness of time.

That was why Melek gave me memories. To ground me. No one person's mind could encompass my lifespan. This was why everything was renewed, presumably every twenty or thirty years. My life would be reset so I could begin again somewhere else. I wondered how many people would welcome that kind of fresh start. No memories of previous mistakes. A whole new life to do again.

Before I came here, I'd been someone else. And someone else before that. And so on. After a while I'd stopped being a person. Now I was just a . . . a receptacle whose purpose was to keep someone else safe. The thing in my head was sleeping now – deeply and dreamlessly – which was probably a very good thing for everyone, but I'd had centuries of some sort of non-life. I'd had husbands – at least two – Ted, and George Torrington. I wondered about Ted. Would I have been removed before he noticed I wasn't ageing? Presumably, there's only so much credit you can ascribe to an exhaustive beauty routine and regular moisturising.

And Lady Torrington, who had disappeared after her melt-down. Not back to England as Clarence had suggested. Once again Melek had spirited me away. Another new name. Another new life.

Random thoughts kept whirling around my head and I couldn't get past them. I stood up and began to pace around. No wonder I'd wanted little Sammy for company. But what a great deal for everyone else. A nice home for the psychopathic god. Who cared about little Tadia, who went into the whole deal for the promise of nothing more than a warm cloak and no goats?

I thought about Melek for a moment. Covering for Iblis. Keeping an eye on me. Resetting the world every time the god escaped. The energy, the effort, the concentration required . . . No wonder she was hard and driven and ruthless and impatient. No wonder she snapped occasionally.

Which was a point. This god thing in my head. For how long could it safely linger here on this earth? Were the old gods still here? I remembered what Iblis had said about *Olympian Heights*, the TV series. That the gods hadn't gone away. That they'd simply reinvented themselves as celebrities and the world continued to worship. To lay offerings at their feet. Again, my mind trembled on the brink of deep mysteries I didn't want to examine too closely. There was so much I didn't know and didn't want to, either.

The thoughts ran around and around my head. I don't know at what point I fell asleep.

Someone tapped at the door. I jumped, woke up, blinked, and ignored it.

They tapped again. I ignored it again.

They thumped on the door. The sort of thump that says the thumper is not going away. I looked up. It was light outside. I'd been asleep for hours and I still had my coat on. And I still didn't know what day it was.

I got up stiffly and opened the door. Melek was standing there. The silence dragged on. It would seem that neither of us was willing to speak first.

Eventually, I said, 'What?'

'I can help.'

I said, 'I'd really rather you didn't,' and went to shut the door.

She stuck out a hefty boot to stop me. 'I can take away the pain.'

'You mean you can fool me again. Twist my mind again. Patch me up again and send me out there. To provide a habitat for something to live in. I'm really nothing but a dog kennel, aren't I?'

'I know this is difficult for you, but you gave your consent. We knew there would be difficult moments and you said you could withstand them. We talked about it for a very long time. Neither of us rushed into things. You thought long and hard before you gave your consent. You agreed to this.'

'I've changed my mind.'

'I'm afraid that's not possible. The two of you are indivisible. You cannot live without her. She left you briefly to heal Iblis

392

and your body began to fail. It was a race to heal him before you died. If she left you, permanently, you would die, and you deserve better.'

'I don't care.'

'Elizabeth, I must make you understand. Do you remember how you felt when you learned your husband had died? Time has, to some extent, blunted your sense of loss. It's still there but you have adjusted and moved on. You can find pleasure in your life. Sometimes it's just a clump of primroses – sometimes it's a new friend, or a good meal. She can't do any of that. Her grief is with her – every moment of every day. Her world is agony to her. Please let me in.'

She went to push the door open. I caught a glimpse of Colonel Barton standing in his window, holding his morning cup of coffee and watching me, his face concerned.

I had a sudden idea. Well – why not? People use me – all the time, apparently – I should use them. I held open the door. 'Come in.'

She walked in and stood in my sitting room. The day was grey and heavy which suited my mood exactly.

Slowly, I took off my coat and went to hang it up, taking my time about it while I considered the options open to me. It didn't take me long to realise there really weren't that many.

I turned to face her. 'I'll consider it on one condition.'

'What's that?'

'You lift the shadow on Mrs Barton's mind.'

I couldn't believe I hadn't thought of this before. She could do it. I knew she could. This was exactly the sort of thing she did. She'd done it to me and she'd done it with Iblis. If she wanted something from me then she could damn well do it to

393

Mrs Barton as well. I saw no reason why I shouldn't get a little something out of this arrangement.

She blinked. I suspected she'd thought I'd want her to get Michael Jones back for me. It wouldn't do her any harm at all to know she could get it wrong occasionally.

She shook her head. 'I can't do that.'

'Goodbye, then.' I went to open the front door.

'Wait. I said can't – not won't.'

I was in no mood for discussion. 'Goodbye.'

'All right,' she said. 'I'll do it.'

'When?' I demanded, rather proud of myself for remembering to tie her down to a specific time or date.

'In a day or two. I am tired.'

I shook my head. 'Then come back in a day or two.' I opened the front door and stood waiting for her to leave.

She stood in the middle of my room looking somehow small and tired. 'Don't you trust me?'

'No.'

'All right. But it will have to be tomorrow.'

'Really?' I said, in a voice which said I didn't believe her.

'I'm tired and I still have an important task to do today.'

I wasn't going to ask what that was.

She made no move to leave. 'Elizabeth – I can make all this go away. I know you won't even consider that at this moment, but think about the way you feel now. It won't ever leave you. Do you want to feel like this in a year's time? Or five? Or ten? For ever?'

'You're not moving me again. I'm staying here.'

'Of course.'

That seemed almost too easy. 'Why should I trust you?'

'You can trust me to do what is right.'

'For whom?'

'For everyone. Including you. You would have died on that hillside. Not on the day we met, perhaps. Or the next day. But very soon afterwards. Exposure. Wild animals. A fall. Blood poisoning from your injured foot. You would have been dead by winter. Now you have a comfortable home. A comfortable life. You are performing a valuable function. I know what you think of her, but none of this is Felda's fault. The love of her life died – she's an immortal and we don't get over these things lightly. Our joy is never-ending but so is our grief. You learned to deal with yours and move on. That is so difficult for us. For Felda, every day is as if she has just learned of Borin's death. Every day the grief rolls right over the top of her. You have seen the damage her emotions can do. You've felt that urge to destroy. She's stuck. She can't move on. She could still pull the world down around her, but, at the moment, thanks to you, she sleeps – and she is content to do so. She is somewhere no one can find her.'

'Is she happy?'

'She is not unhappy. Perhaps one day she will awake and be her former self. Perhaps not. But until then, you are all I have to keep her and this world safe from one another. I need you. No one else can do what you can do. Please help me.'

I thought about it for a long time, staring at my feet, wondering why I would choose to do all this again. And then I remembered her words. 'It won't ever leave you. Do you want to feel like this in a year's time? Or five? Or ten? For ever?'

No. I didn't want that. The weight on my mind was too heavy. This time last week I had been happily preparing for Christmas.

I had been busy and excited – and ignorant. Knowledge is not power.

On the other hand, only an idiot would surrender her advantage. 'Mrs Barton first.'

She nodded. 'All right.'

I waited by the door and after an uncertain moment, she left. I closed the door behind her.

I saw nothing of her for some time. I thought *typical*, and tried to pick up the threads of my life again. I heard nothing from Jerry or Gerald. I was surprised at them but when I thought about it, they'd been Jones's friends – not mine. That's the way of the world. A relationship crumbles and friendships crumble with it. I'd never see Iblis again, either. Or even Nigel. I was completely alone.

The sun came out and we enjoyed a few days of mild weather. I was standing one day, looking out of my window at the people feeding the ducks on the green and crossing in and out of the castle, when I saw Colonel Barton coming up the road and he had Mrs Barton with him. It was so long since I'd seen her anywhere other than sitting in their window that for a moment, I couldn't think who it was. He was carrying their shopping and she was pointing something out across the grass. Her colour – that frail robin's-egg blue – looked more substantial today. I put down my cup and opened my front door just as they climbed their steps.

She greeted me immediately. She knew who I was. 'Elizabeth, my dear. How are you?'

My face felt stiff and unused but I managed my first smile for days. 'I'm very well, thank you, but look at *you*.'

'Oh yes. My doctor changed my prescription and I feel so much better.'

'I'm so pleased to hear it,' I said, and my voice was chokey.

The colonel was unlocking their front door. 'You must come for tea one day this week,' he said.

Her face glowed. 'Oh, yes, Elizabeth. I've been baking.'

'In that case, Mrs Barton, nothing could keep me away. Is tomorrow all right?'

She nodded. 'We shall look forward to it. Scones, I think. With jam and cream.'

I smiled again and backed into my own house before I cried all over everyone.

Melek came that afternoon. I opened the door. We looked at each other for a moment and then I stepped back and let her in.

'Thank you for Mrs Barton.'

She nodded to the sofa. 'Sit down.'

I said, 'No. I've changed my mind. I don't want you messing around with my memories. I don't want safe and secure any longer. Not if it's all a lie. I want to know who I am and I want to remember it. And above all – no more false memories. I know you meant well, but . . .'

'This could be a dangerous path for you. Ignorance was your protection.'

'It's my path. My life. I want to remember things that actually happened. Not what you consider appropriate. You're no better than Sorensen drugging me to get me into his clinic. The only difference is that you drugged me with happy memories.'

'To keep you content.'

'To keep me quiet. Well, no more of that.'

She was silent for a long time, thinking. Eventually, she sighed and said, 'Very well. But – and you would be wise to allow this – I will blunt your memories. They will not carry the same razor-sharp pain. You will know who you are, but not why, and your memories will be hazy. Half-remembered dreams, but you will be at peace. And I will give you back your parents. They are a source of strength to you and you need them. Will you allow me to do that?'

Actually, I thought that sounded a good idea. 'All right.'

She stared into my eyes. 'But you will never remember what happened at Christmas. I can't allow that.'

'What happened at Christmas?'

'When we ate your delicious lunch and fell over each other in the kitchen afterwards, trying to clear away. We played games and Iblis drank far too much and had to be put to bed. The next day Michael Jones was called away and you returned home.'

'Yes,' I said, puzzled as to why she was telling me this. 'I know.'

I woke an hour later, quite annoyed at myself. I really have got to stop dropping off in the middle of the day like this. Fresh air and exercise were the way to go. I'd start tomorrow.

After tea and scones with Mrs Barton, of course.

CHAPTER TWENTY-SIX

I pottered about over the next few weeks, not doing very much at all, really. There was my weekly walk, and visits to the library, mercifully Melek-free. No one ever mentioned the angel books incident, or the Crystal incident, and I certainly wasn't ever going to mention them, either.

My memories subsided. They were there if I needed them – not that I thought I would. Only an idiot goes around poking murky things with a sharp stick.

Jones had disappeared just after Christmas, doing whatever it is he does. I assumed he was finishing off the Ghost investigation. He'd reappear soon enough. He might even talk to me about this one since I'd been involved as well. I was anxious to know whether any more of the 'statues' had died and I particularly wanted to know about Alyson Painswick. She'd lost both parents to violence now and must be feeling so confused and alone. I'd been about her age when I lost my mum. I hoped very much someone was looking after her.

One chilly day, when I'd almost stopped expecting him, Jones turned up. I was doing the washing-up when he knocked at the door. He looked dreadful. The sunglasses were gone but a small scar puckered the skin beneath his eye. He'd lost weight and there were lines of tiredness etched into his face. The Ghost investigation had obviously been a long and difficult one.

'Hello,' I said brightly. 'Haven't seen you for a while. Have you been away? Your eye looks much better,' and stood aside to let him in.

He seemed reluctant to enter. His colour, much darker than usual, curled around him. Usually it would surge towards me whenever we met, but not this time. I knew better than to ask what he'd been up to, but whatever it was, it hadn't been an enjoyable experience for him. He looked drained and weary.

Still standing in my porch, he asked me if I'd seen Melek recently.

'Yes, I think she was here a few weeks ago.'

'You *think*?'

I nodded with more certainty. 'Yes. She was here the other week. Aren't you coming in?'

'And?'

'And what?'

'What did she say?'

'Oh, well, um . . . we chatted a bit . . . you know . . . For heaven's sake, come in. I'm heating the street with this door open.'

He crossed the threshold and stood in the middle of the room. He kept his coat on. He didn't even take off his gloves.

'Name one specific thing she said.'

I blinked in surprise. 'What?'

'Can you repeat something she said? An actual quote? A phrase – anything?'

Worryingly, I couldn't. I'd fallen asleep after her visit and it had been a few weeks or so ago and nothing really stood out. He looked so serious, though, and it was obviously important to him so I took a chance. What did people normally talk about? And he wouldn't know, anyway. It wasn't as if he'd been here for the conversation.

'She asked how I was, what I'd been up to, said how much she and Iblis had enjoyed their Christmas lunch – that sort of thing.'

I thought he was watching me very closely. 'Did she tell you whether Iblis has recovered yet?'

I frowned. 'Recovered from drinking too much? I should think so – that was weeks ago now.'

'Do you have any memory of Christmas at all?'

I laughed. 'Well, of course I do. We ate your delicious lunch and fell over each other in the kitchen afterwards, trying to clear away. We played games and Iblis drank far too much and had to be put to bed. The next day you were called away – about the Ghost investigation, I assume – and I came home.'

'How do you know that?'

'I . . .' I stopped. I'd been going to say, 'She told me so,' which was ridiculous. I tried again. 'I . . .' and found I couldn't think of anything to say.

Jones said nothing. Nothing at all. I couldn't read his colour. I couldn't think what was going on with him.

'What is the matter with you? Why are you in such a bad mood?'

He looked at me. 'I'd tell you, but you wouldn't believe a word of it, so there's no point. But next time you see this friend of yours . . . this Melek . . . tell her I'd like a quiet word, would you?'

I moved towards him and he stepped back as if he was deliberately keeping his distance from me. I wasn't sure he was aware he was doing it. He shoved his hands in his coat pockets and hunched his shoulders. His colour was a solid barrier around him. What was going on?

I could feel my mood darkening to match his. 'What wouldn't I believe a word of?'

'Cage, I don't know what to say to you. I don't know how to treat you. I don't even know if I can rely on you.'

Now I was becoming angry. 'What do you mean you can't rely on me? What have the last two years been all about in that case? Why are you even here if you've just come to pick a quarrel?'

'Believe me, I don't want to be here. I've been instructed to resume contact with you.'

He was telling the truth. He really didn't want to be here. His colour was practically out in the street. Where he obviously wished he was, as well.

'Then I think you'd better go, Jones. You don't want to be here and I certainly don't want you here. Go and take your bad mood out on someone else.'

He stood with his back to the window. 'Or what?'

'What?'

'What will you do, Cage? What world-shattering event will you unleash if I don't do exactly as you want?'

I was utterly bewildered. His colour was a vortex of conflicting emotions. As would mine be, probably – if I had one. 'Look, I don't understand what you're saying or why you're here, or what you want, so I think you'd better go. Come back when you're in a better mood.'

'Sadly, not an option available to me. I've been sent to discuss our future working relationship.'

'I'm not sure I want to work with you any longer. Not with this attitude.'

'Don't be petty, Cage.'

'*I'm* petty? You're the one who's wandered in here looking for a fight. Is that what you're trying to do? You've changed your mind about us working together so you're trying to provoke me into telling you to push off? Because I have to tell you it's worked. Well done. Now go away.'

He immediately threw himself on to the sofa and folded his arms.

Fine. I could do stupid and stubborn as well. I walked to the sink and continued with the dishes. The silence went on and on. I stared out of the window at the pots in my tiny back garden. The bulbs I'd planted were starting to come through. I should be thinking about what to replace them with in the summer. Something bright and colourful. I remembered Ted had been fond of the geranium–marigold–lobelia combination. Red, orange and blue. Very colourful. Perhaps – and here was a daring thought – I could paint the pots as well. Purple and bright green stripes, perhaps. Or purple with green spots. That would be fun and funky. And when I'd done that, I could . . .

'What the hell's this?'

I turned around, keeping my soapy hands in the sink. 'What's what?'

He was holding Sammy's little blue rabbit. Or rather, the little blue rabbit that would have been Sammy's but now wouldn't. Somehow it didn't seem right that Jones should have it. It was a personal thing to me.

'Give me that.'

I flapped my hands to try to get rid of the bubbles and

403

snatched it from him. Now there were bubbles on the rabbit, as well. I carefully wiped them off with the tea towel. 'How did you get this?'

'It was under the cushion.'

I didn't remember leaving it there.

'Whose is it?'

'No one's,' I said, quite truthfully.

'No one's toy rabbit just happened to be under your cushion?'

'That's right.'

He heaved himself to his feet. 'More lies, Cage. You're just full of them, aren't you?'

Still clutching the rabbit, I turned to face him and said quietly, 'There was a time when that remark would have been hurtful and I would have wondered what I'd done to deserve it. Today I don't care what you think. Your opinion is worthless. Please close the door behind you.'

The words hung quivering in the air between us.

He frowned at the rabbit and then at me. 'Why are you all bent out of shape over this, Cage?'

I couldn't answer. I couldn't even look at him. Things were collapsing inside of me. Like a house of cards. Everything was slowly and quietly tumbling to the ground. There was no sound – no drama. I clutched the little rabbit like a talisman and prayed for him to go so I could lock all the doors, go upstairs, cry my eyes out for an hour or so and then . . .

He was looking around. 'Cage . . . do you have . . . is there a child here?'

The cruel irony of it stung me into speech. I tried hard to speak with restraint. Not to let the words tumble out in a humiliating revelation of my utter loneliness.

404

'At one point I had an idea that I would ask little Sammy if he wanted to come here so he wouldn't have to live in the wall any longer. I thought we could be company for each other. I thought we could do things together and he wouldn't be so lonely and frightened, and I wouldn't . . . But very fortunately his mum found him and they were overjoyed to see each other, so that was all right, wasn't it?'

I tried to turn away. I think I thought I would finish the dishes, leave everything neat and tidy and then . . .

'And you bought the rabbit for him? For Sammy?'

'Yes,' I said, impatiently, just wishing he would go.

'Why didn't you get rid of it when you knew he wasn't coming?'

A very good question. When the moment came I just hadn't been able to do it.

'Because if I couldn't have Sammy then I thought I'd have his rabbit instead.'

Did I say that out loud? Apparently, I did, because the next moment Jones was standing in front of me. 'Cage . . .'

'I can't have children,' said a voice I barely recognised as mine. 'Ted and I tried for ages. There were tests. It was me. It was my fault.'

There was a long, long silence. The angry spikes in his colour slowly faded away to be replaced with the usual red and a little gold. His colour reached gently towards me and then he cleared his throat, saying thickly, 'I'm sorry, Cage. It's not your fault. Nothing is your fault. Of all the people in the world, I think you are one of the few who can honestly say that.'

Still clutching the rabbit, I shook my head, staring at the floor because I didn't know where to look or what to do. Or what to say. Or anything, really.

He said softly, 'I expect you'd like to be alone now, wouldn't you?'

I nodded again, actually quite desperate to be on my own.

Briskly, he said, 'Not going to happen, Cage. Go and sit down and I'll make you a drink. Tea or coffee?'

'No . . . I . . .'

He gently pushed me on to the sofa. Then he hung up his coat, went into the kitchen and switched on the kettle. Then he finished the dishes. He emptied the bowl, wiped everything down and hung up the tea towel. Then he made us both a cup of tea. Then he came to sit beside me and put his arm around me. 'You shouldn't be alone right now.'

'I'm not,' I said, pointedly. 'You're here. Still.'

'I'm not going anywhere.'

'Yes, you are.'

'Don't argue with me, Cage. If you and I are to work together, we must agree a few rules. The first – obviously – is no arguing.'

I snorted.

He continued thoughtfully. 'I gave it a bit of thought while I was finishing off the dishes and I see your role as more *assistant* than partner. I'll be the one in charge. I'll devise our strategies, organise our working day, allocate tasks and so on. Your role will be to keep everything clean and neat. Obviously, in this modern age, it is permissible for an enlightened man to allow a woman her own minor area of responsibility, so you can be in charge of refreshments. I'll give you a small budget to manage because that will make you feel as if you have something useful to contribute and – ouch. That hurt.'

'I can't believe you're still unaccustomed to being beaten up by the women you know. It seems to happen a lot and as your potential partner, I have to say I find your inability to learn from your mistakes concerning.'

He reached for his tea. His colour was clearer, lighter, cleaner. Whatever had been bothering him was almost gone.

I leaned against him. 'Why are you here, anyway? Other than to discuss your delusional working arrangements.'

'Oh, yes. I bring good news and bad news. Which would you like first?'

'I don't know.'

'Doesn't matter – it's the same piece of news for both.'

'What is?'

I knew what he was going to say before he said it.

'They've arrested Philip Sorensen.'

THE END

ACKNOWLEDGEMENTS

I'd like to thank Jan for the dinner party menu. She also provided details of the Christmas lunch in *White Silence* and is always my go-to guy in matters foodie.

Many thanks to my agent, Hazel, who hardly emailed me more than three times a day asking when it would be finished. Quail not, trusty agent – 'tis done.

Huge thanks to everyone on the team. (Such excitement when I realised I had a team!)

Frankie – in-house editor and General Supremo.

Bea – who worked particularly hard on this book.

Jo and Shadé – for their magnificent marketing.

Antonia – in charge of publicity.

Sharona – copy editor and all-round good egg.

Thanks also to all those at Headline who work so hard to make my books readable.

Have you read the bestselling CHRONICLES OF ST MARY'S series, the stories of a bunch of historians who jump up and down the timeline investigating major historical events as they happen? (Do NOT call it time travel.)

Or the irresistible spin-off – the TIME POLICE series – featuring Jane, Luke and Matthew, the worst recruits in history. Or, very possibly, three young people who might change everything . . .

To discover more about

JODI TAYLOR

visit

www.joditaylor.online

You can also find her on

Facebook
www.facebook.com/JodiTaylorBooks

Twitter
@joditaylorbooks

Instagram
@joditaylorbooks